Praise for Tony Park

'Break-neck in pace, with narrow escapes from death on every
page, its charm is infectious'
Daily Mail

'Park's obvious role model is that great master of the colonial epic,
Wilbur Smith, whose fans will not be disappointed'
The Times

'An exciting and well-constructed thriller'
Canberra Times

'A thumping good read'
Sunday Sport

'Good writing, memorably exciting...Park sorts out his heroes and
villains with admirable pacing and inventiveness'
Sydney Morning Herald

'He just gets better and better. His descriptions of the southern African
bush and mountain jungles are so vivid you can feel the sun
on your skin and smell the dust and animals'
Sun Herald

Australian writer Tony Park fell in love with South Africa on a short trip in 1995. He is a major in the Australian Army Reserve and has worked in journalism and PR, including six months in Afghanistan in 2002 as PR officer for the Australian ground forces there. Tony and his wife Nicola now divide their time between Sydney and the African bush.

www.tonypark.net

Also by Tony Park

The Prey
African Dawn
The Delta
Ivory
Silent Predator
Safari
African Sky
Zambezi
Far Horizon

TONY PARK
DARK HEART

Quercus

First published in Australia by Pan Macmillan in 2012
This edition published in Great Britain in 2014 by

Quercus Editions Ltd
55 Baker Street
7th Floor, South Block
London W1U 8EW

Cartographic art by Laurie Whiddon, Map Illustrations

A CIP catalogue record for this book is available
from the British Library

ISBN 978 0 85738 794 3
EBOOK ISBN 978 1 78087 419 7

10 9 8 7 6 5 4 3 2 1

Printed and bound in Great Britain by Clays Ltd, St Ives plc

Typeset by Ellipsis Books Limited, Glasgow

For Nicola

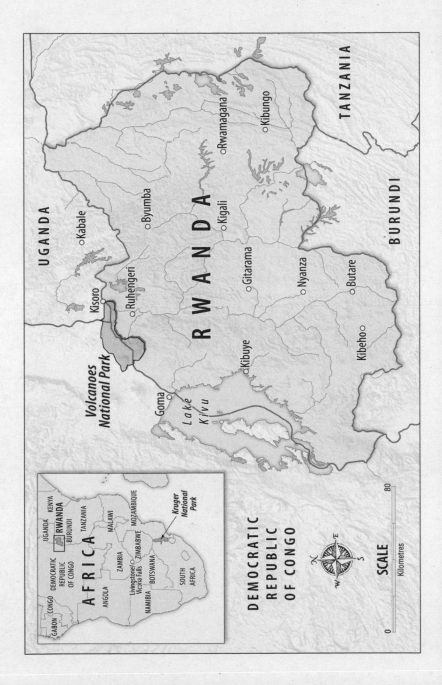

UGANDA

TANZANIA

○Kabale

oRwamagana

oKibungo

oByumba

R W A N D A

Kisoro
○

oKigali

Ruhengeri
○

Volcanoes
National Park

Gitarama
○

Nyanza
○

Butare
○

BURUNDI

Kibeho○

Kibuye
○

Goma
○

L a k e   K i v u

DEMOCRATIC
REPUBLIC
OF CONGO

SCALE
0   80
Kilometres

GABON CONGO

DEMOCRATIC
REPUBLIC
OF CONGO

UGANDA KENYA

RWANDA
BURUNDI

TANZANIA

A F R I C A

MALAWI

Livingstone/○
Victoria Falls

ANGOLA

ZAMBIA

ZIMBABWE

MOZAMBIQUE

Kruger
National
Park

NAMIBIA

BOTSWANA

SOUTH
AFRICA

Glossary

Akazu: literally, 'little house', this small circle of Hutu relatives and friends of President Juvenal Habyarimana and his wife, Agathe, were opposed to power sharing with the Tutsi, and contributed to the organisation of the Rwandan genocide.

bakkie: Afrikaans term for pickup or utility vehicle.

DRC: Democratic Republic of Congo; formerly Zaire.

FAR: Forces Armées Rwandaises; the Hutu-dominated Rwandan national army, in existence until 1994 when the Rwandan Patriotic Army and Rwandan Patriotic Front took control of the country.

gacaca: literally, 'justice on the grass'; a community-based court system introduced to deal with the high numbers of people accused of genocide.

génocidaires: those accused of perpetrating the 1994 Rwandan genocide of Tutsis and moderate Hutus between 6 April and mid July, during which up to a million people were killed.

Habyarimana, Juvenal: Hutu president of Rwanda from 1973 until his death in 1994, when his Dassault Falcon 50 aircraft was shot down by a surface-to-air missile. Also on board and killed was the president of Burundi, Cyprien Ntaryamira.

Hutu: central African ethnic group existing in Rwanda,

Burundi and the Democratic Republic of Congo. The majority tribe in Rwanda (with the others being the Tutsi and the Twa), the Hutu were disenfranchised under Belgian colonial rule, which favoured the Tutsi minority. After 1959, however, the balance of power changed in favour of the Hutu, until after the genocide.

Hutu Power: an extremist anti-Tutsi ideology which spawned several political parties in the lead-up to the 1994 genocide with the aim of excluding or eliminating Tutsis from Rwanda.

ICTR: International Criminal Tribunal Rwanda. UN body formed in November 1994 to investigate and prosecute those accused of genocide and other violations of human rights in Rwanda.

Interahamwe: literally, 'those who stand together', or fight together, this government-backed Hutu paramilitary group was responsible for carrying out the genocide against Tutsis and moderate Hutus in Rwanda.

Kibeho: small town in southern Rwanda which prior to the genocide attained fame as the site of reported visions of the Virgin Mary and Jesus Christ. It was also the site of the largest post-genocide Hutu refugee camp where *génocidaires* and innocent Hutus fearing RPA reprisals sought shelter.

muti: common southern African term for traditional medicine made from plant matter and animal and (in some cases) human body parts.

RPA: Rwandan Patriotic Army. The armed wing of the Tutsi-dominated Rwandan Patriotic Front. Made up of exiled Tutsis, the RPA, led by Paul Kagame, took control of Rwanda following the 1994 genocide.

RPF: Rwandan Patriot Front. Political party formed in 1987 by Tutsis living in exile from Rwanda in Uganda. The RPF took power in Rwanda in 1994, won a majority in the 2003 elections and at the time of writing (2012) the RPF was still the ruling party in Rwanda.

Tutsi: ethnic grouping in Rwanda, Burundi and Democratic Republic of Congo; the second largest grouping in Rwanda (with Hutus in the majority and Twa in the minority). Initially favoured over the Hutu by the Belgian colonial regime, the Tutsi faced reprisal killings and persecution following the 1959 transition to majority rule. Many fled the country for neighbouring Uganda. The 1994 genocide was aimed at eliminating the Tutsi in Rwanda.

UNAMIR: United Nations Assistance Mission For Rwanda. UN peacekeeping force first established in 1993, prior to the genocide, to enforce the terms of the Arusha accords which would have allowed exiled Tutsis safe return to Rwanda.

PROLOGUE

Koh Samui, Thailand, December 2011

The girl looked back over her shoulder and winked at him, then leaned across the pool table, one short but slender leg raised, and lined up the white and the eight balls. A sunburnt Swede on the other side of the green felt, old enough to be her father, leered at her sloppily.

The balls kissed and the black slammed into the corner pocket. The Swede shook his head, laid down his cue and shook her hand. The girl looked back at Mike Ioannou and winked again.

Mike looked at his watch. It was one in the morning. He was alone and drunk. He drained his lukewarm half-litre glass of Singha beer and then groaned as the girl, who had just clinched her fifth straight game of pool, sashayed towards him with a full beer. She'd been working on him all night, in between matches.

'*Kop kuhn*, I think,' he said to her, and reluctantly took a sip. At least this one was cold. *Why me?* he wondered. Well, he surmised as she dragged a stool next to his, he was better looking than the Swede, who had a huge beer belly and was wearing sandals and socks and plaid shorts.

'You look me all night. We go party now?' she said to him, adjusting herself on her seat so that her thigh, most of which was visible thanks to her tiny denim shorts, was resting along his.

'No, thank you,' Ioannou said. He *had* been looking at her all night, but he had no desire to take home a dose of something.

She nudged him with her shoulder, making him spill a little of his beer, which annoyed him. 'You say you from Australia, but you no look Australian. You look Italian.'

He laughed and shook his head. 'I live in Australia now, but my family's from Cyprus originally. You know where that is?'

'No. Maybe you show me one day.'

'Maybe you should go back to your pool table.'

She leaned closer to him and lowered her voice. 'Me no want boom boom, me good girl. We just go dance, maybe play some pool somewhere else, just you and me, OK?'

Her pretence of innocence was oddly appealing. 'You're too good for me – at pool.'

She slapped his back. 'I teach you. Is OK.' She took his left hand in hers and held it up. 'I see you married.' The girl brought his hand to her lips and kissed it. As her lips brushed the gold band he felt her tongue linger on his skin.

'Enough.' He drew his hand away from her.

She looked up, smiling, and fixed on his eyes.'You faithful. That nice.' She lowered her voice: 'Make me so horny.'

Mike laughed out loud and she joined in. 'No thanks.'

She punched his arm. 'Come on. Your friend – birthday boy – he go get his present. Now you all alone. What you do, go home to hotel and play with yourself?'

He couldn't help but laugh. She was fun and her smile was infectious. He checked his watch again and looked around the bar. Ironically, it was called Henry's Africa Bar. He hadn't chosen it and hadn't noticed the sign as he had walked in. It was only once he was inside that he'd noticed the leopard-print wallpaper and carved wooden giraffes. There was a South African flag behind the bar and a framed Springbok's jersey. But that was about where the African ambience ended. The waitresses were all wearing cowgirl hats and garishly coloured riding boots and dispensing shots from mini bottles of vodka slung in leather bandoliers crisscrossing their tiny bodies.

Mike didn't want to think about Africa. He'd come here to try to forget, if only for a few days. He knew that if he did go back to the hotel now, he wouldn't surf porn on his laptop; instead, he'd start going over the transcripts again, agonising over what more he could do to find the men in the photograph, now that he'd identified them.

'I think,' the girl said, loudly enough to break his thoughts, 'time we go now.'

He had a wife and two teenage daughters at home. 'I just don't understand you,' his wife, Helen, had said to him a week ago. It was clichéd, corny even, when he thought about it. He could tell the girl his wife didn't understand him and use it as justification to fuck her brains out tonight.

But he wouldn't do that. His wife couldn't comprehend why and how he had got himself so enmeshed in something that had happened seventeen years earlier in an African country that few people in Australia would have even heard of had its citizens not set about massacring each other on a scale not seen since the Nazi death camps.

He'd taken a job as prosecutor and investigator for the International Criminal Tribunal for Rwanda, the ICTR, to get back to Africa, and to try to do some good. He'd had enough of defending drug dealers and white-collar embezzlers.

Although his parents were Cypriot and he lived in Australia, Mike had been born in Africa, in Rhodesia, now known as Zimbabwe, where his mother and father had owned a supermarket. They had been forced to leave Africa when Robert Mugabe ruined Zimbabwe's economy by destroying its commercial farming sector. In his adopted country Mike had stuck out more because of his funny accent than his looks. Most people thought he was South African and for a while Mike didn't know who he was – a Cypriot, an African or an Australian. His wife was all Australian and couldn't understand why he would want to go back to Africa, least of all to a country like Rwanda. She had gone with him once, to go to a friend's wedding in Bulawayo, in Zimbabwe, and had hated every minute of it.

He didn't want to lose her. He didn't want to seek solace in the arms of a Thai girl half his age. What Mike Ioannou wanted most of all was his life – his pre-Rwanda life – back, working as a barrister in Sydney. He'd been too good at his job. And now he was opening a can of worms that maybe should have stayed closed.

The girl ran her hand up the inside of his thigh. He was wearing cargo shorts and hadn't bothered with underpants. She grinned as she felt him harden, despite his protestations and the amount of beer he'd had. 'No,' he said, though he knew she could sense that his conviction was wavering.

'Yes.' She took his earlobe between her teeth and bit down gently. He groaned.

Mike knew that in two days he would have to confront the reality, the enormity, of what his investigations had uncovered. He rubbed a hand over his face. The girl gripped his arm and tugged.

He tried to resist her. He wanted Rwanda to be over and to go home, once and for all, to his wife and to never see Africa again. He wondered if he could. He wondered if the evil had poisoned him, changed him, so that he could never be normal, never be good again.

But why had he bothered? Did anyone in the world care any more?

'Africa,' he muttered.

'What you say?' the girl asked him. She held him at arm's length, toying with his fingers, tugging on them as she leaned her lithe body back.

'I said, *Africa.* Do you know why people would rise up against their neighbours in a godforsaken little country in the middle of nowhere and murder nearly a million people? Do you know what would make people do that?'

She tilted her head and he assumed her English wasn't good enough for her to comprehend his words or his despair. She let go of his hand and came closer to him. She stood between his spread knees but she didn't touch him. 'I not Thai. I come from Cambodia.'

'Oh.'

'Yes. I here because I got baby, and I no got mother, no got father, no got uncle, aunt, cousin. I got only me to care my baby. I got no family. I know 'bout Rwanda. I know 'bout people killing each other, mister.' She put her hands on her hips and stared at him, daring him to challenge her again.

He felt small and tired. He'd tried to project his anger onto this girl and she'd opened up to him. In her eyes he saw a mirror of his own horror.

He rubbed his eyes again and closed them. When he opened them he saw her gaze had softened. She held out both hands to him, and he took her tiny fingers in his and stood.

'We go somewhere quiet. Not this Africa place. We talk, OK?' she said.

Mike nodded and let the girl lead him outside.

A warm rain was falling and the busy street was choked with yelling drunks and tuktuks beeping their horns. He held her hand as they walked. He would ask her about Cambodia, about Pol Pot and the Khmer Rouge. He wanted to know how she felt – did she want revenge? Did she feel the need to make sense of the madness that had gripped the men who had taken her family from her?

Ironically, he felt more relaxed now that he was thinking about Cambodia. He'd thought Thailand might allow him to escape the horrors, but the truth was that he didn't want to escape, didn't want to forget. He was driven by the need to understand how people could massacre each other, what provoked neighbour to slaughter neighbour.

His head was beginning to throb. Bloody Singha. The stuff tasted like it was fifty per cent formaldehyde. He either needed another one, or a glass of water and a couple of paracetamol. He doubted he'd get the latter.

He was drunk. Too drunk. Something was spinning around his mind – something she'd said inside the noisy bar, but he couldn't quite remember what it was, or why it was nagging at him. He looked down at the ground as he tried to concentrate, letting her lead him. When he glanced up he saw they were well away from the bustle of the main street.

'Where we going?' he slurred.

She looked back at him. 'Quiet place. You say you want talk – we talk.'

'OK.'

What had she said that he wanted to ask her about first? It seemed important.

An Asian pop song started playing as a ringtone. The girl reached inside her singlet top and took the mobile phone from her bra. She flipped it open and spoke into it in Thai. She looked back at him again.

He stopped walking while she spoke, her words staccato, whispered.

It suddenly dawned on him. 'Rwanda.'

She snapped the phone closed. 'What you say?'

'Rwanda.'

The girl started walking, her platform heels slapping the rain-slicked pavement with every step.

'Hey. Wait,' he called after her, hesitating. 'When I mentioned Africa before, and a little country in the middle of nowhere where people killed each other, you said, *Rwanda*.'

She stopped but didn't look back. 'Everyone know 'bout Rwanda.'

'The genocide happened in 1994. You wouldn't have been more than a year or two old. I could have been talking about Burundi, or the Democratic Republic of Congo or half-a-dozen other places in Africa.'

'It lucky guess.' She turned and started walking back to him. She forced a smile and let her hips speak as she swayed expertly along on her platforms.

Mike took a pace back and held out his arms. 'No.'

'Come to me, baby. We talk.' She reached out and grabbed his hands. 'Maybe we boom boom later, yes?'

He brought his arms up sharply, breaking free from her grip. She took two quick steps and pressed herself against him, her tiny breasts flattening against his sweaty belly.

'Get away from me.'

'No, baby. I want you.' She reached up and put her palms on his chest.

'I'm going to ask you one more time. How did you know I was talking about Rwanda?'

She peered around his body, which dwarfed her. 'It no matter.'

'It does matter. I'm going.' He turned and was about to step off the kerb and onto the road when he saw the sedan come around the corner. He heard the whine of its gears as the driver changed down, and the growl as he stamped on the accelerator. Bloody maniac. No headlights either. The girl was behind him. Screw her. Perhaps it had been a lucky guess, but it was too much of a coincidence. The stakes were too high. He needed to get away from her. It could be a trap, someone wanting to know what he knew. But here? He shook his head. No way.

The car screamed down the street. Mike willed it to go faster so he could cross the road and get away from her cloying touch, and the smell of her cheap perfume and sweat. He felt her little hands on his back. 'Enough!'

When he spun around to confront her, he saw the change in her eyes, the set of her pursed mouth. The gap between the top of the kerb and the road was bigger than an Australian street, probably to cope with the monsoonal rains. As she pushed him, hard in the ribs, he started to topple. Silly bitch would kill him if he fell in front of a speeding car. 'No!'

1

South Africa, one month later

A Highveld storm, Liesl Nel thought, was like watching the end of the world, the glories of heaven and the horrors of hell fighting it out across the skies, all played out in three-hundred-and-sixty degree Imax and surround sound.

Liesl drew on her cigarette, closed her eyes and let the nicotine and the deep-bass boom of the thunder soothe her. The lightning penetrated her closed lids, the flicker and the noise that followed reminding her of muzzle blasts and gunfire. When she opened her eyes, the faux Tuscan villas of the estate and the rolling hills beyond were seared white with a burst of light.

She recalled, as hard as she tried not to, how she'd actually thought bodies looked artistic sometimes; the white lime turning the grimacing, reaching cadavers into marble statues. Back then, the camera's viewfinder had been her filter, distancing her momentarily from the reality of the mass grave, though it couldn't block out the smell. That's when she'd taken a cigarette from another shooter, an army photographer, started smoking and stopped believing. That was in 1994. She hadn't stopped smoking – or started believing again – since.

Liesl exhaled and hoped the chill of the rising wind and the first fat drops of rain would blow away the memories and wash away the guilt. It was coming back to Africa that did it; it resurrected the bodies every time. An up-market walled estate on Johannesburg's western outskirts was a world away from the guns and the graves and the killing gangs in Rwanda, but it was still Africa out there, beyond the honey-rendered walls topped with electric fencing. The biometric fingerprint security at the gate and the roving armed response patrols wouldn't save her. She was already dead.

A rap on the window pane startled her, like the *pop-pop-pop* of an AK on automatic. She started and spun around, and saw Sannette laughing. She was tapping a champagne flute against the glass of the French door. 'One more, hey, before we leave?'

Liesl checked her own glass. Empty. '*Ja*, why not.' Booze wasn't the answer, of course, but it sure as hell helped.

A lion roared, but not like in the movies. Richard thought it was more like a wheezy, bronchial groan. Nothing in fiction could portray this continent as it really was. The cat was a long way off, and early with its call – perhaps eager for sex or food. A purple-crested turaco squawked and clucked in the tree above the thatch roof of the surgery. That was more his Africa: annoying birds rather than kings of the jungle.

He looked at the note on his desk. He'd scrunched it into a ball but hadn't been able to toss it in the bin yet. He unfolded it, smoothing it out on the desk calendar blotter left by some pushy drug-company sales rep. *18h00, ten minutes. J.*

He checked his watch and scratched his stubbled chin. It was five-thirty or, as a South African would have written it, 17h30. He picked up the piece of paper and held it to his nose, drawing in his breath deeply. It wasn't perfumed – that only happened in films, didn't it? But he didn't need the scent, or the reminder.

'Mrs van der Merwe is outside, Doctor,' his receptionist, Helen, had said two hours earlier, after she'd knocked and stuck her head around his door.

Helen's husband was a trails guide in the Kruger National Park, as Janine van der Merwe's had been until he'd transferred to the SANParks criminal investigation division. These days he tracked poachers, not game. Rhino poaching was getting out of control in the park and Lourens, Janine's husband, was away from home a good deal. Lourens was used to dealing with predators, of the two- and four-legged variety, and he was invariably heavily armed.

'Tell her I'm busy with a patient.' He had, in fact, been trying to tie a fishing lure.

Helen had raised her eyebrows. He'd stared at her until she'd closed the door. Bloody hell, he realised, it would be all around the staff village by nightfall. He should have seen Janine there and then and told her that it was over, that he'd made a mistake.

Helen had knocked on his door again a few minutes later. 'She's just left. I told her you were still busy with a patient. She left you this.' Helen had passed him the note.

Richard folded it now, instead of crumpling it, and wrapped it around two of his fingers. What to do? he asked himself. He knew the right answer, but he also knew what she wanted him to do. He checked the time once more. Five thirty-two. Decision time soon. There was another knock and Helen entered. 'I've got a tourist in the waiting area, just come in. He thinks he's been bitten by a cobra but he's not quite sure.' Helen pronounced the last three words in what she no doubt thought was a good approximation of an upper-class English accent.

'How can you not be quite sure if you've been bitten by a snake?' he muttered, slipping the note into his top pocket. Helen shrugged, but she'd seen the gesture. She handed him the form with the patient's particulars.

He wondered if she had read the note. Helen was snoopy and gossipy, but would she read a note from a patient to a doctor? Probably.

The British tourist, Raymond Philpott, aged twenty-two, newspaper journalist from Enfield, had walked to one of Skukuza's camping ground ablution blocks, drunk after a lunchtime *braai* and too much beer in the sun.

He slurred his words. 'It – the snake – was on the door handle. I thought it was a bootlace or something, but when I reached out to open the door, it reared up and struck me.'

'I see,' Richard said, adjusting the lamp on his table and holding the man's hand up close to it. 'Big snake, was it?'

'Big enough.' He could tell the tourist felt foolish. 'Like a bootlace, not a shoelace.'

'They're quite active this time of year. It's the summer heat. Most of the snake incidents I deal with are when someone surprises a Mozambican spitting cobra and it spits in their eye. We don't get many bootlace-sized snake bites. What colour was it?'

'Brown. Maybe green. Greeny brown. What do you think it was? My mate thought it might be a cobra.'

'I can't see any evidence of a laceration, not even a scratch, and if you had been bitten or grazed by a poisonous snake you'd be in a good deal of pain.'

'Umm, it feels a bit numb,' Philpott said.

Probably the dozen beers in the sun, Richard thought. The young man's skin was red and his eyes were bloodshot. He'd had a fright, but what he needed now was a litre of water and a lie-down. Richard told him as much.

'You're English?' Philpott said.

Richard nodded.

'How did you end up here?'

Richard sat back in his chair and clasped his hands across his stomach. 'I ran away from the UK to avoid an embarrassing and potentially costly malpractice litigation suit brought on by my addiction to prescription drugs, and this was the only job I could get, giving malaria tests and bandaids to tourists and staff in a dead-end backwater of Africa. The billings are rubbish, but I do get a nice house in the staff village. I had a leopard in a tree in my front yard last week.'

The man blinked his red eyes a couple of times, then started to laugh. 'You're joking, right? Nice one.'

'No, I'm not joking. The leopard was in my front yard. Will there be anything else?' Richard asked. He could see the drunk man was trying to retrace the last couple of steps of the conversation in his mind.

'You were joking about the malpractice stuff, right . . . and the drugs?'

Richard said nothing.

'Well, if you think I'm all right, I'll be off then,' Philpott said. He seemed to have forgotten all about his snake bite. Richard saw him out and told Helen to draw up his bill. He thought about Janine, and how weak he was.

'Goodbye, Raymond. Watch out for snakes in the gents, all right?' he said to the man as he left. He checked his watch. Ten minutes to six. He could make it, and see Janine. Sometimes honesty was the best policy. He'd tell her it was over. Or perhaps he'd do her over the bonnet of her car.

Virunga Mountains, Democratic Republic of Congo

'*Vite! Vite!*' They called him 'Vite' because he was speedy.

Vite ran through the banana plants as fast as he could, but he was young and his legs were short. The illegal charcoal makers who chased him yelled to each other as they tried to outflank him. He screamed in fear. They had just killed his mother with a bullet.

Vite and his family had stumbled into the tree poachers' operation on the edge of the rainforest and the charcoal makers had seen them both as a threat to their work and an opportunity to make some good money. The men operated on the edge of the national park, illegally cutting down native trees and gums that had been planted for timber. Charcoal was the main source of heating and cooking fuel for millions of people and there was never enough of it. The men dug big pits and set their timber on fire, then covered it with mounds of earth and let it smoke until the virgin timber was turned to black charcoal. Vite and his family had also been raiding the gum plantation – for food – so they were competitors as well as a valuable commodity in their own right.

'*A droit*,' one of the men yelled.

Another laughed at the chase. '*Oui. Il est là!*'

Fronds lashed at his face and ears and he panted as he moved through the shadowed labyrinth between the trunks of the trees. A low-hanging bunch of fruit smacked him. He shrieked. There was more gunfire further behind him.

Vite had seen his mother falling, her arms flailing, as the bullets knocked her down. The rest of his tribe had bellowed and cried and scattered as fast as they could. His father, a giant fellow, had charged at the men and tried to retrieve the body of his mother, but the men had opened fire with guns, forcing him and the rest of Vite's family to seek refuge back in the rainforest. Vite had been cut off and his only option was to run into the banana farm. Now they were after him.

The straggly lines of banana plants gave way to the thick green orderly maze of a tea plantation. Pickers with baskets on stooped backs straightened to watch the chase, a welcome break from the drudgery of their job. The tea shrubs were up to the waists of the men who chased him, but Vite was small enough to be completely hidden by them. He slapped the shrubs out of his way as he ran and ran.

The men called to each other, confused now, and even though Vite had the cover of the tea shrubs, he was getting further and further from his home on the mountain. The men had spread out in a skirmish line and some of the tea pickers had seized the excuse to set down their baskets and bolster the ranks as beaters. They yelled and whistled. Vite ran down the hill then up the opposite side. His small heart was pounding and he had stopped screeching to conserve his breath. He had never been this far away from his troop before.

At the crest of the next hill he came to a road. He considered crossing it and pushing further into the tea plantation, which continued just as thick and green on the other side, until he spotted a line of tin-roofed timber huts off to the right. Smoke curled from a pipe in one of them. It would be risky, turning right and running along the gravel road, but it might allow him to outflank his pursuers and double back towards the safety of the forest.

Vite took the road, which soon led him between rows of farm workers' huts and past a smouldering fire. A woman in a brightly coloured wrap, her head in a turban, yelped with surprise as she emerged from her home and saw him darting across her path.

The woman stood there for a second, confused by the sight and the noise, but ducked back into her hut when the two men came pounding along the muddied track that led from the banana farm. One carried a panga, the other an AK-47. The woman knew the killing power of the weapons, each as terrible as the other in its own way. The men slowed. She pointed down the trail. The first man nodded and they set off.

Vite watched this all happen from his hiding place beneath a stack of old mealie sacks behind the hut next door to the woman's. He'd darted around the building as soon as he'd passed her and she hadn't noticed. His little chest was heaving. He could move as fast as his name implied, but not for long. He was used to spending his days close to his mother, perhaps playing with his cousins, tumbling in the grass or climbing trees. He was exhausted and he was hungry.

A dog growled. Vite scrambled towards the mudbricks, dragging a sack with him as partial cover. The dog was mangy, its protruding ribcage studded with fat black ticks. Drool dangled from its bared teeth. It barked.

'Silence,' the woman called. She rounded the hut and looked down at him, then back along the pathway where she had sent the men. She had seen his escape, but she had not betrayed him. The dog growled again and the woman slapped it on the snout. She reached down and Vite cowered from her. He was too tired to run, though, and surrendered to his fate as she placed her hands under his arms and lifted him.

Vite had no idea if there was anyone in his extended family left alive or free. He squealed with hunger and terror, but as the woman brought him to her he started to calm. He clung to her, as he would have done to his mother if she had been there. She was all he knew, and he missed the protective embrace of her long arms. This woman's arms were not as long, and they were not covered in warm hair, but they were black. Vite nestled into her.

The woman made cooing, soothing noises and told him, in French, to be quiet, for his own safety. Vite laid his head against her breast. In the distance was the occasional *pop-pop* of gunshots, but these sounds soon died down. She held him away from her and looked into his black eyes. 'What am I going to do with you, little gorilla?'

Sydney, Australia

Sitting in the Qantas club at Sydney Airport, as unseasonal rain lashed the window, she tapped on the screen of her iPhone and updated her Facebook status: *Carmel Shang now has a chimp named after her. How good is that?*

It was silly, she knew, to post such a cryptic message. Her thirty-nine friends – a pathetic number according to her niece Chloe – would all comment now, asking for more details. It would start up a chain of inane small talk, but Carmel took happiness where she could find it in her life, and Henri's email had made her smile.

There would be little joy waiting for her back in Africa, other than the visit to Henri's wildlife rehabilitation centre in Livingstone on the Zambian side of the Victoria Falls. Although she'd been to the continent fifteen times, nearly always for work, Carmel had never been to the falls, so she was excited about seeing them. And about meeting Henri in the flesh.

They'd first met online, on a web forum called 'Safaritalk', where like-minded people with an interest in Africa and wildlife conservation commented on issues and socialised virtually. Carmel had mentioned that her work had taken her to Rwanda and Tanzania, and Henri had commented that he had grown up in Rwanda. He'd contacted her, via a private message, to ask her what she thought of the country these days, post the genocide of the mid-nineties, and from then on they'd been in regular contact.

Henri had asked about her background, saying that Shang didn't sound like an Australian name to him. She'd explained that she was an ABC – an Australian-born Chinese, the descendant of a Chinese man who'd immigrated during the nineteenth-century gold rush and married a Scottish woman, and that she was as Aussie as they came.

Henri told her he was trying to get his privately run wildlife rehabilitation centre to a point where he could open it to the public, and when she'd enquired about his funding arrangements and offered to help in whatever way she could, he'd invited her to visit next time she was in Africa. He'd cajoled her a bit, and she'd relented. It would do her good, she thought, to spend a bit of time with someone committed to doing good in Africa, rather than just dwelling on past horrors, as she usually did.

Plenty of people, herself included, had tried to make sense of the mass slaughter that had taken place in the tiny central African country, and to try to apportion blame, but Henri had proudly, and at times controversially, stated time and again that he cared more for the innocent animal victims of Rwanda and its neighbouring countries than he did for people who would take up arms against their friends and neighbours.

A little talk bubble flashed up on her screen, informing her that Henri Bousson had just commented on her status. She worked out that it must be about midnight, the night before, in Zambia. She opened the message. *You deserve to have a chimp named after you. Thank you for your support.*

She smiled. She hadn't done *that* much, only donated a few hundred dollars. The chat box popped up on the bottom right-hand corner of her screen. It was Henri. She experienced a little jolt of surprised pleasure.

Hi, he typed. *Where are you, at the airport?*

Yes, she replied. *Late there?*

Oui.

She didn't know what to type next. Her flight would be boarding soon. She would arrive in Johannesburg at about four in the afternoon, stay overnight at the D'Oreale Grande at the Emperor's Palace casino near the airport, then get the Commair flight to Livingstone, Zambia, at eleven the next morning.

I'm looking forward to meeting you, he messaged, filling the void.

Me too.

A lot.

An announcement came over the club's PA, telling passengers the flight to Johannesburg was ready for boarding. Carmel picked up her laptop bag and hooked it over the handle of her small wheeled suitcase. She only ever flew with carry-on – it was too much of a risk and a hassle hoping that checked-in baggage would make it past the Johannesburg baggage handlers intact, let alone all the way to Zambia, Kenya or Rwanda. She held out the phone as it needed to be almost at a full arm's length these days in order for her to see, and tapped the screen as she walked out of the club and onto the escalators.

Me too.

2

Richard took a sixpack of Windhoek Lager dumpies from the surgery fridge where the blood and drugs were kept. Whichever way it went with Janine, he wouldn't want to be stone-cold sober.

Helen had left for the day, which saved him having to answer questions about what he was doing that evening. He still didn't know for sure. The Skukuza doctors' surgery was set on the staff village side of the fence separating the national parks' employees living area from the public rest camp, and the surgery could be accessed by guests in the camp via an entrance on their side. Richard walked through it and into the public area. He'd left his car on the camp side as he had driven to the workshop behind the petrol station to get his flat spare tyre fixed during his lunchbreak and then parked on the camp side to get back in time for an appointment. As he walked to his old Discovery 2, he freed a green bottle from the plastic wrap and used the opener on his key ring to crack it. He'd finished the first before he had driven past the big thatch-roofed Skukuza reception building. He took it slow driving through the gate, as the nightly stream of self-drive tourists hurrying back to camp before the dusk curfew was pouring in. Once he was over the annoying speed bumps he shifted up through the gears to fourth and opened another beer, this time with an opener he'd riveted to the dashboard. As he approached the four-way stop, he'd finished the second bottle and was starting to think a little clearer.

Richard's phone beeped. He fumbled in his top pocket then checked the screen of the cheap Nokia. *Low Battery*, it flashed, then beeped again and died. 'Shit,' he mumbled. He'd plugged it in this morning, but the phone was old and the battery barely held a charge these days. Not good for the camp doctor to be out of contact, but the faux-snakebite victims could damn well wait half an hour while he tried to sort his life out.

He could have turned right before the stop sign and driven through the Skukuza staff village, but it didn't really pay for his patients to see their GP drinking and driving. Sticking to the public roads took a bit longer, but he could drive faster. Although the park's speed limit was fifty kilometres on the tar roads, he had a sticker on the back of the Discovery which showed he could drive at sixty-five. It was handy for emergencies and pressing appointments, such as Janine van der Merwe's breasts.

Richard flicked the top off the third beer as he followed the road towards the Paul Kruger gate. He saw the traffic cop's *bakkie* poorly camouflaged in the bushes and flashed his lights a few times. The national parks traffic enforcement officer, who was there to catch tourists speeding to leave the park via the Kruger gate, stepped out onto the road to flag him down, but then raised a hand and smiled and waved when he recognised the doctor's vehicle. Richard raised his bottle to him in salute, and the man grinned wider. He knew

Ezekial was an alcoholic – took one to know one. Richard had diagnosed himself as borderline, though, which gave him a small measure of comfort. He reflected on what he'd said to Raymond Philpott and smiled. 'Better than being a drug addict, I suppose,' he said to himself.

The beer tasted good and was altering his mind nicely. He'd left the surgery with noble intentions, but they were fading. Fast. He floored the accelerator and crossed the N'waswitshaka River. He thought about Janine van der Merwe's nipples. They were, quite simply, astounding. He'd never, in any examination, professional or not, come across any so perfectly formed, free of lumps and blemishes, and as long and as hard when erect. She liked him to play with them when they kissed. He'd take one between his first and second fingers, teasing it, holding it like a cigarette, and brush his thumb along the tip.

'For fuck's sake,' he said to himself as he finished the third beer. He slowed as he neared the turn-off. What was he doing?

He was becoming aroused. His hormones had always ruled his life. He shifted down to second. The smart thing, he knew, would be to turn around and go home, to stand her up. Perversely, that was also probably the wrong thing to do. Which, he wondered, was the greatest moral misdeed he'd committed with and in relation to Janine: sleeping with a patient, sleeping with another man's wife, breaking off a relationship with a woman who'd told him she loved him and would leave her husband for him, or standing her up now she wanted to talk again? He was a cad, no doubt of it, but he wasn't rude. Richard sighed. The right thing, of course, would be to meet Janine and break it off, again, once and for all.

He turned left onto the gravel road that led to Ten

Minutes – it was a place she'd specified in her note, not a time. Richard knew it well, as did everyone in the Skukuza staff village, so it wasn't a good enough code to fool his nosy receptionist. The broad sandy stretch of non-perennial riverbed was exactly ten minutes' drive from the staff village and it was a favourite hangout for bush *braais* and sundowner drinks after work. The river usually only flowed once a year; the rest of the time there were barely a few pools, which staff kids loved to splash about in. It was like a beach in the middle of the African bush, complete with the odd lion, hyena and leopard patrolling the shore. When he'd first taken the job as the Skukuza GP, Richard had thought it insane to let children play in such a place, but Africa had a way of breeding contempt for danger through familiarity. He hadn't been lying to Philpott when he'd told him he'd had a leopard up a tree in his front garden the previous week. When he'd arrived at Skukuza a year ago, he would have freaked out, but last week he'd sat on the porch taking pictures of it, a cooler box full of beers next to him.

Janine and Lourens had driven around to his house, ostensibly for a look at the leopard, as had several of his neighbours once the word had got around. When Lourens had gone to the toilet Janine had taken the front of Richard's bush shirt in her hands and tongue-kissed him. He'd ground against her, returning the passion and the need. Technically, he reflected as the Discovery bounced along the track, the last minutes of the ten ticking away, he hadn't had sex with Janine, but it was a bit of a Bill Clinton definition. In the past few weeks they'd done pretty much everything else. There hadn't been time in the kitchen while Lourens was relieving himself. He smiled, then shook his head to clear the beer fuzz.

'Fuck it.'

He tossed the empty bottle on the floor of the truck, cracked open a fourth and took a sip before putting it sensibly in the cup holder. He knew what she wanted here in the last golden rays of light, on a blanket she'd probably bring with her. When Lourens wasn't out in the field he often worked nights in the investigations office, monitoring teams in the field. He was fighting the good fight against rhino poachers and his wife was going behind his back. Richard alternated between his ever-present desire for a female body and disgust in himself. He'd served with soldiers in the British Army who'd received the dreaded Dear John letter and back then he hadn't been able to imagine what sort of a man would do that to another man. Now he knew. He had called her and suggested they end the relationship before it went further, but now she wanted to see him again.

'Enough,' he said aloud in the Land Rover as his headlights picked out Janine's Isuzu *bakkie* next to a mound of sand that had been excavated from the river. Richard parked behind a front-end loader. SANParks was quarrying sand to spread on the tar roads. They did it every summer to minimise the effect of the seasonal rains but this January the heavens had brought a deluge that had washed away roads and bridges. The park was a mess and the N'waswitshaka was still flowing strongly even though the floods had mostly subsided. The Isuzu's driver door opened and a long leg, barefooted, swung out.

Janine was pushing forty with two kids, and she pretty much melted his resolve when he saw her in those denim short shorts. He knew she jogged and worked out every day, did whatever she could to relieve the boredom of being at home and unemployed in the staff village. She'd done a degree in marketing or PR or some such thing, he recalled, but affirmative action had closed off most of the plum jobs that once would have been available to white rangers' wives. Janine probably needed someone to tell her she was still sexy, still desirable, and she was – very much so.

Richard ran a hand through his mop of damp salt and pepper hair. He took a moment to consider his current situation. He'd pretty much made a cock-up of his entire life. Sure, the shrinks put the blame on other places, other people, other times, but there was still enough of the soldier in Richard to know that he could have pulled himself together, could have done better. He was a disgrace to his family and a poor excuse for a doctor. And although he knew perfectly well that it was wrong, all he wanted to do was have sex with this woman right now. He took another sip of beer then replaced the bottle in the holder and got out.

He thought he saw her tongue moisten her lips as she walked towards him, hips swaying, feet squeaking in the sand. She brushed a strand of dyed blonde hair from her face. He wasn't keen on sand so his mind drifted to the bonnet of her pickup.

'Richard . . .' she said, stopping just out of reach.

For once in your life, he tried to convince himself, do the right thing. 'Janine . . .'

'No.' She closed the gap between them and reached out to him, putting a French-tipped finger to his lips. He shut his eyes. He was incapable of doing the right thing, he knew it. He smelled her perfume, opened his eyes and felt his body surrendering, betraying him. Why fight it? She wants it. She probably wasn't getting it from Lourens and, if the truth be

told, the man was an arrogant, rude bore. 'Don't say anything, Richard,' she whispered, 'just listen to me.'

He nodded. He kept his hands to himself. He could do slow.

'Richard, I've wanted you since the day I met you, but . . .'

His eyes widened. But?

'Richard, this is wrong. I can't be unfaithful to Lourens
and—'

They both turned at the sound of a big engine revving
hard. They stepped back from each other and Richard felt
himself deflating – mentally and physically. He raised a hand
to shield his eyes from the glare of the spotlights mounted on
the approaching Land Cruiser *bakkie*'s bullbar. Two Africans
in green bush uniforms, R5 assault rifles slung over their
shoulders, stood in the back of the truck. It sped towards
them and for a moment Richard wondered if the driver
intended to run him down. The vehicle stopped just in front
of him, the door opened and Lourens van der Merwe, all six
foot three inches and ninety-five kilograms of him, climbed
out. Richard had given him his annual check-up two weeks
earlier. He was all muscle and very little fat. There was nothing wrong with the man, which was a worry for Richard. He
stood his ground.

'Doc, what the hell's going on, man? I tried your phone five
times but it's switched off. Aren't you supposed to be on call?'

'I am. Problem with . . .'

Lourens waved away the excuse. 'I checked your house then
called Helen. She told me she thought you might be here.' He
looked at his wife for four seconds, no more, his huge hands
bunched into fists at his side; then he looked back at Richard.

Richard was ready. He'd 'milled' during parachute training in the army – put on gloves and tried to beat the shit out

of a fellow recruit who gave as good as he got until the drill sergeant told them to stop. It was all about developing controlled aggression. He'd also boxed a bit for the regiment. He was, of course, older and flabbier now, and Lourens had it over him in weight, muscle and youthfulness. What was coming, though, would do him good, in a masochistic kind of way. Perhaps a few bruises from Lourens might assuage the guilt he occasionally felt for the other husbands he'd wronged.

'We've got a man down. Anti-poaching patrol found some Mozambican rhino poachers. We drilled two of them and we're in pursuit of the third, but they got one of my men. He's taken an AK round to the chest. Chopper's coming and they'll fly him to Nelspruit.' Lourens pointed his right finger like it was a pistol, and fired at Richard's heart. 'But I want you on board.'

Richard nodded. 'I've got my bag in the back of the Discovery.'

'Fetch it. You're coming with me. You can pick up your vehicle later.' Lourens turned and walked back to his truck. He reached inside and talked into a radio handset, in Afrikaans. Richard got his medical bag – an old army medic's pack – and hoisted it into the back of the Land Cruiser. His Afrikaans was basic at best, but he gathered Lourens was talking to the national parks helicopter pilot. Lourens got into the front of the *bakkie* and motioned for Richard to get in the passenger seat. Lourens looked at his wife and spat out a few more words that Richard guessed meant: 'I'll deal with you later.'

'Lourens . . .' Richard began as the Afrikaner swung the truck around in a three-point turn and gunned the big four-litre engine for all it was worth.

Lourens looked straight ahead into the darkness that had descended on the bush. 'Unless it's about my man, I'm not interested. The helo will pick you up on the tar road and you'll go. And my advice to you, *Doctor* Richard Dunlop, is that you keep my man alive and that he stays alive, otherwise people will find out that you weren't on call when we needed you.'

Richard nodded.

There wasn't room for a helicopter to land safely at Ten Minutes, so Lourens had organised the landing to take place on the tourist road nearby, which was turned from night into day by the helicopter's landing light. The journey to the pickup had been quick, leaving no time for excuses or explanations. The helicopter settled. Richard grabbed his backpack from the rear of the Cruiser. 'Are you coming?' he yelled to Lourens over the noise of the chopper's whining engine. The pilot gave him a thumbs-up, indicating it was clear for him to approach.

'No. I've got to get back to the ops room. We'll talk later. Save my man.'

Richard nodded.

He climbed into the chopper and buckled his seatbelt as the pilot lifted off. Richard looked down and saw Lourens was already driving the short distance back to Skukuza. As the pilot, Andre, banked he noticed the headlights of Janine's *bakkie* weaving through the bush. Richard burped beer and the pilot grinned and shook his head.

He'd been for a ride in this helicopter before, out with one of the vets who was darting rhino. The parks people were putting passive transponders in the rhinos so they could track them because a record number had been poached in Kruger the previous year. As a doctor, Richard couldn't understand how people could be so well educated yet still believe in the mumbo jumbo of traditional medicine. Rhinos were being slaughtered for their horns, not to produce a fabled aphrodisiac but rather for the relief of fever and, according to the latest rubbish, as a cure for cancer. The illegal trade in wildlife products was big business and the perpetrators were becoming ever more organised and ruthless.

Through his headphones Richard heard the pilot radioing the anti-poaching patrol on the ground telling him he was inbound with the doctor and would be at their location in four minutes.

'They're not far from Renoster Kopjes,' Andre told him through the intercom. 'These guys are getting more desperate by the day, hey.'

Richard gripped his bag and looked down at the faded camouflage pattern. Funny, he thought, how the combination of the whine of the jet engine and the smell of the burning fuel and the colour of his bag could produce such a response. His skin felt clammy and sweat pricked at his underarms. He felt his heart beating faster. He didn't know if he could do this, didn't know if he could save this man. He saw a strong handheld spotlight being strobed on and off below, guiding them in. The flickering light intermittently caught the shirtless black man on the ground and the glint of the blood as the helicopter began its descent.

Richard saw a movement in the cone of the landing light ahead. 'Hey, look there!'

The pilot nodded and radioed the leader of the anti-poaching unit. 'I've got movement to my front, one hundred metres. One male with a rifle. Looks like an AK, over.'

Richard knew the dilemma. There would be men on the ground wanting the helicopter to follow the fugitive, perhaps the man who had wounded their colleague. At the same time their chief concern must be for the wounded man.

The running man stumbled then fell and, still trapped in the light as the helicopter continued its descent, he turned and pointed his rifle at them. Richard saw the muzzle flash just as the pilot did. 'Holy shit,' the pilot said.

'Put us down,' Richard barked. 'There's a man dying down there.' If it was a chest wound, that wasn't an exaggeration. The pilot nodded and switched off the landing light.

Richard hoped Andre, the young man flying the helicopter, was good enough to land by the comparatively weak illumination of the spotlight that was now being held steady on the road. Richard thought the man holding the light was brave as the startled poacher might aim for it. More likely, though, the Mozambican was running as fast as he could. As they touched down, bumping as the skids hit one after another, Richard heard gunfire over the scream of the rotors. Some of the patrol were in pursuit. He squeezed his eyes shut and forced out the images of the dead who rose up from his nightmares. Now is not the time, he told them, now is not the time.

'Doc . . . Doc!' Andre punched him on the arm. 'Come on, man, get out. I'll keep the engine burning. Go get him, Doc.'

Richard opened his eyes, nodded and grasped the door frame. One of the patrol members, his face streaked with dirt and sweat, his uniform wet with blood, had already opened the door and was beckoning to him. Richard dragged his pack out and ran, bent at the waist, to where the wounded man lay. He unzipped a side pocket of the pack, pulled out a box of disposable gloves and snapped on a pair as the patrol leader told him what had happened. One shot; the bullet had passed through the man's chest and out his back, tumbling on the way as was typical of an AK round, not taking time to smell the roses.

The man was in his mid-twenties, Richard guessed, his abdominal muscles defined, shiny and hard as chiselled stone. He was fit. He'd need to be. Richard peeled back the big, blood-soaked pad of the wound dressing. The man wheezed and winced, as the blood gurgled and frothed from the hole. Sucking chest wound.

A rifle fired nearby, two shots. Richard instinctively hunched down over the patient. His hands shook as he tried to unzip his bag, his latex-coated fingers slick with blood. He pulled out a syringe of morphine and injected it into the man's arm. Taking out another dressing, he bit off the end of the package with his teeth, unwrapped it and then laid the waterproof cover over the wound. The suction from the man's punctured lung drew the wrapper over the bullet hole, sealing it, but Richard knew that the lung could continue to leak air into the chest cavity, causing a tension pneumothorax, which could kill the ranger in a matter of minutes. He pulled a fresh rubber glove from his bag and used his surgical scissors to snip off a finger, then took an IV needle from its sterile wrapper and slid it through the tip of the latex sheath. He plunged the needle through the dressing wrapper and into the man's lung cavity and lowered his head to the improvised one-way valve. He heard the hiss of air through the open end of the finger that told him the lung was now venting outside the man's chest. Next he took out his scissors and cut the man's camouflaged shirt sleeve lengthways, then inserted an IV into a vein in his arm.

A rifle was firing on automatic and a three-round burst cracked around Richard, showering him and his patient with shredded leaves and twigs from the tree above them. Richard threw himself across the wounded ranger. 'Bloody hell!'

The patrol member who'd greeted him was firing back now, yelling to his comrades. Richard heard the helicopter's engine change note. When he looked over he saw the pilot waving to him, urging him to get a move on. 'Help me get him on board,' Richard yelled.

The man nearest him slung his FN rifle across his body and moved to the wounded man's feet. On three they lifted him, Richard carrying him under the arms and the other man holding his ankles. Despite the morphine the man screamed in agony. They took him to the helicopter and slid him through the rear door, laying him on the floor. Richard climbed in after him. 'Will you be all right?' he yelled back to the ranger over the noise.

'Ja. Reinforcements are coming, and that poacher he is running away now. You go.'

Richard nodded and closed the door. Andre lifted off and Richard arranged himself so he could monitor the patient. As he hooked the IV to a fire extinguisher on the fuselage wall, his foot knocked against something loose. It was a pistol. There was an empty holster on the man's belt. He unzipped his medical pack and slid the weapon in. He didn't want it getting lost or stolen at the hospital and he'd take it back to the investigations office the next day.

Richard found a set of headphones and heard the pilot radioing the Mediclinic at Nelspruit, advising them they were inbound with a seriously injured patient who'd suffered a gunshot wound to the chest. The man looked up at

Richard, blinking. There was fear in his eyes. Richard took the injured ranger's hand in his and gripped it, as much to reassure himself as the patient, and to still the shaking. He needed a drink and a smoke, maybe more. No, he told himself. Not that.

He closed his eyes and the waking nightmare began. The sound of gunfire, the sight of red blood on black skin, the man's scream as they'd lifted him into the chopper – these things brought it all back. It was always there, of course, lurking at the dark edges of his consciousness, but now it swamped him. The bodies were rising up, walking towards him, threatening to smother him. He held the wounded ranger's hand so hard he thought he might break the poor man's bones. With his other hand he cuffed away the tears that started to well.

'You OK back there, Doc?' Andre asked in the headphones. Richard nodded, keeping his eyes closed so the younger man wouldn't see. 'How's our man doing?'

Richard opened his eyes to look down at him. He forced a smile for the wounded man's sake. 'I don't know.'

That silenced the pilot. Below them, the darkness of the national park bush gave way to the lamps and cooking fires that dotted the hills of the sprawling informal settlements outside Numbi Gate. They passed over pine plantations and soon the brighter lights of White River and, finally, the provincial capital of Nelspruit, lately renamed Mbombela, came into view. 'Hang in there,' he whispered to the patient and himself.

A trauma team was waiting at the helipad, and as they eased the ranger onto a gurney Richard briefed the surgeon on the drugs and treatment he'd administered. When the man was wheeled away there was nothing else for him and the pilot to do, so they got back in the helicopter and took off again. They flew back to the Skukuza airport, which had once accepted daily South African Airways commercial flights but was now restricted to charters and national parks take-offs and landings. Andre drove Richard back to Ten Minutes to collect his vehicle.

'Hectic night hey, Doc?'

'Yes.' He said goodbye to the pilot and drove back to the staff village. On the way he gulped the open, flat beer sitting in the beverage holder. He was going to need a lot to drink before he'd be able to get to sleep.

Oddly, when he arrived back at his home in Impala Street, the lights were on. As he turned into the driveway he saw a vehicle there. It was Janine's. He never locked his house – it was safe in the staff village – and she must have let herself in.

'Shit.'

She opened his front door as he got out of the Discovery and grabbed his bag. 'I'm sorry . . .' She met him on the pathway.

'What are you doing here, Janine?' Then, when she turned her head, he saw the swollen eye and the beginnings of a bruise. 'Lourens?'

'He didn't hit me, if that's what you think. He never has, but I've never seen him like he was tonight. He only came home once the Mediclinic people told him his man was alive and stable. He cares more for them than he does his family.'

Richard ran a hand through his hair. 'What happened?'

'He sent the kids to their room then pulled his gun out. He didn't point it at me, but I was scared. I had to get out of the house. I tripped when I ran outside and hit my head on the pavement. Richard . . . he said he's going to kill you. I told him nothing had happened, that we hadn't . . . you know.' She put a finger to her puffy eye and started to cry. Richard took her hand and led her inside.

He flicked the lights off and told Janine to sit on the couch. He went to the fridge and stared at the beers sitting there, tempting him, but grabbed a jug of water instead. He poured two glasses and took one to her. 'Do you have someone to stay with . . . a friend, a relative?'

She took the dewy glass in both hands. 'All my family's in PE.'

Port Elizabeth was at the other end of the country. He realised that in the closed community of the staff village word would soon get around about what had happened. Bloody Helen had probably told half the women already. Richard knew the best thing he could do was pack his few bags, throw them in the Discovery and leave in the dead of night. It wouldn't be the first time he'd left a job that way. But what about Janine?

'I can't leave my kids,' she said. 'And he'd kill us all if I tried to take them with me. What am I going to do?'

'Give him the night. I'm sure he'll calm down.'

'I hope you're right, Richard. Can I stay here?'

He didn't want her in his home, but he had no choice. 'The bed in the spare room's made up.' She nodded. Taking the empty glass from her hand as she stood, he couldn't help reaching out to gingerly touch the swelling. 'I'll get you some frozen peas for that.'

She reached up and wrapped her hand around his. 'Thank you. I'm sorry for all of this.'

'Two to tango, and all that.' Gently, he lowered her hand.

'Tell you what, I'll run you a bath and make a cup of tea, all right?'

'You really are a friend, you know that? I think we should have left it at that, but I don't regret any of it.'

He nodded. He showed her to the spare bedroom and turned on the taps in the bathroom's shower. 'I'll be in the kitchen.'

Richard left her and went to the lounge room. His medical bag was on the dining table, where he'd dumped it. He unzipped the bag and took out the ranger's pistol. Easing the slide back, he saw there was a round already chambered. He moved the slide forward again and stuffed the pistol into the waistband of his trousers and went to the kitchen.

While the kettle was heating on the gas range he went back to the lounge and opened the curtains across the window that overlooked his front yard and Impala Street. He saw headlights further up the road, though he couldn't make out the vehicle. As he watched the car he saw the lights go out and heard the engine stop. The vehicle kept coasting along, though, past the house two doors up. When it was outside the senior ranger's home next door, it stopped. A man got out, and although it was too dark to identify him, there was no mistaking the curved magazine of the AK-47 he held by his side. However, the silhouette of the Russian assault rifle was too long. It looked like there was a silencer screwed to the end. Richard had heard that the business of rhino poaching was becoming more and more sophisticated, and it had been Lourens himself, over drinks at a *braai*, who had told the assembled menfolk that the investigations division had recently shot dead a poacher armed with a silenced Russian military special forces weapon.

Richard pulled out the pistol he'd taken from the injured ranger and moved back to the bathroom. 'Janine,' he hissed. There was no answer, and he realised she couldn't hear him over the noise of running water. If he alerted her she might come out with a towel wrapped around her. That might tip Lourens over the edge – if he wasn't already on the other side of sanity.

'Fuck, fuck, fuck,' he cursed to himself.

Richard crept back through his house, the pistol up and ready, the fingers of his left hand wrapped around the right, steadying it as much as he could. He stopped at the window again. The man was walking up the driveway, the rifle still held by his side.

Richard moved to the front door and, with his back against the brickwork, opened it a few inches. He peeked around and looked through the crack. 'Lourens. We need to talk.'

He saw the rifle come up and heard the *phut*, *phut*, *phut* of the silenced rounds leaving the barrel. The wooden door splintered beside him as he pulled his head out of the way, and the lead slugs ricocheted off the kitchen wall inside. 'Lourens, no!'

Richard glanced back through the window and saw the man running across the lawn, rifle up and taking aim.

'Richard?' Janine called. The lounge room was suddenly partially illuminated by light from the bathroom as Janine opened the door.

'Get back.'

The window shattered and Richard dropped to one knee, pushed his hand past a jagged shard of glass and fired two shots, point-blank into the gunman's chest.

'No!' Janine screamed.

Richard stood. He advanced through the remains of the window, smashing the last of the glass out of the frame into the garden. He kept the pistol out in front of him. The man lay face down in the grass and his assault rifle was a foot away from him, where he'd dropped it. He wore black leather gloves and a black jacket and jeans. Lourens hadn't been dressed like that.

Richard used his foot to roll the man over. It wasn't Lourens.

3

It was late January, not October, but as the Berlin Pub was – as its name suggested – German-themed, its owners didn't need much of an excuse to throw an Oktoberfest weekend party, starting on a Friday night. The place was packed and it was, Liesl thought, to use an overused but in this case accurate South African term, hectic.

Instead of a band there was a blond-haired guy in his twenties singing Afrikaans rock and pop to backing tracks he selected from a laptop. The guy was basically singing karaoke, but he had a good voice and the crowd loved it. Liesl guessed many of the patrons had finished work early on the last day of the working week and had been partying since the afternoon.

Sannette squeezed past a stressed-looking waitress and waved to a bunch of people sitting and standing around an outdoor table. A couple of them were dancing.

'Howzit, doll,' said a short guy with a grey crew cut. He kissed Sannette and looked at Liesl.

'Howzit, I'm—'

'I know who you are, Liesl Nel, but the question is, do you remember me?'

She didn't but that wasn't unusual. She met so many people in her line of work, and she'd never been good at remembering faces. People knew her from her by-line and now that she had moved back to South Africa full-time she'd been in this situation more than once. 'Ummm . . .'

'Piet . . . Piet du Toit. From high school in Letsitele.'

'Oh . . . Piet, of course. You're a long way from home. You haven't changed a bit.'

He laughed. She really didn't remember him at all. 'Hey, can we get some drinks over here,' Piet called to the harried waitress. 'What'll it be?'

'White wine, please.' Sannette said she'd have the same. Piet ordered a bottle of Two Oceans sauvignon blanc, a glass of ice and a brandy and Coke.

Sannette said, 'Everyone, this is Liesl Nel, the *famous* journalist from *Escape!* magazine. She and Piet and I were all at school together out in the wilds of Limpopo province, where we grew up. Liesl, this is everyone.'

Liesl waggled her fingers at the crowd of laughing, half-drunk people at the table. Piet had returned his attention to her and taken a step closer. She backed up, but was blocked by a tree. The pub was set in an old house and spilled out down the slope of what would have been the back yard. There were people everywhere. Liesl felt her cheeks start to warm up, and she wiped beads of perspiration from her top lip.

'Hot tonight, hey?' Piet said.

'*Ja*,' she said, but she knew it wasn't the heat.

'I love *Escape!* and I'm a big fan of your writing and your photos,' he said, gazing at her. The drinks came and Liesl was moistening her lips with her tongue in anticipation as Piet poured the wine and added a handful of ice cubes He looked up and she hoped he couldn't see how desperate she was for the drink. Liesl took two big gulps.

'Thanks,' she said.

'You must have the best job in the world, hey, travelling all over Africa, getting to try out fancy new four-by-fours, staying in all those luxury safari lodges. Hell, what a life.'

'It's not all it's cracked up to be,' she said.

Piet raised his eyebrows. 'Really?'

'No. I'm joking, it is the best job in the world.'

He laughed and topped up her glass. She didn't stop him. She'd had two gin and tonics at Sannette's and was just getting started. In fact, there was a high turnover of staff at *Escape!* magazine. It did seem like a fun job, and it was for a while, but spending eight months of every year on the road flying and driving from one part of the continent to the other played havoc with relationships.

'How long have you been at *Escape!* now?'

'A year this time around, but I was there for a couple of years from 2000 onwards.'

Piet nodded, sipping his brandy and Coke. '*Ja*, I won't say I've been stalking you, but I have followed your career off and on over the years. I mean, you were like the most famous person to come out of our school.'

'Oh, I don't know about that . . .'

'*Ja*, no, it's true, hey. I sell insurance, Sannette runs a dress shop.'

'Hey, exclusive boutique,' Sannette interjected. Liesl hoped she might save her from Piet, or introduce her to someone else. He was a nice enough guy, but she knew where this conversation was headed and she wasn't in the mood tonight. All she wanted to do was gulp down her drink, get out of here and go back to Sannette's and open another bottle by herself.

'And then there was you, making the front page of nearly every newspaper in the world with those pictures you took in Rwanda when all those blacks went crazy and chopped each other into little pieces, back in, what . . .'

'In 1994 and 1995.'

'And then Afghanistan. You were wounded in that car bomb, but you kept on taking pictures. Absolutely—'

'And what have you been up to since school, Piet? You said insurance, yes?' She took a deep breath. The guy was only trying to be flattering, and she should be used to it, but he was crowding her – everyone in the place was crowding her. The last thing she wanted to discuss was her photographs. She glanced across at Sannette, hoping for a way out; although her friend was deep in conversation with another woman she must have been keeping an eye on Liesl and Piet, because she caught the look and simply smiled and winked.

Oh my God, Liesl thought, as Piet reeled off his career milestones, *she's trying to set me up.* Liesl would be forty in two months' time and although she told her few close friends that she was perfectly happy without a relationship, they'd all at one time or another tried to set her up with someone. Elise had even tried to set her up with another woman, despite the fact that Liesl was not that way inclined. She could, and did, find a man whenever she needed one. Piet turned back to the table to take the wine bottle from the ice bucket and Liesl caught Sannette's eye again. Liesl didn't need this man, though. 'I am going to kill you,' she mouthed. Sannette grinned and winked again.

'So, where are you off to next?' Piet asked, refilling her glass.

'I'm driving up to Livingstone via Botswana, taking one of the new BMW four-by-fours for a spin.'

'What a pleasure,' Piet said. 'I'm off to a conference at Sun City – that's about as exciting as my job gets.'

She looked at his left hand. 'You're not married?' She didn't think Sannette would pimp her to an attached guy.

He looked away from her for a second. 'Was. My wife died of breast cancer. I've got two girls, thirteen and ten. They're great, but a bit of a handful.'

'I'm so sorry, Piet.' And she was. She saw how he'd sagged a little in the telling of his story. It was the same with her. They said it was good to confront and unburden, but when you had to tell the same tale again and again, it was as though another little piece of you just died. If you said these things too many times, one day there would be nothing left. She put a hand on his arm. 'Really sorry.'

He looked up into her eyes. He was so short. She saw the flicker there and although she did not want to lead him on, she couldn't imagine the sadness of being confronted with the memory of his wife every day in the faces of his two daughters, so she gave his arm a little squeeze. Liesl knew some people would see it the other way around – that Piet's wife was 'living on' through her daughters – but she liked her world better, where it was just her and, except for times like now, no one and nothing to remind her of the horror.

She reached around him and set her glass down on the table. 'Excuse me. Back soon.' Before he protested, she ran her hand lightly down his arm; she'd learned years ago that the key to getting off the hook without a fuss was letting the guy think he was still in charge. He smiled obligingly.

Liesl threaded her way back through the crush of people – even more had arrived – towards the ladies' room inside the bar. An African waitress carrying three plates stacked with huge eisbein and mounds of sauerkraut nearly bumped into her. 'Sorry,' Liesl said.

'Hey, sexy,' a voice behind her said.

Liesl didn't know if the comment was directed at her, but she didn't turn to check. If it was, the man was probably drunk. She felt a hand grab her elbow and this time she spun around.

'Howzit, babe.' The man was ten or fifteen years younger than her. His eyes were bloodshot and he swayed as she wrenched herself free.

'Keep your hands to yourself,' she said.

'Hey, chill, *meisie*,' he said. 'Just trying to be friendly. Come dance with me.' He reached for her again.

'No!' Liesl took a step back, but at the same time the man started to fall backwards, his eyes wide. Behind the man she saw Piet, who was a good eight inches shorter, pull the drunkard by his collar. 'Keep your *fokken* hands off her,' Piet spat.

'Hey, get your hands off me, you fucking Dutchman.' The younger man rounded on Piet with a big swinging punch that Piet, who was not nearly as drunk, was able to dodge.

It was almost comical as the young guy started to lose his balance as his fist sailed harmlessly past Piet's face. Liesl raised her hand to her mouth but her laugh turned to a gasp as Piet, his eyes narrowed and shoulders squared, delivered a short, sharp jab to the other man's solar plexus. He doubled over and coughed, spewing part of his last drink onto Piet's shirt.

'*Fokken soutie*,' Piet spat. His left fist shot up from low down, snapping the man's head back.

'Piet!' Liesl yelled. 'Leave him. It's OK.'

The pub crowd was gathering around them as word spread of the fight. The singer kept singing, but glanced down at the action. People started cheering as the drunk man, blood and spittle hanging from his mouth, took another swing at Piet. Although Piet was older he was quick on his feet and he danced out of range of the coming blow. His next punch caught the drunk man on the chin and sent him flying back towards Liesl. He landed at her feet. She held out her hands in appeal. 'Leave him, Piet. Enough!'

The younger man winced in pain and rolled onto his side. He spat and raised himself on one elbow as Piet stood over him. 'Fucking hairyback,' he spluttered up at Piet.

Piet kicked the man in the ribs then grabbed a handful of his hair, lifted his face and punched him again. 'Shut up, you fucking *rooinek soutpiel*.' Others broke from the mob, seeing the fight had gone too far, and two men grabbed Piet's arms and pulled him back. The other man looked like he'd passed out.

Liesl turned and ran.

'Liesl!' she heard Sannette call behind her.

Liesl was gasping for air as she weaved through the chaos of the crowded car park. She ran up the steep driveway to the street where Sannette had parked her Santa Fe people mover.

'Liesl, come back. It's over,' Sannette urged. 'You've had a fright. Piet's a good guy, hey?'

Liesl stared at her friend. '*Bliksem*, he nearly killed that poor guy!'

'That *Engelsman* was trying to molest you. I watched you going to the ladies' and saw what happened and I sent Piet to save you from that *soutie*.'

'I didn't need saving, Sannette. Especially not by Piet! That guy was just drunk and stupid, that's all. And listen to yourself . . . *Engelsman*, *soutie*. The guy's not a "salt prick" with one foot in South Africa and one foot in England, he's a South

African, like you and me. OK, sure, he's an idiot, but he's not an excuse for tribal warfare to break out.'

'You heard him, Liesl. He called Piet a Dutchman, and worse.'

'So? He was *drunk*.'

For an instant she'd almost let her guard down when she pictured Piet at home in his empty Tuscan mansion on some estate trying to work out how to raise two teenage girls. Her heart really had gone out to him, and then an instant later he was kicking the shit out of a helpless, if stupid, man on the ground. The anger inside people, the harm that ordinary people were capable of, never ceased to scare her. That's why they were better off avoided.

'So? He got what he deserved,' Sannette said.

Liesl shook her head.

'Come, let's go back to the party, Liesl.'

It was the last thing she wanted to do. Her idea of fun wasn't watching two guys beat the shit out of each other. Also, she couldn't tell Sannette but the sight of the blood pouring from the drunk man's nose and mouth made her want to either vomit or burst into tears. She hadn't, as she told people who asked, given up reporting on war zones because she'd been offered a better deal by *Escape!*. She'd been fired by the wire service she worked for in Afghanistan because she'd broken down in the field after an American soldier on the patrol she'd been accompanying had taken a bullet in the neck. Oddly, as she'd been in the Humvee when it had been hit by an IED – an improvised explosive device as the Americans called roadside bombs – the sight of her own blood hadn't fazed her nearly as much.

'I'm tired, Sannette, really tired. You go back to the party. I'm sorry.'

Sannette put her hands on her hips and glared at her.

'I know you want to set me up with Piet, but it's never going to work. I'd feel like a fool going back in there now. I couldn't speak to him after what just happened.'

Sannette's shoulders slumped and she opened her arms. '*Ag*, come here, sis.'

Liesl fell into her friend's embrace and had to swallow to hold back the tears.

'It's OK, babe. I didn't want to say anything, and I know we hit the wines a bit last night, but you looked so tired this morning. I'm worried about you.'

A man walking through the car park wolf-whistled in their direction. 'I don't sleep a lot.' Liesl gently broke the embrace and brushed her hair from her eyes.

'I'll drive you home.'

'No, I don't want to keep you from your friends, and I'd be miserable company tonight. I'll call a cab or something.'

Sannette opened her handbag and fished inside. '*Eish*, but you've been away from South Africa for too long. This isn't London. Here, doll, take my keys. Drive home. The gate thingy's on the key ring. I'll be too pissed to drive home by the end of the night anyway. Make yourself at home and if you're still awake when I get back we'll open another bottle to help you sleep.'

'I can come get you if you give me a call,' Liesl said taking the keys.

Sannette waved her hand. 'No problem at all. I'll get one of the girls, or maybe Piet, to drive me home. You go home and put your feet up.'

Liesl reached out and placed her hand on Sannette's forearm. 'You really are a pal. Thank you, and I'm sorry again, hey.'

'Your loss,' Sannette grinned. 'Now, be a good girl and run on home. I hardly ever get a night out away from the kids, so I've got some serious *jolling* to do.'

Liesl waved goodbye to her friend and looked around the congested car park. She pushed the unlock button alarm fob on the car key and saw the flash and heard the beep of Sannette's people mover. There was something else on the key ring and she held it up to the glare of the security lighting as she walked to the car. It was a small can of pepper spray. Liesl got in the car and slid the seat back; she was several inches taller than Sannette. She adjusted the mirror and saw the crumb-littered back seat and the discarded junk-food wrappers. She'd wanted to drive the BMW to the bar, but Sannette had cajoled her into coming with her, perhaps fearing she'd try to pull out early. 'Besides,' Sannette had added, 'that Black Man's Worry is a prime hijacking target. I wouldn't drive around in that thing if you paid me.'

It was barely two kilometres from the complex that housed the Berlin Pub back to Featherbrooke Estate where Sannette and her family lived, just down the road from the Silver Star Casino. There seemed to be casinos everywhere in South Africa these days. When Liesl was growing up, in the apartheid era, casinos were only allowed in Swaziland and the black homelands – places where supposed decent, upstanding Afrikaners went to indulge in sinful gambling and to have sex with black people. She had hated living in a society where the government tried to dictate morals to its people and regulate where and how they lived, but in the new South Africa people lived behind brick and electric fences and carried pepper spray and pistols to the shops and the neighbourhood casino. Maybe she should have stayed in London, although even in that city there'd recently been rioting and looting. No, it wasn't Africa, or youth unemployment, or disenfranchisement; it was just people and their stupid bloody tribes.

She backed out of the car space, weaved around a couple of girls staggering arm in arm, and drove through the estate the pub was in. If she'd married a man like Piet, she wondered, would she have ended up in one of these places? She knew she couldn't keep roving and trying to dodge the horrors that lived inside her – that had almost got her killed in Afghanistan – but nor could she bring herself to settle down. She wondered, not for the first time, if there was much point in her existence at all.

Liesl stopped at the security barrier and an African guard pressed a button to raise the boom gate, allowing her to leave the complex. She waved back to him and wondered why there was security on an estate where anyone could come and go as they pleased to visit the local pub. The traffic lights in front of her turned orange so Liesl planted her foot. She swung the wheel to the left and made it through just as they turned red. Behind her she heard a horn hoot. She checked her rearview mirror and saw a red Volkswagen Golf had followed her through, running the red light and causing the driver of a *bakkie* coming from the right to brake hard. It had been the *bakkie* driver beeping his horn at the Golf.

She shook her head. She reckoned the number-one danger in Johannesburg wasn't crime, it was bad driving. Liesl eased off the accelerator, expecting the maniac in the Golf to overtake her. Instead, he stayed behind her, though the driver of the *bakkie*, a burly male with a mullet haircut and moustache, leaned on his horn and blared abuse out the window as he passed the Golf, and then her. Liesl added road rage to her list of top risks in this sprawling, crazy city. She'd be glad to escape this zoo and get back out into the wilds of Africa, where the man-eating animals were much safer to be around.

Ahead of her Liesl could see the left turn onto Furrow Road, which led to Sannette's complex. The lights were green, but this time she didn't rush it. She heard an engine being revved hard and checked her wing mirror to see the little Golf suddenly accelerate and fly past her. She shook her head again at the driver's unpredictability. Still, it was a Friday and the end of the month – pay day for most people – so it was possible this car's driver had had more than a few drinks. She couldn't see who was behind the wheel as the windows were heavily tinted.

Without indicating, the Golf veered suddenly back in front of her, cutting the turn so finely that Liesl had to brake hard. This time she thumped the centre of the steering wheel, although there was no hooting. She didn't know where the damn horn was on Sannette's car. '*Poephol!*' she yelled instead. Ahead of the Golf the light was still green, but the car's brake lights flashed red, forcing her to again apply her brakes ferociously.

Liesl couldn't overtake, as her left-hand turn was just ahead. What was this idiot doing? Next, he put on his left indicator.

'Oh, great,' she muttered. He'd nearly taken her out when overtaking her, just so he could make the same turn as her, in front of her. She fiddled with the indicator lever and found the horn. She pushed it. The sound was tinny and unimpressive. The Golf slowed even more. He was taunting her, which made her heart beat quicker. 'Come on, come on. Please don't stop at the robot,' she willed him. Co-workers had laughed at her, years ago when she'd first moved to England, when she'd called traffic lights robots. She wasn't laughing now.

Just as it reached the lights, which were still green, the Golf stopped suddenly. Liesl didn't see the flash of the brake lights, so she had no warning. One minute it was moving, the next it was stationary. She stood on the brake pedal of Sannette's people mover and everything seemed to slow.

She saw the Golf looming in her windscreen; saw the driver's door open and the man jump out onto the roadway; felt Sannette's car fishtail as she tried to veer left around the smaller car and miss the man on the road. She almost made it, but the kerb on the left side was too high for the low-clearance people mover to mount and when she hit it she careened back to the right.

I'm going to die, she thought as the nose of Sannette's car ploughed into the back of the Volkswagen. The airbag exploded in her face as she was thrown forward. Looking to the right, wincing from the pain in her neck, she saw the man who had caused all this walking, almost casually, towards her with a black pistol in his hand.

Liesl reached for the keys in the ignition and pulled them out. She scrambled to the left, over the gearstick and around the passenger side airbag, which had also inflated, towards the passenger door. She felt for the tiny can of pepper spray on the key ring. As she pushed the door open with one hand she twisted and depressed the yellow button on the can.

She felt a breeze on her face as she scrambled and heard the man cry out, swearing, at the same time as she felt rather than heard the nearby impact of two bullets. One smashed through the plastic dashboard on her right and zinged off some metal, while the other punctured the passenger airbag as she tumbled forwards onto the road. Opening the door had created a draft that blew the irritating pepper spray away from her and into the face of the gunman. She kept pressing the red button, but heard the last of the spray escape the canister. She fumbled with the keys as she crawled along the road, manoeuvring them until a key was protruding between each of her fingers when she made a fist. She'd learned the move in a self-defence class years ago, and she would fight this bastard to the death.

Except he had a gun and, as he wiped his streaming eyes, he moved around the back of the car. Liesl got to her feet. To her left was a drainage ditch and beyond that the electric-fence-topped wall of a housing estate. She'd be silhouetted against the ochre-coloured wall whichever way she ran. She turned and darted to the front of Sannette's car so that it was between her and the gunman. He was blinking and his hand was wavering as he tried to focus through the pain of the chemicals in his eyes. He fired again and the bullet whizzed past her head. They were stopped on Hendrik Potgieter, a busy road, and she could see a car cresting the hill, its headlights on high beam as it raced down the slope towards the intersection with Furrow. The driver would have seen the Golf stopped at the robot and the people mover behind it. No one stopped for anyone or anything out of the ordinary in Johannesburg, especially at night. Liesl ran up the road, into the path of the oncoming Mercedes.

The driver honked and blared the horn and Liesl waved frantically. The car swerved. Liesl tried to yell and point to the man in black. She made it across the road and would have kept on running if she hadn't heard the screech of rubber and the sickening thud of the Mercedes slamming into the man who had just tried to kill her.

4

Carmel Shang took a Diet Coke from the minibar in her room in the D'Oreale Grande Hotel and poured it into a glass.

Ten years, two months and, oh, about four or five days ago, she would have set to work on the miniature bottles of alcohol as well, but she'd been sober all that time and the temptation wasn't nearly as strong as it once had been. However, nights away from home, in the anonymous cocoon of a hotel with a drink at her fingertips, were difficult. Fortunately, as always, there was work to do.

Carmel took her laptop out of her carry-on bag and turned it on, then fossicked in the bottom for the power cord.

She retied the fluffy bathrobe and sat down at the hotel room desk. The shower had been reviving and, while the tiredness was creeping up on her, she knew the worst thing she could do for her jet lag was succumb too soon to the lure of the double bed. Carmel connected to the hotel's free wireless service and opened Outlook. Sipping her Coke and scrunching her toes on the carpet, she waited for her thirty-two messages to download. As soon as the first message chimed its way into her inbox she opened it, read it and began to reply. She answered every message – or deleted it if it was spam as it arrived. The download was faster than her replies though, and she could see a message from Henri Bousson waiting for her. It was tempting to skip ahead and open it, but she didn't. She was thorough and methodical in everything she did; it was what made her a good prosecutor.

She replied to her mother, telling her that yes, she had arrived safely in South Africa and was flying to Livingstone in Zambia the next day. She reminded her mother that her email contact would be sporadic over the next few days, and during the two weeks she would spend in Rwanda, as the GPRS and 3G phone systems were erratic. It was partly true, but also partly an excuse. She would be busy – too busy for personal stuff.

There was a knock at the door. 'Room service,' a man called.

Carmel moved to the peephole and looked into the hallway. The African man had a trolley and wore the uniform of the hotel. She pulled her robe closed tighter, then slid the safety latch aside and let him in. She told the man to put her meal on the desk and signed for the stuffed chicken breast and salad, leaving him a ten rand tip. The man thanked her and left. She'd counted on the service being slower. The food could wait under its cloche until she was finished with her messages.

The next one up was from her personal assistant, Ros. Carmel opened it.

Hi Carmel, hope the flight wasn't too terrible. Just wanted to let you know that the subpoenas have all now been sent. Cheers, Ros.

'Good,' Carmel said out loud, and typed the same one-word reply, adding, Thanks.

Finally, she got to Henri's message.

Bonjour again. If you get this before you leave for Livingstone, I just wanted to say again how good it is that you can take time out to visit us. Please don't think it's just about the dona-tion – as kind as it was, I am very much looking forward to meeting you. I hope you don't mind, but I have taken the liberty of booking us a cruise on the Zambezi for the afternoon of your first day. If you are too tired we can postpone it, but I would recommend it. The river is beautiful. Little Carmel the chimp is looking forward to meeting you, I am sure.
Rgds, Henri
Henri Bousson, Director, The Second Chance Wildlife Rehabilita-tion Centre, Livingstone, Zambia

Carmel reread Henri's message. It was an indulgence, deviat-ing via Zambia instead of flying straight to Rwanda, so what difference would a cruise on the river make? She was going to enjoy herself. Apart from a three-night safari in the Serengeti two years previously, she hadn't had an actual holiday or more than a weekend's break in four years. There was always too much work. Besides, she thought as she sipped her Coke, she didn't like having too much time on her hands, too much time to think.

She hadn't thought that her donation had been all that sig-nificant, and wondered if Henri paid this much attention to all his donors. Perhaps he was struggling for funds. Carmel sent Henri a short reply saying she looked forward to seeing him at the airport, then she clicked on the first of the many case files she needed to review. She might be indulging in a short break from tomorrow, but there was still work to be done.

As she cut into her chicken she read about a panga, wielded with enough force to sever a baby's head and then cleave halfway through the body of the mother who had been carrying the child on her back. Carmel had ordered the chicken because as well as not drinking alcohol she hadn't eaten red meat in seventeen years.

Richard smoked a cigarette as the detectives, one black and one white, from the Nelspruit Murder and Robbery Squad interviewed him. A crime-scene photographer strobed the front garden with the rapid fire of his flash.

'You can't think of anyone who wanted to hurt you?' the black detective, Mabunda, asked again.

Richard glanced at Lourens, who stood by Janine's *bakkie* with his arm around his wife. She was still visibly distressed. 'I want to go home,' she'd said after Richard had calmed her a little. Half of Impala Street had come out at the sound of the gunshots, but most had since returned to their homes. Richard had called Lourens on his mobile phone and told him there was a dead man in his front garden and it might be best if Lourens came and collected his wife.

Richard had wondered, briefly, as he'd stood over the body of the man he'd killed, whether the man with the cut-down silenced assault rifle had been sent by Lourens to kill him. Contract killing was as common as it was cheap in South Africa. But Richard had quickly dismissed the idea. Lourens had pulled a gun on his wife and he was a bombastic, macho man. If he wanted a man dead he'd do it himself, then face the consequences afterwards. Before he'd hung up, Richard had told Lourens that, for the record, he had not had sex with his wife, which was pretty much the truth, and that if

Lourens pulled a gun on Janine again Richard would shoot him. Lourens hadn't responded, but when he'd arrived Janine had run to him and he had wrapped his big arms around her and kissed her and apologised.

Once he'd arrived, Lourens had looked at the body and said, 'I don't know him.' He'd said nothing to Richard about the evening's earlier events, or about the condition of the wounded ranger.

'What about the rifle?' Richard had pushed.

Lourens had rubbed his chin. '*Ja*, I know about these things. We've got one of these in the armoury that we took off a poacher, but this one's not ours.'

'How can you be sure?'

'It's there – I checked it earlier this evening when I was thinking about shooting you.'

'So,' Detective Mabunda continued now, 'if you can't think of anyone who would want to kill you, Doctor, then what are we to make of this man opening fire on you with a silenced military rifle without provocation?'

'You're the detective.'

'Do you gamble, Doctor Dunlop?'

'No, I have bad luck.'

'Drugs?'

'What do you mean?' Richard scratched his ear, then lowered his hand. He knew cops were trained to look for telltale body language.

'I mean, do you keep prescription drugs in your home?'

'Oh, right. Yes, I do as a matter of fact. I keep some in my medical bag, which I lock up at night when I'm home.'

Mabunda looked around the living room, which was

littered with shattered glass from the gunfight. 'That bag over there, on your couch?'

'Yes.'

'Unsecured.'

'Yes, I was out saving a man's life tonight. Been a bit hectic.'

'Do you keep large sums of money in your home, or jewellery?'

'I'm broke, Inspector, and I believe less is more when it comes to accessorising.'

'Why are you making jokes, Doctor Dunlop?'

'I don't know, because no one seems to be laughing.'

Detective Mabunda left him to go back to the body, where the white member of the duo, whose name was Lutz, had found something. Richard thought about the line of questioning, about who might want him dead. A couple of husbands, perhaps. He'd never dealt in England, or falsified prescriptions for addicts, or been otherwise involved with other criminals. He'd only supplied drugs illegally to himself. He was a one-man train wreck and had decided early on not to take on any passengers. He was clean now, but it wouldn't take the police too much effort to find out about his history.

Lutz held up a plastic bag, which he gripped in rubber-gloved hands by the extreme tip. 'White powder. About ten grams, I think. Care to speculate on what it might be, Doctor?'

'A fit-up, by the look of it,' Richard said. South Africa had a justifiably bad reputation for violent crime and home invasions, but that sort of thing happened in Johannesburg and Durban, not in the staff village in the Kruger National Park. The man lying dead in the flowerbed had come to kill him and, by the look of it, plant a bag of cocaine somewhere at the scene of the crime. A drug deal gone wrong, the police and newspapers would speculate, once the first cop or reporter did a bit of googling and found out Richard Dunlop's form.

Richard suspected many, if not all, the residents of the staff village knew something of his past in the UK, but no one so far had been indiscreet enough to say anything to his face. They all knew how hard it was to get a GP to come out to the park, and how high the turnover rate was for the ones that did come. He was sure many idealistic young doctors fresh out of college might think it a plum job – living in a nice house on the banks of the Sabie River in a veritable garden of Eden. They'd think there was little or no crime – and they'd be pretty right if you took out casualties in the war against poachers and tonight's little episode – and plenty of excitement.

In fact, there was very little excitement, which had been one of the reasons Richard was drawn to the job. Most of his patients were the park's staff and their families, and beyond check-ups and malaria tests and the odd sprained limb, there was nothing too dramatic to keep a keen doctor interested. The tourists who came to see the doctor were the paranoid, such as Mr Philpott the snakebite victim, and the mundane – travellers' trots, and a stupid Australian man last week who'd stabbed himself in the palm with his own pocket knife. That was all fine by Richard. He didn't do blood if he could help it. The slick skin of the ranger with the chest wound had reminded him why he'd turned to drugs all those years ago. He didn't want to go back there, but if he'd been alone in the house tonight, instead of in the presence of a would-be mistress, a jealous husband, a police squad and a dead assassin, he might have been tempted to take out the wounded ranger's gun, chamber a round and raise it to his lips. He'd contemplated suicide before, but talked himself out of it. What use, he asked himself, was a half-hearted attempt as a cry for help if there was no one to hear the cry? And he didn't really think he was brave enough to actually go ahead and just do it.

'*Yissis*, but that chick driving the Merc should get a medal, hey,' Piet said.

Liesl sat in the passenger seat of Piet's Land Cruiser Prado. She could see his knuckles were cut and swollen from the beating he'd given the man in the pub earlier. Sannette stood at the open door of the four-by-four, holding Liesl's hand. Liesl couldn't bear to look back at the police cars and the ambulance and the flashing lights that bathed the crime scene. The woman who had run down and killed the man who'd shot at Liesl was being comforted by her husband, who'd arrived on the scene shortly after the police.

'We'll get you home just now,' Sannette said. 'I spoke to the officer in charge and she said you should be able to leave soon, once you talk to the detectives.'

'I've already told the police everything I know,' Liesl protested.

Piet put a hand on her knee. 'It won't take long.'

Liesl shook her leg, shrugging off his touch. She wanted to be alone. With a bottle. She looked up at Sannette. 'He followed me from the pub – but I was driving your car.'

Sannette shook her head. 'No one wants me dead – not even my husband. Besides, look at us, Liesl, I've got black hair and you're blonde – no one would mistake us for the same person. This was just a Joburg thing – a carjacking.'

'*Ja* but he didn't tell me he wanted the car, or my purse, or order me to do anything, he just looked at me, raised his gun and fired.'

'These people . . .' Piet said, but trailed off when the uniformed African female police captain walked over. Two men in plain clothes followed her.

'These are the detectives, Miss Nel. They'll talk to you now.' Liesl sighed.

Vite clung to the woman who had rescued him from the hunters. He nuzzled her bosom, searching out the milk that he should have been getting from his mother. But his mother was dead.

'*Non*,' the woman chided him. Instead, she held a baby's bottle and pushed the rubber teat into his mouth. Vite gulped the strange-tasting milk. The woman had two children of her own, aged three and five, and they reached up for the little gorilla's black feet and played with his toes. Vite kicked as he drank, causing the young girl to squeal and run out of the hut.

Vite finished the bottle and wailed for more. The woman told him to hush, then carried him out into the sunshine. She walked to another hut and left the two small children with a wizened woman who came to the door and tut-tutted when she saw the orphan baby gorilla in the woman's arms. The woman carrying Vite shrugged, then set off up the path towards the road that led from the village of Ngiko down the N2 to the distant city of Goma and the *muti* market, where people would buy and sell most any type of animal, dead or alive, for food, *muti* or for pets.

After the police and Lourens and Janine had left, Richard took a beer from his refrigerator, sat down at the desk in the second bedroom of his staff house and switched on his laptop. He noticed a red smear on the blotter under the computer.

Richard inspected the underside of his hand and saw a gash. He must have cut it on a shard of glass. It wasn't serious, but he got up and washed the cut in the bathroom sink while he waited for the slow computer to boot up. He looked down at his shirt and saw that it, too, was stained with blood, as were his trousers. Blood. How he hated it.

As he sat back down the computer chimed to life and Richard opened his email program. He wouldn't be able to sleep after the night he'd had. He hadn't checked the messages on this private account for four days – there was rarely anything of interest for a man who was hiding from nearly everyone he knew. He scrolled through the multitude of offers of Viagra and penis enlargements, and Nigerian bank scams, and ignored the jokes from the few remaining friends who had his address. His cursor hovered over the one entry that might mean something. It was an email from the war crimes prosecutor, Mike Ioannou, dated three days earlier.

The subject line of the email read: *Summons to appear before the International Criminal Tribunal, Rwanda*. He clicked on the message and read it. When he finished he rocked back in his swivelling office chair and thought about what he had just read. He took a long sip of Scotch and then typed '*Escape! magazine*' into the Google search field.

Jet lag woke Carmel at four in the morning. It always happened when she flew from Australia to Africa. Knowing that she wouldn't be able to get back to sleep, she got up, showered and returned to reading her case notes and Mike's investigation notes.

She still couldn't believe Mike was dead, killed by a hit-and-run driver while on holiday in Thailand. The Australian Federal Police were assisting the Royal Thai Police in the investigation, but the latest information Carmel had was that there were no further leads on the identity of the driver. Given who Mike was, and the nature of what he'd been investigating for the ICTR, the Feds were taking it very seriously indeed. When the police went to Mike's hotel room to collect his effects they found the room had been burgled. His camera was lying on the desk, but an empty laptop bag indicated that his computer had been stolen.

Carmel had been given responsibility for Mike's caseload, including an ongoing investigation he'd been carrying out but keeping pretty close to his chest. She scrolled down to the list of witnesses who had been subpoenaed by Mike to attend the ICTR hearings in Arusha or to give written depositions. She still couldn't quite believe the two names that confronted her again from the screen – Liesl Hannelie Nel and Doctor Richard Edward Dunlop.

In her early years as a lawyer Carmel had served in the Australian Army as a legal officer. In 1995 she'd been sent to Rwanda as part of a UN peacekeeping mission. She had met plenty of civilians, including journalists and photographers, but it was an uncanny and, frankly, unnerving coincidence that Mike Ioannou, in his capacity as a senior ICTR prosecutor, had been interviewing a man she'd thought she'd loved in Rwanda seventeen years ago, and a woman she had once wanted to kill.

She and Richard had met at an officers' mess dinner in Townsville, before Rwanda, and not long after he'd arrived in Australia on his exchange posting from the British Army to the Australian Army Medical Corps. He'd sat next to her and looked incredibly dashing in his mess uniform, and she'd been pleased to have someone so charming to talk to in between the toasts and the formalities. She usually found these dinners a bore. She wasn't so much on the outer because she was a woman – there were a few other female officers on the brigade headquarters staff – but as a lawyer she was expected to take good-naturedly the same old litany of lawyer jokes each time there was a social gathering.

He'd wanted to know about her, not what an army lawyer did but what sort of music she listened to, what her taste was in the arts, where she'd grown up. He was interested in her, and she in him.

She'd had a couple of boyfriends at university but had been too preoccupied with meeting her parents' high expectations to devote much time to relationships and they had run their natural course. She prided herself in being cautious around men, a trait she believed served her well in the presence of so many alpha males on an army base. In fact, she had set herself a personal rule of not falling for a military man. Her long-term plan was to finish her enlistment in the army and then move into private practice. She had served in the army reserve while at university and enjoyed military life, but only envisaged her time as an army lawyer as a stepping stone.

But there was something about Richard; perhaps it was that he was British and wouldn't be in Australia for long. She wasn't the sort of person to have a one-night stand or a brief affair with an exchange officer virtually passing through the base, but thinking about it now, many years later, she wondered if she had dropped her guard and become friends with him *because* she knew he would only be around a few months and therefore there was no risk of her becoming involved with him. Or it could have been his eyes.

He had asked her if she had ever scuba-dived and she had confessed that although she had lived all her life in north Queensland, on the edge of the Great Barrier Reef, she never had. He had cajoled her into doing a one-day dive and she had loved it; afterwards they had gone for a meal. He'd talked about medical school, and the rigorous training he had undergone to become a member of the British Army's parachute regiment and she had liked the way he combined the strength and fitness of a paratrooper with the brains of a doctor. And he was unlike most of the other officers at the brigade, who were career soldiers. Richard was working off a return of service – an obligation to the army to serve as a doctor for as many years as the military had supported him through university and medical school. Although he was only in the army for a limited time, he had nonetheless done some of the toughest training imaginable. He was a driven man who seemed to apply himself to the nth degree in everything he attempted.

Carmel stared at the screen of her laptop but couldn't force herself, just yet, to go back to the business of reviewing Mike Ioannou's notes. Damn Richard.

Was that it, she wondered; was it because she'd held out for so long? There had been more dates: movies, a day trip on the ferry to Magnetic Island, a visit to a local art gallery. Had he pursued her because he never gave up? Was she just another challenge to be conquered?

One night, after they'd been to see *Schindler's List* at the cinema, he'd suggested that instead of finding a restaurant they get some takeaway and a bottle of wine and drive up Castle Hill.

'Sure,' she said to him, as they stood on the footpath outside the theatre. She felt her pulse quicken a little. Castle Hill was the sort of place teenage couples went to make out.

'It's so hot, I thought it might be a bit cooler up there,' he said quickly, as if reading her mind.

They were just friends, she'd told herself at the time. He hadn't once tried to make a move on her. But she loved his company and his friendship, and she saw the way that people, other women in particular, looked at him, and them, as they walked down the street. They stopped at a takeaway shop and bought a barbecued chicken, then at a liquor store for a bottle of chardonnay and a couple of plastic glasses. They got into Carmel's second-hand sun-bleached Ford Capri convertible and took Castle Hill Road to the top of the three-hundred-metre-high granite hill that dominated the waterfront town. She had the top down and the moving air was a welcome relief from the heavy humidity.

'I told you it would be nicer up here.' Richard opened his door as soon as she pulled up, and got out. He walked to the railing of the lookout and stared out over the lights of Townsville and across the glassy sea to Magnetic Island.

She got out as he was coming back. She felt awkward, not knowing if they should sit in the car, or outside somewhere. She looked over at him and saw that his eyes were fixed on her. 'Beautiful,' she heard him say.

'The view? Yes, I suppose it is. I walk up here for exercise sometimes, and . . .'

He walked around the front of the Capri to her. She stood on one side of the open car door and he on the other. He leaned across it and touched her cheek with the back of his hand.

His fingers were scalding. 'Richard, I . . .'

He leaned closer and kissed her. Carmel threw her arms around him, the door between them uncomfortable and awkward as their lips locked, but she couldn't wait. They laughed as he came around to her, and she leaned back against the bodywork as he pressed his body against hers. She loved the feel of his muscles under her hands for the first time, the smell of him this close, the taste of his mouth. She felt his hand on her breast. Her nipple responded and she reached for him.

'Blanket?' he murmured.

'Uh-uh, sorry.' There was nothing in the boot of her car except the flat spare tyre she'd been meaning to change.

'No matter,' he whispered. His hand moved lower, pressing her, touching her through the thin cotton of her sundress and her pants underneath. She felt how hard he was and it was more than the tropical heat that she could feel in her cheeks.

He broke from her, reached down and hit the passenger seat release so that the back folded and the seat slid forward. He eased himself into the back seat and held out his hand to her. 'Come.'

She brushed damp hair from her eyes. For a moment she hesitated. This was not how it was supposed to be. He leaned forward and took her fingers in his, and she yielded to him. 'It's too cramped,' she giggled nervously as she let him lead her in.

'Not if you sit on top of me.'

She climbed in, holding the hem of her flowered dress up so she could straddle him, revelling in the flash of lust in his eyes as she did so. Carmel had never had sex anywhere other than a bed, and it had rarely been satisfactory. She leaned over him, her black hair curtaining his face, and kissed him deeply as she ground against him.

'Carmel?' he whispered in her ear as they kissed.

'Mmm?'

A short pause, and then: 'I think I love you.'

'Me too. I want this, Richard.'

Gently, he lifted her off him and she was momentarily jolted with disappointment until she saw his grin as he reached into the pocket of his cargo shorts and produced the condom. He kept eye contact with her as he unzipped. She lifted her legs and wriggled out of her pants, then climbed on top of him again.

He undid the top three buttons that ran down the front of her dress and freed her breasts from her bra. She rocked her head back as he took each of her nipples, in turn, into his mouth. Carmel felt his hands on her again, the slight hilltop breeze cooling the skin of her bottom as he lifted her dress so he could grab her as she lowered herself onto him.

She had cried, burying her face in his shoulder, when the release came. She had worked so hard at school and university to please her parents, focused on being a good daughter and a good officer and not allowing herself to be led astray by the soldiers who had tried, and she had never had a man say he loved her. He held her tight, and the significance of the shift in her world had been illuminated by the glare of headlights coming up the hill. They had laughed as they scrambled back into the front seats and drove off, the warm breeze drying her tears of happiness. Back in her flat, off the base, they had drunk the wine and eaten, and made love again, and Carmel had climaxed, again and again, and understood, when she woke to find Richard beside her, what life was really about.

There was a knock at the door. Carmel grabbed a tissue from the box beside the hotel bed, wiped her eyes and opened the door. The room-service waiter wheeled in the breakfast she had ordered. She tipped him, blew her nose when he left, and went back to work.

When the senior prosecutor in Arusha had given her responsibility for Mike's cases, he'd informed her that Ioannou had been investigating a new lead into the downing of Rwandan President Juvenal Habyarimana's jet plane on 6 April 1994 – an event that had sparked 1994's infamous genocide. Habyarimana and the president of neighbouring Burundi, Cyprien Ntaryamira, had both been killed, and the Hutu extremists in the government had claimed that Tutsis had been responsible and had used the event to whip the Interahamwe – the Hutu extremist militia – into a killing frenzy. Subsequent enquiries, Carmel knew, had determined that while it was still not known exactly who had downed the aircraft, it was actually more likely to have been Hutu extremists, as a result of Habyarimana's decision to accede to the Arusha peace accords and allow expatriate Tutsis to return to Rwanda. Carmel got the clear impression from her superior that Mike had been operating on his own on this one, as the investigation of the president's death was out of the ICTR's terms of reference.

She continued to read over the summary of Mike's telephone conversation with Richard as she ate her breakfast. The file note said the conversation had taken place just three weeks earlier. Also in the file was a copy of a subpoena addressed to Richard at a post box at Skukuza Rest Camp, Kruger National Park, with a note that Richard had been emailed the subpoena just a few days earlier. She'd been to

Kruger, South Africa's flagship national park, twice.

She had to admit that the thought of bumping into him on this trip held some appeal – just so she could slap his face and remind him what a bastard he'd been to her back then.

Carmel's anger abated as she started to read Mike's notes. It was Richard's version of that fateful day at the Kibeho refugee camp in south-western Rwanda. The words transported her back in time, and the cold, creeping memory of the horror started permeating through her body.

5

Rwanda, 1995

It was, Captain Richard Dunlop thought, a painting by Hieronymus Bosch in living, breathing and dying three-dimension.

Death was all around them, in sight, sound and smell, defiling all the senses at once. Richard looked into the eyes of the woman he'd just injected with morphine. Her breath rattled as she died. It had been pointless trying to save her. She was too far gone.

Richard pulled his bloodied rubber gloves off and glanced up over the sandbag parapet to take in the scene from hell.

The sky was clouded with black smoke and grey ash from the burning of the damp thatch huts that had dotted the cleared hills of the Kibeho refugee camp. There'd been rain that morning and a drizzle might have made it through had the blanket of smoke and burning grass not been so thick. Over and above the burning smell there was the acrid stench of cordite drifting from gun barrels, and the pungent odours of blood and perforated bowels and intestines. A few of the Australian soldiers, hard-looking infantrymen who called themselves diggers, had been sick.

Out on the surrounding hills Hutu refugees lay dead and dying. As Richard watched, a ragged skirmish line of RPA soldiers in East German camouflage fatigues, gumboots and berets moved down the slopes on another sweep. Women, children and mostly old men rose from the grass and the piles of rubbish and corpses and took flight, like grouse startled by the noise of the beaters. Rifles were raised again and voices called target indications. Men laughed as they fired, trying to hit the runners before they reached the safety of the UN compound.

'Can't we do *something*, boss?' A twenty-one-year-old Aussie medic looked at him with eyes rimmed the same red as his bloody hands. They'd all asked themselves and each other the same thing at one time or another through this bloody day. Richard didn't know which was the greater madness, the greater evil – the men out there in the camp doing the killing, or the decree that the armed and ready UN peacekeepers must stay behind their barbed wire and sandbags in the Zambian compound and do nothing. They had been ordered, literally, to stand there and watch, and count the bodies, while unarmed civilians were shot dead in front of them.

And the RPA knew it. The commanders and their foot soldiers knew the peacekeepers were under orders not to intervene. So they taunted them – had done all morning. They made a game out of the killing.

The woman who had just died had almost made it to where Richard and the Australian and Zambian peacekeepers were based. She had already lost an arm below the elbow – hacked off with a panga in an earlier melee – and she had wrapped a discarded shirt around the stump as she staggered towards them. A Rwandan Patriotic Army, or RPA, soldier had put a bullet in her back, a lucky shot – for him – from a couple of hundred metres away. She had fallen and Richard was sure she was dead, but she pushed herself up to her knees and reached out to them with her one good hand, beseeching them.

An Australian infantryman had slung his F88 Steyr rifle over his back and vaulted over the sandbags. His mate had followed him and they zigzagged through the bodies. The RPA were still firing at scattered, running refugees who had taken flight, but the diggers had ignored the gunfire. Three RPA soldiers, including the man who had shot the woman, had also broken into a trot, and were running down the hill to try and reach the woman before the Australians could get to her and take her back to the safety of the Zambian compound. The UN outpost was an abandoned two-storey brick convent whose buildings were arrayed around an open courtyard fortified with wire and sandbags.

Richard had watched the race to see who would reach the woman first, the UN soldiers or the RPA.

'Go Snowy, go Greeny!' one of the other Aussies had called from the barricade.

The Australians had charged on, burdened with the weight of flak jackets, webbing gear, weapons and the blue Kevlar helmet that signified their membership of UNAMIR, the United Nations Assistance Mission For Rwanda, one of them almost falling as he slipped on garbage or guts or excrement – the ground was littered with all three. But the soldier had righted himself and he and his mate had reached the fallen woman, who had slumped onto her belly again. Her back was arched as she reached out to her rescuers. They'd shown heroism worthy of a gallantry medal to bring her back into the compound, and their comrades had given half-hearted cheers, and now the woman was dead. Their actions had been for nothing, but even so, more soldiers were sallying out in search of the living.

Richard took out his cigarettes. He'd be lucky to get in two or three drags before the medics brought over the next mutilated Rwandan. He lit it, took just one pull, then saw his female Australian Army counterpart bent over a man, sliding an IV into his arm. Richard ground out the smoke on the side of his boot – the bottom was covered in shit – and put the fag end in the pocket of his British Army-issue trousers, feeling guilty he'd lit up in the first place. Two soldiers laid another woman on a blood-soaked stretcher at his feet.

'Panga wounds to the back and neck, boss,' one of the diggers said. Richard pulled on fresh gloves and as he worked, checking the field dressings the soldiers had applied, he glanced out over the camp. Irate RPA soldiers yelled threats and insults at the two men who'd repeated Snowy and Greeny's act of bravery. Despite the futility, they couldn't give up.

It was a bizarre situation. The infantrymen in the peace-keeping force could not open fire on the RPA or use any force to stop them from going about the business of herding and killing their fellow countrymen. The Australians could only fire back in self-defence. If a civilian managed to reach the Zambian compound, then they were deemed to be under the protection of the UN peacekeepers. If a wounded person was reached first by the peacekeepers, they could be taken back to the compound. The RPA had refrained from shooting directly at the peacekeepers, though there was risk from wildly aimed shots into the crowd. The race to save a life had been played out many times already. For every man, woman or child the peace-keepers could dash out and save, many more were killed. In the peacekeepers' favour, they didn't have to venture out far from the compound to find people to treat – the Hutu refugees were being shot and hacked almost on the compound's doorstep, and many others had been slashed by razor wire when the crush of panicked refugees pushed them against the defences of the UN laager.

The Rwandan government and the UN had been trying to close down the remaining Hutu refugee camps for months, since the RPA had taken control of the country. Among its estimated one hundred thousand inhabitants, the Kibeho camp held mostly innocent Hutus who had fled in fear of reprisals by the invading RPA, but it was also home to a rump of hardcore Hutu *génocidaires* who had left their escape to Zaire too late. They ruled over the moderates and innocents in the camp with the same combination of threats and violence that held sway in other camps across the border in Zaire.

When Richard had arrived a day earlier he and the Australians had set up a casualty clearing post, or CCP, to carry out health checks on the Kibeho residents as they made their way out of the camp, and while things had begun peacefully enough, some hardcore elements had tried to force their way into the Zambian compound to escape the RPA troops who were drawing the noose on the camp ever tighter, trying to force more and more people through the CCP at the same time. The CCP had relocated to the relative safety of the Zambian compound as the RPA began shooting to kill.

It was confusing. Some said that armed refugees had opened fire on the RPA and the new government troops had fired back, thus sparking what was fast turning into a spree of reprisal killings. Others said the RPA soldiers had started the killing. Gunfire was constant now, with Hutus being killed and wounded continually in front of the peacekeepers.

Richard had been too busy treating wounded people and was beyond caring how or why the madness had begun. He focused his attention on the young woman on the ground in front of him. She might have been pretty, but if she lived she would be forever scarred from the slash that had very nearly severed her carotid artery. The blow had been aimed downwards and had cleaved into the muscles of her shoulder and cracked her collarbone. She wailed as he lifted the field dressing. With the medic's help he squirted Betadine solution into the wound, eliciting further yells. He'd seen people stagger into the compound speechless, with missing hands and horrific wounds, but the screaming always began as soon as the shock started to wear off. Richard gave the woman an injection of anaesthetic and opened a suture kit.

'Hey, you peacekeeper dogs! Hey!'

'Tie the dressing on her and get her to the ambulance,' Richard said to the orderly. The Australians had a couple of six-wheel-drive Land Rover ambulances that had been ferrying the wounded to Kigali for two days now. It was a difficult business, deciding who would go to the capital. They had to be cases that were serious enough to warrant further surgery, but not so serious that the person would surely die before reaching an operating room.

Richard stood and looked over at the man who had called out. He was an RPA officer and he was dragging a woman towards the UN compound by her hair. The woman's mouth was bloodied, presumably where he'd struck her, and she limped from a bullet wound in her right thigh that had soaked red the once bright yellow and green wrap she wore. She said nothing as he half-dragged, half-marched her in front of him, the pistol in his other hand pressed in her back.

'Hey, you pathetic dogs. Look at this. Look at this woman. She is a Hutu – her people massacred nearly a million Tutsi. Who do you think you are, trying to protect these killers who have fled justice?' The officer slurred his words and staggered a little. Richard wondered if he was drunk or stoned, or both.

Soldiers were standing behind the sandbags, their rifles at the high port with bayonets fixed, ready to take aim and fill the loud-mouthed RPA officer with lead if he snapped a shot in their general direction. The officer stared at them, then pushed the woman to her knees. 'Well, who do you think you are?' the officer screamed at them.

'Let her go,' one of the Australian medics yelled. 'You bastard!'

The officer threw back his head and laughed. When he was finished he wiped his bloodshot eyes with the back of his hand and rammed the barrel of the pistol into the woman's temple. The force pushed her head to one side.

'No!' Richard yelled.

The officer pulled the trigger. Blood spurted from the woman's head as her body slumped to the ground. The man turned his back on them and walked away.

Richard could see the fingers of the infantrymen curling tighter on the triggers of their raised rifles, imagine the sight pictures they were taking – a dozen black circles trained on the officer's back as he wobbled away in search of another victim to sate his need for revenge.

As Richard turned to look for his next patient he saw Liesl

Nel, the South African civilian news photographer, step from the ruins of the church. She had taken pictures of him treating several victims, spending most of her time and attention getting shots of him working on a girl aged about eight who had been slashed with a panga across her back. The camera she held was fitted with a long lens, perhaps a three-hundred-millimetre zoom. She strode through the rubbish towards him.

'Did you get that?' Richard asked, gesturing with a flick of his head towards the departing RPA man.

Liesl nodded. The camera was shaking in her hands.

'Good.'

She looked down at the blood on his hands and reached out to his chest and unbuttoned the uniform pocket. They were fellow smokers and she knew where he kept his cigarettes with the lighter in the packet. She took two out and put one in his mouth and one in hers. She lit them both and replaced the pack in his pocket. Her hands were still shaking. 'The Aussie soldiers have been trying to stop me taking pictures. They say it's just inflaming the RPA.'

Richard shrugged. 'It's your job. Someone needs to show the world what's going on here. Don't be hard on the soldiers. They're trying to do their job, and they don't like it. Some of them – me included – would like the RPA to get enraged enough to open fire on us. I'd like to take a few of the bastards with me.'

'Brave words.' She exhaled smoke into the air. 'They'd kill us all, though. You know it. There are too many of them.'

Who do you think you are? the officer had taunted them. Richard knew it was a good question, and one none of them could answer. He felt the bile rising in his throat and swallowed it down. There was another victim being laid at his feet. Liesl stepped back and took photos of him and the medic as they worked.

The double hell of it was that the drunk or stoned RPA officer was right. Some of the people being slaughtered today were, more likely than not, guilty of mass murder themselves. It was so bloody impossible to make sense of. The Hutu were the majority tribe in Rwanda, the Tutsi the minority and once the ruling elite. Rwanda's civil wars and unrest had been going on since the 1950s with the balance of power ebbing and flowing between the two tribes. The Tutsis, who were cattle herders, had been initially favoured by the Belgian colonialists who had taken over Rwanda from its former German rulers after the First World War. The Belgians introduced identity cards which labelled a person by their tribe, adding to the segregation of the population. This disadvantaged the crop-growing Hutu majority, but when Rwanda gained independence after the Second World War the Belgians had tried to atone for the perceived unfairness by backing the Hutu majority in the post-colonial government. More than seven hundred thousand Tutsis had fled Rwanda since 1959 when Hutus had risen up and killed thousands of their Tutsi countrymen.

The latest tsunami – you couldn't call it just a wave – of bloodshed had been sparked by the downing of an aircraft carrying the presidents of Rwanda and Burundi and the death of both leaders.

After President Habyarimana's death the majority Hutu tribe had risen up again and, egged on by the Interahamwe militia, had set about eradicating the country of all remaining Tutsis, as well as the moderate Hutus who had opposed their dead leader. Richard knew from the briefings he had received that this refugee camp was supposedly home to as many or more moderate Hutus as those who were in the Interahamwe and *génocidaires*, but it was impossible to know for sure. State radio had egged on the killings, denouncing all Tutsis as cockroaches who had to be exterminated. The total number of people killed was still unknown, but it was feared to be close to a million. Even the women he'd treated and watched die today could have been murderers.

Richard and the Australian peacekeeping force he was attached to, as a medical officer on an exchange posting, were part of the second rotation of UN peacekeepers to try to make sense of the genocide. The first rotation had had to deal with the clean-up of hundreds of thousands of bodies and then make a start on repairing equal numbers of hacked, beaten and shot people.

The RPA, and its political wing the Rwandan Patriotic Front, had successfully taken over the country, putting an end to the mass killings, but not for long. The RPA's Tutsi soldiers had returned from years in exile in Uganda and Kenya only to find in many cases that their entire families had been killed, their women raped before death, their homes destroyed and their wealth looted.

The UN, late to act and hamstrung when it did, had not been able to prevent the slaughter of the Tutsis, but, ironically, it was doing its best to ensure protection and safe passage out of Rwanda for the perpetrators. Camps such as Kibcho, where Richard and the Australians were deployed, had been set up as refuges for Hutus fleeing the vengeful RPA. Those who had stopped in the refugee camps had thought they would be safe, but they were wrong. It seemed that the power of an eye for an eye was stronger than the UN's. But even though Richard knew the history was as complex as it was bloody, he could not reconcile the violence that he was witnessing as justifiable in any way.

An orderly had crossed the barricade to check on the woman who had been shot in the head. Richard looked at the soldier, who shook his head and stood there numbly, the woman's blood on his hands.

The man Richard turned back to treat was perhaps in his late fifties or early sixties. He wore what had once been a good suit but was now stained with red mud, blood and human waste. It looked like he'd crawled from his attackers. The left side of his face was masked with blood and the white of his skull was visible beneath a flap of skin. His right arm had been crudely bandaged. Worse than these wounds, however, was revealed as Richard prised the man's hands away from his belly. Dark blood welled from beneath a soaked towel. A young girl, perhaps eleven or twelve, kneeled in the mud beside him, weeping.

Richard was aware of Liesl off to one side, shooting pictures of him with the old man. The battery-operated motor wind of her Nikon wasn't distracting, but she was. He forced himself to concentrate.

'Doctor,' the man said in accented English, 'I am dying, yes?'

The girl spoke rapidly and tearfully in French, and Richard's schoolboy translation was that she was telling the man he would be fine and the doctor was here to help him.

Richard ignored both of them. He would be the judge of whether the man was dying or not, and if he could be fixed. Richard ordered the medic to start an IV drip and rolled the man over to check for an exit wound; there was none. He was probably right in his self-diagnosis. The man gripped Richard on the arm.

'I have something for you. It is important,' he said.

'I need to treat you first.'

'No . . .' With his ebbing strength the man pushed Richard's hand aside and reached into the inside pocket of his suit coat. Richard knelt beside him and opened a fresh dressing. With a trembling hand the man produced a photograph. He held it out to Richard.

The colour print had been folded and the shiny surface had cracked in a line down the centre. It was now smeared with the man's bloody fingerprints. Richard glanced at it quickly. He registered two black men, dressed in camouflaged uniforms and berets, and a white man in a two-piece khaki safari outfit. The white man was holding a weapon of some sort, a rocket-propelled grenade launcher. While the faces of the white man and one of the black men were visible, neither of them were looking towards the camera. The other man had his back to the camera.

'Do you know what this is, what this picture means?' the wounded man asked, trying to clutch his belly. The medic held his hands aside while Richard cut away the man's shirt.

Liesl had moved beside them, still taking pictures.

'No.' As fast as Richard could soak up the blood it welled out from the wound. He pressed the pad down on the wound and passed the tapes of the dressing around the old man's back as the medic lifted him a little. 'There's a bit too much going on today for me to take a guess.'

The old man nodded. 'All that is going on around you today, all these people dying, all the innocents who have been killed already, all that has happened in this country of mine is because of this photograph.'

Richard didn't care about the cause of this madness. Hutu, Tutsi, they were one as bad as the other, he thought. He'd sat through the intelligence briefing before he'd left Australia with the medical contingent, and listened to Carmel's legal briefing about rules of engagement, but at the end he'd still have had trouble answering which tribe was responsible for which outbreak of violence, and which had the moral high ground, and why the armed UN peacekeepers manning the sandbags and wire around him couldn't stop a soldier from shooting an unarmed woman in the head in front of them.

'This white man . . .' the wounded man said, holding the photo up to Richard's face, 'he is . . .'

Liesl's camera clicked and flashed.

'Look,' Richard brushed the proffered picture aside, 'I don't care who the white man in the picture is. All I care about right now is getting you patched up and out of here, back to Kigali.'

'This man is evil, he is . . . S—'

The man coughed and a spray of blood hit Richard in the face. 'He's arresting!'

'Papa!' wailed the girl.

When they could do no more, Richard stood and peeled off his bloodied gloves and tossed them aside.

'No! Do something, please, Doctor,' cried the girl in English. 'Please!'

Richard looked down at her cradling her dead father's head, her tears streaming down her face. He had to move on to the next patient. He turned and started to move away, but something made him stop. He looked back and saw the girl's face, tilted up to him.

'Where is your mother?' he asked her.

'Dead, Doctor.' Her body was racked with sobs.

'Do you have any other family?'

She shook her head.

Christ, he thought. There was nothing he could do, technically. They couldn't transport a relatively healthy child, orphan or not, back to Kigali. She would have to stay with her own people.

'They were trying to kill us, Doctor,' the girl said, wiping her eyes with the back of her hand.

'Who, the RPA?'

'*Oui* . . . yes,' she said, 'but also the people in the camp. It is the bad men here, inside Kibeho, who shot my father.'

Richard ran a hand down his face. 'Do you have other family here?'

The girl shook her head. 'I have nowhere to go, Doctor. I think the bad men will want to kill me now.' Her thin body sagged next to her dead father, as if she was too tired to run and had accepted that her fate now was to be the same as the rest of her family's.

Richard looked around. There was an infantryman named Jackson; he carried a Minimi squad automatic weapon. Jackson had his machine gun perched on a sandbag wall. 'Come with me,' he said to the girl.

'Private Jackson,' Richard said, leading the girl by the hand.

Jackson looked over at him, his face grim. 'Doc?'

'This is . . . what's your name?'

She looked up at him. 'Collette.'

'This is Collette, Private Jackson. We're going to look after her.'

'Whatever you say, boss.'

Richard led Collette to the soldier and she sat down beside him in the shade of the sandbag wall, drew her knees up to her chest and rested her face down between her knees.

'Don't let anybody harm her or take her away,' Richard said to the soldier.

Jackson nodded. 'No worries, boss.' It wasn't the infantryman's job to guard a child, and if anything it would hamstring him further, but Richard sensed the big man was more than happy to be given an order that he could understand and would quite possibly give his life in following it.

Liesl stood by, her camera hanging loose in her right hand. Her face was white. Richard walked back to her. 'What was that man talking about before he died?' she asked. 'Why did he keep holding up that picture?'

In his effort to try to save the man, Richard had momentarily forgotten about his ravings. Richard saw the man's hand had opened as he'd died. The crumpled, blood-smeared picture was on the muddy ground. Two infantrymen, called by the medic, walked over. One grabbed the man's arms, the other continued walking towards the feet. Richard thought he should pick up the picture, but as he started towards it, the second soldier trod on it. As the soldier crouched to grab the dead man's ankles Richard could see the photo was stuck to the bottom of his boot, along with a smear of blood and human excrement. He was tempted to grab it anyway, to peel it off the sole, but the medic called, 'Doc! Little kid – she's lost an arm and is bleeding out.'

'I'll tell you later,' Richard said to Liesl as he ran to where the medic was bent over a screaming girl of no more than seven.

He fought back the tears as he ran. Richard didn't care who'd started this madness. He really didn't.

6

The convoy of Land Rovers, painted white for UN service, rolled in through the gates of the former Rwandan Army military academy on the Avenue de l'Armée in Kigali, where the Australian peacekeeping force was based. Captain Carmel Shang moved to the window of the office she shared with the army public relations officer and photographer on the first floor of one of the red-brick buildings in what the soldiers referred to as 'Club Med Kigali', and looked out at the mud-spattered vehicles coming in.

More wounded from Kibeho had been dropped at the Kigali Central Hospital up the road, and the troops were now, finally, returning to barracks. Carmel could only imagine the horrors they'd seen. She'd been to Kibeho herself two days ago, to help set up the casualty clearing post. It was before the mass killings had begun, but she'd seen the chaos as the movement started from the camp; people moving in shoals, like fish, across the grassy hills and being crushed against the slicing razor wire of the Zambian compound as they'd tried to claim sanctuary from the encircling RPA troops.

Carmel headed downstairs, but hung back, watching him. She saw Richard climb down out of the cab of a truck. His hair, too long for the liking of the task force's regimental sergeant major, was awry, and his uniform was darkly stained – with blood, she presumed. He was talking to a female doctor.

Carmel thought he was one of the most beautiful men she'd ever seen. Beautiful probably wasn't a good word to describe a man, but his features were aquiline rather than chiselled, his hands soft rather than callused. She didn't think him effeminate – not in the slightest – just, well, beautiful. She thought that when – if, she corrected herself – people saw them together as a couple they'd think her the lucky one. And she was lucky. He was smart, compassionate, funny, sexy *and* he made her orgasm every time he made love to her.

Across the crush of people, over the noise of barked orders from a platoon sergeant, he saw her and winked. Carmel blushed, knowing what she'd just been thinking.

A section of infantrymen dismounted from a Land Rover troop carrier. Some lit cigarettes, all of them seemed listless, shocked. One, a private named Green – Greeny to his mates – started walking towards her. He carried his rifle by the pistol grip, the barrel pointing down. As he came closer Carmel nodded a greeting. She saw that his uniform was also stained with blood. He scratched himself under his arm with his left hand. His face was streaked with dirt and dried sweat. He smelled of rotting meat and shit.

'Why?'

'Private Green,' she said in reply.

'Tell me, *ma'am*, why. You're the lawyer.'

They were probably about the same age, although he might have been a year or two younger. She'd only graduated university and law school the year before. Greeny had joined the army straight from school and was a generally exemplary soldier, although he had a hot head. She knew all this because she'd defended him, back at his base in Townsville, when he'd been brought up before his company commander on a charge of assaulting a lance corporal. The lance corporal had chosen to slip in a jibe about Greeny's girlfriend during a dressing-down. Private Green had king-hit his superior, breaking his nose. The lance corporal was a bully – borderline psychopath, Carmel reckoned on the quiet – and had since been discharged from the army. The word around the barracks was that after the incident with Greeny a few of the others, a couple of other NCOs as well, had sorted the bully out. Greeny was still guilty, but given the circumstances, the fine and seven days' restriction of privileges had been a good result. Green had been grateful at the time, relieved not to be sent to the military correctional establishment at Holsworthy in New South Wales.

'What do you mean, Rick?' she asked, recalling his first name and trying the friendly approach, hoping that might work. Carmel had joined the army as a lawyer and, like other professional people taken into uniform because of their jobs, such as doctors, psychologists, PR people, nurses and padres, her officer training had been limited to a six-week 'knife and fork' course, designed to teach them the basics of soldiering and which way to pass the port at a mess dinner. He hadn't addressed her respectfully as he should have, but Carmel knew respect was something that had to be earned from these hard men, not demanded.

'I mean, *ma'am*,' and the word was said as an insult, 'why does the fucking *law* say we can't do anything when we see some cunt shooting a defenceless woman in front of us?'

Carmel took a breath. She knew the words were designed to shock, and she knew his temper. She saw the vein pulsing in his neck, the free fist clenched, the other hand tightening on the grip of his rifle. 'It's the UN that makes the rules, Rick, and it's our job to enforce them. You know that.'

'The UN? More fucking lawyers. I just can't get my fucking head around it. We watched them kill women and children. Hundreds of them, thousands—'

'I can imagine how hard it must have been for you.'

He took a step forward, teeth gritted. 'No, you can't. You're back here at headquarters like those fuckers in the UN in New York. All in your fucking ivory tower, you—'

From the corner of her eye she saw him coming to her. She didn't want to need him, but she did, and he was by her side. 'Everything all right here?'

The private turned and glared at him. Green's chest heaved, his breath exiting his nose audibly. 'You were there, Doc. Tell her. Tell her what happened because we were following the fucking rules.'

'A lot of people, hundreds, maybe thousands, died. But Captain Shang didn't make the rules, if that's what you're insinuating.'

'Fucking lawyers.'

Richard moved between her and Green and, without touching the soldier, he was in his face and staring him down. Maybe an inch separated their noses. 'That's no way to speak to an officer, Private.'

Green didn't move, but Carmel saw his Adam's apple bob. Richard was a doctor and an officer, and he was also three inches taller and maybe ten kilograms of muscle heavier than the rangy infantryman. He also wore British Army parachute wings on the right sleeve of his camouflage shirt. 'We've all had a tough day, Private. I suggest you go back to your section and talk it over with your mates. There's no sense in trying to find someone in our own ranks to blame for this madness. Understood?'

Green looked back at Carmel and she had to fight her urge to step back, to turn from him.

'Under*stood*?'

This time he nodded. 'Yes, sir.' When Green looked back at her it wasn't in anger. The rage had passed. He blinked a couple of times and she thought she saw his eyes glisten.

'Greeny! Get over here,' the platoon sergeant called.

The soldier took a step, then glanced back at Carmel. He swallowed. 'Ma'am . . .'

'It's alright, Rick. Get back to your mates.' Carmel allowed herself a breath.

'You didn't need to come to my rescue,' she said when the private was out of earshot.

'I know. But I got off on it.'

She smiled, but couldn't hold it when she noticed the blood on him again. 'We've been getting reports and I saw some of the wounded coming in earlier. It must have been terrible, Richard. We can talk about it later if you like.' She wondered if he wanted to touch her as much as she wanted to touch him right now. She wanted to hug him and draw his face to her neck and breast and tell him that it was all right, the only thing that mattered was that they should have as much time together as possible.

And the way he looked at her now, despite being tired and filthy and blood-spattered, was the way he'd looked at her that night up on Castle Hill. She knew what he wanted, what he needed. He didn't need to talk. He needed her, and she needed him. The chemistry was still there, even in these bizarre circumstances. They'd kept the affair a secret from everyone else in the brigade back in Townsville, and been lucky enough to both be deployed to Rwanda on the same rotation.

'I don't need to talk about what happened today,' he said. 'I just need to feel bloody human again.'

'Tonight?' she whispered.

'Yes. Might be late. They'll need a hand here, then I've got to go see someone.'

'Who?' Carmel asked.

'One of the civvie photographers. That South African girl, what's her name, from *Global News*.'

'Liesl Nel,' Carmel said. 'She's very pretty.'

'I hadn't noticed,' Richard said. The corners of his mouth curled.

'Very funny. I'll wait up for you.'

'Bad lawyer.'

'Only for you,' she said.

7

Liesl had made herself as at home as she could in what had once been the manager's office in a bank building in the Avenue de la République. The bank, robbed and looted during the genocide a year earlier, had never reopened and had been taken over by the NGO Rescue the Children, that had organised for Liesl and several other journalists and photographers to visit Rwanda.

The trade-off for the transport into the shattered country was that Liesl and the others would cover the work of Rescue the Children; however, she was also free to shoot and file as much general news as she wanted. Some of the others had found hotel rooms around town, but Liesl quite liked the peace and the illusion of protection the bank's thick walls gave her. The manager's old room was sparsely furnished and a bit of a mess, with dirty clothes everywhere. There was a bathroom out back, which had been for the manager's use, and the water had been reconnected. One part of the building she refused to go to, however, was the old vault; it was said that the bank's Tutsi tellers had been executed there.

Tonight, she was working late, developing negatives and printing the pictures she'd taken at Kibeho in the accountants' office, which she and the other photographers had turned into a darkroom. Alone in the comforting gloom, the horrors of the day's events materialised in front of her as the chemicals in the trays did their work. She'd already developed, printed and transmitted the picture she knew would be on the front page of newspapers all around the world tomorrow. It was of the RPA officer holding the pistol to the head of the screaming woman. The second frame, where the woman fell to the ground, blood spurting from her head, was more dramatic, more confronting. There would be few countries where both shots would be shown. People in the west had a morbid fascination with Africa's dark, crazy soul and the endless run of wars, famines and massacres it spawned. They would read and tut-tut about the killings in Rwanda over breakfast, but while it was OK to be told several hundred thousand people had been slaughtered, it was not OK to see the blood, to see someone actually dying.

On the flipside, when she looked at her own work dispassionately she would take the side of the world's editors in preferring the shot of the man holding the pistol to the woman's head, her mouth wide with the unheard scream. Knowing that she died in the next instant made the image all the more powerful, whereas the frame of her falling, blood spurting from the wound, was more gory than emotional. Editors would want readers moved, not throwing up into their cornflakes.

The images appearing in front of her now, which she pegged to the line in the darkroom to dry, were mostly of the British doctor Captain Richard Dunlop in action just after the shooting. Although it was unfair of her to single out the British army officer from the Australian unit he was working with, he was a good-looking man and she had some nice frames of him treating the little girl with the wound on her back. The child's eyes glistened in hopeful gratitude as she looked over her shoulder at the brave white doctor who had come to save her from the intertribal conflicts of her own people. At least that was how a corny, news-hungry subeditor would see it half a world away. Liesl knew enough about the history of Rwanda to know that the conflict between the Hutu and the Tutsi had been encouraged by the Belgians who'd colonised the country and sought to conquer it by dividing the two peoples, favouring one over the other. And as brave as Richard Dunlop and the Australian medics and soldiers had been today, the fact was that the UN had arrived too late to stop the initial genocide, and was now powerless to stop the next round.

Liesl hadn't expected to end up back in Africa so soon. She'd left South Africa for London two years earlier, at the age of twenty-one. She'd done well at school and had intended to go to university, but when her father had organised an internship on a regional daily newspaper at Nelspruit, the *Lowvelder*, Liesl had loved the work so much that she'd put off going to varsity in favour of taking the full-time job she was offered on the newspaper. She'd trained as a journalist, earning the praise of the subeditors and her editor, and at the same time she'd pursued the interest she'd had in photography since her thirteenth birthday when her parents had bought her a Canon single-lens reflex camera.

Working as a journalist, even on a conservative Afrikaans provincial newspaper, had exposed Liesl to places, peoples and issues she would never have encountered on her parents' sprawling citrus farm back near the small town of Letsitele, near Phalaborwa. She'd covered strikes and demonstrations and learned more about the black campaign for majority rule than she would have sitting at home watching the pro-government SABC news on television. She'd also seen first hand the effects of the government's tools of persuasion: tear gas, rubber bullets and the sjambok. Liesl's parents lived a life of privilege, as had she, but she couldn't agree with her father's steadfast defence of the apartheid regime. After two years on the *Lowvelder* she'd applied for and landed a job on the liberal English-language paper, the *Rand Daily Mail*. Her father had been outraged, her mother indulgent, and Liesl had left for Johannesburg.

She pegged up a series of prints of the old Rwandese man in the suit, the one with the bullet wound in his belly, who had gone on and on about a crumpled photograph before dying.

Liesl had seen bigger protests and far more violence in Soweto than she had in the Eastern Transvaal, including demonstrators killed by police gunfire and ANC dissenters executed in the most horrible way by their own people with the feared 'necklace', a tyre filled with petrol and thrust over a person's head and then ignited. It had been shocking, and she had been hardened to the realities of death and torture very quickly, but as she looked at the series of images drying in front of her now she realised the intertribal and interracial fighting that had gone on in her country paled into insignificance compared to what was going on in Rwanda.

People she'd met in England, after leaving the *Rand Daily Mail* for a job at the *Global News* wire service, thought South Africa's problem was racism, and that all of the other conflicts that had ravaged the rest of the continent were the legacy of white colonialism. That, she mused as she looked again at her hero shot of the day – the officer pointing the gun at the woman – was bullshit. It was so much more complicated than that.

Yes, the Belgians had favoured the Tutsis over the Hutus for decades and this had contributed to the animosity that had manifested itself in civil war and genocide, but the Belgians had only been able to conquer and rule because the tribal divisions had already been there. Even on the *Mail*, where most of the other journalists were English-speaking South Africans, she'd had to endure snide remarks and jokes about her Afrikaner background. The English speakers complained, because it was true, that the National Party government and big corporations favoured Afrikaners over the *rooinek*, or rednecks, as Afrikaners called English speakers. Tribal divisions ran as deep in the white population as they did in the black, and while they didn't manifest themselves in mass killings these days, the English and the Afrikaners had fought a full-scale war against each other back at the turn of the century.

Liesl sighed. It was all so bloody depressing.

'Liesl? Hello?' she heard a man's voice call from the foyer of the bank, which had been converted into a makeshift lounge room with an odd assortment of kitchen stools and armchairs scrounged from other offices and houses. The tellers' counter was a bar, littered with mostly empty liquor bottles and unwashed wineglasses.

Speaking of Englishmen, she thought, smiling to herself. 'Just finishing up in here. Make yourself comfortable, I'll be out in one minute.'

Liesl pegged up the last of the prints, took off her rubber gloves and left the darkroom.

'Howzit?' she said, opening the door that led from behind the counter to the waiting area.

'Hi there.' Richard tapped the pistol in the holster on his hip. 'I've come to make a withdrawal.'

She laughed. 'This is a surprise. I was just looking at you.' She hadn't meant it to sound like a come-on, but she thought that perhaps it did. It was like when she'd taken his cigarettes out of his pocket for him. She had done so because his hands were bloodied, but even amid all that death and suffering she'd quietly enjoyed touching him.

She'd gotten straight to work developing her images once she'd returned late that afternoon and, like him, hadn't had time to shower or change. She was suddenly self-conscious. 'Have a seat,' she said, motioning to one of the tubular steel-framed chairs.

'Thanks. I was wondering if you had any pictures of that old man who died today – the one with the photograph.'

'You said you were going to tell me what it was he was saying to you about that picture.'

'It was important to him.' Richard closed his eyes for a couple of seconds, then opened them. 'Something about the picture being why all this was happening. And someone was "evil".'

'Everyone's evil in this country,' Liesl said.

'I can't argue with that. Do you have any pictures of him?'

'Sure. They're just drying. They'll take a few minutes or so. You can have a look through them when they're ready. How about a drink while you're waiting?' Liesl went to the counter, boosted herself up with her hands so that her belly was on top and she was leaning over into what had been a teller's station. She reached under the benchtop and found a hidden half-full bottle of Captain Morgan Spiced Gold Rum. She straightened up and held it out to him. 'This OK? Everyone else is out, but when they're here they drink everything in sight. Bloody journos, hey.'

'Fine, thanks.'

'No ice.'

'Life really is hell in Africa, isn't it,' Richard said, taking the glass.

His chin was stubbled and his uniform was filthy. He ran his fingers through his thick, unkempt hair. She glanced at his left hand. No wedding ring. The rum warmed her insides. Pushing a strand of hair away from her eye and tucking it behind her ear, she noticed that he was watching her every gesture, trying to read her. She wondered if he could tell that she had just realised how long it had been since she'd had sex. Too long. She was hit on by soldiers from the various peacekeeping forces on an almost daily basis. Occasionally she was tempted, but she knew that sleeping with a soldier would only cause complications. The way she felt in this moment, though, made her think that this doctor might be worth the complication. It was odd, feeling this way after a day spent witnessing death, but she did. 'So, why aren't you serving with the British forces here?'

'I'm on an exchange posting with the Aussies. I like them. They're good people. Your accent's quite soft. Are you based in the UK?'

She nodded and took another sip. 'I ran away from Africa, from the things I didn't like about my country, but now my work brings me back here, and even though I'm happy South Africa now has a black president, I look at this place and I wonder what future there is for my home. When Mandela goes we might end up with people like they had running Rwanda.'

He finished his rum and she topped up his glass, then hers. She wrinkled her nose. 'Hey, no offence and all that, but I think you need a wash, man.'

Richard sniffed under his arm, then scratched it. She laughed. 'Yes, I know,' he said. 'Also I think I've picked up some lice or fleas from the camp.'

'Ewww,' she teased.

Laughing, he said, 'I'm actually half-decent when I scrub up . . . and don't have lice.' He suppressed a yawn. 'Sorry. Busy day.'

'I know. I watched you. It's funny for me – I'm an eyewitness to death and tragedy. I take pictures and I write about it, but I'm never part of it. I watched you with that little girl, the old man, all the others, the ones who lived and the ones who died. You hardly ever stopped.'

'When you reached in my pocket for my cigarettes, how did you know that was where I kept them?'

'I told you. I watched you.'

He downed his rum again. He was drinking quickly, maybe to forget, or maybe for the same reason she wanted another drink. Courage. She did what she had to, said what she had to, in order to get the picture and the story. Politeness and meekness were not traits that suited a news photographer, and a journalist had to have the courage to ask the questions no one else would. Sometimes, not always, she went for a man in the same determined way she went about getting a story or a picture. Liesl was curious about the pictures he had come for, but her interest in him was overriding her news sense at the moment. She poured two more tots.

'There's a bathroom just through there,' she said, point-ing to a connecting door, 'out behind the manager's office, which is where I stay. Why don't you shower while the photos dry and I'll get them off the line for you?'

He checked his watch and nodded. 'OK. Thank you.'

She got up and showed him to the bathroom. 'There's soap and shampoo there – I hoard all the little bottles from every hotel I stay in – and a towel on the rack.'

'Thanks.'

She lingered in the doorway. 'Just call if you need anything else.'

'Will do.' He started unbuttoning his uniform shirt and she closed the door. Liesl leaned against it and exhaled.

Richard turned on the hot tap and stood under it. African showers, he'd learned, took an age to warm up, and by the time he'd washed his hair the water was warm enough for him to need a little cold.

He thought about Carmel while he lathered his body and wondered how long it would be until Liesl thought up an excuse to knock on the bathroom door. He didn't consider himself a vain man, but he'd learned how to read women at an early age.

Carmel was pretty and smart and single and he loved mak-ing love to her. They'd been sleeping together for several weeks and he was sure she enjoyed the illicitness of their affair. It would have been no big deal if their fellow officers had known of it, but Richard was happy that she wanted to keep it a secret. It did add a sense of spice and urgency to their stolen couplings.

Richard stared down at the mix of blood and grime

cascading off his skin and down the plughole. The image of the RPA officer executing the woman seared his mind and he shut his eyes to try to make it go away. But he heard again her pleas and the man's laughter. Liesl had been there too. How was she dealing with it? he wondered. Perhaps it would help if they both just talked. No, he remonstrated with himself, that would just cause complications. There would be more booze, and he'd be late for his rendezvous with Carmel.

The only thing that worried him about Carmel was her clinginess. She'd dropped more than one hint that she saw them continuing their romance after he returned to England. 'I've always wanted to travel to the UK and my stint with the army will be up in eighteen months,' she'd said.

'Carmel, I could be posted anywhere in the world – you know what it's like. After the army I'm thinking about Médecins Sans Frontières or something similar. I want to see more of the world, not be tied down.'

She'd nodded supportively and not pressed the issue. It wasn't that he didn't want to settle down with *her* – he just didn't want to settle down at all. He thought that if he did settle into an ongoing relationship it might be better if he found a partner who was likewise nomadic in her work life. It was partly his fault, for telling her, in a moment of weakness, that he loved her.

Above the pounding of the shower he heard a knock on the bathroom door. 'Everything OK in there?'

He slid the shower curtain open. He knew he should say that yes, he was fine, thank you very much. He knew that he shouldn't have had more than one drink, and that he should just dry off, get dressed into his filthy uniform, take what pictures she had and go. The old man had fought through his pain to stress the importance of the photo and perhaps it would make sense to the military intelligence people in the UN mission, but the original had been lost. He knew Carmel was waiting for him. He wanted to do the right thing, but the words wouldn't come.

The door opened. He turned his head and saw in Liesl's eyes what they both needed to do to forget this terrible day.

His silence seemed to embolden her. She lifted her T-shirt over her head as she crossed the floor. He saw she'd already removed her hiking boots and socks. Her fingers were at the button at the top of her jeans. She kept her eyes locked on his as she slid her jeans down, tugging her pants at the same time. She wasn't drawing it out, or teasing him. He knew what she was feeling. It was a need, nothing more. Naked, she stepped over the rim of the bath. He felt himself growing hard as she wrapped her arms around him and he felt her breasts pressing against his back. She kissed the back of his neck. 'Clean me.'

Richard turned his body to her, wishing he was a stronger, better man. They kissed, drawing it out as he moved her into the stream of water. He broke from her and pushed the wet hair from her face and squeezed some shampoo into the palm of his hand, then massaged it into her hair.

She turned from him and lifted her face so he could kiss her again as he worked her hair into a lather. As the water rinsed her he stayed behind her, taking the soap and rubbing it over her chest, breasts, belly, and into the tangle of her pubic hair. She pushed back against him and his cock slipped between the cleft of her cheeks as he reached under her and soaped her some more. Richard dropped the soap and let the water rinse his hand. Liesl groaned as he slid the length of his middle finger down over her hard bud and then into her. She reached behind her, groping for him, encircling him.

Richard felt his arousal boiling inside him, but wasn't ready for this to end yet. He dropped to his knees, pulling himself from her grip. He turned her, so her back was against the tiled wall, and pushed her legs apart. She grabbed his shoulders to stop from slipping as he retrieved the soap and slid the bar up and down her legs. Richard was addicted to women – the touch, the smell, the taste of them. He buried his face in her and revelled in the soft folds of her as the water cascaded down off her body onto him. She ran her fingers through his hair.

When he sensed Liesl was close he stopped and stood and felt the added rush from seeing the naked longing, close to begging, in her eyes. He smiled.

'Bastard,' she whispered.

He grabbed a handful of wet hair and pulled on it, drawing her head back so he could kiss her neck. 'Bitch.'

Liesl groaned again.

Carmel didn't like him talking dirty to her, so Liesl's muttered profanity was like a shock to his system, bringing him back from relationship land to the world of raw, animal fucking. He loved it. He spun her around again so she was facing the wall and reached around her, spreading her with his fingers and grazing her clit as he pushed against her.

'Fuck me,' she said again, her right cheek pressed against the tiles. She hadn't mentioned protection and his lust had overcome his common sense. She put her foot up on the rim of the tub and he entered her from behind, driving up into her in one hard thrust.

'Yes.'

'Beg,' he said.

'Yes, please. More . . .'

Liesl cried out.

Carmel drove the Land Rover through the streets of Kigali. The padre, an Anglican minister named Michael, was in the seat next to her, and a soldier, their bodyguard, was sitting in the back. All three were armed with F-88 Steyr assault rifles.

'To tell you the truth, while I'm not pleased, it's good to actually be doing something. I know that's a terrible thing to say,' Michael said.

Carmel didn't reply. She gripped the steering wheel so hard it hurt her palms. She wanted to scream, but couldn't in front of the minister without having to provide an explanation. She didn't understand why Richard was taking so long to get back to the barracks, and resented having to go out looking for him. She drove down Avenue de la République and turned into the car park of the old bank where she knew Liesl Nel and some of the other media people were camped.

Carmel nodded to a security guard sitting on an old bar stool by the gate and he touched a hand to his cap. She hated this and the irony was that she'd volunteered to break the news to Richard when the signal had come into the communications centre. She'd made the call to London, to the point of contact that had been included in the message.

Carmel came to the glass door of the building but couldn't see inside because of the old bedsheets that had been tacked up inside to act as makeshift curtains. She knocked.

Liesl opened the door. 'Hello? It's um . . .'

'Carmel. Captain Carmel Shang. I'm the UNAMIR legal officer. We've met.'

'*Ja*, of course. Can I help you with something?'

The fair-haired South African woman was barefoot, in a T-shirt and a pair of shorts. Her hair was wet. Carmel sniffed the air and was fairly sure the smell was marijuana smoke. A man inside coughed. 'Is Captain Dunlop here?'

Liesl took a step back and looked over her shoulder. Carmel peered in as the door was opened wider. Richard was sitting on a tattered armchair in the midst of a messy lounge area. He stood and ran a hand through his hair. 'Carmel, Padre . . .'

'Can I come in?' Carmel asked, fighting to keep her voice businesslike.

'*Ja*, of course. Would you like a drink?' Liesl asked.

Carmel took in the two glasses and the near-empty bottle of rum on a rickety coffee table.

'Mightn't be a bad idea,' Michael whispered behind her.

'No, thank you,' Carmel said.

'What is it?' Richard asked.

She thought his cheeks were colouring. She looked at his hair again – she loved his hair – and saw that it was wet, like Liesl's. Carmel started to feel light-headed as the clues littered around her fell into place. On the far side of the tellers' counter she saw an open door and an office converted to a bedroom. The sheets were rumpled and two wet towels were draped over the door.

'Richard, your father's dead,' Carmel said.

The padre stepped out from behind Carmel. 'Richard, I'm so sorry for your loss. We're making arrangements now to get you home to England.'

'I . . . how . . . ?' He looked at Carmel and she almost felt sorry for him.

'It was a heart attack,' the padre said, stepping forward

and putting a hand on his arm. Carmel felt the emotion rise up inside her. She wanted to cry but knew she couldn't.

'Richard, I'm so sorry,' Liesl said.

Carmel looked at her and wanted to slap her face.

'Right,' said Richard. He turned to Liesl. 'Best be off then.'

Carmel wanted to punch him, to pound on his chest with her fists and hurt him. He didn't deserve their sympathy. 'The funeral's a week from today.'

'Right,' he said again.

He was all English stiff upper lip and understatement, she thought. As Richard came to her she saw how he was unable to meet her eyes. 'Yes,' Carmel added. 'I spoke to Juliet, she's helping your mother with the plans for the service.'

He stopped, already past her but not looking back. 'Juliet?'

'Yes, you remember Juliet; the nurse you've shared a flat with for the past year. She answered the telephone at your parents' house when I called. Apparently she drove up as soon as she heard the news. Juliet asked me to pass a message to you, telling you how much she loves you.'

8

Zambia, 2012

Carmel looked out the window of the Commair Boeing 737–400 as the aircraft started its descent to Livingstone Airport. Far off to her right she could see what looked like a line of smoke rising from a fissure cut into the African bush. It was, she realised after gazing at it a while, spray rising from the Victoria Falls.

Apart from that sudden drop into the massive rent in the land, the geography here seemed very flat compared to Rwanda, which from the air looked rumpled and scrunched, like an unmade bed. The valleys and folds of Rwanda had flooded with blood and they still hid bones. Zambia, she knew, had suffered decades of corruption and mismanagement, and the verdict was still out on its newly minted government, but if they had to choose between graft and the other major sociopolitical malaise that had infected much of Africa – war and genocide – then she imagined the people who lived in Livingstone would probably prefer the former.

Carmel forced the thoughts from her mind and stretched out her legs – she'd been lucky enough to move to a vacant seat in the exit row after take-off. She raised a fist to her mouth to stifle a yawn. The images from the files came back to her. A couple of the men she would be prosecuting in this next round of cases in Arusha were Tutsis – former mid-ranking officers in the RPA who had taken part in the slaughter of Hutus at the Kibeho refugee camp. The men were scapegoats, arrested so the government could claim it wasn't just settling old scores with the Hutu *génocidaires*. She wondered if the men were guilty of more than killing unarmed people – as if that wasn't enough – and whether some other transgression was behind them being offered as sacrifices.

Carmel remembered the trucks coming back from Kibeho, and the soldier, Rick Green, who had challenged her. It was a telling moment in her life. She had never felt so helpless, so bereft of words – a scary proposition for a lawyer – as when that infantryman, stained with blood and grime, had challenged her to make sense of the law under which the UN mission operated. It was, she long ago realised, the reason why she had come back to Rwanda to work as a prosecutor for the ICTR. She'd needed to make sense of what had gone on and to try to right the wrongs that the UN assistance force had been unable to stop.

Recalling that incident with Greeny also dredged up painful memories of Richard coming to her rescue. The complete and utter bastard.

She'd found it hard to trust any man after the way he had betrayed her. After her tour in Rwanda was up she had returned to her posting as the legal officer at brigade headquarters in Townsville. The day-to-day work of prosecuting or defending drunken absent-without-leave soldiers bored her, and the scenarios put to her on the monotonous round of field and command-post exercises seemed to her to bear no relationship at all to the myriad complex legal challenges a real UN deployment had presented to her and the soldiers who had endured the horrors of Rwanda.

A captain in the 2nd/4th Battalion of the Royal Australian Regiment had come to see her one day, to talk about a soldier who had been arrested after a brawl in town, and he had noticed the UNAMIR plaque hanging on her wall and the photograph of a huge silverback mountain gorilla.

'I was with the first rotation,' he'd said, moving to the photo to take a closer look. 'We didn't get time to go sightseeing and tracking gorillas.'

'My tour was like a holiday,' she'd replied flippantly.

He'd asked her out and she'd said yes. Carmel lived in a small, lonely one-bedroom flat off base. She'd fended off many subtle and not-so-subtle come-ons from other officers, but despite his shaved head and lean body, there was something vulnerable about Dan that attracted her. And he'd been to Rwanda.

Over their first dinner she finished most of the two bottles of wine they'd ordered, plus two gin and tonics. He joked about her tolerance and she thought it a compliment. She let him take her to bed that night and revelled in the feel of his hard body under her fingertips. They talked afterwards in the dark, her head resting on his chest, about their time in Africa. She asked him, the booze talking, if he'd been affected by the bloodshed she knew the first contingent had encountered.

'We did OK, my boys and me,' Dan said. 'I was a platoon commander and I knew every man I deployed with. We were a team, you know?'

Carmel nodded, but it hadn't been the same for her.

'At night,' Dan continued, stroking her hair, 'we'd sit around, and after the formal debrief and orders for the next day we'd just talk – about the stuff we'd seen. Pretty emotional shit sometimes, but it helped, you know?'

She didn't. The headquarters where she worked was a collection of individuals thrown together from various units. They hadn't trained and lived together for months on end prior to Rwanda, as Dan and his infantrymen had. There wasn't the same camaraderie or the same opportunity to talk or even cry together. Each night Carmel had retreated to her single room, left to her own thoughts. She hadn't seen what Dan and his boys had seen, had rarely ventured out past Kigali, but in a way that made it even harder for her to get her head around what had gone on in the country.

'What was it like for you?' Dan asked.

'Oh, fine . . .' She was tired by then, sated by the wine and the sex. 'I spent most of my time in the headquarters. I didn't see as much bad stuff as you did, and I went sightseeing – gorilla trekking.' He let it go and she lay there, eyes wide open, staring at the ceiling as he drifted off to sleep.

She moved in with Dan two months later and they married within a year. They told each other and anyone who would listen that the frequent absences from each other as they went off to different army exercises and courses were good for their relationship. The truth, however, was that Carmel found it increasingly hard to deal with the weeks of lonely nights without Dan. Her drinking increased and there was more than one day she had to call in sick, unable to face the glare of day. She and Dan would go out to dinner to celebrate one or the other's return home and he would end up chastising her for slurring her words too soon, or being too tired for sex. He eventually suggested she seek help and she abused him.

The more Dan tried to help her, the more resentful she became. When they were home together he started spending nights out socialising with other officers – boys' nights out. She was, Carmel realised, an embarrassment to him, and the realisation just made her feel more morose and crave more alcohol. Dan had always been fit – a requirement in his job – but he started going for longer runs in the morning and long marches in the cool of the evening dressed in his shorts, trainers and T-shirt, but carrying a full pack and webbing. He told her he was getting in shape to attempt the gruelling Special Air Service selection course. He told her it would be good for his career, but Carmel knew enough about the army to understand that an intelligent, hard-working young captain would do better in the battalion than in the SAS where promotion opportunities were rare. She wondered if the real reason he was volunteering for special forces was to get away from her.

Dan passed selection for the SAS and, after completing a string of courses that kept him away from Carmel for months, he was sent to East Timor, where an Australian-led UN intervention force was re-establishing order after the vicious infighting that followed the fledgling nation's decision to break from Indonesia.

There were no vacant postings for legal officers in Western Australia, where the SAS was based, so Carmel stayed in Townsville, marking time at the brigade headquarters. By the time Dan returned from Timor she had decided to leave the army and try to get a job in a civilian law firm in Perth. 'I never intended to stay in the army long term.'

'Don't do it for me, Carm,' he said when she told him of her decision.

'What do you mean?'

'I've been thinking while I've been away. It's not worth it. I'm not happy, you're not happy. I'm just going to keep being posted away with the army. You're from Queensland – your family's here. You'll be miserable if you move to Perth.'

'Shit,' she said. 'Is there another woman?'

He looked her in the eye and shook his head. 'No.'

And she believed him, which made it all the more difficult to deal with. He wasn't leaving her because he'd fallen for someone else – he just didn't want to be with her. 'It's not worth it,' he'd said.

After Dan left that last time, she spiralled out of control, and her colleagues at the headquarters noticed it. There was an embarrassing incident after a mess dinner where she fell into the base swimming pool, fully dressed, and had to be carried home. She had brief affairs with two other officers, and the gossip about the drunken, promiscuous lawyer became a running joke on the base. The senior legal officer from 1st Division headquarters called her into his office and recommended she seek professional counselling.

Post-traumatic stress disorder, or PTSD, from her time in Rwanda, had been the diagnosis from the civilian psychiatrist the army sent her to.

'Me?' She was surprised. 'But I was just a lawyer. I saw some people who'd been wounded and some bodies, but I wasn't a doctor or a nurse or a soldier. I didn't really see the suffering.'

'Maybe not,' the doctor, a man with kind eyes, assured her, 'but you carry guilt for what happened. You didn't see the killing and you didn't write the rules of engagement for that operation, but you were stuck in the middle of it. You had to tell men they couldn't protect innocent women and children. You had to advise your commander to sit on his hands and watch genocide take place. It's no wonder you're drinking to try to forget all that.'

The whispering and sniggering continued when word got out that Carmel would be leaving the army with a compensation payout for PTSD. She knew what the others at headquarters would be saying, because she'd said the same things to herself. How come she, a legal officer, could get a compensation payment for PTSD when she'd never seen someone put a gun to an unarmed African's head and pull the trigger; when she had never had to lift a half-rotten corpse and feel the skin of the hands come off in hers like black gloves; when she'd never had to unblock the blood and hair and skin from the toilets inside the Kigali hospital which Tutsis had been held over while their throats had been slit. She felt a fraud and a failure as she marched out of Lavarack Barracks in Townsville for the last time.

Her parents did a fair to middling job of hiding their disappointment when she moved back into their house in the Brisbane suburb of Redcliff. They hadn't expected her to stay in the army forever – and would have been happy to see her leave to take up a position in a civilian law firm sooner, but they were tight-lipped at her announcement that she'd left without another job to go to. Carmel caught up and partied with some old friends from school, most of whom were married with children. On a night when four of the girls had been able to escape their babies and husbands, Carmel ended up passed out on the floor of a nightclub toilet. Her friends found her and poured her into a taxi home. When she woke up she realised it wasn't just the booze that was making her head throb. She had smashed her forehead on the tiles and been left with an ugly bruise and abrasion. That morning she fronted a job interview with a Brisbane firm specialising in local government work. The partner grilling her clearly didn't buy the 'walking into a door' excuse, but as he flicked through her résumé, he planted an idea in her mind.

'I see you were in Rwanda with the army. I've got a friend who's off to Arusha in Tanzania soon to work as a prosecutor on the genocide tribunal crimes.'

Carmel had left without the job but with a new resolve to do something about her life. She had gone to her first AA meeting that night.

The passengers beside her on the flight to Livingstone, a pair of Germans in matching khaki safari outfits, were craning across her to see out the window. Carmel leaned back to give them a better view. The pilot had banked left and was taking his time, tracking along the Zambezi River, heading upstream. Carmel looked down and saw a shadow moving across an open patch of ground. She suddenly realised it was a giraffe, in the Zambezi National Park, on the Zimbabwean side. It made her feel good for a few moments, thinking about a gentle creature happy and, hopefully, safe in its element. It was, she thought, a good omen.

It had been hard and confronting work coming to terms with the demons in her life, and she'd learned to take comfort in whatever it was that cheered her. Seeing animals in the wild was one of the things that gave her pleasure. On an early trip to Rwanda, Carmel and some of the other lawyers on the team had taken time out to travel to Ruhengeri in the north of the country to see the mountain gorillas made famous by the

American researcher Dian Fossey. Carmel had seen the gorillas during her tour of Rwanda with the army, but the second visit had been more memorable. Ironically, she'd learned more about the depravities of the genocide as a prosecutor combing files long after the events of 1994 than she had when she had been on the ground in the country. Contrasting what she knew of the daily litany of crimes against humanity – murders, torture, rape and mutilation – with the gentle actions and serene stares of these huge but generally harmless primate cousins of man had soothed her jagged soul.

She had rebuilt her life, finding strength in the courage of the survivors of the genocide and, though the ICTR trials were drawn-out affairs, in moments of justice when a key *génocidaire* was finally convicted. The media in Australia had taken an interest when her name appeared in wire-service copy about the Arusha trials, and her parents, who saved every profile article about their prosecutor daughter, were once again proud of her.

The pilot banked to the right and right again, crossing the river and heading downstream, towards Livingstone and the falls themselves. The Zambezi River was a peaceful grey green, its surface broken into eddies and channels by small islands of granite. Somewhere below her, she guessed, was Henri's house. He'd described it as being upriver of the falls. She wondered what it would be like to live on the edge of one of the world's most beautiful rivers. She'd canoed the Lower Zambezi from a camp below the dam wall at Kariba, and had visited Victoria Falls once before on the Zimbabwean side, but she'd never had the chance to go upriver. She was looking forward to it, and to seeing Henri's collection of rescued animals and birds.

As the aircraft's wheels squeaked on the tarmac Carmel noticed a movement in the grass bordering the runway. A troop of baboons was running alongside them. It made her sigh with contentment; at last she felt like she was truly back in Africa.

Liesl turned off the N1 at Polokwane and followed the bypass to the R71 towards Magoebaskloof. That would take her on to Tzaneen and the road to the only place in the world she had ever felt truly safe: her parents' home. But she wasn't looking forward to visiting them.

Sleep had come hard after the attempted carjacking, and Sannette's kids had been up early making a racket. Liesl reckoned she'd had no more than three or four hours' rest. She had dosed herself with coffee, ignored Sannette's pleas for her to stay another day, and got into her borrowed BMW four-wheel drive and set off for the Lowveld. She had been glad when at last she'd broken free of the morning commuter traffic and passed Pretoria, but her mind was still churning.

Liesl had stopped at the Total Petroport twenty kilometres north of the capital city and ordered a cheeseburger at the Steers restaurant located in the bridge over the dual carriageway. While waiting for her burger she'd checked her emails on her iPhone. She'd scrolled back through the last few days' messages and found the summons to appear before the International Criminal Tribunal in Rwanda. As Liesl had reread it the restaurant manager had had to ask her twice if everything was all right with her order. She'd looked up and mumbled that everything was fine.

As she barrelled along the R71 through the open countryside Liesl's phone rang in the console. It was the shrill, stuttering chirp of a woodland kingfisher. She checked in her rear-view mirror for traffic cops then picked it up. 'Liesl, hello?'

'Howzit, Liesl,' said Sarah, the telephone receptionist from *Escape!*.

Liesl considered responding with news of the attempt on her life and the summons to travel to Tanzania to testify in a war crimes court about things that had scared her so bad that she still woke up sometimes with tears rolling down her cheeks. But instead, she said, 'Fine, and you?'

'*Ja*, you know, same as always here. Sorry to bother you but there's been this *oke* pestering me all morning trying to get your cellphone number. I told him to send you an email, but he said he needs to speak to you personally. He sounded really agitated, like some kind of stalker.'

'Really? I could use a stalker. My love life is *kak* these days,' Liesl said. Sarah laughed. She was twenty-two, blonde and skinny. She could afford to laugh.

'He says he's a doctor, so he could be a good catch.'

'Really? What's his name?'

'*Doctor* Richard Dunlop.'

Liesl wondered if she would have remembered him so clearly, so immediately, if it hadn't been for Ioannou and the follow-up email from the ICTR.

'Are you still there, Liesl?'

Not really, she thought. She was in a shower in Rwanda seventeen years earlier. '*Ja*. Do me a favour and SMS me his number please.'

When the phone beeped a few seconds later Liesl scrolled to the message and selected the number. She pressed send without slowing her car down from a hundred and thirty kilometres an hour. She was exceeding the speed limit, but that was nothing new for her.

'Doctor Dunlop,' the voice said, as deep as she remembered. 'It's Liesl Nel here. How are you?'

'Someone tried to kill me last night.' Asking someone how they were came naturally to her, ingrained by her parents and reinforced a million times since during her travels throughout Africa. It was the height of rudeness in African culture to come straight to the point, to say what was really on your mind, and they hadn't spoken in years. Richard was an Englishman so his bluntness shouldn't have surprised her, but it rankled. 'Are you still there?' he asked her.

'Yes. Me too,' she said.

'You too? Someone tried to kill *you* as well?'

'Yes. This is weird, Richard. Did you get a summons from the Rwandan criminal tribunal as well?'

'Yes. An email a few days ago, but I only saw it last night.'

A Mercedes with dark tinted windows was looming in her mirror. Normally she would have geared down and planted her foot. She didn't like people tailgating or passing her. Uncharacteristically she touched her foot to the brake pedal and moved into the yellow lane on the left, allowing the car to pass her. As it did, she peered through the dark glass, suddenly afraid she might see the barrel of a gun pointing at her. The driver didn't even glance at her. She exhaled. 'Do you think it's related?'

'I don't know. Maybe,' he replied. 'Where are you now?'

'I'm on my way to my mom and dad's place. It's a farm in a little place called Letsitele, about an hour from Phalaborwa, but you probably don't know—'

'I know where Phalaborwa is,' he interrupted.

'OK. I know from your phone number you're in South Africa. Where are you and what are you doing in this country?'

'I'm working in the Kruger National Park and the rest is a long story. We need to meet.'

She pursed her lips. Liesl wasn't used to people telling her what to do, but in this case she was thinking along the same lines as Richard. But, God, it had been so long. The last time they'd seen each other had been bizarre.

'*Ja*,' she said. 'I only have a day, then I have to drive to Botswana on a job.'

'I'll come to you. A man visited my house and tried to put several bullets from a silenced rifle into me. All of a sudden I have an urge to see more of Africa.'

She didn't laugh. Instead, she told him briefly about the attempted carjacking, adding that the man who had tried to kill her had also used a silenced weapon.

'Is that normal for a Joburg carjacker – to use a silencer?' Richard asked.

'I don't know. But I do know he seemed more intent on killing me than taking my friend's *vrot* old people mover.'

Liesl gave Richard directions to her parents' farm and told him to call her when he got close. They ended the call and she thought again of the crazy circumstances that had brought them together the first time. It felt almost the same this time around.

Richard hadn't studied psychiatry, but he'd read somewhere there was a term for what he and Liesl had done all those years ago – survivor sex. The problem was that there had been collateral damage from this acting out of their frustrations and fears. He sat at the kitchen table in his house in the

Skukuza staff village and thought about how his deployment to Rwanda had changed his life.

Carmel had said nothing to him on the drive back to headquarters and it hardly seemed appropriate to discuss his love life back home in England in front of the padre. Richard had been on a Canadian C-130 out of Kigali the next morning and had caught a British Airways flight from Nairobi to London.

His tour in Rwanda would have finished a month after he received the news and his attachment to the Australian field hospital would have ended two weeks after that. When he returned to the UK the British Army decided it wasn't worth the cost of an airfare to send him back to Africa or Australia for just a few weeks. He'd written a letter to Carmel, trying to explain things, but she hadn't replied. Seventeen years later, Richard still felt guilty.

He wasn't due to go into the surgery, as he had already told Helen to clear his calendar for the day so he would be available to the police investigating the shooting. As he drank a lukewarm cup of coffee his maid delicately picked shards of glass off the floor and put them into a plastic bucket.

Richard went to his bedroom and pulled out a slightly mildewed green canvas travel bag from the top of his wardrobe and put it on the bed. Gulping down the last of the bitter coffee, he took four shirts from their hangers, a pair of khaki trousers, two pairs of shorts, two T-shirts and two pairs of socks and dumped them in the bag without folding any of them. He was wearing trousers, a short-sleeved shirt and leather hiking boots. Raiding the bathroom for necessities, he dropped the lot into a camping toiletry bag. In the top drawer of the bedside table was his passport and an envelope containing two thousand US dollars. There was also an unopened blue plastic packet of condoms with a red ribbon logo on them – freebies that were available throughout the national park in a bid to get the staff to practise safe sex. He pocketed all three, zipped the bag up and had a quick look around the bedroom. There was nothing else he would need or miss. He travelled light in life, always had.

'Bye, Flora,' he said to the maid. He took her hand and palmed over a thousand rand which he'd taken from his wallet.

She looked down at the notes and her eyes widened in surprise. 'Goodbye, sir. When are you coming back?'

'Probably never.'

Vite felt warm and safe nestled against the breast of the woman. She carried him on her hip and he wrapped his arms around her neck. On her head she balanced a basket of small black-spotted bananas as she walked along the muddy verge of the rain-slicked potholed road.

The whining engines and belching smoke of passing motor vehicles had scared him at first, but the woman had murmured to him and that, and her body heat, had soothed him. He shrieked when the woman suddenly broke into a jog – not easy with her burdens – and turned his head into her armpit when she climbed into the back of an open pickup truck.

Two children on board laughed and squealed at the sight of Vite and they poked and prodded him, making him shriek as well, adding to the cacophony. The woman cuddled him closer and kept him away from them. Vite peeked at the children. The vehicle lurched off into a cratered road and he was scared all over again.

The noises around him grew louder as more and more

vehicles began passing them. The woman took out a spare *igitenge,* one of the colourful printed wraps worn by women, and swaddled him in it, so he couldn't see out. Vite didn't know whether to be relieved or even more terrified now that he couldn't see what was going on. He whimpered and she said to him, 'Hush.'

At last the vehicle stopped and the woman climbed down out of the truck. Her bananas were passed back to her and she arranged them on her head while Vite cowered under the wrap. Through a gap in the material, as the woman walked, Vite glimpsed more humans than he had seen in his entire life. They were everywhere.

Vite felt humans brushing against him as the woman squeezed her way into a crowded market. He heard her voice and that of a man. Their talk was rapid, back and forth. At last she moved the coloured veil that was hiding Vite's face. He was inside a room whose darkness and fetid smell was made closer and hotter by the outside sun superheating the corrugated-iron roof and walls. Flies buzzed around them. Vite saw the wide eyes of a man and he blinked back at him. The man reached for him, grabbing Vite under his arms, and Vite shrieked and bared his teeth.

The woman said nothing as the man took Vite. Vite kicked and screamed and wriggled, but he was small and the man's black hands were big and strong and sticky. He was held, but not lovingly or with care, as the woman had for these past few days. Vite cried for his mother.

'*Il s'appelle Vite,*' the woman said. She didn't reach for him or touch him, or try to soothe him. Instead, she took the wad of grimy notes the man had taken from his pocket and tucked them into her blouse.

As his eyes adjusted to the gloom, Vite recognised the shapes and forms around him. On a crude timber shelf nailed to the wooden supports of the hut was the gigantic head of a mountain gorilla. The silverback's massive severed hands were next to him. Hanging from a hook, attracting the flies and draining red blood into a cut-down drum, was a dead chimpanzee.

Vite shrieked.

9

Henri Bousson could have sent his driver to pick up Carmel Shang from the airport, but he was looking forward to meeting her too much.

He waited for her among the throng of tour operators and drivers in the arrivals area of the grandly named but underwhelming Livingstone International Airport. A trickle of passengers from the Commair flight started appearing, but Henri knew, from personal experience, that people travelling on non-Southern Africa Development Community passports would be queuing for a visa and that there would, most likely, be only one immigration officer assigned to the lengthy process of accepting payment, receipting, entering and stamping those visas. He'd lived in Africa all his life so he couldn't be surprised or annoyed that Zambia was any more or less bureaucratic and inefficient than anywhere else on the continent.

She looked attractive in the pictures he had seen of her on her Facebook page and the news media features he'd found about her online, which was another reason why he had made the decision to come to collect her in person. There had been a portrait shot, professionally taken and used to announce her employment by the ICTR, but the more flattering images came from an article about her work in an Australian women's magazine. The photos showed her in tourist khaki, kneeling in the midst of a troop of mountain gorillas in Rwanda; in a prosecutor's black robe outside the Rwandan criminal tribunal in Arusha; and, his favourite shot, her sitting on a white leather lounge in her apartment in Brisbane, in a white T-shirt and denim shorts, with her legs tucked up under her while she sipped a cup of tea. The idea was to capture the sum of the subject in words and images – crusader for justice, friend of wildlife, and attractive, self-assured independent woman. Only the eyes in the at-home picture – uncertain, nervous, perhaps unsure of the merits of embarking on a PR exercise, and alarmed at the impending glare of the camera's flash – betrayed the truth about Carmel Shang.

Henri had been in Rwanda at the time of the genocide as well, and he knew what the experience did to people. He was sure that Carmel Shang did what she did, in her work and private life, because of what she had done or failed to do in that time of darkness.

A brace of Americans in matching greens and browns, floppy bush hats and unmuddied boots stumbled into the arrivals hall and were pounced on by a protective guide who shepherded them away from the pack of touts and taxi drivers who waited for each flight in the hope of bagging a stray independent tourist.

Henri saw her, and his breath caught in the back of his throat. She *was* attractive, and she was here. She pulled a carry-on wheelie bag with a laptop in a matching case slung around the handle. The sudden realisation that she was really here, in the flesh, excited him. He walked up to her, his hand extended. 'Carmel?'

'Hi. Henri?'

'*Bonjour*. How are you?' He took her hand in his and held it. 'You're much . . . forgive me, but you're much younger than you look in your photo.'

She laughed. 'And you're taller than I thought you'd be, even though I couldn't find any pictures of you on the net and your Facebook pic is a chimp!'

'Ah, so you've been checking me out online, *oui*?'

He held onto her hand and took in her dark eyes. They were already flirting. He felt it in his heart again, the flutter of excitement. He was so very glad she had come to him.

Doctor Aston Mutale reread the article in *The Citizen*, the daily Johannesburg English-language tabloid. GIVE HER A MEDAL was the headline that had been plastered across the front page. *Motorist runs down carjacker who tried to kill famous photographer*, continued the shout line.

Aston threw the newspaper down on his desk in disgust. He had known there would be media coverage – the woman was not exactly a household name, but some of her photographs would have been reprinted along with her obituary, and the magazine she worked for was popular among whites. Carjacking was, he knew, a common enough offence for the story to be buried, but the twist in the bungled hit had propelled it to the front page.

Liesl Nel would be confused and worried now, and she would also be on her guard. She would be harder to kill. Aston picked up his mobile phone and tried Tryford's number for the eighth time. Not available. There had been no

SMS confirming that the British doctor in Skukuza had been killed. Aston had used Tryford before and considered him a good man, reliable. Both Tryford, whom Aston had dispatched to kill the white doctor, and Lawrence, who had been run over by a passer-by before he'd been able to kill the Nel woman, had been good soldiers, dependable men. It was inconceivable to think they had both failed in what were fairly straightforward missions. His business partner in Rwanda would not be happy.

Aston had a good business of his own in the Johannesburg suburb of Roodepoort, running his traditional healing practice, but it was just a front for the real source of his income. Aston worked as the middle man in South Africa for an international syndicate that smuggled live animals out of the country, a particularly lucrative business. Mostly these were exotic animals – birds and reptiles – for the benefit of private wildlife collectors abroad. The latest boom market was the oil-rich Gulf states, in particular the United Arab Emirates. The traditional markets in Europe were still struggling to recover from the global financial crisis. Any *mzungu* with enough money to afford a private zoo had been burned in the GFC. Aston also did a nice sideline in protected plants, particularly cycads.

As well as using *muti*, traditional medicines made from herbs, plants and the various body parts of different species, to treat his patients, he also supplied his cures to a growing international clientele of wealthy Africans living abroad, and shipped the occasional rhino horn to China and Vietnam via his underworld contacts in Thailand.

Aston was a man who dealt in traditions, but the nature of his diverse business interests meant that he'd had to embrace technology. His laptop chimed, signalling a new email. It was from his long-time business partner, who used an email account with the ironic name of wildlifelover3231. Aston opened it. They were good friends, but the message was businesslike and coded as usual.

Have a line on that marmoset in Kg. Have a doctor who would like this one as a pet. Also, new request from collector has just come in. Where can we get some dogs that like to hunt?

Aston typed a reply, fast, with two fat fingers.

I can organise purchase of marmoset and transport to you if that suits. Dogs??? Are you joking my friend? Will keep my ears and eyes open.

A marmoset was a small monkey originally from South America that was legally available to trade and own in many countries. They made good pets, but Aston knew his partner was not really referring to a marmoset – there was no money in the legal trade in animals – but to a gorilla. This was particularly exciting news. Mountain gorillas did not come onto the market every day. In Rwanda and Uganda the remaining gorillas were monitored on a daily basis, but things were less controlled across the border in the Democratic Republic of Congo. He'd read a media report recently about a female being shot by charcoal poachers and her baby presumably kidnapped. He assumed this was the animal in question, and that it had been smuggled across the border from the Congo to Rwanda.

Rereading the second request made Aston suck in a noisy

breath through his teeth. '*Eish*,' he said out loud in his surgery. It appeared that his partner had a client who wanted to buy some painted dogs – also known as the African wild dog or painted hunting dog. These animals had once roamed sub-Saharan Africa but there were now only about two and a half thousand of them left on the continent. As an endangered predator and something of a cause célèbre, they also tended to be intensively researched and monitored, which would undoubtedly pose a problem for Aston. The dogs were extremely efficient predators – far more so than lions, leopards and cheetahs – but as a result they were not popular in small private game reserves as they could quickly wipe out a stock of herbivores, such as impala, kudu, zebra and wildebeest. Despite education and conservation campaigns, there were still many cattle and sheep farmers who wanted a return to the days when the painted dog was considered vermin and could be legally shot on sight. Because of their huge home ranges the dogs often roamed outside of southern Africa's national parks in search of food. It would be impossible, Aston thought, to capture a pack inside a national park, and almost as difficult to find and trap some outside on private land. On the upside, if there was some way they could track down and capture a pack and smuggle them offshore, then Aston and his business partner could probably ask any price they wished. There was no precedent for such an order, and no benchmark that Aston was aware of.

There was a knock on his door. 'Yes?'

Elizabeth, his willowy Lozi receptionist, opened it. 'Mr Musanga is here, Doctor.'

Aston forced a smile. Elizabeth had been his mistress for the past six months. She was tall, but a little too thin for his liking. He would have to keep an eye on her health. 'Show him in.'

Musanga had the virus. But Aston didn't tell his patient that he had HIV-AIDS and would probably die. No one could tell for sure, unless they took the test, and Musanga, understandably, did not really wish to know his status. It would bring shame to him if he had to tell his wife, who had recently given birth to their fourth son. No good could come of knowing you were going to die and could no longer support your family or look forward to your children supporting you into old age. As he entered Aston's room, Musanga was beset with a coughing fit, and his lungs rattled with the aftershock. Aston noted the blood on the grimy handkerchief that Musanga stuffed back into his pocket.

'Still bad I see, my brother,' Aston observed. 'Sit down.' He checked Musanga's eyes and put his hand on his back. 'Breathe in for me. Did the pepper bark help?'

Musanga drew a breath. 'A little, *baba*,' he exhaled.

'You will need more,' Aston pronounced. He went to the line of small wooden drawers he'd had built into one wall of his surgery. He took out a ten-centimetre length of grey bark, curled from where it had been stripped from the branch, whose diameter had probably been no more than one centimetre. This batch had come from the Kruger National Park, one of the last two remaining stands of the tree in the wild in South Africa. It was worth a small fortune. The dwindling resource had pushed the price up dramatically in recent years. Pepper bark had always been used to treat coughs and colds and other respiratory complaints and, as these were common in sufferers of the virus, the relief the ground-up bark, taken in a tea, gave them also provided them with hope.

Aston told his patients that pepper bark was, in fact, a cure for the virus, which justified the huge mark-up he applied to the cost of the bark, which he sourced from poachers in Limpopo Province and Kwa-Zulu Natal.

Musanga nodded. 'I will try the pepper bark again, but I don't think it is strong enough *muti*. There must be something else I can take, something else I can do.'

Aston sat back down in his chair and interlocked his fingers across his ample belly. He nodded slowly then leaned forward conspiratorially. He lowered his voice. 'Yes, you can do something else.'

'Go on,' Musanga said.

Musanga was like most of the patients who came to Aston looking for a miracle cure to the virus. If Aston had found himself in Musanga's position he would have had himself tested and gone to a clinic. But he didn't give Musanga this advice. Musanga was an ignorant taxi driver – a man of little schooling, but also one whose job demanded steel nerves and arrogance. Such men fought turf wars with AK-47s and risked life and limb on a daily basis. Musanga didn't want to be told to do the sensible thing – to go to the clinic and have his life taken from him with the results of a simple blood test. He wanted the magic cure, whatever the risk or the crime involved – they all did. So many patients in Musanga's situation paid the *inyanga*, the doctor, for justification.

Aston's father and his father before him had been *inyangas*. Aston had, after completing his service in the army, gladly taken on the mantle of traditional healer, but by then he had already seen too much of the world and learned too much to believe in most of the cures his ancestors had peddled. Aston had learned that medicine was money. He supplied a service and commodities for which there was an escalating and limitless demand.

'What must I take, *baba*?' Musanga said, filling the silence that Aston had intentionally created.

Aston knew what he would do if he had the virus. He would go to the clinic and he would get the anti-retrovirals and he would watch his diet and try to stay fit and healthy. But he knew there was something else he would do – and Musanga wanted a green light to try that magic as well. 'A child. A virgin. Take it, use it, cleanse yourself in its purity.'

Richard drove north through the Kruger National Park and tried to let the animals and birds he encountered on the way take his mind off the events of the past twenty-four hours, and of seventeen years earlier.

But those years were never really far from his mind, and no matter how hard he tried to numb his brain, once night fell and he slept, the images would return: the blood, the bodies, the fear in people's eyes. Most harrowing was when the faces of the children he witnessed orphaned rose up, in distress just like Collette, the girl whose father had died that terrible day at Kibeho. He took some comfort from the fact that Collette had made it out, but he wondered how many of those other terrified children had survived.

It would have been quicker for him to exit the park at the Paul Kruger gate and make his way through Hazyview to the R40 and drive north outside the park. However, the heavy January rains had damaged the road through Bushbuck Ridge, and traffic control points at the works sites and the usual risk of collision with a kamikaze minibus taxi convinced him to take the scenic route instead.

He stopped at the Tshokwane picnic site on the road between Skukuza and Satara and got out to eat the apple and drink the Coke he'd salvaged from his near empty refrigerator before leaving. The normally bustling pit stop had been gutted by the floods and was still closed to the public. Whether as a result of mother nature or mankind, Africa always seemed to do things the hard way.

Back on the road he saw some impala and a breeding herd of elephant on the drive north to Satara, and slowed to negotiate a traffic jam of game viewers and private cars that were jockeying for better positions to see four sleeping lionesses. Cameras flashed in the greyness of the morning when one of the cats rolled onto her back. Richard weaved through the vehicles and planted the accelerator again.

Liesl.

He wondered how she had aged. She'd been a bloody good-looking girl when he'd met her. The memory of her stirred him as he savoured the details of their one night together, starting in the shower. He'd had many women since, but few of the situations had matched the intensity of that time with her. The encounter had come to nothing – he had lost touch with her as soon as he'd left Kigali – and it had ended the parallel relationships he'd been leading with Carmel and Juliet.

Funny, he thought. He'd been on the verge of writing to Juliet from Rwanda, to end it with her because of Carmel. He had loved Carmel, he knew that now – or he had at least been as close to finding true love as he had before then or since. There was something about Carmel that he missed more than all the other women who'd passed through his life. She'd been totally devoted to him and it could have been this virtue that had scared him. He hadn't really been ready to settle down back then, and now, given the mess he had made of his life, no one would want to domesticate him. He didn't miss Juliet at all, but he still felt bad about hurting Carmel.

Around Satara the bush thinned to more open savannah. The summer rains had prompted the annual mini migration of herds of zebra and wildebeest from one side of the narrow national park to the other. It wasn't a patch on the massive movements of animals across the Serengeti in Tanzania and the Masai Mara in Kenya, but the high densities of game were a lovely sight. Much of Kruger was bushy so it was nice to be able to see across greater distances and take in the sight of long lines of animals slowly on the move. The scene helped him justify his own nomadic ways, which he was resigned to these days. It was time for him to move on again, once he'd sorted this business with Liesl and worked out who had tried to kill them.

As he came into mobile phone range again his phone beeped. He checked it and opened the SMS. *RU OK?* It was from Janine. It was nice of her to ask, but Richard seriously hoped she wasn't already trying to rekindle something with him now that she had presumably calmed her husband down. He pulled over. *Fine. Going away for a week*, he lied.

An hour later, Richard stopped to refuel the Discovery at Satara Camp. Tourists milled around outside the camp shop, checking the large map of the area and the coloured magnetic discs that signified animal sightings. Inside he weaved between people shopping for souvenirs and campfire meals and bought another Coke for the road before continuing north to Letaba.

As he drove he thought that he probably should have

shaved before meeting Liesl's parents. No, he corrected himself. He wasn't there to impress them with his prospects – he had none bar his qualification, and few assets other than the battered Land Rover he was driving and some cash in the bank that was dwindling fast. His mother had died three years after his father, and the sale of the family home had not come at a good time in the market's cycle. What money he did inherit from the sale, after the mortgage was paid, was long gone, spent on nearly fifteen years of boozing and womanising.

He was making good time, so he bypassed Letaba Camp, turning left at the crossroads, and headed towards Phalaborwa Gate. A kilometre down the road he rounded a bend and stamped on the brake pedal.

A male lion stood defiantly in the middle of the road, not moving as the four-wheel drive skidded to a halt and stopped no more than a metre away. He glared at Richard in silent reproach at the speed he'd been doing; Richard shuddered involuntarily at the creature's piercing yellow eyes.

Another male, its luxuriant rusty mane fringed with black like its brother's, emerged from the long grass by the side of the road. Richard could feel his heart beat faster as the cats wandered past his front bumper bar. Africa, he thought. He knew he was safe in the car, but he'd also seen the damage lions could cause. He'd worked at a clinic at Chirundu on the Zimbabwe–Zambia border for a while and had stitched an African game scout's scalp together after a one-eyed lioness had dragged him out of the unzipped tent he'd been sleeping in. The man had been lucky a colleague had been able to get to his AK-47 and shoot the lioness before she finished him off for good. She and her three subadult cubs had taken a liking to human flesh and had killed two other people from a village near Kanyemba and a cook from a safari operation. Richard had been lost in his self-absorbed thoughts, but the lions were a timely reminder that danger could be waiting, literally, around the next corner, and that it wasn't only two-legged animals that killed on this continent.

Richard carried on, keeping his speed down, and made his way back up north to the Phalaborwa Gate, situated about halfway up the western border of the national park. The security guard at the boom checked his ID and waved him through.

A kilometre from the gate Richard indicated left and turned into the car park of the Kruger Park Spar supermarket. He went in and grabbed a plastic basket and filled it with three cans of Coke Zero, two bottles of water, a Bar-One and a packet of rusks. He didn't know if he'd be sleeping at Liesl's parents' place, or if he'd have to find a B & B somewhere. He might be breakfasting on the road the next morning for all he knew.

As he queued at the checkout the people around him were all speaking Afrikaans. The language was common among the staff in the Kruger Park, but the younger staff, in particular the Africans, tended to favour English. Phalaborwa, however, was a mining and army town, and the language of the old regime still ruled here out of necessity because of the diverse mix of cultures employed in the town. The slim woman with blonde ringlets in front of him glanced back at him and smiled. Her singlet top showed off her brown shoulders and her denim mini gave him a nice view of her legs, which were flattered by the high-heeled sandals she wore. Ahead of her was an African woman with a plastic Pick'n'Pay shopping bag tied over her hairdo, to protect it from the rain outside, and a cute little daughter standing in a near-empty shopping trolley. The child stared at him. Richard poked his tongue out at the little girl and the white woman, who was glancing at him every now and then, smiled at the girl's laughter. Steady, Richard told himself.

Women had been neither his downfall nor his saviour in life. More a temporary refuge. He was, he knew, a bit of a joke among the few friends back in the UK who had stayed loyal to him, and those of even fewer number he'd allowed to get remotely close to him in Africa. The married men he knew thought he had a great life, but the women fell into three camps. There were the busybodies who tried to match him with every thirty- or forty-something single friend they had; the lecturers who told him it was time he grew up and settled down; and the sisters who winked and laughed at his antics and probably thought he was actually gay. He'd had sex with women from all three groups.

The blonde woman paid and pushed her trolley slowly out to the car park. She was lingering by the tailgate of a battered old Toyota Condor as he came out with his bag. She caught his eye and smiled at him. Richard forced himself to keep on walking past her.

10

Henri Bousson handed a five-thousand kwacha note to the uniformed guard on the boom gate at the Livingstone Airport car park. The guard asked Henri a question and he replied with a phrase that provoked a deep laugh. From reading her *Lonely Planet* guidebook, Carmel thought the language might be Lozi in this part of Zambia.

Henri closed the electric window and smiled across at her. 'He asked me if you were my new wife.'

Carmel raised her eyebrows. 'And what did you tell him?'

'I told him you were a very important donor to my fledgling wildlife rehabilitation project and that you should be treated and addressed with the utmost respect and not be the subject of crude jokes.'

Carmel laughed. 'Yes, it sounded just like that.'

'They're good people here,' he said. 'They like a joke and I like Zambia. It's rugged and run-down enough to feel like the real Africa, yet it's relatively stable politically, and economically the country has undergone a mini boom in recent years.'

Carmel nodded, pleased he'd stopped the innuendo before it escalated. He was a handsome man, but she did feel a little vulnerable alone in the vehicle with him. She'd imagined she would be picked up by one of his staff – a guide or a driver, perhaps collected with a group of other guests or donors. 'Yes,' she agreed, 'but I've read that Zambia's newfound prosperity is largely due to the decline across the river in Zimbabwe. Wasn't Zambia's agricultural sector kickstarted by white Zimbabwean farmers who fled, and the tourism industry's really only "boomed", as you put it, since Zimbabwe's nosedived?' She was a lawyer and a prosecutor. She argued for a living.

'True on all counts, but I still like it. Perhaps it's more to do with the heart and soul of the country than its balance sheet or record on human rights.'

I've done it again, she thought. 'I didn't mean to offend.'

He looked at her and grinned. 'No offence taken. I like a good argument – to be challenged is to be alive.'

They sat in silence for a minute or so. 'It's lovely and green here, and the view of the falls and the river coming in was great,' Carmel said, trying to be more polite. Well-meaning friends had told her that when she met a new man it was like watching the Spanish Inquisition in action. She questioned their assertions, probed their backgrounds and tried to categorise and file them within the first few minutes. The observation by her friends had angered her at first and then, when she'd realised it was true, saddened her. But it was true and it was how she protected herself.

'You're not married?' Henri asked her. 'I just realised I never actually asked.'

'No.' While Carmel would quite like to have a man in her life, her real regret was not having children. She doted on her sister Sarah's ten-year-old boy and seven-year-old girl, but it wasn't really enough. She didn't, however, want a child badly enough to go through the process of finding a sperm donor and raising one on her own.

The questioning of prospective boyfriends was, she told herself, a means of saving time and avoiding a broken heart. But maybe she was subconsciously repelling the men she'd been set up with, or had chanced upon. Besides, it was easier to be alone than to open up and let someone get close to her and learn of her past problems – and she certainly wasn't about to change her ways to accommodate a stranger in her life.

'And you?' she asked Henri.

He shook his head. 'No, never. I could say that I never found the right woman, but that would be a lie. I've met quite a few wonderful women and I probably should have married one of them, but to be honest my work always came first. I know that sounds terrible.'

'No, not at all. I'm probably guilty of the same thing. It's nice to hear someone be honest about it. You don't say it like you regret it.'

He glanced at her, making eye contact. 'I don't regret anything in my life. I have met women who say they could put up with my solitary ways, and my animals, and my constant travelling through Africa, but I doubt any of them could. Also, I wonder sometimes if there is room in my life for another person. Perhaps I am subconsciously turning them away. Sorry, I am talking too much.'

Amazing, Carmel thought. It was as though he'd been eavesdropping on what she'd been thinking. It was time to change the subject. 'So, how is the chimp refuge going?'

Henri nodded. 'It is good. As you no doubt know, chimps are not endemic to Zambia, but this country is something of a conduit between southern, east and central Africa. Chimps are smuggled through here, to Mozambique and South Africa from Tanzania and the Democratic Republic of Congo. Sometimes the police and customs officials intercept them, but in most cases they are bribed to turn a blind eye or they miss them. Mine is not the only chimp sanctuary – there is another better-known one in Zambia, and also one in South Africa, but sadly there are enough animals either seized or handed in by owners who have tired of them to fill half-a-dozen such places.'

'It's amazing an animal as big and noisy as a chimp could evade the notice of a customs inspector.'

Henri took a hand from the steering wheel and waved it in the air. 'This is Africa, Carmel. The smugglers sometimes hide the animals in their trucks or aircraft, but in other cases they are declared, but the name of the creature on the paperwork and the crate is changed to something legal. Wildlife traders will tell the authorities they are moving a vervet monkey or a marmoset – species that are not protected, and are legal to own as pets – and then pay the customs officials not to take a close look. I am telling you, quite seriously, that many border officials wouldn't know the difference in any case.'

'Incredible.'

The car in front of Henri put on its hazard lights and slowed down. He did the same thing. Carmel saw a man in green overalls and a beret waving his hand up and down, motioning for the motorists to stop.

'Army?' Carmel asked.

'*Non*. ZAWA – Zambian Wildlife Authority. This boom gate is the entrance to the Mosi-Oi-Tunya National Park. Sadly there is not much game left here – some elephant and giraffe and a few buck – but most of it has long since been poached. There are also a couple of rhino here under twenty-four-hour guard. They are replacements for others, which were shot by poachers not long after being reintroduced here.'

Carmel had read about the park. Henri spoke to the national parks man in Lozi. The ranger looked into the cab and saluted her. She returned the gesture and he waved them through. 'You seem to know everyone here.'

'It is a small community and, like I said, I like it here, and the people. I was born in Africa, and that makes me an African. I drive this road every day – sometimes two or three times – and this man and his friends, they stop me every time. Some whites get infuriated with the meaningless bureaucracy and the pace of life on this continent, but I always say that if one does not like Africans then one should not live in Africa.'

They drove on, lush green bush watered by the summer rains flanking the roadside. Henri slowed to a stop and looked to the right. Carmel peered around him but saw nothing. 'What is it?'

'Giraffe.'

'Where? Oh, now I see it.' It was amazing how such a tall creature could blend in so perfectly with its surroundings. She knew from her previous trips to Africa that it would take her a few days to get used to spotting animals in the bush. Her eyes and her brain were conditioned to the city. Her horizon was the multistorey office block opposite hers; the only predators she had to watch out for were badly driven taxis and tourists on foot stopping in the middle of the Mary Street Mall to consult their guidebooks.

By the time Carmel had found her camera in her daypack

the giraffe treated them to one more look of lofty disdain and moved deeper into the trees.

'Damn it.'

Henri smiled and started the engine again. 'I will find you another one.'

'*Merci*,' she said. Henri was a big guy; heavyset without being fat, and muscled without being muscle-bound. Somehow she'd thought he would be slighter, gentler. When he reached over to adjust the air conditioning the left sleeve of his T-shirt rode up a little and she glimpsed old blue ink, though couldn't make out the pattern of the tattoo. His hair was dark but flecked with grey. She wondered how old he was. Closer to fifty than forty, she guessed.

They passed through a second boom gate at the exit to the small national park. Beyond the fence Carmel noted an immediate change in the vegetation. There was more open grassland, lines of straggly maize, and far fewer trees. Habitat destruction, she knew, was the biggest threat to so many species of mammals in Africa. But the reality was that people and animals had to live side by side.

'It's not all like this,' Henri said, taking in the view with a sweep of his hand and reading her mind once again. Her married friends said this happened all the time – that one partner would start talking about something the other had been thinking. 'There are still some properties where the natural vegetation remains. Like mine. And here we are.'

The carved wooden sign hanging from a metal brace said *Kubu*. 'It means hippo in the Lozi language,' Henri said.

Immediately they were surrounded by mature trees and thick riverine bush. The narrow dirt road meandered in loops that in some cases seemed to go back on itself. 'I had a tree expert work with the engineer who built this road,' Henri continued. 'I wanted to cut down as few mature trees as possible. As a result, my "driveway", as you would call it, cost me four times the price of a straight road, but I think it was worth it, yes?'

'Oh yes, definitely!' Carmel said. 'These trees are beautiful.'

The thickness of the vegetation made her first glimpse of the Zambezi from ground level even more exciting and grand. As the road gave way to a gravelled circular driveway, she could see the river beyond the house, sparkling enticingly at the edge of the view. She almost wanted to run to it. Once they pulled up, an African man in khaki safari shirt and shorts and rafter sandals strode up to the four-wheel drive and opened her door for her.

'Carmel, this is Elvis. He's my senior guide.'

They exchanged greetings and shook hands as Carmel got down from the truck. Elvis opened the back of the vehicle and took out her bags.

'He'll take them to your room. Come through to the main house. You must be dying for a drink.'

'Sounds good,' she said.

Henri led the way past a fountain and then down a flight of four grey stone stairs. The house was painted a pale blue, with a slate roof. At its centre was a pair of heavy, arched, ancient-looking doors. With their stained brass studs and sturdy crossbeams they looked like the ornate examples she'd seen in Zanzibar.

Henri pushed them open. As Carmel came up behind him she had to raise her hand to her eyes. The Zambezi River filled most of her view, across an open-plan living room. She walked inside, mouth open.

'You like?' Henri asked.

She turned to him. 'My God, it's so incredibly beautiful. I can't believe you actually *live* here.'

'Yes, my little piece of paradise.'

Carmel looked back at the river, once again transfixed by the view.

'I'll show you around if you like.'

She nodded. The building she was in, though it was the size of a three-bedroom home, was not so much Henri's house as his entertainment area, he explained. There was one guest bedroom off to the side of the sprawling lounge area, a kitchen with walk-in pantries, a coldroom and a freezer, and a library. On the riverfront side of the building was a long line of concertina glass doors, instead of a solid wall. A long, low mahogany coffee table piled with guidebooks, novels, and travel and fashion magazines fronted an equally long upholstered chesterfield which would easily seat eight people. The walls were painted the same pale blue as the exterior, which gave the room an enhanced feeling of coolness under the high-vaulted ceiling and a trio of spinning fans.

Henri led her out onto the narrow strip of lawn that separated the entertainment area from a fifteen-metre infinity pool. The inviting waters provided a seamless transition to the river beyond. On the other side of the river was Zimbabwe and the Zambezi National Park.

'There are many more animals on the Zim side,' Henri said, following her gaze. 'Though I am afraid poaching continues to take its toll. Still, I am sure we will see some elephant at least on our cruise.'

'That would be wonderful.' Carmel followed him along a stone-flagged path to their right and greeted two maids on their way to the kitchen. Beyond a stand of bush and trees was a mini version of the blue house, as she already thought of it. Henri walked up a wooden staircase onto a wide verandah and slid open the glass door. When Carmel reached the top of the stairs she felt the chill blast of air conditioning from inside.

'This is your suite.' Inside was a king-size bed in a room that was almost as large as her one-bedroom flat back in Brisbane. Elvis had been there ahead of them and Carmel saw her daypack and bag had been placed on a carved wooden chest at the foot of the bed. The bathroom was proportionally grand, as was the spa bath. Through another door Henri showed her to an outdoor shower with a wall screening it from the main building but not from a view of the river.

'This place is over the top.' She meant it as a compliment, but she saw his face crease.

'You think I am a millionaire or something?'

Carmel didn't know how to respond.

'And you are asking yourself, perhaps, why did I donate money to such a man and his animal rehabilitation project, yes?'

'No . . .' But he was right. The thought had just been forming in her mind.

'The truth is that this is an illusion, Carmel. Yes, I am fortunate to live in such a beautiful home, for now, but I will probably have to sell it soon.'

'Why?'

'The rehabilitation centre has drained my personal savings. My fortunes have been up and down over the years, but like many people I was hit hard by the financial crisis in 2009 and 2010. I lost a good deal of money on my investments. I set up the chimpanzee project when times were good and I had money to spare, but keeping it going has cost me dearly.'

'So that's why you went public, appealing for donations?'

He looked out at the river, as if ashamed to meet her gaze. 'Yes. I ran the centre for seven years without anyone knowing about it. I registered it as a charity two years ago so that I might raise enough money to feed my animals and provide them with veterinary care. I do not want anyone's pity, but if people do donate money to my foundation I can assure them that every penny goes to the animals – none of it is taken by me for my own use. My books are available for anyone to peruse – the operation is totally transparent.'

'Yes, I think that's a good idea.'

'Now, if you want to change or freshen up, the boat will be leaving in an hour's time. And tomorrow you can give me a lawyer's opinion of my accounts.'

'Sounds wonderful, but you don't need to show me your books.'

'Please, I want to.'

Henri left and closed the door behind him. Carmel felt the jet lag drawing her towards the crisp cotton sheets and fluffy pillows, but she knew she should fight through it. Besides, she didn't want to waste a moment in this place. She stripped and walked outside to the shower. It was a liberating feeling, standing naked in sight of a river in Africa. The summer sun was hot on her shoulders as she turned on the taps. She got under the spray before it heated up too much, revelling in the feel of the cool water sluicing the grime of the flight from her. When the hot came through she wet her hair and lathered it with shampoo. She turned and felt the sun on her breasts as she arched her back to rinse her hair.

What harm was there, she reasoned, if Henri could afford to keep this magnificent place? Whether he knew it or not – and she suspected he did – she had already contacted the accountant whose link was on Henri's website and checked out his financial records for herself. She'd satisfied herself he was legitimate before transferring five hundred Australian dollars to the foundation's account. She would also make sure she received the itemised accounting of how the money had been spent.

Also, Carmel thought as she squeezed the conditioner into her palm and massaged it into her hair, she would hate it if this attractive, sensitive man with the mysterious tattoo turned out to be a crook. She was having too good a time already in his company. If he was in serious financial trouble she wondered how she might go about helping him get out of it. What would it be like, she mused as her eyes were once again drawn to the river, to live in a place like this?

Vite sweltered in a cage in the tin shed at the back of the village market.

Around him were the twitters, chirps, hisses and cries of other caged animals and birds. Some he dimly recognised from his short life in the wild, but their combination and proximity were driving him crazy. He shrieked and cried for his mother.

When he made too much noise the man came into the storage room and jabbed a pointed stick through the wire mesh of the cage. Vite yelped even louder at the pain the short, sharp stabs caused him, but he was smart. In time he learned that if he kept quiet the stick would not come into the cage, and the pain would be avoided.

He watched the man when he came and went, noting how he unlatched the cage opposite him, across the narrow corridor of beaten earth. The man reached in, and when Vite saw the sleepy python in his hands he cried in terror and shrank back against the bars of his cage. The man laughed at Vite's fear as he dumped the snake into a bag, tied it shut and walked out of the storeroom.

Since the day he could first remember Vite had been terrified of serpents. Whenever one of his family had come across one, they would shout out an alarm call, letting them all know there was danger. Vite couldn't be quiet until the thing was gone. When the room was empty he stared at the latch on the open cage.

Wiggling his hand through a gap in the mesh of his cage, Vite was able to easily reach the latch that held his door closed. He was still very young, but his arms were long and he would grow into them in time. He found the piece of wood wedged into the hole. Vite grabbed it in his fingers and tried to move it. It was knocked in tight. He heard a noise and pulled his arm in and shrank back to the rear of his cage.

The man walked back in, pausing in the doorway. He looked around, then turned and left, closing the door behind him.

In the darkness, Vite reached his hand out through the gap again and began worrying at the stick. After a while it started to move.

11

Richard raced along the R71 at a hundred and twenty kilometres per hour, past a game farm enclosed by a high electrified fence to stop animals from trying to leap out. When he started encountering citrus farms, they too were protected by high-voltage fencing, though this was to keep monkeys and baboons out.

Richard passed the Gravelotte Hotel and knew from the directions he'd written on the back of an envelope that he was getting close to Liesl's parents' place. He pictured the farmhouse as a rather modest whitewashed place, lovingly tended to but a little run-down. Liesl had run away from this snoozing corner of the country in search of excitement, he remembered her telling him in one of their few conversations.

'*Fuck me,*' she'd said to him in the shower.

A half-hour later Richard crossed the Letaba River and knew he'd gone too far. She'd warned him about this. He pulled over to the side of the road and took out his mobile phone and the envelope. He was supposed to take a right turn to a place called Eiland Spa. He'd seen no such sign. He dialled the number.

'Liesl, hello?' she said.

'It's Richard. I'm geographically embarrassed.'

'*Ag*, shame,' she said. He told her he'd just crossed the river, so she told him to turn around and take the first left. Richard thanked her and hung up. He remembered the soap cascading down her spine as she arched her back.

When Richard got to the turn-off he saw the sign to Eiland Spa, but noted with some small satisfaction that it was only visible from this side. If there had once been a sign to the spa from the other direction, it had gone missing. In Zimbabwe, when he'd worked there, he'd found it difficult finding his way around Harare and had been told by a local that people stole the road signs and melted them down to make coffin handles. AIDS was the only growth industry in that part of Africa these days.

Richard drove the required number of kilometres on the road and came to the sign sponsored by a chemical company that announced, *Red Star – Tokkie and Elize Nel*. He turned left and was immediately surprised. Instead of the rutted farm road he'd expected he crunched along a gravelled drive flanked by an honour guard of tall palm trees. Off to his left were neat rows of grapefruit trees that stretched as far as he could see. Unfolding on the right was a lush tropical garden arrayed around a perfectly manicured lawn. A wayward sprinkler sprayed the right side of his dirty Discovery and a few drops splashed his face.

Ahead and to the left was a dam the size of a couple of football pitches. Richard slowed to check out what looked like incongruously placed granite boulders in the water. One of them submerged. When he stopped he saw a plume of spray exhaled, followed by the wriggling ears and whiskered snout of a hippopotamus.

'Bloody hell.' He counted a dozen of the massive creatures, bobbing up and down. A few sets of beady eyes turned to him and followed his progress as he cruised slowly along the driveway. A grey heron took flight from the grassy dam wall and flapped slowly across his path and into the sky. In his peripheral vision he caught a brief glimpse of a multicoloured little malachite kingfisher darting among the reeds at the edge of the water.

The house, when it came into sight, was like something out of *Gone with the Wind*. Although only one storey and whitewashed, it wasn't the humble shack he'd envisioned. Far from it. A trellis woven with vines and dripping with fruit jutted out from the clean lines of the sprawling house and shaded a long dining table surrounded by what looked like a couple of dozen chairs. Flowers bloomed everywhere and he counted at least three African gardeners, all of whom waved to him.

At the end of the drive was a four-car garage with a Land Cruiser, a Mercedes sedan, a Hilux pickup and a BMW four-wheel drive. All of the vehicles looked new. Richard pulled off onto the grass and switched off the engine.

He leaned across to the front passenger seat to get his baseball cap and was startled by a rap at the window. He turned to see a blonde woman tapping on the glass. Where had she come from so quickly? He opened the door. 'Hello.'

'Hello, hello, hello! Welcome! You must be Richard, *ja*?'

'Yes. How do you do?' The woman was beaming and looked happy and healthy in a white tennis shirt and shorts. Her hair was cut short and streaked; she was older than he was, but she looked in terrific shape.

'I'm Liesl's mom, Elize.'

'No,' he said, and he was only half joking. 'You're far too young.'

'*Ag*, you're a smoothy all right. I can see we're going to get on very well.' Elize took his arm and led him from the Land Rover. 'Come, come, Prudence will get your bags. Come inside.'

Richard let himself be led into the dark, cool hallway of the house. Rooms and more corridors fanned off the passageway. A man in a two-tone grey and khaki shirt, bush shorts and boots with long grey socks emerged from what appeared to be a home office. 'This is my husband, Tokkie,' Elize said.

Tokkie looked much older than his wife, his brick-red face lined from years in the sun, his eyes set in the farmer's permanent squint – or was that distrust? Richard wondered.

'Hello,' Tokkie said, and his handshake was so firm it was a relief when the man let go.

'Liesl's showering,' Elize explained. 'She and I only just finished playing tennis. I'll get the girl to make tea.'

Richard wished the woman hadn't mentioned the word 'shower'. Elize disappeared into the kitchen and started speaking to a maid in Fanakalo.

'So, you knew my daughter in Rwanda?' Tokkie said, and waved Richard into a velvet-upholstered armchair.

'Umm, yes, briefly. I was there with the army.'

Tokkie raised his eyebrows. 'Army. I thought you were a doctor.'

'I was a doctor in the military. Parachute Regiment.'

Tokkie gave a grunt and Richard wasn't sure whether it was disdain for Richard's inability to carry on in some specialised field of medicine and open up an expensive Harley Street practice, or out of some kind of innate Afrikaner respect for military service. He'd found that when South Africans of his age or older found out he'd served in the army they opened up to him a little more. National service in the apartheid era had created a shared bond amongst the male population.

'I didn't want her to go to that place – Rwanda.'

'I don't think any of us particularly wanted to go there. It was . . .' Even though people had been asking him about Rwanda for seventeen years he still hadn't come up with the right words to describe the madness and the horror, but also the frankly fascinating array of injuries he had treated and the procedures he had performed in the field. He'd had more trauma-surgery experience in those few weeks than an emergency room specialist might encounter in a lifetime. 'It was . . . an experience.'

'She volunteered to go. To take pictures. Those people . . . what they did to each other in that country . . .'

Richard nodded. He imagined Tokkie had seen service on the border, in Namibia – the old South-West Africa – or perhaps Angola. He would know about death, and about the people who revelled in it.

'It changed her, you know,' Tokkie continued. 'She came back like some of my soldiers did. That place took her innocence away.'

Richard wondered why the old man was confiding in him like this. Perhaps he couldn't with his bubbly, attractive wife who had kept the home fires burning while her man had been away fighting the communists.

Elize came back into the room. 'Richard is a *doctor*, Tokkie. Did Liesl tell you that?'

Tokkie harrumphed. 'In the *British* Army.'

'Yes,' Richard said, 'but I promise not to mention the war.'

Tokkie stared at him.

'The Anglo–Boer war, that is.'

'I understood the joke. My grandmother died in a concentration camp, along with two of her children.'

'Right.'

'My grandfather was a commando. He was one of the "bitter-enders" who never gave up. When the English finally caught him, they hanged him.'

'Right.'

The maid walked in, carrying a silver platter. 'Tea is served,' Elize said. They all settled into armchairs around a glass-topped coffee table while Elize poured, forcing a big smile.

'Howzit, Richard?'

Richard turned his head at the sound of the woman's voice, and stood at the same time. His elbow collided with the china teacup Elize was passing him. The cup clattered off the saucer and fell onto the carpet. 'God, sorry.'

'Prudence!' Elize called.

Liesl smiled. 'Nice to see you again, Richard. No blaspheming here, either, please.'

Richard looked at the spilled tea, the scowling father, the mother's strained smile, and the woman who had just entered. 'Sorry, again.' He'd seen her picture in the magazine she worked for, but her headshot was very small, and black and white. It didn't do her justice. 'Liesl, hi.'

They shook hands. Her grip was firm, like her father's. When he'd tried to remember how she looked when they'd had their encounter in Rwanda, he'd found her twenty-something face wouldn't come to him. The magazine photo had her in sunglasses and a bush hat, almost as though she was wearing a cheesy disguise. When he'd thought of her over the years, the memory had been more visceral than visual. He could recall the heat of her breath on his neck; the feel of her fingers on him; the glory of her gripping his body with hers; the pure, illicit thrill of surrendering to his own weakness; the intense arousal of the way it had unfolded – her taking the initiative. He could recall many of the details, but not her face. He studied it now.

She gave a small, patient smile. 'You haven't really changed. Your hair's still too long for a soldier.'

'Lucky I'm not a soldier any more.'

Her hair was different – longer; her body seemed lean, muscled even. He'd remembered her as soft – not chubby, but carrying a mix of remnant baby fat and a young person's disregard for alcohol and foods forbidden later in life. This Liesl looked like she worked out in a gym. Where there once had been girlish curves there were now chiselled, perhaps even brittle edges.

'We need to talk,' she said.

'Tea, my girl?' Elize asked.

'No thanks, Mom. Richard and I need to chat in private. We'll take a walk in the garden.'

Elize had started refilling a fresh cup, brought in by the maid who was now on all fours, dabbing at the stain. Elize looked up at Richard.

'Thanks, Mrs Nel.' He took the cup carefully and added milk and two sugars. He excused himself, taking a sip as he followed Liesl out the open French doors into the lush garden.

'I see you've made a good first impression on my folks,' she said.

He snorted a laugh. 'I think your father wants to shoot me.'

'His bark's worse than his bite – although you were a British soldier . . .'

Richard lengthened his stride and fell into step with her, spilling a little of his tea. She was taller than he remembered. Still a cracking good sort. She wore jeans and gym shoes, and a simple white V-necked T-shirt.

'So, Richard, someone tried to kill you too?'

'Yes.' A near-death experience was one way to stop him thinking about sex, he supposed. 'An African man dressed in black, with a silenced assault rifle. Hardly your garden-variety South African home invasion. He had a bag of cocaine on him, which I suspect he was going to plant at my place, to make it look drug related. The kids in Nelspruit go mostly for Mandrax and weed. Coke's a bit out of the bush league.'

She stopped under a knob-thorn tree. 'Would planting drugs on you have been a plausible way to cover up the real reason for your death? Would the cops consider you part of a drug deal?'

'If I said yes, would you think less of me?'

'It doesn't matter what I think of you. Do you always make jokes at inappropriate times?'

'Always. Is it true a good journalist never asks a question she doesn't know the answer to?'

'Yes. But I've also done some things over the years I'm not proud of. I know what it's like to look for a way out.'

He didn't ask for more information. He was in no mood for group therapy. He'd been there, done that. It hadn't worked, although he had slept with a fellow addict. The sex had been rubbish, but that hadn't really mattered. It had fed one of his addictions for an hour, and that was all that mattered to him at the time. 'You're convinced you weren't just the victim of a botched car-jacking?'

'It's why we're here now, isn't it?' she replied.

'Point taken.'

'We're here because of that war crimes investigator, Mike Ioannou, the one looking into the Rwandan war crimes, aren't we?' she said.

'I can't think of another connection,' Richard admitted. 'He told me he would be in touch with you – that he wanted to see if you had copies or negatives of the pictures you'd taken. I take it he did?' He sipped his tea. He wished it was Scotch.

'Yes,' Liesl said. She folded her arms across her body. 'That was about two weeks ago. He seemed very insistent. He emailed me then called me at work in Cape Town. He said he would get a warrant, from the war crimes tribunal or whatever it is, if I didn't comply. He was quite pushy. I told him all my old files of prints and negs were at my parents' house, and that I was off to Namibia on assignment the next day and wouldn't be able to get back here to Letsitele for two weeks. I was hoping it would all just go away, but then a few days ago the subpoena came.'

Richard recalled his own phone conversations – two of them – and the emails from Mike Ioannou. 'He was a man on a mission, all right.'

'What did he ask you? And how did he find you?'

Liesl motioned to a wooden bench under a jacaranda tree. They sat and Richard rested an arm on the seat back and turned to her. He told her that Ioannou had been reviewing old media coverage of the aftermath of the Rwandan genocide, the massacre of the Tutsis, and the follow-up revenge attacks by Tutsis against Hutus. Ioannou had come across two of Liesl's photos in an old edition of *Newsweek*, the picture of the RPF soldier holding his pistol to the head of the woman, just before he shot her – this had been on the maga-zine's cover – and, inside, a much smaller image of the old man holding out a photograph to Liesl's lens while Richard tried to treat him.

'He googled me and tracked me down. Not easy, consider-ing the number of jobs I've had. He wanted to know what the man had said to me, and who was in the picture.'

Liesl nodded. 'I remember that shot. You couldn't really see who was in the photo he was holding – it was too small – but it was the dying man's eyes, wide and crazy, that made the picture. I remember some subeditor supposed that the picture was of his slaughtered family and made up the accompanying caption.'

'Yes, that's right,' Richard nodded. 'It made no sense. If you think about it, why would he have been holding out a pic-ture of his dead relatives? The men being shot and hacked up that day were the perpetrators of the initial genocide. Ioan-nou said he'd had the same thought. I got the feeling that he knew the identity of the man holding the picture, but when I asked him he was evasive. He said something like, "I can't confirm that." He wanted to know if I could remember what was in the picture.'

'Did you? Remember?'

Richard shrugged. 'A bit. It was of three guys – two black, in uniforms, and one white guy in safari get-up. They were holding what looked like an RPG – a rocket-propelled gren-ade launcher.'

Liesl closed her eyes. '*Ja*. I sort of remember that too. It cer-tainly wasn't of his wife and kids. He was really agitated, too, hey?'

'He was. Ioannou asked me to recall what he said. All I

can remember was the guy saying something like, "This is important." Ioannou asked me what happened to the picture and I told him it had been ground into the blood and shit and mud in Kibeho by some soldier's boot, and that I'd had more important things to do than retrieve it. He asked if I could give a more detailed description of the picture and I said I couldn't, but I told him that I was pretty sure you had zoomed in closer on the picture and snapped a couple of frames of it. I'm sorry, Liesl.'

'Ag, no matter. He would have tracked me down and asked me anyway,' she said. 'I told him when he called me that I did remember zooming in on the picture because I thought it might have been important to the story – that we could have used it as well as the image of him holding it out. But when I developed the negatives I saw it was just a bunch of guys standing around, so it didn't fit the story of the day.'

They both sat in silence for a few moments.

'I've tried hard over the years to forget that day,' Liesl said eventually.

He didn't reply to that, but he knew what she meant. He'd tried everything. Booze, sex, drugs, coming back to Africa – nothing had worked.

'Can I ask,' Richard said, 'why you were so sure the attack on you in Johannesburg was related to all this, and not random?'

'I just got an email, from that lawyer woman. Your old girlfriend, Carmel. She told me she was taking over from the other guy, Ioannou, and that I should be very careful. She said I should pay particular attention to my personal safety and be wary of strangers.'

'Funny, she didn't send me a warning.'

Liesl shrugged. 'Perhaps it slipped her mind.'

'Yes, perhaps. So, have you found the picture?' Richard asked.

'Yes.'

'After all these years? That's impressive. I can't find a matching pair of socks.'

'You're a man, and I'm guessing single, right?'

He nodded.

'I'm a woman. All of my negatives, from when I still used film, are filed and archived in date-ordered boxes. Also, that set was particularly important for me – it was the first time I'd had my work used around the world, and the first magazine cover I'd had.'

'*Newsweek*. Not a bad debut.'

'I printed it. It's drying now. We can scan the negative later and that will give us an electronic copy, but I wanted to see a print as well.'

Richard was surprised by her calm. 'Someone possibly tried to kill you for this picture, so you came home to your parents' place, found the negative, printed it, hung it out to dry and then went and played a game of tennis?'

Liesl shrugged and stood up. 'I already know what's in the picture – three guys and a rocket launcher. I saw it on the enlarger while I was printing it. Waiting for it to dry isn't going to tell me anything. Shall we go take a look at it anyway?'

He followed her inside and carefully set the cup and saucer down on a table as he entered the house. He could hear Tokkie and Elize talking in the lounge room, in Afrikaans. He couldn't help but wonder if he was the subject. He hadn't made a good impression but, then, he hadn't been trying to.

Elize might have been impressed when Liesl told her she was inviting a doctor around for tea, but any initial kudos his job brought with him disappeared fast once people learned of his history. He followed Liesl down a corridor he hadn't seen earlier and slowed as he noticed the row of framed prints on both sides.

'Yours?'

'*Ja.*' She waved a dismissive hand without looking back at him. 'My folks framed all of them.'

Richard paused. 'I recognise some of these, and not just the Rwanda ones. They're very good.'

He moved past the Rwanda images quickly. He tried not to notice the image of the RPA man about to execute the unarmed Hutu woman. That moment would be with him for as long as he lived. He hoped there wasn't an afterlife, because he didn't want to relive that moment forever. It was an odd choice of picture, he thought, for a mother to hang in the family home, but on the other hand it had been her daughter's crowning moment.

As Richard took in the rest of the gallery he saw a continuing theme. Misery. There was the other picture, which he'd seen in a half-dozen UK newspapers, of the Afghan man holding the body of his child, killed in a coalition airstrike, arms outstretched towards Liesl's lens. The agony and confusion on his face was palpable. Likewise, the frame of the British Army medic holding up a saline drip in one hand and calling for assistance with the other captured a moment of heart-wrenching hopelessness.

Towards the end of the display the subject matter and the mood changed. The final frame from what could be described as Liesl's 'war period' was a front-page clipping from the South

African broadsheet, the *Sunday Times*. BRAVE SNAPPER KEEPS ON SHOOTING AFTER BOMB BLAST, screamed the headline. Below it was a series of graphic shots of US soldiers treating wounded comrades against a backdrop of smoke and fire. The last shot, taken by someone with a less steady hand, showed Liesl, her face and left arm covered in blood, her clothing singed, still holding her Nikon in her right hand, pointing out towards the photographer as she knelt on a roadside, a Humvee blazing behind her. Her eyes and mouth, the position of her camera hand, seemed to echo the beseeching of some of her other subjects. Although wounded herself, Liesl was still trying to capture something before she went. Richard remembered the story, and how gutsy he had thought she'd been.

After that, the pictures were of wildlife: magnificent shots of the big five – lion, leopard, elephant, buffalo and rhino – as well as cheetah and wild dog, and whales off the South African coast. There were also four covers of *Escape!* magazine framed, and Richard assumed the cover pictures were Liesl's.

'Coming or not?'

'Coming,' he said.

At the end of the hallway Liesl opened a door and Richard smelled flowers and talc. There was a single bed and a poster of Duran Duran on the wall. 'This is my room. My mom never changed it after I left home. It is almost like I died and she's one of those crazy old *tannies* who set up a shrine to her lost daughter, don't you think?'

'That's one way of looking at it, though your mother doesn't seem like the mad aunty type to me.'

'The darkroom's through here.'

They went into what Richard presumed was once an en-suite.

'I was photography crazy when I was a teenager,' Liesl explained. 'My parents were very indulgent, so they said they would turn the en-suite into a darkroom if I was happy to use another bathroom. We have five, so it wasn't exactly a hardship.'

Liesl switched on the light, reached up and started pulling down a series of prints. Richard couldn't help but notice that the first half-dozen or so were pictures of him, at work on victims of the Kibeho massacre. Liesl placed them face down on a bench and then took down the close-up of the photo the man had been holding out to her.

She turned to him, but lowered her eyes. 'I just wanted to remind myself what you looked like.'

'I recognised you as soon as I saw you,' he said. 'But then I had seen your picture in the magazine.'

She shrugged. 'Well, here it is.'

He took the print from her and walked back out into her bedroom. Richard stared at the black man whose face was visible, and the one white. Even with the recent reading he'd done online about the war crimes tribunal, and the books he'd read about the massacres, he recognised neither of the men, and the third had his back to the camera. He looked at the weapon the white man was holding. He'd thought it was an RPG, but now he saw it wasn't.

Tokkie Nel walked into his daughter's room, his eyes taking them in, and the neatly made single bed. He gave a little nod as if reassuring himself all was above board. 'Everything all right?'

'*Ja*, Poppa, of course.'

Tokkie took a pair of reading glasses out of the pocket of his shirt. 'This is the picture you were looking for?'

'*Ja.*'

Richard handed the print to Liesl's father.

Tokkie studied the picture. 'Is this taken in that awful place?'

'Yes, Poppa.'

'I didn't think they were that sophisticated up there with their military.'

'What do you mean?' Richard asked.

Tokkie held the picture out and pointed to the white man. 'Why's this *oke* holding a SA-7 surface-to-air missile?'

12

Henri's guide, Elvis, started the outboard motor and reversed away from the Zambian bank of the Zambezi River. Henri's house looked even more impressive from the water, Carmel thought.

The afternoon clouds had cleared and sunlight glittered on the wide, green, fast-flowing waters. As Elvis turned and headed out into the current, a cormorant took flight from a polished red granite rock, rippling the surface.

'The birdlife is fantastic here,' Henri said over the noise of the outboard. The seats on the boat were wide enough for two people, with three down each side, but Henri was seated across the narrow centre aisle from Carmel. The boat itself was flat bottomed and aluminium, with an awning made from green ripstop canvas. Henri reached for the cooler box. 'We have gin and tonic, white wine, rosé or beer and some soft drinks.'

'Just a Sprite, please. I don't drink.'

Henri popped a can and poured lemonade for both of them into pewter wine goblets. 'To Africa.'

She raised her glass and clinked with him. 'To Africa. Thank you so much for showing me your home.'

He took in the river with a sweep of his hand. 'This is where I feel truly at home.'

'But you're from Rwanda, originally, yes?'

He looked out towards the far bank for a moment. '*Yes*. It was my home, but I think that if Africa is in your blood, then where you live, inside which borders, doesn't really matter. It's interesting that you raise the subject, though, because I wanted to ask you about your work. It sounds fascinating from what little you've told me of it.'

Carmel shrugged. She didn't want to sound boastful, or to bore Henri, but she was proud of what she'd achieved, of the criminals she'd put behind bars, of the justice she had served. 'A lot of it is fairly mundane, sorting through papers and witness accounts.'

'*Oui*, but the stories in those papers must be so horrific. How do you cope?'

It was a question often asked, to which she hadn't yet found a proper answer. She felt at ease, though, with this stranger, and she answered honestly. 'I think I need it.'

He had an animated face and when he raised his eyebrows high and fast, the comicality of it disarmed her, and made her feel safe to continue. 'It does sound funny, I suppose. I was there, as a legal officer with the Australian Army, when some of the follow-on massacres took place at Kibeho. I saw dead bodies but I didn't actually see any killing myself; though I heard plenty of stories. I think I need to be reminded, constantly, of how completely and utterly these people were failed by the government, by the UN and by their neighbours. It helps keep me strong. Does that make sense?'

'Perfectly,' he said with such empathy that she couldn't regret her sudden revelation.

It was true, she thought as she looked for the hippo Elvis claimed had just submerged off to port, she had become hardened to the gruesomeness of the witness statements, but that hardening had not made her callous – it had forged her like a samurai's blade. Her heart had been melted and hammered and cooled time after time until she felt as though she could fight through any plea for clemency, dispatch any argument about following orders. She needed the horror to keep her focused on her mission.

'There!'

She followed Henri's finger and saw the wriggling ears and snorting snout break water in their wake, not fifteen metres behind them. 'That must have been close,' Carmel said.

'Elvis has lived on the river all his life. He knows what he's doing.' The guide gave her a thumbs-up.

Carmel felt a buzz from a combination of jet lag, sun and the soporific effect of being on the water that was almost like being tipsy again. It felt good.

'What are you working on at the moment?' Henri asked her.

'Quite a few cases.' She didn't really want to talk about work now. She didn't exactly regret opening up to him, but she didn't want to reveal any more. It made her feel vulnerable. It was normally her asking the questions when she met a man for the first time.

'But surely all the big men of the genocide are behind bars now? After all, it's been seventeen years, yes?'

Carmel felt her hackles begin to rise. There had been too much criticism from uninformed 'experts' about the pace of prosecutions and the fact that the tribunal should have wound up years earlier. 'People just don't understand the magnitude of what happened. There are thousands of people still waiting to be tried. Many have been dealt with by the Gacaca.'

'What's that? To tell you the truth, I left Rwanda fifteen years ago and have not followed events there for a long time.'

Carmel explained that defendants judged to have been foot soldiers in the massacres, as opposed to those who had given the orders and organised the Interahamwe and other citizens to rise up against their fellow Rwandans, had been sent before local village courts, Gacaca, which usually sat in the place where the defendant was from, or where the crimes had been committed. The Gacaca, which meant 'Justice on the Grass', was made up of a panel of people from the area who more often than not knew the accused personally or had lost relatives to them.

'In many cases the accused are given sentences involving community work. It's often hard labour, such as digging wells or clearing land for farming or building a road, but it's nation-building as well. Sometimes the work gangs include both Tutsi and Hutu, but the feedback I've seen is that the work gives the men an outlet, and a chance to think about what they've done, and to atone.'

'And the big fish?' Henri asked again.

'Well, more than eighty have been tried by the ICTR, but we're still looking for several others. I'm afraid many were able to get out of Rwanda soon after the massacres took place. One of the first UN interventions was by French troops who gave protection to thousands of Hutus who fled Rwanda because they feared reprisals from the returning Tutsis. Among the legitimate refugees, there were also some of the organisers of the genocide.'

'That's shameful,' Henri said.

Carmel shrugged. 'The tribunal recently called on several African countries, including Zambia, to take a more active role in helping track down the perpetrators of the killings. Interjurisdictional cooperation between African countries is a nightmare.'

'I see. So who is your big priority right now – your white whale? There must be someone you want more than all the others?'

Carmel bit her lower lip. Much of her work, by its nature, had to be kept under wraps, especially while a case was being prepared or an investigation carried out. 'It's not so much a person as a group of people.'

'Really? Are they Hutu or Tutsi? I do know that the tribunal has tried to be seen to be fair by prosecuting Tutsis as well as Hutus, even though the Tutsi are now back in control of the government.'

It was a simplified summation, but accurate enough. 'To tell you the truth, we don't know what tribe or even what country they're all from. They're a bit of a mystery, this small gang of three that I'm looking for at the moment.'

'Why these three?' Henri asked.

'I'm not exactly sure. I don't even know their names.'

His expressive face creased. 'You're searching for phantoms?'

'They may as well be at this stage.' Carmel felt uncomfortable about saying any more about the investigation she had inherited from Mike Ioannou. That was another death she was having trouble coming to terms with.

Henri seemed to be waiting for her to say more, so she took her binoculars from her daypack and scanned the far bank. 'I am sorry if I seemed like I was prying. I imagine you cannot talk too much about your work,' he said.

She lowered the binoculars. 'No, it's fine, Henri. There's really not much more that I could tell you if I wanted to. All I know is that a man ... a colleague of mine who put a lot of work into identifying these men is no longer on the case and now I've been given the job of finding them. It's a bit daunting.'

'I can only imagine. Look!'

Carmel raised her binoculars again and swung to where Henri was pointing. 'Elephants!'

'*Oui*. How many do you think, Elvis?'

'Ah, five, I think, boss.'

'Yes, the same herd I saw two days ago. They have a small calf with them. Can you see it, Carmel?'

She focused and tried to peer through the thick riverine bush. 'Yes. Got it! Oh, my. Isn't it tiny. It's beautiful.'

Elvis cut the engine and let the boat drift with the current.

This was what she craved, what she had come to Zambia for. She knew that one of the few things that could make her forget about her work, and the terrible things human beings did to each other, was to lose herself in Africa's wildlife. True, this sometimes involved her witnessing more killing, but there was something pure and honest about a cheetah killing an impala to feed her cubs. There was a sense of purpose to death on the plains and in the bush, a feeling of balance in nature that was missing from the madness of human slaughter.

'I will never tire of watching these creatures,' Henri said.

'I know what you mean.'

'They may come to us tonight,' he said.

'Really?'

'Yes. They swim from the Zimbabwe side, from the national park, to our side, because they know that beyond the river-front lodges there are maize farms. The farmers don't like it, but the elephants can't resist. There is conflict – sometimes a farmer has had enough and he shoots an elephant.'

'That's terrible,' Carmel said.

'That is life,' he said gently. 'Man and nature cannot live side by side easily. So much of my work is picking up the pieces – animals orphaned because their parents were a problem, others run over by cars, birds poisoned. It never ends.'

It pained her to hear the despair in Henri's voice when they were witnessing such a beautiful spectacle. The matriarch of the small elephant herd was leading her daughter, her grandchild and her own tiny new calf down to the water's edge. A big bull tailed them, on spec. The matriarch tested the air with her raised trunk. She then sucked water up into it and drank from the Zambezi.

All the elephants had waded into the water and the younger ones seemed tentative, but when the matriarch walked further out into the flow the little ones followed her, until all were swimming.

'Are they going to cross?' Carmel asked.

'Yes,' said Elvis.

He started the outboard again and turned and motored across the elephants' intended path so that they were upstream, with the setting sun in the pinking western sky behind them. Carmel snapped away with her camera as the elephants paddled across the wide river, their trunks held up like periscopes.

Carmel realised she was taking the same picture over and over again, so she laid her camera in her lap, accepted a refill of Sprite from Henri and just sat back and enjoyed the spectacle of the herd crossing an international boundary.

Elvis kept the boat upstream, and far enough away from the elephants to avoid spooking them. When they neared the Zambian side he increased the throttle and hooked around downstream of the herd and nipped into the wharf at the base of Henri's house.

'Quickly,' Henri said as he jumped off the boat and tied it to a post. He held out his hand and Carmel took it as he helped her onto shore. 'Leave the cooler box and your things. Elvis will bring them. Come, let's go.'

Barefoot, as she had slipped off her sandals in the boat, she ran alongside Henri, across the manicured lawn, giggling nervously at the prospect of tracking wild elephants. They passed the main building and the two separate suites on the far side until they were within sight of the western fence of the property, which ran along what looked like a creek that flowed in a deep gully down to the Zambezi.

Henri held up his hand. 'Quietly now . . . here they come. Hear them?'

The light was fading and the sky was a neon red. Carmel was as far from city civilisation as could be, and she loved it. She stopped and heard the sloshing of the giant creatures leaving the water, and the rumbling of their bellies as they urged each other on.

'I see them,' she whispered.

Henri nodded, and stood still, beside a tall jackalberry tree. 'My neighbour fenced her property on the far side of the stream, so we have left a corridor for the elephants and any other game in the area to move to and from the river.'

Carmel nodded. 'That's great.' The fencing was tacit

acknowledgement that the elephants would visit the Zambian side and raid the local farmers' crops, but it was pointless trying to fence the entire riverbank. It was an acceptance of wildlife, she realised, though not a solution to the villagers' problems. Right now, however, she was just content to watch these huge creatures, blackened from the water like commandos on their cross-border raid, silently creeping past her and blocking out the sunset.

'Beautiful, *oui*?'

'Oh, yes,' she whispered. Carmel took a step to one side to get a better view and stood on a sharp stick. 'Ow!' She lifted her foot and momentarily lost her balance.

Henri grabbed her free hand to steady her. 'OK?'

Carmel nodded, and checked her foot. It was fine. He gave her hand a little squeeze and she returned the gesture. She was amazed by how quiet the elephants were as they moved up the narrow confine of the stream. She was also surprised by how soft Henri's big hand felt. He had relaxed his grip. She knew it was time to let go, but she didn't want to.

Henri eventually released her hand and moved to the fence as the last of the elephants passed them. She followed him.

'That was fantastic,' Carmel said. 'I've never been so close to them on foot before. I can't believe how big and yet how quiet they were!'

'Their feet are like big sponges, you know. They creep around everywhere.'

The last elephant disappeared into the deepening shadows. Carmel didn't want the moment to end.

'Come, dinner will be ready soon,' Henri said.

They walked back across the lawn to the main building where Elvis was waiting for them. He had placed Carmel's daypack and sandals by the coffee table. 'Your phone is beeping, miss,' he said.

'Thanks, Elvis.'

'I'll get us some water and some snacks,' Henri said.

Carmel opened her bag and took out her iPhone. She was a little annoyed that she had signal here on the banks of the Zambezi. She saw she had received three new emails, one of which made her pulse quicken. It was from Richard Dunlop. She had sent him a message advising him that she was taking over Mike Ioannou's investigations, but it had irked her that she had to have any dealings with him at all. Would his reply be friendly, jovial – as if he hadn't cut her heart out and stomped on it – or would he be contrite over the way he'd treated her, or perhaps embarrassed to hear from her again? It didn't matter. It was just work, she told herself.

She looked over her shoulder to make sure Henri was still in the kitchen. He was chatting and laughing with a plump African lady who, judging by her apron, was the cook. The smell of roasting chicken wafted out. Carmel was starving, but her stomach was churning for another reason.

She looked at the subject line of Richard's message: *Urgent – need to talk about threats*. Carmel opened the message.

Hi Carmel,

Someone tried to kill Liesl Nel and me last night. We have the photograph that Mike Ioannou was asking us about. I tried calling his mobile number and got his wife – or should I say widow. When you emailed Liesl you might have cc'ed me and mentioned your fellow investigator appears to have been murdered.

Sorry if this sounds terse, but I am. Terse and tense.

Liesl and I have no idea who the men are in the picture, but

when you open the attachment, have a look at the weapon the
white man is holding. I thought it was an RPG, as I told Ioannou.
Liesl's dad says it is a Russian-designed SA-7 man-portable surface-
to-air missile. Does this mean anything to you?

Please tell us what is going on and what we should do.

How are you, by the way? I still think about you.

Regards,

Richard

At the bottom of the message was his South African mobile
phone number, and an icon for a jpeg picture. Carmel moved
the cursor and clicked on it. The download started.

It was a big file – too big to fit on the phone's small screen
and she hadn't had the phone long enough to work out how
to make the image fit the available space. Instead, she had
to shuffle the cursor up and across. She moved it until the
frame was at head height with the first of the three men in
the picture. There was a black man in uniform on the left.
She shifted the cursor to the right. The next African man was
also in camouflage uniform and sporting one of those jaunty
French military-inspired berets that looked like you could
land a helicopter on it, but he had his back to the camera so
she couldn't see his face.

All Carmel knew about the photograph was from an email
Mike Ioannou had sent to their superior in Arusha which had
said that he was trying to track down an enlarged copy of
the picture Liesl had taken at Kibeho, of a dying man holding out another picture. Mike had said that he believed he
had ascertained the identity of the dying man, who had some
involvement in the plot to shoot down President Juvenal Habyarimana's aircraft. While the man holding the picture was

dead, Ioannou had theorised that the people in the picture might also be connected to the plot, and might still be alive. Given that it was a picture of a picture, taken in the midst of a massacre, and that the man holding the original was probably shaking and dying at the time, the quality was surprisingly good.

She didn't recognise the black man whose face she could see, but felt sure she would be able to find someone in Arusha or Rwanda who did. She shifted the cursor until the left shoulder and arm of the white man came into view.

'You are not working, are you?'

Carmel started, and lowered her head, moving the phone out of Henri's line of sight. 'No, no . . . nothing really.'

Henri passed her a glass of iced water. 'The curse of those devices is that you can never truly escape, can you?'

'You're right.'

'Nothing serious, I hope? You look a little worried.'

'No, everything's fine.' She needed to sit down. Richard had said someone had tried to kill him and Liesl. My God, she thought, did this mean Mike's death was really related to what he'd uncovered in his investigation? She knew his questions about the dead man holding out the photograph to the camera had caused some commotion in Arusha, but she was still getting on top of what it was all about.

She had been ordered by the chief prosecutor in Arusha to keep him up to date on anything and everything she was able to piece together about Mike's leads. Carmel slipped the iPhone back into her pack.

'Well,' Henri spread his hands, 'dinner is ready.'

They took seats opposite each other at a dining table out on the verandah. It was a gorgeous setting, with the Zambezi glittering in the darkness and frogs calling in the background, but Carmel couldn't relax and enjoy it. She pushed her food around her plate.

Henri dabbed his mouth with his linen serviette. 'Do you want to talk about it?'

'What? Umm, no, everything's fine.'

Carmel took a mouthful of chicken. It was delicious, and she concentrated on enjoying it. When she looked up she saw he was still sitting quietly, his plate empty, watching her. She finished chewing and swallowed her food. 'It's this investigation I've inherited – the one I'm working on.'

'It's causing you worry, I can tell.'

She knew it would prey on her mind all night, and that she would be terrible company. Perhaps it might help to get his opinion; after all, he had been born in Rwanda and had been there at the time of the genocide. It was a long shot, but he might even recognise the two people in the picture whose faces were visible. It was a candid shot, as none of the men was looking right at the camera, and Carmel wondered if it had been taken covertly.

'Would you be interested in having a look at something for me?'

'Of course.'

13

The red sun was hovering close to the tops of the mopane trees as Liesl and Richard drove back towards the farmhouse. Not knowing what else they could or should do, Liesl had suggested Richard might like to see her parents' game farm. Liesl drove an old open-top Land Rover game viewer, which bounced along the gravel road.

'I was expecting a hundred hectares of fenced bush with a few zebra and kudu,' Richard said.

She laughed. 'Yes, people who haven't been here before are surprised when they find out Poppa owns four thousand hectares of bushveld.'

'Apart from buffalo, are there any animals your father *doesn't* have?'

Liesl grinned. She was saving the best until last. 'We'll see.' The afternoon light was glorious even though this time of year was normally frustrating for a professional wildlife photographer. Once the rains began, the sky tended to be cloudy early in the morning and late in the afternoon, which were the prime times for shooting in the dry season. The so-called golden hours, just after dawn and just before dusk, were a rare occurrence in the summer, and not to be wasted – even in the face of death threats.

Within the game reserve were a few large enclosures, usually used when new animals were brought in, in order to acclimatise them to their surroundings before they were let loose into the rest of the park. Liesl came to one of these and stopped. She climbed down out of the game viewer, went to the rear of the vehicle and lowered the tailgate. 'Come give me a hand, please.'

Richard looked around.

'You're safe here – well relatively.' He got down and she walked to a big marula tree. 'I need you to help me with this.'

'Bloody hell.' Richard stared down at the dead impala ram behind the tree. 'What happened to him?'

'Shot, half an hour ago, by Koos the game reserve manager. He knew we'd be coming.'

'I hope you don't expect me to gut and skin and *braai* this. Is this some kind of Afrikaner initiation ceremony?'

'No.' She held a hand up. 'Listen . . .'

From the other side of the fence she heard the high-pitched yelps and barks. She grinned when she saw Richard's eyes widen as the first of the dogs bounded up to the fence. Soon the animal was joined by three other adults, and then eight pups. Liesl noted the dogs were in fantastic shape – much better than they'd looked in the photos her father had sent her when they'd first been brought to the farm. Their coats, a palette of black, brown, white and mustard, were shiny and free of ticks and mange.

'Wild dogs! Bloody hell, Liesl. What's your dad doing with these?'

'I'll explain, but first we need to prepare dinner.' Liesl instructed Richard to take the dead impala's hind legs, while she took the front. They heaved the ram up into the back of the Land Rover, then Liesl climbed back into the vehicle.

'Stay there and get the gate,' she said. 'There used to be seven adults in this pack and they roamed the area between here and the Kruger park,' she went on.

'That's a big distance,' Richard said to her through the open window.

'*Ja*, but wild dogs have a huge range and the pack needs to eat every day. That doesn't endear them to livestock farmers or game farmers, but the pack used to roam through my parents' property every few months and my folks were willing to live with the loss of a few impalas and kudu in exchange for having one of Africa's most endangered predators as visitors. Not everyone's as sympathetic, though. As you probably know, painted dogs were considered a vermin up until recently and nearly wiped out.'

Liesl started the engine of the Land Rover and drove the few metres to the gate. The dogs were yelping excitedly and leaping up on their hind legs at the prospect of food. 'OK, open the gate then slide it closed once I'm inside. Don't worry, though – they won't try to escape as they know I've got their food.'

'I'm not worried about them escaping, I'm worried about being mistaken for the first course.'

She laughed. 'Relax, Richard, there's never been a recorded incident of wild dogs attacking a human.'

'Not recorded because the victims never lived to tell the tale.'

'Open the gate, chicken.'

Richard frowned, but slid the gate open then rammed it shut again as fast as he could once Liesl had driven inside.

'Are you sure you're safe in there?' he called.

Liesl clambered over the rear two rows of seats to the open load area at the back of the game viewer. She unfastened the tailgate, kicked it open then started to slide the dead impala out. The alpha male and alpha female of the pack were ready and eager to help her. As they grabbed the impala's snout and forelegs, Liesl snatched up her camera and started shooting it. Then she slung the camera around her neck and jumped down.

'Liesl!'

She waved to him. 'Come in, Richard. It's fine. They won't hurt you.'

Liesl stayed about four metres from the pack, mostly to avoid being splattered with blood and gore rather than out of any sense of fear. She knew the dogs were totally engrossed in feeding and couldn't care less about her. When she looked up momentarily from the viewfinder she saw Richard slide the gate open a fraction and then squeeze through the tiny gap. She went back to her job, crouching and moving to capture as many frames as she could of the dogs tearing the impala apart.

The pups were now old enough to feed from the carcass themselves. When they were younger the adults would have left them in the den with a babysitter, gone out and made a kill, scoffed it, then returned home and regurgitated part of the meal for the pups to eat. Now the adults let the pups in for their share. It was a gory feast. Liesl snapped a pup making off with a trail of intestines that looked like butchers' sausages.

Liesl sidestepped as one pup chased the other, bearing a leg bone, and nearly tripped her over as it brushed past her. She pulled back a little then dropped to the ground.

'Liesl!'

She ignored Richard's shout, willing him to be quiet. She had a fantastic angle, looking up at the alpha female and two of the other adults playing tug of war with the remains of the carcass. The light was perfect. It wasn't the same, she knew, as if she'd caught the kill in the wild, but as stock pictures these would be worth something. She might even see if she could get the *Escape!* editor to do a story on her father's work with the local conservation people to get the pack back up to strength.

Within three minutes there was nothing left of the impala save for a bloodstain on the grass. The dogs carried off the remaining skin and bone into the bush inside the enclosure. Liesl stood and brushed herself down. When she looked at her hands she saw they were shaking. It wasn't the excitement of seeing the dogs in action, or being so close to them; it was the blood and bone. When she watched things happen through the viewfinder she was calm, detached, professional. Afterwards, when she thought of what had happened, what she'd seen, she started to unravel.

'Well, that was amazing,' Richard said.

She felt unsteady on her feet and his voice sounded distorted.

'Liesl? Are you OK?'

Liesl turned and walked over to the Land Rover, opened the driver's side door and sat down heavily. She set her camera down on the passenger seat then wrapped her arms around herself, but no matter how tightly she gripped, she couldn't stop the shakes from taking over her whole body.

Henri Bousson studied the picture on Carmel's iPhone and

she looked over his shoulder at the image of the white man in the group for the first time.

The man had blond hair. Although he was wearing a khaki-coloured civilian safari suit he had the hard eyes, straight bearing and muscled arms of a military man. He was holding the weapon that Richard had said was a surface-to-air missile launcher.

Henri sucked a breath in through his teeth, then shook his head. 'No, I'm afraid I don't recognise any of these people. There were plenty of gun runners in Rwanda and the neighbouring countries in those days, though – they're still there today. Someone is always killing someone else in that part of Africa.'

Carmel took the phone and had another look. There were other investigators in Kigali, locals as well as foreigners, who could try to identify the men in the picture. It was important enough, apparently, for someone to kill to try to keep the image, and the testimony of those who had been there when it had been taken, away from the tribunal. She wondered what she should do about Liesl and Richard. The irony of her position – that she should find herself responsible for the safety of two people she'd once wanted to shoot – didn't escape her.

'I could help you identify them, I think.'

She looked up from the phone's screen. 'How?'

Vite wiggled and jiggled the wooden peg with his fingers until his long arm ached from being stretched for so long. He shook the peg some more and when he pulled, this time, it started to move.

Vite paused, all of his senses alert for the sound of the

man returning. When he was certain all was quiet he slid the loosened peg from its metal home. He pushed against the cage door and it squeaked. Vite paused again. When no one answered the rusty cry he pushed the door all the way open and climbed down. His cage was sitting on another and when the cobra inside it reared up and hissed at him, Vite's little heart nearly exploded from his chest. Had he known he'd been sitting atop a snake for so many days, he might have died of fright.

He scampered along the dirt floor of the prison to the steel door where the man came and went to check on his captives. Vite pushed the door. It wouldn't budge.

Vite banged on the metal and to his surprise it started to open. He thrust his hand through the gap at the edge, into the shaft of light that pierced the gloom, but before he could squeeze out he felt hands grabbing his arm. He was lifted off the ground and when the door opened fully he found himself staring at a white man.

The white man spoke to Vite's captor in an angry tone. Vite wriggled and struggled, but he was no match for the two humans. They carried him not back to his cage, but to a wooden box on the floor. He kicked at the sides and tried to grab the timbers to stop them putting him inside, but they beat down on his hands and forced him in. Vite squealed as the lid was nailed shut. He felt himself lifted and saw cracks of light between the slats of the box as he was carried outside and the box was dropped on something that clanged. An engine started. Vite felt himself moving, further and further from his home.

Aston's mobile phone vibrated in his top pocket. The woman

opposite him was worried that a workmate, a former close friend whom she had fallen out with, had placed a curse on her which was preventing her from falling pregnant.

Aston had just prescribed a root infusion to help her conceive, but the woman was now complaining about a hacking cough, tiredness and night sweats. He could hardly tell her to go have sex with a virgin, as that cure for AIDS didn't work with women.

'It's probably nothing – just a tummy bug or a virus. Perhaps something you ate?' Aston said.

The woman nodded vigorously and looked relieved. 'Yes, I am sure that is it, Doctor. Thank you so much.'

'It is only a pleasure,' he said, and stood to end the consultation. The woman stood and opened her handbag. 'Please, pay my receptionist on the way out. I am sure you will be fine and that you will soon be coming back to me to report your good fortune.'

'Thank you, Doctor.'

The phone had stopped vibrating. As Aston closed the door he slipped the phone from his pocket. The number of the missed call was withheld, which was normal in this line of business. Aston waited. The phone rang again.

'Yes?'

'The Englishman went to the woman's parents' farm in Letsitele. He's there now,' said the man Aston knew as Jan Venter. It was no doubt an alias, but that was fine. Jan was ex-South African special forces, a close friend of the boss and very good at his job, whether that was reconnaissance and surveillance, or killing. Aston had no doubt that had he sent Jan to kill the photographer and the doctor they would not be alive, but it would have been too much of a risk. South

Africa might be, in theory, the rainbow nation where all colours lived side by side and race didn't preclude or guarantee access to any job, but the fact was that carjackers and home-invading drug addicts tended to be black rather than white. Had Jan failed in the spectacular way that Aston's other two would-be assassins had failed, there would have been a good deal more police interest in the two attempted murders than there was currently. Aston was using Jan to gather intelligence and oversee the surveillance of the two targets who were, somewhat embarrassingly, still alive.

'We know that she keeps her photographic files at her parents' home. By now she will have found the picture and printed it,' Aston said. He was fishing. He wanted to hear how the white man would tackle the problem.

'This isn't some poor Afrikaner farming family. There will be computers in the house . . . a scanner. She will have sent the image to the people who want it. It's too late,' Jan said.

'Maybe yes, maybe no,' Aston said, his mind racing. 'It is not good that things have progressed this far, but we cannot afford to fail.'

'*You* can't afford to fail,' Jan said.

'The man and the woman are as important as the picture – their testimony is what makes the photo so crucial.'

'You're talking about a big operation. The parents would have been shown the picture, perhaps been told what the man and woman know. If we want to contain the damage we need to go large, hey?'

'I'm not sure I follow you,' Aston said.

'Oh, I think you do. Farm invasions happen every day in South Africa, and they're bloody.'

Aston thought about the fallout that would occur from

murdering a wealthy farming couple, as well as their daughter and the doctor. It would be big, but manageable. 'There's no way you could make it look like an accident?'

Jan laughed into the phone. 'Four people? *Fokken* big accident, *bru*. The man and woman went into the family game park today. Might have been able to finish them off and feed them to the old man's lions or wild dogs, but accident . . . no.'

Aston's eyes widened. 'Did you say wild dogs?'

'*Ja*,' Jan said. 'I've been doing my homework. There was a piece in the local paper a month ago about the old man adopting a pack of twelve wild dogs. Crazy *oke*. Where I grew up we used to shoot those *bladdy—*'

'Shut up. Keep the place under surveillance, I have another job for you.'

'I'm listening.'

'I want those wild dogs. All of them. Alive.'

There was a silence on the end of the line and Aston wondered if the signal had dropped out. 'Serious?'

'You heard me. The dogs.'

More silence. '*Ja*, OK, but it'll cost you. I'll need drugs, dart guns, that sort of thing. I can't put an operation like this together tonight.'

'You've got two days. I know a vet in the Lowveld and I'll SMS his number to you.'

'And the family? The man and the woman?'

'Go large,' Aston said. 'If you get a chance to take out the man and the woman before we get the dogs, then take it.'

'*Ja*, all right. I want a hundred thousand for the lot,' Jan said.

'Rand?'

Jan laughed into the phone. 'Dollars. US.'

'Fifty,' Aston said.

'Seventy-five thousand, no less.'

'Deal. But when it comes time to clean the farm, I want you to do it. I can't afford any more failures. The boss is watching us all.'

'With me, failure is not an option. That's why the boss sent me to help you,' Jan said.

Aston hung up and tried to calculate how much he could charge for a dozen wild dogs. Anything he wanted, he guessed. A pack that big must include pups and he could charge a premium for the little ones. But the dogs, no matter how lucrative, were his secondary concern.

As Jan said, the Nel woman's parents would know some of the story of the photo by now, and the image itself would have already been emailed. He could probably stop the picture going further if he acted quickly. He typed a quick email into his computer then picked up his phone again. It was time to put the contingency plan into action.

He dialled a man he knew in Livingstone, Robert Banda, another ex-soldier, down on his luck. The man had poached rhino in Hwange National Park, across the Zambezi in Zimbabwe, and had boasted that he'd killed a park ranger.

It was short notice, but when the call finally went through, on the third attempt, the man said he was available and would happily do the job for the two thousand US dollars Aston offered. He was so staggered at the amount that he didn't even think to bargain it upwards.

Carmel sipped her coffee as Henri explained how he might be able to help her identify the men in the picture. He said that from the look of the thick vegetation in the background the picture had probably been taken either near the Virunga Mountains or Nyungwe National Park.

'I know both areas well. As I said, my parents made their fortune growing tea, at Gisokoro near the Nyungwe Park, and we were regular visitors to the Volcanoes National Park. I actually met Dian Fossey when I was a boy.'

'Really?' Carmel was impressed.

'Yes. My father was in Ruhengeri on tea business and we met her in a bar. She gave my father an earful about growing tea, and he agreed to make a donation towards her research. I think she would have thrown it back in his face if it wasn't so generous!'

Carmel laughed, as did Henri. 'That's good, but I still don't know how you can help identify the men.'

'Not me, but perhaps people I know, still living and working in the national parks. Before the situation deteriorated, I worked for a few years as a guide in both parks. It's where my love for wildlife began. I used to escort foreign researchers into the remote areas, even though there were few who made it to Rwanda, and fewer still who stayed once the fighting became more intense. We had farms around Ruhengeri as well, and my father would send me to check on them. There was a lot of illegal cross-border traffic at the time, from Uganda and Zaire, as it was known then. There were animals – gorillas and chimps – being killed for bushmeat and their babies sold as pets, but there were also arms shipments coming and going. Some of the whites I knew back then were involved in both trades. It was shameful.'

'You think you might still have some contacts there?'

He shrugged. 'Maybe. Ruhengeri was a strong base of Hutu

Power, the movement that whipped people into a genocidal frenzy against the Tutsis. As you would know, Hutu Power had the backing of the Rwandese Army, so it could be that the military men in your picture were meeting in that area, near the mountains where the gorillas live. It's remote, and on the route to and from Zaire.'

'Well, I have very few leads to go on. We should talk about this more,' Carmel said.

He nodded. 'But now I think it is time for bed.'

'You're right,' she said, thankful for his thoughtfulness.

Henri stood and walked over to a side wall and pushed some buttons on the house's alarm system. From a side table beneath the alarm box he took a rechargeable torch. 'I'll show you to your room.'

Robert Banda rubbed the infusion of crushed leaves and roots into the skin of his chest and belly, then smeared some on his cheeks and the top of his shaven head for good measure.

Doctor Aston had prescribed the *muti* to him two years earlier, when the *inyanga* had visited Livingstone to collect the rhino horn Robert and his brother had taken from an animal in Zimbabwe's Hwange National Park. Aston had said the *muti* would protect him from rangers' bullets on his future forays.

And it had worked. The next time Robert had ventured into Zimbabwe, to hunt for buck in the Zambezi National Park on the other side of the river, he and his brother had been surprised by a foot patrol of rangers. His brother had foolishly brandished his handgun, a Browning 9mm pistol, and the rangers had opened fire. Robert's brother had been killed, but Robert himself had been unharmed, because he had used the *muti*. He'd taken his dead brother's pistol and fled, making it back to Zambia.

He checked the pistol in the moonlight, in the yard of his small house. He slid back the slide and let it go, chambering a round. It reminded him of his days in the army, under Aston's command. It was good to hear from the big man again and to be trusted with such an important job. He would not let the doctor down. He slid the pistol into the waistband of his jeans, then took out his green parka and put it on back to front. Robert got onto his Yamaha 125cc motor scooter and kicked the starter. It took him three attempts to get it going. He would buy a new bike with the money he was about to earn. It would better suit his image as a gangsta. Women would love it. Robert pulled on his helmet and let out the clutch. The bike puttered and chugged, but sounded better when he revved the throttle hard.

He left Livingstone and headed out towards the Mosi-Oi-Tunya National Park. He knew the house where the Frenchman lived, as his mother still lived in the village nearby. Several years earlier, when the Frenchman was building his mansion on the river, Robert had worked as a construction labourer. He had mixed cement for the bricks that had built the sprawling entertainment area and the attendant suites. He knew the Frenchman's living quarters were on the eastern side of the property, and the guest bungalows were on the far side of the living area. This was the side he would enter from, via the creek that the Frenchman and his white woman neighbour had stupidly left open to the river, creating an elephant highway.

Robert didn't want to be remembered by the Zambian Wildlife Authority guards on duty at the entry to the park, so he turned off the road onto a dirt trail before the ZAWA checkpoint. Half a kilometre further on was a turn-off that led to the road that ran along the park fence. Robert turned left and motored slowly until he came to the gap where the fence had been cut and the wire mesh flattened. It was a well-known entry spot for the men who set their snares in the park.

Robert turned off the engine, got off the bike and pushed and lifted it through – grateful for once that the machine was so puny. Once through he started it again and followed the fence until he came to one of the game-viewing roads. He knew there was little likelihood of encountering a ZAWA patrol this late at night. If he did, he had his pistol. The mix of excitement and fear emboldened him, and he gunned the engine. On the far side of the park he found a similar break in the fence and repeated the procedure. Soon he was back on the tar road, having successfully evaded both checkpoints.

Robert slowed as he neared his mother's village, not because he wanted to see her but because of the huge dark shapes ambling across the road, blotting out the stars in the process. He stopped and revved his engine. One of the elephants paused and looked at him, shaking her great head so that her big ears flapped noisily.

He felt his heartbeat quicken. He hated these animals. They were off to feed on the crops the people in his mother's village grew. They would trample and gorge on the food that was meant for the humans. If Robert had been armed with an AK, instead of the pistol, he would have killed the big matriarch then and there, and hacked out her skinny tusks. Instead, he waited, holding his breath, until the old cow led her clan across the road and into the bush on the other side.

The Frenchman was part of the problem, Robert thought

as he cruised past the entrance to the man's property. All the people of his mother's village knew that the reason the elephants were able to get to their crops so easily was because of the unfenced corridor along the creek line that separated the Frenchman's property from his neighbour's. Robert would have liked to have killed the Frenchman as well, but orders were orders. It wasn't unusual to hear gunshots at night – people sometimes fired a shot or two to scare away elephants – but if the man was woken by the shot and came out of his suite and saw him, then Robert would have to shoot him in self-defence. Aston would understand.

Robert eased the bike onto the dirt verge and stopped the engine. He wheeled the bike ten metres into the bush and laid it down in the long summer grass so that it would be invisible from the road. He took off his parka – it was warm now that he had stopped riding – and placed it over the bike as an extra covering. He touched the butt of the pistol for luck, and imagined the bulletproof field radiating from his body, thanks to Aston's *muti*. This would be better than killing a rhino or an elephant. If the woman was sleeping he might try to smother her with a pillow rather than shooting her. Perhaps there would be time for him to have some fun. The thought excited him.

He slid down the steep bank of a cutting made by a creek that fed to the Zambezi and smelled the pungent odour of fresh elephant dung. Yes, this was where they had crossed and passed through. Robert walked along the edge of the trickling stream, hopping from rock to rock when he could, and trying not to lose his shoes to sucking mud when he had to step onto the softer ground. He scanned the sky, looking for a suitable tree.

As he'd hoped, the *mzungu*'s staff had been lax in pruning the higher branches of the taller trees that ran along the fence line. There was the occasional report of a leopard in the area, but Robert imagined the white man wouldn't be too worried at all if one of the cats was able to climb a tree, then walk along a branch that overhung the electric fence and jump into the protected compound. A white person would probably welcome such an invasion. A villager would lament the loss of a goat or a dog, and then set a trap to kill the leopard. Robert found a suitable jackalberry, climbed it, crawled along the branch, then, hanging from it by his hands to lessen the distance to the ground, let go and landed softly in the grass. All the *mzungu* with houses and lodges on the river had boats too, for game viewing and fishing, so Robert planned on making his escape via the water. The outboard might be locked away, but he could drift with the current until he found a jumping-off place, then circle back for his motorcycle. He had thought of everything.

Robert stayed crouched in the moon shadow of the tree for a few moments, listening. There would be a nightwatchman somewhere on the property, probably dozing near the expensive four-by-four the Frenchman drove. Robert stood, slipped the 9mm from his belt and crept towards the nearest bungalow. As he drew closer he heard the hum of an air conditioner and saw all the lights were out. It was three in the morning. She would be asleep.

Carmel's mouth was dry when she awoke and in the near total darkness of the room she suffered a few seconds of disorientation as her sleep-deprived brain tried to work out where in the world she was.

Bloody jet lag.

She swivelled her head until she saw the luminous digits of the clock radio: *3:08*. She groaned. Now that she knew where she was, the worries she'd taken to bed with her flooded her mind again. She groped on the bedside table for her iPhone and switched it on.

Robert Banda heard the ping of SMS messages arriving on a phone. His heart, already pounding with anticipation, lurched at the noise. His hand rested on the handle of the sliding door.

His confidence suddenly left him. What if the door was locked? What if she got up and switched the light on? What if she screamed? Could he get away in time? Was he stupid to think the Frenchman would not be woken by the gunshot and come running? The boat landing, he now realised, was at the other end of the property, nearly three hundred metres away. He would never make it – and he might cross paths with the white man as he came to investigate the noise.

Robert wanted to run, but then he thought of the money, and his mother, all alone since his father had died of the virus. Robert was the man of the family. He had to be strong. And he had used the *muti* prescribed by Aston.

Plus, if he failed, Aston would surely have him killed. Robert slid open the door.

Carmel looked up from the screen of her phone as she heard the shush of the door on its slide. The curtains twitched.

If it was Henri he would have knocked, surely.

She couldn't remember locking the door.

Carmel saw an arm and made out the dark silhouette of the pistol. She rolled.

Henri Bousson had never shot anyone in his life, but he felt a strange sense of calm descend over him as he wrapped the fingers of his left hand around those of his right, which held the Colt .45 calibre pistol tight. The thing was American, a cannon, and he had bought it for its stopping power.

Henri was on the grass, feet planted firmly apart. The intruder was above him, about a metre off the ground, on the paved verandah. The man was silhouetted against the moonlit trees.

The man had his hand on the door to Carmel's bungalow and started to slide it. He reached inside for the curtains.

Henri briefly thought about calling a warning, but he didn't want to lose the advantage. He squeezed the trigger twice, quickly – the way they did it on the cop shows on DSTV. The pistol kicked in his hand, as he knew it would. Henri saw the man spin and drop, and then he was running up the stairs leading to the verandah as the body hit the ground.

Carmel screamed.

'It's me, Carmel!' Henri kicked the man, a short, savage jab in the ribs. The intruder's gun was on the tiles and the African reached in the air for invisible help as the life rattled from his body. Henri glanced at the spreading stains on the man's shirt. One plumb in the heart and the other probably passed through both lungs. The air hissed from the body with frothy bubbles of blood as he died.

Henri stepped over the body, pistol held high. 'Carmel? You're safe now.'

He switched on the light and saw her, cowering by the

side of the bed, half wrapped in the sheets and duvet she'd taken with her when she'd rolled. Clever girl, he thought. She peered up at him.

Henri strode across the polished concrete floor to her and held out his free hand. She took it and when he lifted her to her feet she threw herself against him. He wrapped his arms around her. She didn't cry, but shivered in his arms.

'It's all right,' he said, and breathed in the scent of the shampoo from her pre-bed shower. She was warm from the covers, but he saw the goose bumps on her arms beneath the sleeves of her T-shirt. She wore a checked pair of pyjama shorts. Henri freed an arm and pulled the duvet from the floor, then extricated himself from her and wrapped her. He sat her down on the bed. 'Stay here. I'm going to check for others.'

'No. Stay with me, please.'

He looked into her eyes. 'I will. You're safe now.'

14

Richard read the message on the screen of his BlackBerry:

> Richard,
> A man with a gun tried to break into the place where I'm staying
> last night. I'm sure it's related to the attacks on you and Liesl, and
> the death of my colleague Mike Ioannou. I'm flying to Rwanda to
> try to find out who the people in the photo are. I need to interview
> you both. You need to get to Arusha ASAP and report to the ICTR.
> They will take care of you until I can get to you and take your
> depositions. Please take care.
> Carmel.

Richard read the message again. He'd showered, put on the
same clothes he'd been wearing the day before, and found
his way from a guestroom through the labyrinthine maze of
corridors to the kitchen. The cook was there early, and he'd
asked her to make him coffee. He sipped it as he considered
what he should do next.

'Morning.' Liesl wore a blue silk robe. 'Please may I have
some tea, Prudence?'

Richard looked up from his phone. 'Someone tried to kill Carmel last night.'

'Oh my God. Is she OK?'

'She can still email,' Richard said.

'So it's not just a coincidence.'

'No.' The night before, over drinks and then dinner, Richard had tried to convince Liesl, and himself, that as bizarre as it seemed, the attacks on them had been random and unrelated. He theorised that the man who had tried to kill him was a drug dealer and user who was trying to steal whatever was in his home. Even as he'd formulated the story he could see its holes. Why would a drug dealer risk entering the Kruger National Park, and how would he have known where the doctor lived?

'Maybe it was a hitman hired by one of your ex-lovers' husbands?' Liesl had said, her mood brightening after her near meltdown in the wild dogs' enclosure.

'Now that does make sense.'

She had smiled, which pleased him. Her parents were good people and they'd fussed over him without making him feel uncomfortable, seemingly warming to him after Tokkie's initial frosty reception. After Liesl had gone to bed her father had lingered, offering him a Scotch.

'Like I said before, I knew soldiers who couldn't handle what they'd seen, what they'd done in Angola. You're a doctor – do you think Liesl is sick in that way?'

'I myself was diagnosed with post-traumatic stress disorder,' Richard said, swirling the golden liquid around the glass, relishing the siren call of the ice and the cool on his fingertips. He craved the release, every day. It was just a matter of degrees. 'I still don't think I'm over it – and maybe

I never will be. It's very possible Liesl's suffering from the same condition.'

Tokkie stood up from his chair and walked out of the room. Richard wondered if he was unable to deal with the fact that his daughter had PTSD, but he returned a couple of minutes later. In his hand was a pistol. 'You were a doctor, but you were a paratrooper as well.'

'Yes.'

Tokkie held out the pistol to him. It looked big, heavy and workmanlike. Maybe Russian, Richard thought. He took it, found the magazine release and thumbed it, and let the magazine fall into his left palm. He pocketed it, pulled back the slide, checked the chamber was empty, let the slide go, then fired the action with a click.

'It's a Makarov,' Tokkie said. 'I got it in Angola off a dead Cuban.' Richard guessed from the coldness in the older man's eyes how the Cuban had died. 'I've got a .357 Magnum, Elize has a small .22 and there is a hunting rifle in the pantry. I don't know how to heal my daughter's mind and heart – I'll want to talk to you more about this later – but for now I am worried about her life. We're not going to let anyone hurt her, Richard.'

Richard had nodded and Tokkie had gone to bed. He had followed, but had not slept well with the lump of the pistol under his pillow.

Liesl sat down at the kitchen table and Prudence placed a tray with a small teapot, cup, saucer, milk jug and sugar in front of her. Richard read the message aloud as Liesl poured her tea.

'She wants us to go to Arusha?'

'So it seems,' Richard said.

'What do you think?'

'I don't think the answer to all this is in Tanzania, or here.'

Liesl took a sip of tea. 'I'm worried that us being here is putting my parents at risk. I want to hide, but I don't know where. Should we go to the police?'

Richard shrugged. 'I don't know what the South African Police could do, but sure, yes, we should probably tell them what we know.'

'Do you think it will do any good?'

'No, not really. I think the only way we can sort this out is to find out who is in that photo, and why it's important enough for someone to want to kill us for finding it.'

'I wish I'd never kept those negatives,' she said. 'I don't want to be a part of this, Richard. This isn't our war.'

He didn't want it either. He was more angry than scared right now. He'd carved out a nice little nomadic life to help him escape the tragedies and fuck-ups of his past, and now someone was doing their best to bring that peaceful life to an end. Richard wouldn't have been so angry if it was just him. He'd earned a bad death, several times over, and if someone put a bullet in his head in the middle of the night, not too many people would mourn him. But it angered him that Carmel and Liesl, two women he'd cared for in different ways, were also on the killers' list, and Collette, the daughter of the dead man who had shown them the photo, might also be in danger.

Tokkie walked into the kitchen, dressed in his farmer's uniform of shorts, short-sleeved shirt, boots and long socks. 'I just overheard what you said.'

Richard sipped his coffee. 'What do you think we should do?'

'Leave.'

'What?' Liesl said.

'It's not safe for you to stay here,' her father said.

Richard was surprised at the old man's bluntness. 'Why?'

Tokkie rubbed his eyes and Richard noticed now they were red, with dark bags underneath. He saw, too, that Tokkie's boots were caked in mud and there were grass seeds and burrs in his socks. 'I got a call last night from my head of security. There was someone in the game reserve.'

'Poachers?' Richard asked.

Tokkie poured himself a cup of coffee, black with no sugar. 'That wouldn't be unusual – we get them quite often, either setting or checking their bloody snares, or with their dogs. If we catch them, we arrest the poachers but shoot the dogs. This was different.'

'How so, Poppa?'

Tokkie looked at Liesl. 'My security guys are good. They woke Koos, the manager, when they found fresh tracks and they then started following whoever it was who broke in. It was only one person, a man wearing expensive boots with deep, new tread on them – unusual for one of our local *tsotsis*. They followed the tracks to a gap in the fence – the warthogs dig holes under the electric fences quicker than we can fill them in. Whoever was in slid back out again and then took off in a vehicle – a Land Cruiser by the look of the wheel tracks. They woke me at three this morning and I went out.'

Richard hadn't heard anyone waking in the house, but given its size that wasn't surprising.

'We did a sweep along the fence line, and out the front of the house. The scouts found the same footprints coming

right up to the house. When I questioned a few of the workers this morning a couple remembered seeing a Land Cruiser
with Gauteng plates being driven by a white man slowly
along the road late yesterday afternoon. No one drives slow
on that road.'

'Could have been someone from Johannesburg looking for
someone's place,' Richard ventured hopefully.

'I've got three neighbours in a ten-kilometre stretch and
I already called all of them this morning. No one's had any
visitors from Joburg,' Tokkie said.

'But how could they – whoever *they* are – know that I'm at
home, or that Richard is here too?'

Richard thought about it. Whoever was after them – if
indeed someone was and this wasn't all still a train of coincidences – might guess that he and Liesl would link up. He
didn't recall anyone tailing him from Skukuza, but then he
hadn't been looking.

'I'm sure there was no one following me here,' Liesl said. 'I
was the only car on the road from Gravelotte.'

Richard's phone beeped. He was wondering if Carmel
was going to send another message, telling them what they
should do. He checked it, but annoyingly, the email read:
Wayne Hamilton commented on your photo. Bloody Facebook. He
wished he'd never signed up for the thing. He hadn't updated
his profile for months. He didn't particularly want everyone who knew him knowing where he was all the time. The
thought hit him. 'Are you on Facebook, Liesl?'

'Yes, isn't everyone?'

'What's that got to do with anything?' Tokkie asked.

'When was the last time you updated your profile?' Richard asked her.

'Just yesterday, but . . . wait a minute. Do you think that's how they're tracking me – us?'

'What did you say on Facebook?'

'Nothing. Just something about having a bad night's sleep.' She got out her phone and scrolled to the app. '*Kak*. There's a message on my wall from my friend Sannette, who I was staying with in Joburg. She's asking if I got to my parents' place safely. Hell.'

'How many friends do you have and do you know them all personally?'

'I've got more than two thousand. I get a lot of people I don't know who like my photographs,' she said defensively. 'How many do you have?'

He said he didn't know, although he did – eighteen.

'Whoever was on the farm last night is the same person who was checking you on this Facebook thing, *ja*?' Tokkie asked.

'Yes, Poppa.'

'Well, put something on there now. Tell Sannette you arrived safely and that you're looking forward to spending a few days here. Say Mom's putting on a big dinner for you tonight. We'll invite some people around.'

'But you want us to leave . . .'

'I don't *want* you to leave, my girl,' Tokkie took his daughter's hands in his. 'But I don't want them to get you, and it now seems like they know you are here and are watching you. If they've been watching our place they will know Richard is here too. I'm worried they're going to try to kill you both here.'

Richard was still puzzled by one thing. 'Why would this person go into the game farm? Wouldn't they assume that Liesl and I were here in the house?'

Tokkie thought about the question. 'We have a little lodge there – a kitchen and bar area with some small rondavels. We use it as a family retreat and we advertise it online as a camp for hunters. We do some bow hunting on the farm when we need to reduce our antelope numbers. Whoever is after you might have thought you were staying there.'

'That shows they've done their homework,' Richard said.

Tokkie nodded. 'I don't think you're dealing with amateurs.'

Jan Venter raised the high-powered Swarovski binoculars as one of the electronic doors of the multi-car garage next to the farmhouse opened. The Land Cruiser reversed and Jan focused and saw the farmer sitting behind the wheel.

He appeared to be alone. Nel had left early in the morning, just after six, and had returned two hours later. Jan guessed the old man had gone to check on the farms and his other businesses, which included a cardboard-packaging plant, a juice-making factory with sprawling packing sheds and the local bottle store and service station, which one of his sons owned and ran. The Nels seemed to own the town, and they obviously had eyes everywhere.

Jan had noticed the extra patrols by a local armed-response security company's *bakkies* earlier that morning, roving up and down the road between the citrus farm and the game farm, following the pre-dawn commotion when they realised they'd had an intruder on the farm. He had to admit he was begrudgingly impressed at the tight ship they ran; the Nels were no fools. From his vantage point on a high hill on the Nel family's game farm, located across the road from the farmhouse, he could watch all the comings and goings from the family home.

After checking the wild-dog enclosure and the safari camp on the game farm by foot in the early hours of the morning, he had left via the same crawl space that he'd entered, and driven his Land Cruiser, which he'd rented in Johannesburg with a fake ID, five kilometres from the Nel farm. When he'd come to a gum plantation he'd driven another kilometre in off the road and then bundu-bashed deep into the forest, where he'd left the vehicle. He didn't care if someone found it and stole it – he would have other vehicles arriving in a couple of days' time – and he knew his ride had been compromised. Jan had then trekked back from the forest and entered the game farm again via a different warthog scraping, a kilometre from the first, and had taken care to cover his tracks as he'd moved slowly to his observation point. When he'd seen old Tokkie Nel and his scouts checking the spot where he'd first entered, and inspecting the ground for tracks, he'd realised he had underestimated the farmer and his staff.

Jan had set up a hide, a green ground sheet strung between two trees to provide shelter from the sun and rain, and camouflaged it with branches. He made a note on his phone of the time Nel left home, and scanned the grounds of the farmhouse for signs of the doctor and the woman. The man's Discovery and the woman's BMW X5 were both still parked on the lawn outside the garage.

When the four-by-four was out of sight, headed in the direction of Letsitele, Jan scrolled through his contacts for Aston's number and called him.

'Yes?' said the *Inyanga*.

'They're still in place. I checked the dogs last night, as well. I've confirmed their location and number. Security is not so tight in that part of the farm, not like the rhino and sable enclosures. Also, the dogs aren't far from the main road. If you want to do it properly, there is an airstrip on the farm, so you could land an aircraft and fly them straight out.'

There was a brief pause. 'I want to do it properly. I'll organise the vet and a helicopter.'

Jan smiled. Proper meant costly. Costly meant more for him.

'You can get up now,' Tokkie said.

Thank God, Richard thought. He eased his cramped body up off the floor of the Land Cruiser, where he'd been sandwiched between the front and rear seats, hidden under a blanket. Behind him, Liesl was throwing off her cover from where she'd been curled up in the comparatively more comfortable flat cargo space of the vehicle.

Richard saw a big tin-roofed shed and heard the increasingly high-pitched whine of a turbo engine. He looked around. 'Where are we?'

'This is Dad's packing shed,' Liesl said. There was fast-paced activity all around. Trucks were coming and going, bringing grapefruit from the orchards and leaving with cartons full of the produce.

'I spoke to the police on the phone before we left,' Tokkie said. 'They're going to send out patrols to keep an eye on us and try to track down whoever was driving that Land Cruiser. It's a long shot, but if I hear anything I'll let you know.'

The vehicle rounded the end of the shed and Richard, now sitting upright, saw the blue Squirrel helicopter sitting on a concrete pad outside its purpose-built hangar. He shook his head in disbelief. Tokkie had told them he was going to fly them out of Letsitele, but Richard had assumed they would be going to an airstrip to get on a light aircraft. It seemed the farming business was going strong.

'Who's flying, Poppa?'

'Marthinus.'

Richard looked at her. 'He's one of my brothers,' she said, 'the one who owns the local Spar supermarket in town.'

'Is there anything your family doesn't own around here?'

Liesl ignored Richard's jibe as Tokkie stopped the car out of reach of the helicopter's spinning blades. Its hot exhaust sent out a heat haze that whirled in the downwash. Richard smelled the burning fuel and it reminded him of helicopter rides in the army. He paused at the bumper and took Tokkie's outstretched hand.

Tokkie leaned close to Richard as he crushed his fingers in his hand. 'I'm putting my only daughter in your care,' he yelled into Richard's ear. 'I would rather have her with me, but you two have to lose yourselves just now. If anything happens to her I'll hold you personally responsible and me and my four sons will find you.'

Richard didn't laugh. He knew it wasn't a joke. 'Yes, sir.'

'My boy Marthinus will take you to Wonderboom Airport in Pretoria. We've got a house in the city, so you two can stay there until we get this thing sorted. Get her to put more stuff on that Facebook thing. I want whoever is after my daughter to try something so I can kill him.'

Richard nodded. He knew the old man was serious.

Tokkie said a few words into Liesl's ear that Richard couldn't hear, then the father and daughter hugged and kissed. Richard climbed into the back of the helicopter with Liesl, and Tokkie slammed the door shut behind them. Marthinus turned back to check on his passengers as Liesl handed Richard a headset. As they were buckling up, Marthinus lifted off.

Richard looked down and saw the sunburned, lined face of the old farmer. He waved but he wasn't smiling. Richard turned from the perspex window and saw Liesl was staring at him. She had her hand resting palm down on the middle seat that separated them. Richard put his hand over hers and gave it a squeeze.

Carmel sat in the main lounge area of Henri's house with her laptop on her knees, typing an email to her superior at the ICTR in Arusha, outlining what had happened to her, Liesl and Richard, and asking what protection the tribunal could offer.

Two detectives from Livingstone and a posse of uniformed Zambian police had been trampling around Henri's place throughout the morning. Henri spoke with them now, in Lozi, on the verandah. It seemed to Carmel they were nearly done. An undertaker had already taken away the body of the gunman.

Henri shook the detectives' hands and escorted them out to the gravel driveway. He came in as Carmel was hitting 'Send'.

'That didn't go too badly,' he said.

She closed the laptop. 'You seemed to get on well with them.'

'I know most of the local cops. They're good men, and not as corrupt as people might think. Also, they know the dead guy.'

'They do?'

'He was a petty criminal and sometime poacher. He'd done

a couple of stretches in prison. The police are convinced he was here to rob or assault you.'

'But I *told* them about the Rwanda connection, and the attacks on my two witnesses,' Carmel said.

Henri shrugged. 'Like I said, they're not bad guys, but neither do they want to increase their case load unnecessarily. It's much easier for them to close the case off – one criminal caught in the act of breaking and entering, and killed. Nice and simple, *n'est ce pas*? They've offered, reluctantly, to put a man with an AK-47 out front for the next few nights while you're still here, but that's more a favour to me. I'll end up having to transport him to and from town and feed him. I'm happy to do so, but . . .'

'But you don't think that's enough?'

He shrugged again. 'You tell me, Carmel. If you think there is a gang out there trying to assassinate you and your star witnesses because of a picture, and something you all may or may not know, then what do you think we need to do about it?'

She thought about his question. He didn't really need to do anything at all about it – it wasn't Henri's problem, but he had already offered to assist her investigations in order to identify the men in the photograph. She wondered if he was looking for an excuse to get back to the country of his birth, and perhaps a bit of adventure.

'*I* need to get back to work as soon as possible. I'm sorry, Henri, but I'm going to have to cut short my visit. I can't be sightseeing while people are in danger. I need to work out a way to get to Richard and Liesl quickly, and I need to find out who is in the photo and why it's so important.'

'*D'accord*. Then I want to come with you, to Rwanda. Allow

me to volunteer my services to your tribunal. It's high time I did something to help my birth country. It would be my honour.'

Carmel was touched by his sense of chivalry, and she owed Henri her life, but the lawyer in her was already finding a hundred reasons to refuse his offer.

'Whatever you say, Carmel,' he said before she could reply, 'I am going to Rwanda. I have business there, as of this morning.'

'You do? What's so important that you all of a sudden want to go back?'

'I received an email from an animal welfare group we work with in Rwanda. Someone came across a baby chimp in a market in Gisokoro, near Nyungwe National Park. He's been taken to a refuge in Ruhengeri, but he can't stay there because they don't have a large enough enclosure for him, and he can't be returned to the wild. It appears the little fellow was stolen from his troop by a trader, who probably planned to sell him as a pet or, worse, for medical experiments.'

Carmel frowned. 'And do you go and personally collect every rescued chimp that ends up in your rehabilitation centre?'

Henri spread his hands. 'Ah, you are too good an investigator. You have caught me out. No, the truth is I usually just oversee the shipments and leave others to do the dirty work, but I do want to get back to Rwanda to meet the people from this rescue organisation. And I have, in the past, personally transported chimps. And I *am* concerned about your safety, and whether you think you need me or not, I *know* I can help you identify the people in the picture.'

Carmel let what Henri was proposing sink in. She was still

shaky from the aftershock of what had nearly happened to her last night. She felt out of her depth with this investigation and she wished Mike Ioannou was still alive and that she was going about her normal business of prosecuting *génocidaires* who were already in prison. She was comfortably zealous dealing with crimes that happened seventeen and eighteen years earlier, but she had never had someone point a gun at her.

Despite her fear, she knew she could dig deep and see this investigation through, but right now, as she looked at the handsome Gallic bear of a man waiting for her to accept his offer of help and protection, she knew that she wanted him beside her.

'Rwanda's what passes for a free country in Africa these days. I can't stop you from travelling there,' Carmel said.

'Then I'll take that as a yes.'

15

Jan had watched the farmhouse all day and noted the extra security patrols and the police cars cruising past the farm every three hours. The police and the undertrained security guards couldn't help but fall into a pattern. It would still be easy enough to get what he wanted.

He'd had little time to get bored. He had been on his mobile phone so much that he'd needed to pull the portable roll-out solar panel from his pack to charge it.

Jan had spoken to the vet whose contact number Aston had given him. The man had dismissed him at first and said that he might call Jan back. The vet had been cautious, and had obviously called Aston to check out his credentials, and then phoned him back. When Jan had told him he needed him to be available with his dart gun, enough M99 to tranquillise a dozen small animals, and possibly an aircraft within two days, the vet had said, 'Not possible.'

'Talk to the man in Joburg,' Jan had said, meaning Aston. 'Ask him how much money's involved.'

Again the man had called him back after just a few minutes. 'OK. I can do tomorrow. I have to be at an anti-poaching seminar in the Kruger Park the day after, so tomorrow would be better for me.'

'And the aircraft?'

'I've used a helicopter in the past. I've checked with the pilot, he can also do tomorrow.'

Aston got off the phone to the vet, again. The white animal doctor was a nervous man, as well he should be, Aston thought. The risks, but also the rewards, were higher for him than if Aston had been using one of the gangs of Mozambican poachers he sometimes employed.

The vet needed to be repeatedly assured that security was tight and that the money would be worth him betraying his profession. In the eyes of many South Africans the vet would be considered a far worse criminal than a poorly paid black poacher armed with an AK-47. But Aston had to pay the vet far more to use a dart than he would have paid the hunter who used a bullet.

The vet and his tame helicopter pilot – someone else many whites would have gladly lynched, even though it was they who had nearly wiped the rhino out through big-game hunting by the early twentieth century – had delivered five rhino horns to Aston so far. The vet had begun his foray across the line into crime by shooting a white rhino in the Letaba Ranch game reserve, on the northwestern border of the Kruger Park. He'd used a dart full of the opiate-derivative drug M99 from the helicopter and had then landed and sawn off the horn. Afterwards the vet had administered Naltrexone, the antidote to the M99, and the rhino had lurched to its feet, little worse for wear, as the helicopter had taken off.

Aston had later told the vet he had been foolish, but the

man had been indignant, claiming that it was better to leave the rhino alive. The action had salved the man's conscience and, as he had pointed out, it made sense from a commercial point of view as the rhino would eventually regrow its horn and they could target it again in the future.

'You have betrayed yourself,' Aston had said.

The man had not understood his foolishness, so Aston had had to explain it to him, with the patience of a father talking down to a smart but naive child. 'It is not new, taking down a rhino with M99 in a dart gun. It is done by others because it is quieter than a bullet. By reviving the rhino, though, you have told the landowners and the police and the national parks' criminal investigations division that the person who darted that rhino cares for animals. Who cares for animals yet knows how to load and fire a dart filled with potentially deadly drugs? A veterinarian. You have narrowed the police's search for you, and established a modus operandi by which they will find you.'

The white man had suddenly grown paler.

These days, when the vet shot a rhino with M99, he didn't revive it. Aston knew that once men crossed the line that separated criminals from law-abiding citizens there was no going back, and there was no such thing as degrees of right and wrong. It was the same as being an *Inyanga* who was prepared to deal in the strongest *muti*. Some traditional healers, particularly the female *Sangomas*, who were spiritualistic diviners and healers rather than physicians and herbalists like Aston, would publicly deplore many of the treatments Aston prescribed. Other *Inyangas* stopped short of prescribing illegal cures. But Aston knew that many of those same healers who expressed revulsion at the rape of a child to cure

AIDS, or the killing of wild vultures, or the removal of a person's eye or internal organs while they were still alive, were secretly envious of his decision to cross those particular lines. The whites decried the killing of vultures – repugnant birds in Aston's mind – but everyone knew that sleeping with a dead vulture's head under one's pillow gave one the ability to foresee next week's lottery numbers, thanks to the vulture's extraordinary eyesight in life. Likewise, there was no *muti* stronger than that made from human body parts – especially when taken from the donor while they still lived. The power was in their pain, and in their screams, as an eye was gouged from their face, or in the last minutes of life as their belly was slit or their chest cleaved.

What Aston thought was criminal was the actions of *Inyangas* who resorted to digging up bodies from cemeteries or paying mortuary assistants for body parts. Aston had held the beating heart of an albino boy in his hand and the tortured screams of the child had filled the organ with immense power. There was no substitute for harvesting the proper way – from a live donor.

Aston had seen worse things in Rwanda during his time there as a soldier and peacekeeper. The Rwandans had killed because of jealousy and because they were incited to rage and murder by short-sighted, greedy politicians. Aston could not countenance killing for such trivial reasons. If he killed an albino it was to ensure a Mozambican fishing village's catch was better this year than last; if he took an eye from a child it was to help a big man, an important man, recover from a disease. If a paying customer could cure his AIDS by screwing a girl a few years earlier than her uncle or father would have done anyway, then what was the problem?

Aston checked his watch. By now he should have heard from Robert Banda, his paid assassin in Livingstone. He dialled the man's number, but the call went through to voicemail. He scrolled through his phone's address book and found the number for a detective inspector at Livingstone Police Station. The man was a valuable business contact who had overseen the movement of ivory from elephants killed in the villages along the Zambezi River through to Mozambique where it found its way, via Aston's networks, onto Chinese ships in Beira harbour.

'*Ensha*, how are things in Zambia, my friend?'

'*Ensha*, Aston. Ah they are fine, and are you well in *e-goli*, the land of gold, my friend?' the policeman chuckled.

'Ah yes, I am fine. I was just calling to see how things are going in Livingstone. Have you been busy lately?'

There was a pause while the inspector deciphered Aston's question. 'Ah yes, my friend. Very busy. Just last night a man was killed while trying to break into the Bousson property, upriver from the falls. Do you know it?'

'Ah, the crazy do-gooder Frenchman who runs a private zoo? I have heard of him.'

The detective laughed again. 'Yes, he is the one. Although he calls his place a "rehabilitation centre". The intruder was armed with a gun and it appears he was trying to break into the room of one of the Frenchman's guests, to rob her or maybe rape her. Bousson shot and killed him.'

'I see,' Aston said. He felt the anger rise in him, until it seemed to grip his heart and squeeze it. 'Thank you, my friend. I am sure Livingstone is better off without this criminal.'

More laughter. 'Indeed, my friend, indeed. Is there anything more I can help you with?'

Aston thought about the offer. 'No, thank you.' It was clear, from the succession of failures by the imbeciles he had employed, that if he wanted this thing done properly he would have to dirty his own hands.

No matter, he thought to himself. He remembered looking down at the albino's heart and feeling the warm blood that soaked his own hands and arms. It was time for him to regain control, and to feel that power once again: the power that came from the scream.

He knew the woman, the Australian lawyer, would be heading to either Arusha or Rwanda next. He hoped it was the latter. It would be poetic justice to end this thing where it began. He recalled the once grassy hillside in Kibeho, where the Hutu refugees had died in their thousands, and the streets of Kigali and every other town and village across the country, littered with dead Tutsis. It was in Rwanda that Aston had first heard the scream, where he had first crossed the line.

Twenty-two-year-old Private Aston Mutale took off his blue Kevlar helmet and wiped the sweat from his brow. He had been lifting dead bodies, along with Private Chinamasa, all morning, but it was only now, as Chinamasa went to relieve himself and Aston pulled his cigarettes from his pocket, that he had the opportunity to really look at one.

It was a woman. Young. Not attractive, but someone had seen fit to impregnate her. Her stomach was heavy with the baby, but a vicious blow from a panga had nearly severed her head and had ended her life – and presumably the child's moments later. Aston wondered how long it would have taken the baby to die. She had been dead some time – days, perhaps, but he had now seen enough corpses to tell the difference between a stomach bloated with foul gases and a pregnant belly.

Aston had joined the army of the Republic of Zambia to escape the poverty of his life in Livingstone, and hopefully to save enough money to set himself up as an *Inyanga*. Aston's father and his father before him had been traditional healers. His father had wanted him to go to university and study white man's medicine, as well as the old ways, but Aston's marks had not been good enough. And so he had found himself in the army, in the strange African country of Rwanda. Aston didn't really understand the reasons behind the slaughter, but he knew for certain that the inhabitants of this country were all mad. Possessed, perhaps.

The other soldiers in his platoon knew of Aston's background, and that he had been studying the preparation of medicines, talismans and curses. They came to him for advice and treatment, and for protection against the evil that lived in every street and building and tree and heart in Rwanda. Aston couldn't charge his fellow soldiers too much – their pay was as bad as his – but all the same he had amassed a tidy sum allaying the coughs and colds and sexually transmitted diseases and fears of his comrades in the 'Zambatt', the Zambian Army battalion attached to UNAMIR, the United Nations Mission in Rwanda.

Aston's father had counselled Aston from an early age that it was wrong to dabble in the darker side of traditional healing.

'Yes, but how will I know which *muti* is right and which is wrong?' he had asked his father.

His father had placed a hand on Aston's shoulder and said,

'All men know the difference between right and wrong, Aston. It is up to them to make the choice.' His father was a healer, but he was also a devout Christian who went to church every Sunday. Aston had been raised in the same way.

He knew, of course, that it would be wrong to kill or hurt another person, or to dig up a freshly buried body to harvest its eyes and organs to make *muti*, but his grandfather had muttered occasionally, much to the chagrin of Aston's father, that these were sometimes the only ingredients that would truly cure or protect someone with serious ailments or problems.

In the distance was the sound of gunfire, like the crackle of dried grass burning. Aston had been scared at first, when the RPA had begun the killing of the Hutu refugees, but he'd soon become numbed to the sounds, sights and smells of death. He knelt down beside the dead woman.

Her hands were raised, as if grasping at her assailant, or for her god. Rigor mortis had captured the terror and pain of her death. Her eyes were wide open, though virtually invisible behind the mass of crawling flies. Aston noticed that the pale skin of her right palm had been laid open and three fingers of her left hand had been lopped off. These, he knew, were what the doctors and medics called defensive wounds. He'd seen many such wounds. The woman had raised her hand to ward off the first blows of the panga and the instinctive, though futile, gesture had ensured she had died in even more pain, watching her own blood flow as her attacker delivered the killing blow to her neck.

Aston reached behind his back and felt for the bayonet that fitted to his FN self-loading rifle. He slid it from its sheath while he looked left and right again. No one was watching him, save for the eyes of a dead child, a girl of maybe eight or nine who had been killed by her own kind, friends and family perhaps; crushed to death under the feet of thousands of Hutus who had surged up to the Zambatt perimeter when the Tutsi soldiers had begun firing. Many such innocents had been trampled and others had been wounded or killed when they had been pushed into the compound fence and slashed by its razor wire.

Aston turned from the eyes. He ran his thumb along the bayonet's edge. He had never used it in action, only against straw-stuffed dummies during training. All the same, he kept the blade finely honed. A healer had many uses for a good knife. Aston reached for the woman's blouse. He pulled it open and stared for a moment at her swollen breasts. He laid the tip of the bayonet between them and lightly drew it down over her skin until he felt the bone of her sternum drop away, at the top of her distended belly.

He glanced up and down the line. His fellow soldiers were engaged in a score of different vignettes of horror. Private Chinamasa had been dragged off by a sergeant to help another man carry a wounded man to the Australian medical team. Aston knew he had to be quick. He drew a deep breath and slid the bayonet into the dead woman.

A gush of foul-smelling air hissed from the woman's stomach and Aston turned his face from the stench. He'd been expecting it, and although he was now well accustomed to the odour of death, there seemed something particularly horrible about this. Perhaps it was the dead child's spirit leaving. Aston drew the blade down towards her groin, opening her, until he could see the lifeless foetus curled in the womb.

The rush Aston felt as he dropped the bayonet and reached

in and scooped the dead child from its mother was incredible. Even from his limited training he knew of many illnesses and ailments that could be cured with the by-products of this unborn child. Healers spoke of these things, but how many ever actually got their hands, literally, on such a tiny body? Aston knew he had to be quick. He set the baby – he saw now it was a boy – back into the cavity that had once sustained it, and used his bayonet to free the nearly full-formed child from the umbilical cord. He looked around him, at the litter and corpses, and saw a square zip-up bag made of thin, cheap PVC. He undid it and tipped out its contents. Aston scooped the foetus out of the mother again and gently lowered it into the bag and zipped it up.

As he walked back to the compound carrying his grizzly souvenir, the words of his father came to him. '*All men know the difference between right and wrong, Aston . . .*'

He knew what he had just done was wrong, but all the same it excited him and he felt a power he had never known in his young life. His grandfather would probably understand how he felt right now. He had looked into the old man's eyes and seen a strength he'd never found in his religious father. He knew the old man had the courage and the power to do what needed to be done.

The light was fading and the flicker of fires silhouetted the few remaining ramshackle structures still standing. This country had gone to hell, which made what Aston had just done somehow less shocking in his mind. He had not killed the child or its mother, and although he knew his father would have been appalled at the way Aston had defiled the woman's body, he consoled himself with the knowledge that the *muti* made from the unborn child would benefit many people in need. For himself, he had taken a step in a new direction on his path to becoming a fully fledged healer. He could not turn back now. He had felt the power. He had liked it.

'Aston!'

He turned and saw Private Chinamasa running towards him, high-stepping over the body of an old man, still to be recovered.

'Did you hear the news, Aston?'

Aston shook his head, and slowly moved the zippered bag behind him, out of Chinamasa's sight. 'We are leaving tonight,' Chinamasa said. 'The platoon commander just told me. We are being relieved.'

'That is good,' Aston said, quickly turning his thoughts to the transportation of his prize. There was a sergeant back in Kigali whom Aston had helped with a treatment for the sores that had returned to the man's spear. The sergeant worked in air movements and logistics, loading and unloading the C-130 Hercules aircraft that shuttled from Lusaka to Kigali, bringing in the Zambatt's supplies. 'I can get anything into this country – and out of it,' the sergeant had boasted.

Later that night, when the tired Zambian contingent finally made it back to Kigali, Aston went to the mess hall in the military academy barracks.

'Hey, you know we have no food at this time of night. You are not allowed in here,' said one of the cooks, a middle-aged corporal dressed in camouflage trousers and a stained white singlet. The man was the shape of a football. Aston doubted there was such a thing as a thin cook in any army.

He held up his bag. 'I need to put something in the freezer.'

The cook planted his meaty hands on his indiscernible

hips. 'You cannot put whatever you wish in *my* freezer. Get out of here, soldier.'

Aston walked up to the fat man. Leaving aside the fact that Aston felt this bloated Idi Amin impersonator had no right to tell him what to do – Aston had, after all, been out on the line dodging bullets and collecting dead and dying Rwandans all day – he felt emboldened by the power the item in the bag had given him. He felt indestructible. Aston stopped a pace from the corporal and stared into his eyes.

'You're the so-called *Inyanga*, aren't you?' the corporal cook asked. The man was trying to be brave, but Aston noted his blinking eyes, and the tongue darting out to moisten fat lips. The cook reached for a small gold crucifix hanging around his neck. 'I don't believe in your mumbo jumbo, you know. The others might, but I'm not afraid of you.'

Aston leaned in closer, until his nose was just millimetres from the cook's. 'Open your freezer.'

The cook tried to hold Aston's gaze but blinked again, turned his face and took a step back. 'All right. But what is it you have in your bag?'

Aston set the bag down and unzipped it. From it he took a package wrapped in newspaper and tied up inside a plastic shopping bag. He held it up to the cook. 'Do you want to see?'

The cook shook his head.

'It's just meat. But it's mine. Touch it and you won't live to regret it.'

The cook regained some courage and squared up again, puffing out his chest. 'Are you threatening me?'

'Yes.' Aston walked out the door.

When Aston went to the kitchen the next day to retrieve his frozen parcel it was there, but it was plain as soon as he looked inside the bag that the newspaper around the foetus had been unwrapped and clumsily replaced.

'Where is the cook?' Aston asked a private standing behind a counter, sharpening a carving knife on a steel.

The man shrugged. 'I don't know. He said he was feeling ill this morning, not long after reporting for duty.'

Aston's heart began to beat faster and he felt the dread rising inside him. If the cook went to the commanding officer, Aston would be finished. 'Thanks,' he murmured to his fellow soldier. He stuffed the package back in the bag and walked briskly outside. He walked past the old Rwandan officers' candidate dormitories to the transport compound, where the quartermaster's store was located. Soldiers in T-shirts and camouflage trousers were hosing down army trucks, cleaning away the filth of this decaying country in preparation for the vehicles to be sent back to Zambia.

'Sergeant.'

'Hello Aston,' the noncommissioned officer said from behind his desk, smiling but not rising. The quartermaster sergeant was Aston's business partner, but he was also his superior.

'I have a parcel – frozen goods – that needs to get onto this afternoon's flight to Zambia please.'

The sergeant rocked back in his chair. They were alone, so he had no need to lower his voice. 'Space is at a premium now we're packing up. The aircraft is full already.'

Aston lifted the bag. 'It is small. I thought we could find a small cooler box and seal it inside.'

'I haven't seen a decent cut of meat in this entire godforsaken country,' the sergeant said, 'so I won't ask what it is. Who's going to collect it at Lusaka?'

'My grandfather, Sergeant.'

The sergeant frowned. 'But I thought your family lived in Livingstone. That's about five hundred kilometres.'

'It will be worth the journey for him, Sergeant.'

'Really? And how much will it be worth for me?'

Aston wasn't completely sure what the cargo would go for, though he imagined that his grandfather would be able to command top dollar for the tiny body parts, whether he used them for himself or on-sold all or part of the child to other healers. 'A hundred US dollars.'

The sergeant gave a low whistle, then sat up straight and fixed Aston with a cold stare. 'A hundred and fifty.'

Aston shrugged. 'It's not that important.' He turned to leave the quartermaster's office.

'Hey, hey . . . all right. Don't go.'

Aston looked back. 'Yes?'

'OK. A hundred and twenty-five. Yes?'

Aston pretended to think for a few seconds. The sergeant would have been a terrible gambler. 'Yes, all right. And one more thing, Sergeant. Would you like to make an extra hundred dollars?'

The sergeant leaned back in his chair again, feigning nonchalance. 'I suppose so.'

'You're in charge of the medical supplies, right?'

Aston clicked on the internet browser icon of the laptop in his surgery and typed in, *Johannesburg to Kigali flights*.

While he waited for the results to come up he thought about the cook. It had been many years ago, but it had been another step along the path that had led him to where he was now. Taking the baby from the dead woman's womb had been one thing, but up until then Aston had never killed a human being before.

The newspapers in Zambia reported the tragedy a few days later, of how a corporal, so traumatised by what he had seen in Rwanda (even though the fat cook had rarely set foot outside the compound in Kigali) had sought refuge in drugs – morphine carried by the Zambatt's medics – and apparently accidentally overdosed.

Through the transport sergeant Aston had also met a white man in Rwanda – a man with hair so pale and eyes so blue he could almost have been an albino. The *mzungu* was also in the import-export business. It was said he moved weapons into the country and shipped out live animals to other foreigners who paid a fortune for such things. The three had gone into business, and Aston had worked with him ever since. The white man was the boss – not because of some outdated colonial legacy but because he was a man to be feared.

16

Liesl's father had arranged for a driver to be waiting for her and Richard at the grandly titled Wonderboom National Airport outside the old three-storey red-brick terminal building.

'Do you want to hole up in Pretoria?' Liesl asked as she waved goodbye to her brother, who was waiting for the helicopter to be refuelled before flying it back to Letsitele.

Richard shook his head. 'I was thinking OR Tambo International Airport.'

'*Ja*. Me too.' Liesl gave the order to the driver as he loaded their meagre luggage into the boot of the Mercedes.

They slid into the back of the black limousine and for Richard the soft leather seats and the air conditioning were a godsend after the vibration of the helicopter and the Highveld sun streaming in through its perspex windows.

'Are you all right for money for airfares?' Liesl asked.

'What?' Richard was already losing himself in thoughts of planning the next leg of his trip, and in that sense Liesl had read his mind. 'Oh. Yes. I've got plenty of credit on my card.'

Liesl had taken her netbook out of her daypack and opened it on her lap as the driver headed south towards Johannesburg. She tapped away at the keys. 'I can't see a direct flight but there's Kenyan Airways to Nairobi and then a connection with them to Kigali. How does that sound?'

'Fine,' he said.

'All right, I'm going to book. Do you want me to book for you too? You can pay me later.'

'No thanks,' Richard said. 'But if I can use your computer I'll do mine straight after.'

'OK,' she said.

Richard stared out the window and watched the latest crop of walled residential estates whizzing by. More and more of Johannesburg's residents were moving further out of the city in a bid to escape the crime and congestion, but all they were doing was taking the problem with them. In between each new estate a new 'informal settlement', as people called shantytowns these days, had sprouted. Every new home needed a maid and a gardener or two, and these were more often than not illegal immigrants – Zimbabweans, Mozambicans and Malawians who set up their tin and cardboard shacks as fast as the developers could squeeze out their faux Tuscan villas. There was no running away from poverty, Richard thought.

'I've booked,' Liesl said, 'and I checked availability. There's room for you as well.' She handed him the netbook.

'Thanks.'

Liesl rested her head against the seat and closed her eyes. Richard looked at her. She was as beautiful as she'd been in her twenties – probably more so now she'd matured into the prime of womanhood. He wondered if he should have pursued her, both back then and now.

However, he realised it was too late.

He tapped away at the computer and managed to extricate his wallet from his back pocket without disturbing her and entered his credit card details to pay for the airfare. The cost was extortionate and would eat up most of his savings, but as he was paying for an international fare at such short notice it was only to be expected. 'What the hell,' he muttered as he selected a business-class multi-leg fare. That *would* wipe out all his savings, but he was feeling fairly fatalistic. He pushed the confirm button and imagined his money disappearing into the ether.

Liesl's lips were parted and her breaths were deep and audible. She was fast asleep, so Richard took the opportunity to open his Gmail account and begin composing a new message. Fortunately his address book was stored as it had been years since he'd emailed Jason and Denise Clemenger and he wouldn't have remembered their address otherwise.

Dear Jason and Denise,
I know it's been years since you've heard from me but I'm coming to town and was hoping you could put me in touch with Collette. I'd very much like to see her. It's very important.
Regards,
Richard

He was able to see the message successfully sent just as Liesl opened her eyes. He shut down the program. 'Sorry, hope you didn't mind but I just checked my email.'

'No problem.' Liesl stifled a yawn and looked out the car's window. 'Hey, we're almost there.'

The driver pulled up outside the international departures terminal and helped them unload their bags onto a trolley. Liesl waved away a porter in an orange uniform and tipped the driver. Richard, who got his wallet out too late, realised he had hardly any cash on him. Where he was heading wasn't a place one could travel cheap, and he suddenly regretted his extravagance in booking the business-class flights.

Richard pushed the trolley into the terminal building and slowed to a stop. Liesl checked her watch. 'The flight to Nairobi's not until just after midnight,' she said. 'It's only four now. We've still got about six hours until we need to check in.'

'Yeah, right,' Richard said. He was looking at the departure boards.

'There are plenty of restaurants and bars in between the international and domestic terminals, or we could always get a day room at one of the airport hotels.'

Richard turned from the board and looked at her.

'Hey – don't get any ideas. I wasn't suggesting . . .'

'No,' he said, 'I didn't think that.'

'Then what, Richard? Why are you looking at me like that?'

This wasn't going to be easy. He glanced up at the electronic board again. 'Liesl, my flight's boarding in just over an hour. I have to check in and go through immigration and—'

'What?'

'I'm sorry.'

'Where the hell are you going?'

Richard weighed up whether or not to tell her. He looked at his watch again.

'Richard? Talk to me. I thought we were in this thing together. I thought you said you wanted to come to Rwanda to sort this mess out and find out who's been trying to kill us?'

He grabbed his daypack and his holdall. He couldn't meet her eye. 'I don't recall saying any such thing.'

She put her hands on her hips. 'I can't believe this. You're running away?'

Richard shouldered his pack and lifted his bag. He met her stare. 'I've got some things I need to do, that's all.'

'But I . . .'

He could see the mixed emotions on her face and he hated himself for not having had the guts to tell her sooner. She was hellbent on flying to a country that neither of them knew any more and blundering about, like a foreign journalist or photographer would, until she got her story or it killed her. He didn't work that way. He guessed she wanted him with her, for support or help or whatever – she was far too independent to have said protection. Collette, on the other hand, was hopefully safe and Richard wanted to make sure she stayed that way. She could provide valuable information that might help them, but he didn't want Liesl dragging her into the limelight through a media story about the events of 1995 and of the recent attempts on their lives. 'Stay safe, Liesl.'

'Stay safe!'

People had slowed pushing their trolleys or suspended their goodbyes to watch. She was causing a scene. 'I have to go.'

Liesl dropped her hands by her sides and clenched her fists. She lowered her voice. 'At least tell me where you're going.'

If he didn't move soon check-in would close. He thought about how much she should know. 'England.'

'Back to where you came from? I wouldn't have thought your job prospects were too good there.'

He tried to ignore the barb, but it found its mark. It didn't comfort him to think she'd followed at least part of his blighted career. 'It's not what you think, Liesl.'

'Yes, it bloody well is. I was a fool to trust you. You left me behind once before and you're doing it again.'

Left me behind? He wondered where that had come from, but didn't have the time or the inclination to open up some old wound. What did she expect, that he'd call her and ask her out on a date after she'd been instrumental in breaking up his relationship with Carmel? If she had also thought she had some sort of claim on him, then he'd set some record in male blundering back in 1995, losing a fiancée, a girlfriend, a lover and a father in the space of about forty-eight hours. 'Goodbye, Liesl.'

Richard turned towards the check-in counters and walked away.

'Coward,' he heard her say behind him. He kept walking.

Liesl stood there fuming, watching Richard disappear down the wide corridor and around a corner. She scanned the area and saw a porter and beckoned him with a wave.

'Yes, madam?'

'Did you see that man I was with just now?'

'Ja.'

How could he not, Liesl thought. She'd attracted the attention of half the bloody terminal. She hated herself for losing it like that almost as much as she despised Richard right now. 'Go through to the departure desks, please, and check which flight he's checking in for.'

The man looked around him. Liesl reached into the front compartment of her daypack and pulled out a red fifty-rand note and waved it in front of him. It was five times the going rate for a porter. 'Yes, madam.'

'Don't let him see you.'

'Of course.'

Liesl moved away from the centre of the concourse to the CNA and bought herself a newspaper. The porter was back in less than two minutes.

'The Qantas flight, madam. To Sydney. He just went through.'

'Not London, not BA?'

'No, madam. British Airways check-in is at the other end of the terminal.'

She gave him the money and the man walked off, his step light. At least someone was having a good day. Richard, the bastard, had lied to her. What did he think, that she was going to come chasing him through the boarding gates like some mad stalker? She was better off without him. Apart from his foppish good looks she didn't know what she'd seen in him. He'd seemed principled and courageous, but perhaps war just brought out the best in some people.

Liesl went into the open-plan cafe and bar at the end of the terminal, sat down and ordered a brandy and Coke. She opened her netbook and clicked on Outlook Express. When the messages downloaded she was surprised to see one from Richard.

Dear Liesl,

Sorry. I wanted to tell you, but thought it was best to just slip away. Carmel is on her way to Rwanda as well. You have her email, but I've attached her mobile number at the bottom of this message. It might pay to touch base with her. She's looking for the same thing as us, and will have better resources and hopefully some protection.

R.

Great, Liesl said to herself as the waiter set down her drink. I'm not doing this by myself, I'm doing it with Richard's old girlfriend, who hates me.

While Aston was waiting for his Gucci luggage to be wrapped in cling film – a free service provided by Kenya Airways in an attempt to thwart Johannesburg's notoriously light-fingered baggage handlers – he saw the woman.

He watched her kick her pack along the polished floor as the economy-class queue inched painfully slowly towards the check-in desks for the Nairobi flight. Aston's Rolex said it was just after 10 pm. He was checking into business class so he moved to the counter virtually as soon as the men operating the wrapping machine were finished. When he had checked in and been issued his boarding pass, he walked between the counters towards immigration, but lingered in the corridor before the security checkpoint so he could use his mobile phone. He dialled the number of Jan Venter, the mercenary.

'*Ja*,' the man answered after one ring.

'Are you watching the farmhouse?'

'*Ja*, of course.'

'Any change?'

'No, it's all quiet.'

'Yes,' Aston balled the fingers of his fist so tight that he felt his fingernails dig into his palm. 'I know it's all quiet because the doctor and the photographer woman are not there.'

'What do you mean? I've been watching them all day and half the night. They went nowhere. Her Facebook page says she's at home looking forward to dinner with her parents.'

'Well, I've just been watching the woman check in to a flight bound for Nairobi – the same flight I'm on.'

There was a pause on the other end. '*Jissus*. What about the man?'

'I don't know,' Aston said, 'and neither do you, obviously.'

'I'll go in close tonight; find out if he's still there.'

'No! You have done enough damage already. Stay in position and be ready to hit the place and get the wild dogs on my command.' There was another pause on the other end. Aston fancied the man was bridling at Aston's tone. As well he should. Another damned incompetent.

'Very well. If I see the doctor, how can I contact you?'

'SMS me. But I doubt the woman would have left alone. Just stay in place and try not to fuck up anything else.'

Aston ended the call as the woman emerged from economy check-in and walked past him. He followed her into the queue for security, showing his boarding pass and passport.

'You can go through the express queue, sir,' the female security guard said to him, pointing to a dedicated lane and X-ray machine.

'No, it's fine,' Aston said. The woman shrugged.

Aston moved into the maze created by the bollards and barrier tape, and caught up with the woman. He was close enough to smell her perfume. Opium. Addictive; deadly.

The woman stopped at the X-ray machine and unzipped her daypack, taking out her netbook and placing it in a plastic tray.

'Shoes,' the security guard at the metal detector said to her, pointing to the woman's boots.

Aston had already taken his laptop out and placed it in a box on the roller conveyor. The woman turned and smiled at him. 'Sorry.'

He beamed at her. 'No problem at all. Take your time. We

have only bad food and warm drinks to look forward to on the other side.'

She smiled back at him. Aston took out his cellphone and coins and his Mont Blanc and put them in the tray with his computer.

As he moved through, the woman was grabbing her things. The X-ray operator kept the baggage pumping through and Aston saw the woman was having difficulty grabbing everything. 'May I?'

'Oh, thanks so much,' she said.

Aston picked up the tray containing her high-heeled boots and walked with her to a line of seats.

'That's why I never wear my high heels on business,' he said. She laughed, and he sensed it was a type of release for her. She must be nervous. She should be.

'Thank you,' she said, taking the boots from him.

'I'm sorry, I know you must get this a lot, but I've seen your face before, haven't I? On television, or in the newspapers?'

She hesitated a moment, but he knew his smile would disarm her. 'I'm a photojournalist. I write for *Escape!* Maybe you recognise me from that?'

'Ah, of course. I've read your column. I love wildlife and I'm a keen photographer.'

'Really?'

'Yes, some black people can take pictures and like to camp in the bush.'

'God, I'm sorry, I didn't mean to infer—'

She had played into his hands. He laughed loud and hearty, enough to draw a glance from the security guard. 'I'm just joking. No offence taken.'

'Well,' she said, zipping up her bag, 'none intended, believe me.'

'Are you on the Nairobi flight?' he asked as they queued for the next stop, the immigration officers.

'Yes.'

She was being guarded, but he wanted to draw it out of her, to get her to trust him. 'I am going to Nairobi, too, then connecting to Kigali, in Rwanda, tomorrow morning.'

'Well, have a safe trip,' she said, then purposely scanned the row of counters looking for the next available immigration officer.

Aston noted her body language and her clipped tone. She wasn't going to reveal her onward destination, although he was certain she was going to the same place as he was. It wasn't a good thing if she nosed around too much and got too far into the country, but on the other hand it might make his job easier.

With both the lawyer and the photographer in the country at the same time, he would be sure of killing at least two of the three people he needed gone. He would ensure Liesl Nel told him where the English doctor was before she died.

17

Just before she'd boarded the flight to Kigali, Carmel had received a brief email from Liesl on her BlackBerry advising her that she was at OR Tambo Airport in Johannesburg and would be catching the late-night flight to Nairobi.

Liesl would arrive in Nairobi tomorrow morning and get the early flight to Rwanda, which meant she was only a day behind Carmel and Henri. Carmel was annoyed. She liked people to do what she told them, not what they thought was best, particularly when it came to legal matters. She'd advised Liesl and Richard to travel to Arusha, where the tribunal sat, and the last thing she needed was for Liesl to be blundering around Rwanda. Liesl had made a point in her email of saying that Richard was not with her and was not coming to Rwanda. Carmel was still wondering what that was all about as the Kenya Airways Embraer 170 entered Rwandan airspace.

The pilot had been cruising in the clear blue sky above the clouds to escape the worst of the turbulence thrown up by the mountains and hills that punched the atmosphere like jubilant freedom fighters.

Henri was next to her, lost in his Kindle ebook reader.

There were only two seats on either side of the aisle, and the aircraft was new enough for the seats to be of still-clean leather rather than fading greasy fabric.

The flight attendants in their red slacks and white shirts dispensed Tusker beers and a nose-wrinkling beef stew and rice to the passengers, who seemed to be mostly business-people. Carmel had caught snippets of French, but Henri had nodded to the men with crew cuts in front of her and whispered: 'Belgian. They still think they own this place.'

The fasten-seatbelt sign pinged on as they descended once more into the grubby clouds. Africa was beckoning again, drawing them down into the buffeting gloom. Raindrops streaked the windows and Carmel shivered.

When they reached the bottom of the clouds she was surprised to see how low they were. It was almost as if the pilot was following the course of the valleys, as the crowns of most of the hills were lost in a mix of cloud and fog. The line between earth and sky, heaven and hell, was blurred in foggy grey.

Below it was green.

South Africa and Zambia were verdant at this time of year, swapping their dusty winter khakis for drab olive, but the endless undulating hills of Rwanda were a rich emerald cut by venous roads of blood red running slick from the misting rain.

Henri had switched off his Kindle once the descent began and he looked across her now, out the window, lost in his own thoughts. She wondered what memories this place provoked in him, and whether they were nightmares like hers.

Kigali appeared, improbably perched on a cluster of hills. Walled villas ruled from the high slopes, and more modest homes of rendered concrete, and rickety shanties, tumbled down into the valleys. From this height, it seemed not a square inch of land in the capital was left unoccupied.

Carmel drew a sharp breath, whose real cause was masked by an accompanying lurch as the Embraer bounced through a pocket of malevolent air. It wasn't turbulence, it was memory that was rushing up to meet her. The hills were either side now, the slick dark silver of the runway reaching up to catch them and draw them into the vortex of remembered evil and sadness. The first time she'd flown into this airport was in a C-130 Hercules military transport aircraft, seated on a red canvas webbing seat opposite Richard. She'd wanted to grip his hand as they landed, but they'd made a conscious decision not to sit next to each other, as their romance was a secret and they were serving in different parts of the task force – Carmel at headquarters and Richard with his medical unit. When all the peacekeepers had boarded and filed to their cramped seats in the Hercules it was an ironic twist that they'd ended up sitting facing each other. Some of the soldiers had feigned boredom or disinterest and sat with heads lolled back and eyes closed. Richard winked at her every now and then and she tried to stop herself from blushing. She really had thought she had found true love with him. She bit her lower lip.

'Mi-6 helicopters – Russian.' Henri pointed to where the trio of giant striped dragonflies sat, rotors down as though crouched and ready for action, outside a hangar on the left.

Carmel wasn't interested in military aircraft or their provenance. Sure, the Rwandan national army, the Forces Armées Rwandaises, or FAR for short, and the Interahamwe had been armed with Soviet AK-47s, but so had their opposition, the

RPA. Just as the genocide hadn't been about religion, it had also borne no links to that other great killer, ideology.

'Have you ever been to the genocide memorial?' Carmel asked as the Embraer's engines came down from the reverse-thrust high and the airliner turned towards the terminal.

'No, have you?'

'No. I never seemed to have the time and, besides, I always thought that since I'd seen the aftermath for real, I didn't need to see it laid out again in humidity-controlled display cases.'

Henri looked into her eyes, perhaps wondering, as she was, why she'd raised the subject of the memorial. 'And now?'

'I think maybe I need to see it,' Carmel said. 'I've focused on the perpetrators and the victims for years, and while I've read about the causes, I think it would help me to take a fresh look at the theories about how it happened.'

Henri was silent. Carmel thought that they were both prob-ably experiencing the same strange sensation. They'd spent much of the past seventeen years trying to forget what they'd seen, but they both knew they would be forever haunted by it as well.

Outside on the tarmac an African man in waterproof gear was guiding the pilot to his parking spot with precise waves of his hand. Carmel wondered, as she always did, if pilots actually paid any attention to these waving guys on the ground. After all, a GPS and a computer had brought them from Kenya, so was it really necessary to have a poorly paid man with a glowing wand to point you to a big painted num-ber on a runway devoid of other commercial aircraft? Was the man with the wand an anachronism from the days when aircraft had propellers and compasses, or was he a failsafe?

The world had assumed that Rwanda would autopilot itself into some sort of vaguely acceptable democracy in 1994, after the Arusha Accords, but that had just been wishful thinking. The warring parties had been guided, on and off, to the negotiating table, but the people with the glowing wands had ultimately turned their backs and the country had crashed.

The engines sighed and the seatbelt light flashed and pinged off, but the businesspeople were already on their feet opening overhead lockers and retrieving laptops and snapping out the handles of wheelie bags. The handful of tourists on the flight collected their daypacks and duty-free bags and shuffled forward.

Carmel and Henri let the other passengers bustle past them and waited until the aircraft was nearly empty before finally standing and retrieving their bags. Carmel was frightened by the task ahead. Someone, an individual or a group of people, was killing to protect a secret. She carried a residual dread of this country, but at the same time she felt her heightened state right now might be something else as well. Her heart was beating and she could feel adrenaline coursing from her heart out to her fingertips. Was she *excited* too? she wondered.

Rain still pelted the window, but the pilot had parked close to the terminal – no more than a hundred metres. 'I thought we were going to have to make a run for it. That's why I wasn't in a hurry to get out, in case the rain eased,' Henri said, putting a brave face on his reluctance. But at the foot of the covered staircase that had been driven up to the aircraft's door was a bus, its engine idling. Carmel and Henri ignored the impatient and accusatory glares from the other passengers, who were already on the bus.

'Crazy,' Carmel said as the bus lurched off on its short

journey to the terminal. 'We could have walked.'

As she looked out over the glistening runway Carmel recalled a story she had heard from an Australian soldier who had been on the first flight into this very same airport after the genocide, when the UN had finally got its act together and sent in the peacekeepers.

'The first thing we saw, as we walked down the rear ramp of the C-130,' the soldier had told her, 'was a mangy dog, trotting across the tarmac with a human head in its mouth.'

Now a country that had once imploded, with neighbours turning on each other and beating babies to death against brick walls and hamstringing women with panga slashes so they couldn't run away from rape and torture before their executioners finished them off, thought enough to put on a bus to transport thirty people a hundred metres to the airport terminal because it was raining.

Inside the terminal, Carmel knew the drill, which made it marginally easier to deal with the nonsense of African bureaucracy. To save time, she and Henri had filled in an application for a Rwandan visa online and received a letter of authorisation. Instead of presenting this to the visa payment counter, they first had to join a queue of people who were being triaged by a roaming bureaucrat in a suit. Waving the confirmation letter wasn't enough. Each passenger had to wait while the man in the suit, as polite as he was deliberate, examined their passports and visa confirmation letters. Only once he was satisfied that each applicant had spelled his or her name correctly did he allow them to move to the visa payment counter. Eventually it was Carmel's turn. Once at the counter, another man checked her passport, letter, name and numbers and then took her sixty US dollars. After that, she sidestepped two paces left to an attractive woman with braided hair who checked her passport again and stamped the visa.

Thanks to the time all this had taken, Carmel didn't have to wait to collect her checked baggage. She grabbed her bag off the carousel and loaded it onto a trolley and waited for Henri to catch up and collect his luggage. Carmel led on, past the customs officers, who were there more as a formality than to fleece visitors or returning residents of phantom duties, but she was stopped short by the sight of a man with a knife in his hand.

Carmel's brain told her that it would be very unlikely for a thief or madman armed with a blade to be waiting in ambush inside the airport's *cordon sanitaire*, but neither would her mind ever be totally free of images of white bone laid bare beneath red slash wounds.

'Your plastic bag, please,' the man said, smiling an apology.

Carmel's heart dropped back a gear when she saw that instead of a knife blade the man carried a pair of scissors. 'Excuse me?' she asked.

'I am sorry, but non-biodegradable plastic is banned in Rwanda.' He pointed at the clear plastic wrapping around her wheelie bag.

'Oh. OK. That's new.' Carmel waited while the man bent to her bag, carefully but quickly snipped through the layers of plastic wrap, then balled it and tossed it in a rubbish bin.

'And plastic bags?'

'Also banned, madam.'

'That's fantastic,' she said, meaning it. Too much of Africa was awash with plastic 'flowers' – countless millions of cheap plastic shopping bags. In isolated areas, such as South Africa's national parks, the park shops had been able to ban plastic bags in favour of paper, but Carmel had never heard of a first, let alone third, world country serious enough about the environment to ban plastic packaging.

'The plastic bag ban has been in force for a couple of years now,' Henri said as the security wrapping was removed from his bag. It's a great idea. Somehow symbolic, too, I think, of the change in rule here.'

A man dressed in black trousers and a long matching smock trimmed at the cuffs and hem with orange embroidery stood holding a sign with Carmel's name on it. She walked to him, smiled and introduced herself.

'I am Lucien,' he smiled back. 'Please let me take your bags.'

They followed Lucien out of the terminal. The rain had eased, but they walked briskly to avoid the light drops towards a minibus with the Hôtel des Mille Collines' stylised three hilltops on the side. They climbed in and said hello to the driver as Lucien loaded the baggage then took the front passenger seat. 'Welcome to Kigali,' he said. 'This is your first visit?'

'No.'

The silence that followed Carmel's answer was enough for the two men up front. Perhaps they were relieved that she and Henri weren't first-timers, with a million questions they wanted to ask about the genocide. The four of them settled into the companionable silence of veterans.

Carmel looked at the backs of the men's heads and wondered, as she invariably did when she returned to this blighted country, what their stories were. Had they been active participants or unwilling accomplices in the genocide? If they weren't *génocidaires*, had they done nothing to stop the killing? Were they Hutu or Tutsi? Despite her repeated visits she'd never been able to correctly guess on a first meeting. Were they Tutsi returnees, or were they one or two of the remarkably lucky Tutsi survivors of the murderous rampage of 1994?

Lucky? No, that wasn't the right word. She knew from the interviews she'd carried out with survivors that many felt the opposite. Carmel remembered one woman in particular who had been forced to watch as her two children, a boy and a girl aged four and seven, were slaughtered in front of her. The woman had been raped and then hacked at with a panga by the drunken Interahamwe man who had killed her children. She had been left for dead, minus a hand and with a brutal gash on the side of her neck. The man had been too high or too inebriated, or both, to do the job properly. 'I wish I had died, with my children,' the woman had told Carmel. 'Then my pain would have ended. Instead, I will carry it all my life, until it finally kills me.'

'What are you thinking?' Henri asked.

She shrugged. 'The usual. And you?'

He nodded. 'The stories, the images I have of that time . . . it's hard in some ways to connect it to how the place is now, but when I see a familiar building or street, then it's so easy.'

'I know what you mean.'

She had come here with other lawyers from the ICTR who hadn't been in Rwanda for the genocide or its aftermath, and it had been impossible to answer their questions, to convey what she'd seen, to provide the explanations they sought. With Henri she didn't need to analyse or shock or console or explore. They had both seen the horror. It didn't make it any easier to live with, but at least they didn't have to talk about it.

'Look,' he said, pointing out the window, 'the twenty-first century. Perhaps it will be better for my country than the twentieth.'

Carmel looked at the big digital billboard, broadcasting a succession of mini videos promoting Japanese cameras, a local hotel, a Korean car brand. Carmel hadn't seen this form of advertising anywhere else in the world, and guessed it probably would have been banned in Australia as it would be too distracting to drivers.

Horns blared around her as the Kigali traffic closed in on them. Banning plastic bags to protect the environment was probably an easier goal for the Rwandan government than getting people to drive more safely, she thought. Motos – small motorcycles used to transport fare-paying pillion passengers – swarmed around the minibus like bothersome tsetse flies, their riders in bright yellow vests sounding their horns with annoying regularity.

The setting sun, filtered through wood smoke and the belching exhausts of Kigali's battered and ill-maintained vehicles, painted the clouds a rich gold and glittered off new, glass-clad office buildings. In between the towers were one- and two-storey walk-ups, their walls covered with more traditional handpainted murals advertising mechanics' garages and washing powder. The old and the new sat side by side in a fascinating montage.

The driver entered the big Place De L'Unité National roundabout and weaved his way across three ragged, shifting lanes of traffic until he came to the Avenue de la République exit that took them further up a hill, towards the more expensive part of Kigali, home to government residences and the administrative district, the foreign embassies, and the Hôtel des Mille Collines.

A security guard raised a boom gate and they drove through the gates. 'The Hotel Rwanda,' Carmel said, using the common name for the Mille Collines. It had been bestowed on the hotel after the movie, *Hotel Rwanda*, about the manager who had provided sanctuary there to hundreds of Tutsis and moderate Hutus during the genocide.

Carmel could see even before entering that the hotel had undergone some renovations and extensions. The foyer of the hotel looked pristine, except for the muddy footprints on the polished white floor tiles, apparently left by the group of six bedraggled-looking tourists who were checking in ahead of Carmel and Henri. Carmel picked up the familiar Australian accents as one of the women asked about getting her boots washed.

While she was waiting, Carmel took out her iPhone and checked her emails. There was nothing from the ICTR in Arusha. She was annoyed, as she'd marked her message to her boss, an English barrister and full-time UN employee named Kellie White, as high priority. The subject line had read, *Witness protection – life threatening*, so it was unlikely Kellie could have ignored it. In the email Carmel had outlined the recent attempts on the lives of Liesl and Richard, and her own close brush in Livingstone. Carmel had also suggested the ICTR communicate formally with the Thai police and urge them to re-examine the death of Mike Ioannou in the light of the three failed attacks. It was clear someone was trying to kill everyone with any information about the photo Liesl had taken.

'What is it?' Henri asked, perhaps seeing the annoyance in her face.

'Nothing, and that's the problem.'

'Are you Australian?'

Carmel looked up from her phone to see the man who had addressed her, one of the group of tourists, a man with short silver hair. 'Yes.'

'Here to see the mountain gorillas? We've just been up gorilla tracking. It was awesome, but pretty muddy.' He laughed.

A cleaner was busy mopping up around the party, not even waiting for the group to finish checking in. Carmel remembered human cadavers lying where they had fallen in Ruhengeri, where these tourists had just come from; bodies left like litter; a food source for feral dogs and birds of prey. 'No.'

'Oh,' said the man who, rebuked, went back to his companions.

'You've never seen the mountain gorillas?' Henri asked her.

'I have, but we're not here to sightsee, Henri.'

'We should go anyway,' Henri said. 'They are amazing creatures.'

Carmel lowered her voice. 'I hardly think we have the time, given what's happened lately.'

Henri shrugged. 'I still have to go to Ruhengeri, near the Volcanoes National Park. That's where the rescued chimpanzee is. He was smuggled across the border from Congo and is being kept there. Maybe you should book a trekking permit and make the most of our visit?'

Carmel was amazed that Henri could be talking of viewing primates when she was about to embark on an investigation that could lead them both into more danger. She wondered whether he fully appreciated the seriousness of the situation. Perhaps it was time to tell him everything she knew – everything that had happened so far, to Mike, Liesl and Richard.

The Australians finally got their room keys and moved off, leaving a fresh trail of mud on the tiles. The cleaner, who had been hovering nearby, followed their spoor to the lift. Carmel wondered what kind of mess the hotel must have been when there were a thousand or more people crammed in here hiding from the Interahamwe.

'Shall we meet at the bar for a drink in, say, half an hour?' Henri asked once they had checked in.

Carmel checked her watch. She had more work to do. There were more emails to be sent, including one to the investigators in Arusha who also hadn't replied to her request for information about the identities of the men in Liesl's photo. She half wondered if there might be some communications problem at the ICTR – if the email server was down. It seemed as though all contact between her and her employers had been suspended. She was tired, but she needed to eat, and it would be more pleasant – even more reassuring – to be with Henri than sitting alone in her suite eating room service food. Besides, she could always keep an eye out for emails on her phone at the bar. 'All right.'

Getting out on the second floor, Carmel was greeted by a fresco of a lion on the wall. The decoration was new, and seemed slightly out of place to her. Try as she might, she couldn't get her head around the idea of people visiting Rwanda as tourists; of the country as a big-game safari destination. She knew about the role of research and tourism in stopping the decline in numbers of the endangered

mountain gorillas, but to her a word-association game beginning with Rwanda always ended with death.

Carmel located her room and tipped the porter who had
carried her bags into the room. When he left she opened the
sliding glass doors and stepped out onto the narrow balcony.
The sky was a darkening red now, the valley in front of her
dotted with lights. Off to her left a squadron of kites wheeled
and dived over a construction site. The sight of the birds sent
a chill down her spine. They, and the crows, had been everywhere in 1995, feeding off the rotting flesh of dead bodies.
She wondered what was drawing these birds, and hoped to
God the construction hadn't unearthed more bodies. It was
possible, she knew, as mass graves were still being uncovered
all over the country.

She leaned her elbows on the balcony railing and wondered if she had done the right thing, coming straight back
to Rwanda. The sensible thing would probably have been to
go to Arusha and set the creaky, squeaky wheels of the UN
in motion. She would have been safer there, but what of the
others involved in this thing? Whoever was trying to kill the
people who had seen that photo had the power to reach across
continents. Carmel knew the answer to who was behind this
thing was here in Rwanda.

It was hard, being here again. She knew that each time
she visited part of her had hoped she would never again
have to set foot in this country and that, paradoxically, at
the same time she had always known it was her destiny to
return. Rwanda had cost her the love of her life, and probably a chunk of her sanity. Her descent into alcohol abuse
and losing her job . . . it all stemmed from her desire to forget what she'd seen and who she had become. It had defined

the second half of her life. Africa was in her blood now, not in the form of a love potion, but as an addictive, poisonous drug that was consuming her. Perhaps this time, once this was done, she would be able to go through withdrawal and free herself from Africa's hold.

As she looked out over the city she felt the fear and sadness rise inside her. She took deep breaths to try to control it, but her grief began to surface again. On its crest were the images she had tried hardest to forget – the body of the baby exhumed from the latrine pit in Butare; the corpses in the church, locked inside by their priest who then stood aside as the Interahamwe tossed in hand grenades; the look on Richard's face when he realised he'd been caught out. This place held nothing but bad memories for her, yet time and again she dashed herself against it.

The sobs came from deep within her and they shook her body as the tears rolled down her cheeks. She clung to the balcony railing to stop herself from falling.

Henri sat at a stool at the hotel bar, which was a rectangular island under a large thatched shelter by the pool. Even though it was dark, a couple of young Rwandan boys, their fat bellies attesting to their parents' wealth, were locked in a ceaseless pattern of bombing into the water, climbing out, running up the grass and jumping in over and over.

The whore on the far side of the bar smiled at him again, over her umbrella-decorated Coke. He gave what he hoped was a polite but uninterested smile, but she took it as an acknowledgement and slowly ran a finger up and down the dewy side of her glass. He remembered this place back in late '94, when the pool was nearly empty from the Tutsis who'd stayed here and used cleaning women's buckets to scoop out the water to drink and cook with. The Belgian chef who ran the restaurant on the top floor also ran prostitutes, and it was a given that if you wanted to eat in the Hotel Rwanda the meal came with a girl as a side order. And you had to pay the chef for both.

Times had changed. The hotel's foyer and rooms had undergone a facelift so that the place looked like every other bland Sofitel or Ibis or Holiday Inn around the world, and most of the hookers had moved downstairs to this pool bar, where they now preyed on visiting western businessmen and local fat cats.

He was relieved when he saw Carmel walk across to the bar. He stood to greet her, and took her hand, to show the prostitute once and for all that he was taken, and because he liked the feel of Carmel's smooth skin.

'Enchanted.'

'Kiss it and I'll slap you,' she said.

He laughed. 'Are you all right?'

'Yes, why?'

Her eyes were red and her face looked tired, as if some of the life had drained from her body through her tear ducts. This place had that effect on returnees, he remembered. 'No, nothing. It's just that I know it can be trying, coming back to this part of Africa.'

She shrugged. 'Is that Primus you're drinking?'

He nodded. 'Would you like one?'

'No thanks, but I remember it. Watery. I'll have a Coke Light, please.'

He ordered, then asked: 'Where are you going to start your search tomorrow?'

'The Ministry of Justice.' She took a long sip of her drink and half wished she was weak enough to have alcohol again. 'I know one of the country's senior prosecutors. We worked together for a while, even though the ICTR and the local authorities haven't always seen eye to eye.'

Henri shifted on his bar stool so the working girl couldn't keep catching his eye. 'To tell you the truth, I haven't paid much attention to the prosecutions. What's the problem – I thought you would have all been on the same team, no?'

'Yes and no,' Carmel said. 'That's a bit simplistic. We – that is the ICTR – are primarily concerned with prosecuting the big men behind the genocide, the architects of it, and those responsible for inciting the people to kill. Sure, we're after some of the mass murderers, but we just don't have the resources or the time to prosecute every killer. That's being left to the Rwandan judicial system and the Gacaca village courts. There were more than a hundred thousand people indicted for crimes relating to the genocide.'

'That's quite a backlog. But why is there friction between the ICTR and the Rwandan judicial system?'

'Rwanda still has the death penalty, but the ICTR doesn't. There's a strong feeling in Rwanda that those most respons- ible for the genocide may live out their days in comparatively comfortable prisons in The Hague, while the middle-ranking killers will be executed. It doesn't seem fair to many people.'

'And what do you think?'

Carmel slumped forward a bit. 'I can see both sides. I'm duty-bound to stick to the letter of the laws I work under and prosecute to the best of my ability. I've been involved in the incarceration of a few very bad people. I don't believe in the death penalty, but I can understand how incensed some people here may be at the outcomes from the ICTR. I mean, there are women in Rwanda, Tutsis and Hutu women who were married to Tutsi men, who were gang raped during the genocide by men who were known to be HIV positive. They were spared a bullet or a blow from a machete so that they would die of AIDS, in long-lasting shame. That is some evil shit, and yet the organisers of this evil who are in the ICTR detention facilities are getting three meals a day and anti-retrovirals to keep their HIV under control. Is that justice? I don't know.'

'What makes you think the people who want to stop your investigation into the photo are here in Rwanda, and not elsewhere?' Henri asked.

'It's just a hunch. Most of the stuff in Mike Ioannou's files is about his interviews with Liesl and Richard, but Mike spent a lot of time in Rwanda over the last few months. He kept his cards close to his chest, so no one really knew what he was up to, but he was digging around here.'

Henri nodded. 'And what makes you think this white man in the photograph would still be in Rwanda after all these years?'

She shrugged. 'I don't care if he is or isn't, or what colour he is. The man in the picture, holding up the picture of the white guy and the others, told Richard Dunlop that everything that had happened in Rwanda was because of this photograph.'

'It could be nothing.' Henri waved a hand in the air. 'Perhaps the old man was trying to big-note himself so that he and his family would get preferential treatment. The RPA was trying to round up Hutu criminals at Kibeho, as well as disperse the innocents and force them to go home. Perhaps the man feared for his life, if he was arrested.'

'Perhaps,' Carmel concurred, 'but that doesn't explain why

someone is trying to kill everyone who saw that photo and heard the old man's story. I need to find out who he was and who the people are in that picture. Look, if you want out, that's fine by me. I shouldn't be involving you in any investigation anyway. Please, if you want to go and collect your chimp tomorrow and go back to Zambia, that is totally fine with me, Henri.'

He shook his head. 'No. No way. I want to come with you, to help if I can, and I stand by my earlier offer – and I do believe I can help you find that white man. I'm sure I can find my old contacts in the mountains; if not, the people looking after the chimp may be good sources of information, which is why you should go there with me.'

'To the Volcanoes National Park? Gorilla country?'

He saw she still wasn't convinced. 'Yes. Ruhengeri, the major town near the park, was a stronghold of Hutu Power. If there are powerful Hutus responsible for the genocide still in hiding somewhere, they could be there. It's an easy place to get lost in. Also, many of the *génocidaires*, both big fish and little fish, escaped through that region to Goma, across the border in the Democratic Republic of Congo, when the Tutsi army returned and took over the country.'

'I hope this investigation doesn't lead us into the DRC. There's no way I'd be able to go over there, and I have no contacts or jurisdiction there. Ironically, the country where most of the war criminals are now living in exile is one of those we don't have an extradition treaty with.'

'I'm pleased you just said "us",' Henri said. 'I'm still in this with you, Carmel. But now we must eat.'

'Spoken like a true Frenchman.'

18

It was well after dark when Liesl's plane landed at Kigali International Airport. She'd been mildly annoyed to find the overweight but well-dressed Zambian businessman who had struck up a conversation with her at Johannesburg Airport was on the same flight as her again to Rwanda.

When she climbed into the Hôtel des Mille Collines mini-bus she took the rearmost seat and sat her backpack beside her to stop him from squeezing in. He was polite, and had done nothing improper, but all the same he gave her the creeps.

'I know it may seem forward of me,' he said to her as they queued behind a couple of American tourists at the hotel while they waited to check in, 'but would you care to join me for a drink in the hotel bar after you've freshened up? I promise you, it is simply to talk about Rwanda – in case you need any help with your itinerary or your travel articles. My name is Aston, by the way.'

'No, thank you,' she replied, and was then saved by the clerk on reception.

'Well, if you change your mind . . .' Aston said after he'd been issued his key.

'I'm fine, really.' Liesl lingered by a stand of tourist bro-chures at the end of the counter. When the lift doors closed on Aston she said to the man behind the counter, 'Excuse me?'

'Yes, madam?'

'I have an acquaintance staying here. Her name is Carmel Shang. She arrived earlier this evening.'

'Yes, madam.' The clerk tapped his computer keys and checked the screen. 'She is in room two-one-two.'

'Can you call her please?'

'Ah, she and the gentleman have gone out to dinner.'

'Gentleman? Really? Do you know where?'

The clerk shrugged. 'I am not sure. They asked about the American Club, which was located across the road from the hotel.'

'Yes, I know it,' Liesl said. She'd been drunk there many times. 'You said "was"?'

'Yes, madam. The American Club has closed. It is now an Indian restaurant. I also recommended Chez Robert to the lady and gentleman, so if they are not in the Indian restau-rant they may be in the French one. It is also nearby.'

'Thanks.' Liesl took her bag upstairs and found her room. She went to the bathroom, splashed water on her face, brushed her teeth and took her hairbrush from her daypack and ran it through her hair. Rummaging in her bag, she found the half-jack of vodka she'd bought at Johannesburg airport, unscrewed it and took a couple of slugs.

She left her room and went back down through reception and out into the night. She was pleased Carmel and whoever she was with had gone out as it would mean she could get another drink without bumping into the creepy Zambian in the hotel bar, or being forced to order room service. Liesl walked into the night. The temperature had dropped and she felt a slight mist on the breeze.

'Howzit,' Liesl said to the security guard as she walked past the booth at the entrance to the hotel. He smiled and touched his cap. She knew the club – or restaurant as it was now – was just across the other side of the roundabout. She didn't feel in danger; Rwanda had a reputation for low street crime now that the population had got mass murder out of its blood.

She forced herself to remember to look left instead of right when crossing the road, then headed over. She passed a trio of fairly badly interpreted statues of mountain gorillas. Her emails to her editor and to several tour companies who advertised regularly with *Escape!* had paid off. One of the operators had agreed to comp her – to give her complimentary accommodation – at a lodge just outside the Volcanoes National Park, and her long-suffering editor had agreed that the magazine would cover the five hundred US dollars for a gorilla-tracking permit. The tour operator had had a cancellation for the day after next, so fortune was smiling on her. She had paid her own airfares, but figured she could claim them back later on expenses. Her father was organising to transport the BMW loaner back to Johannesburg. It was ridiculous that she should have to work while attempting to find out who was trying to kill her, but despite her parents' wealth, Liesl was serious about her financial independence. Besides, her father would kill her if he knew where she was.

Liesl was on edge as she walked down the darkened Avenue du Roi Baudouin, but the nervous tension was almost intoxicating. It was, she realised, like being in pursuit of a good, hard news story again. If she found out the significance of the photo she'd taken all those years ago and if, say, it led to the prosecution of some major war criminal, then she might have an even bigger story she could sell to one of the broadsheets back in South Africa, or even to one of the big international news agencies. She'd left that world because she could no longer cut it, but she missed it too.

What had once been the simple whitewashed walls of the American Club were now decorated with coloured light bulbs and a painted sign that said *Royal Garden Restaurant.*

Liesl walked down the same old steps, but the place had undergone a Bollywood makeover. The basketball hoop was still up, but tables had encroached onto the court. The small pool in the corner, in which she'd once ended up after being thrown in by a marine, was now a rather neglected water feature. The food, however, smelled better than the greasy chips and burgers and burnt barbecue.

She hadn't seen Carmel Shang in seventeen years, but she recognised her at the outdoor table straightaway. It was only partly because she and the guy were one of only two non-African or non-Indian parties in the half-full restaurant. Carmel still had that ice-maiden lawyer look about her, and her part-Chinese heritage meant her skin and lustrous hair were slow to age. Her face was a little pinched and drawn – no fat there – but her mouth was still sexy and pouty and her dark eyes were just as accusatory as they'd been all those years ago. Liesl took a deep breath and walked over.

Carmel stayed seated. 'Liesl.'

The man stood. 'Hello. My name is Henri Bousson, how do you do?' He held out his hand.

Liesl thought the politeness and smile were a little forced and wondered what Carmel had said to him about her. Still, she took his hand and returned the smile. He was handsome, whoever he was.

'Please, won't you join us?' he said.

Liesl let Henri seat her, briefly enjoying his old-fashioned manners even if they were a bit of an act. She noticed the pointy icicles in Carmel's eyes. 'Good flight?'

Carmel banished the small talk. 'You shouldn't be here,' she said.

Liesl was tired and dirty – she hadn't showered since she'd left her parents' place the previous morning. She'd known this meeting wasn't going to be easy but this woman was already doing her best to piss her off. 'Someone tried to kill me, and Richard, because of your crusading.'

'It's not "crusading", Liesl, it's the law.'

'Well, you know what they say about the law . . .'

'It is, as the English say, an ass?' Henri picked up the bottle of South African red and held it over Liesl's glass. She nodded. He poured. 'The goat vindaloo is very good.'

Liesl noticed they were halfway through their meals and her stomach rumbled. She called the waiter over. 'I'll have the goat vindaloo, please. And another bottle of the red.'

Henri smiled at her, and Liesl saw the frown deepen on Carmel's face.

'What are you doing here? What do you hope to achieve exactly?' Carmel asked.

Liesl took a sip of wine and put her glass down on the table. 'I'm actually here on a work assignment, to photograph the mountain gorillas. I might go see the chimps at Nyungwe National Park as well, if I have time.'

'We're going to see the mountain gorillas also,' Henri chimed in.

Carmel looked at him. '*We* are not. Listen, if you're planning on conducting some amateur investigation—'

'You said in your email that you wanted to see me,' Liesl interrupted, 'and then you subpoenaed me – well, here I am.'

'I directed you to go to Arusha, where the ICTR's offices are.'

'Well, then I'll kill two birds while I'm here. You can ask me whatever you want and then I'll go ahead and get my work done and then fly back to South Africa and wait until whoever is trying to kill me gets the job done properly. OK?'

'What do you think of the wine, Liesl?' Henri asked.

She looked at him, wondering what he was trying to do. Defuse the tension, she guessed. 'It's all right. It's a Nederburg; you'd pay about fifty rand for it in South Africa.'

Henri sighed. 'I just paid fifty US dollars for it here. This country has become so expensive. Have you travelled much in this part of Africa? You are a photographer, yes?'

Carmel sat back in her chair and folded her arms. Her meal was only half-eaten. Liesl wondered why this Frenchman was flirting with her. What had he said his name was? Bousson? Yes, that was it. Something clicked in her memory. 'I know your name.'

He shrugged and raised his hands, then went back to his curry. 'It is possible. Your magazine covers matters of wildlife conservation, and that is my business as well.'

'Yes, that's it. You own the animal rehabilitation place in Zambia – Livingstone, right?'

'*C'est moi.*'

'How do you fit into all this?' Liesl asked.

'Henri has come to Rwanda to collect an orphaned chimp which he's going to take back to Livingstone to try and integrate it with his captive troop,' Carmel said before Henri could answer. Liesl couldn't help but wonder if she was trying to keep her attention away from Henri. Perhaps there was something between the lawyer and the scruffily attractive Frenchman.

'And that's all?' Liesl looked back to Henri, who in turn looked at Carmel, as if waiting for permission to speak.

'That is *all*,' Carmel said. 'I'm tired, and I don't share Henri's enthusiasm for the curry. Please excuse me, Henri, I'm going back to my room.'

Henri shifted his chair back and wiped his lips with the serviette. He gave Liesl an apologetic tilt of his head and began to get up.

Carmel put a hand on his shoulder. 'No, stay. Finish your dinner and your *expensive* wine.'

Henri looked from woman to woman, as if trying to work out what the most chivalrous course of action was.

'No offence, Henri,' Carmel said, reaching in her handbag and pulling out some US dollars, 'but I need some time alone right now. I have work emails to do and I need to think about tomorrow. Liesl, shall we talk over breakfast?'

'Yes, *ma'am*.' Liesl raised her hand in a mock salute.

'Goodnight,' Carmel said.

Henri sat back down.

'I see she hasn't changed,' Liesl said.

Henri topped up her wine. 'You two know each other, outside of the investigation Carmel is conducting? She told me there was a photographer involved, but not that you two had met previously.'

'You could say we have some history. Not good history.' Liesl looked around the restaurant. The place was doing OK for a week night, but it had lost its character. As the American Club it had been a place of intrigue, where western spies and

Rwandan officials met and shared secrets, and death-weary aid workers and journalists blew off steam and cried into their beers before going back to the hotel to try to fuck away their guilt and grief. 'I wonder what we should call this place now – "the American Indian Club"?'

Henri drained his glass then shook his head. 'No, that is not politically correct. How about "the Native American Club"?'

Liesl laughed out loud and slid her glass across to him for a refill. He emptied the bottle as the waiter brought a second, along with Liesl's goat curry.

'Hey,' she said, chewing her first mouthful, 'I don't know if it's just because I've been eating airline *kak* for the past two days, but this tastes fantastic!'

'I told you it was good.'

'Hmmm,' she said, her mouth full. He poured more wine. She liked his eyes.

'So, you took the picture that has become the centre of so much controversy?' he said.

'Yes. I wish I hadn't. It was a good shot, but it was eclipsed on the day by another I took, of an RPA soldier executing a woman.'

'Terrible times.'

She looked across at the pool and remembered falling in. Despite all the death, there had been wild times. Was it wrong to say good times? Probably, she thought. She wondered where Richard was and what he was doing. Fucking coward.

Henri filled the void of her silent reverie. 'You were a photographer. A difficult job for a woman at the time?'

She scoffed. 'No one could accuse you French of being politically correct, could they? It was like any male-dominated profession – hard at first for women to be accepted, but eventually we turned out better than most of the men doing the job.'

'What makes a woman a better photographer?' he asked. 'Charm?'

She laughed and drank some more of her wine. She wanted to feel the numbness, but she also needed to take this handsome, but arrogant man down a peg or two. 'God no, there's little room for charm in news photography. But there was a difference, I found, between men and women shooters. The men would want to be there first, to push their way past the police tape, or past the soldiers, to get in close and get the strongest, bloodiest, most dramatic pictures.'

'Isn't that what it's all about?'

She pushed her plate away. She had wolfed down the food. 'Yes and no. The strongest image is not always the first, or the closest, or the most graphic. A woman is more likely to stand back for a moment – sometimes all it takes is a second – and look at the whole scene, not just the body on the ground or the crashed car or whatever it is. We'll look at the people on the edges of the disaster; the crying loved one, the dead child's abandoned toy, the laughing soldier. A man will bully his way into the centre of the action. Am I making sense?'

'You are.'

'Good. Then pour me some more wine, so I can get back to being senseless.'

He smiled as he poured. 'You seek escape. It's not unusual.'

'You shunned the limelight when *Escape!* did the story on you. I couldn't place you when we met, but I remember hearing about you now. We sent a journalist and a photographer up to your place to do a story on your volunteer program, and the editor was pissed off when they came back without a picture of you.'

'I value my privacy, and I don't rescue animals for personal aggrandisement or profit.'

'So the story said,' Liesl said. 'Instead, all we got were dozens of frames of pretty young female volunteers working with chimps and other endangered animals. Is that why you do it?'

'For the endangered animals?'

'You misunderstood.'

He placed his glass down hard enough for the wine to slosh, and a few drops spattered the tablecloth. 'No, I didn't misunderstand your question. You seriously think I run a wildlife rehabilitation centre in order to have sex with young female volunteers?'

'You're a man, aren't you?'

He raised his hands. 'I give up. Enough of the interrogation. It seems you are as good a journalist as you are a photographer.'

She liked him, she decided. 'What's your relationship with Carmel?'

'What do you mean?'

'You know what I mean.'

'She is one of our donors. She came to see my animals and that is when a man broke into my property. He had a gun. I have never had an intruder before. Carmel believes he was there to kill her.'

'*Ja*, well, there's a lot of that going around at the moment.'

'So I gather. But why would someone want to kill you and her and this other man over a seventeen-year-old photograph?'

'That's what I'd like to find out. The bottle's nearly empty. How about another?'

'But of course,' Henri said, smiling at her across the candles.

Richard rolled over. The bedside clock told him it was 4.33 am. There was no way he could get back to sleep. The woman lay on her side, softly snoring.

He swung his legs over the edge of the bed and walked naked to the bathroom. As he urinated he looked across to the mirror and saw his eyes were bloodshot and his grey-flecked stubble was approaching beard status. When he ran his hand over his chin he could smell her. 'Bloody hell,' he said softly.

The jet lag had woken him, but some of the substantial amount of alcohol he'd consumed on the Qantas 747 was still circulating through his body – enough to let him know that while he wasn't technically suffering a hangover, it wasn't far away. His brain was fogged in, and so, too, was the city of Sydney when he parted the curtains and looked out the seventh-floor hotel window.

He switched on his laptop then rummaged in his pack for his nylon rugby shorts and pulled them on while he waited for the computer to boot up. The arch of the Harbour Bridge was visible above the layer of fog, as was the top of Sydney Tower, off to his right. It was as if the structures were floating in a sea of cottonwool. He laced his running shoes as the email program opened.

There was a message from 'Clemenger, Jason and Denise'. He clicked on it.

Hi Richard, long time no hear, mystery man. Where are you? In Australia? Collette is living in Sydney and I'm sure she'd be interested in seeing you after all this time. Will we see you?

There was a mobile number for Collette, and a message of love from Denise, Jason Clemenger's wife. The couple lived on Sydney's upper north shore, a short commute by train from the city, where Richard was staying. He didn't know, though, if he would have time to see them. It was their daughter he needed to talk to. He wrote the phone number on the hotel notepad and was about to dial it when he remembered what time zone he was in.

He typed a quick note of thanks to Jason and Denise and the tapping woke the woman behind him. She groaned. 'What time is it?'

'Early. Go back to sleep . . .' Embarrassingly he couldn't remember her name, but noticed her bag beside the table. The luggage tag read, *K Driver*, and it came back to him, '. . . Katrina.'

She groaned again. 'I can't sleep. My body thinks it's midday. God, how much sleep did we get? A few hours?'

'Something like that.' There had been a spare seat between them on the flight, in a row of three. She was South African, from Durban originally, a green-eyed bleached-blonde beach girl who'd moved to Noosa Heads, in Queensland, with her husband and two children. She'd divorced him when she'd caught him cheating with his secretary. She'd been home to South Africa on a two-week trip back to care for her mother, who had just come out of hospital. Richard had noted that she kept her tan in good shape, and her arms.

Their flight was due into Sydney at three in the afternoon, but Katrina had told him she was planning on staying in Sydney for a night rather than getting a connecting flight through to Brisbane.

'I guess it's good to break the journey, but isn't it only an hour's flight to Brisbane?' he'd asked her.

'Yes, I could easily go all the way through, but I never get to spend a night away from home all by myself.'

She had booked a hotel, which was more than Richard had done. He'd welcomed the small talk on the flight as she'd matched him drink for drink, and had even found himself laughing a few times. She'd twirled her hair while she talked and reached across the empty seat a couple of times to lay her hand on his arm when she was making a point. He'd known he shouldn't entangle himself with her, but he couldn't help it.

Richard picked up the T-shirt he'd worn on the flight from the floor and put it on. It stank, but it would only get worse on the run. He slipped the room's key card into his shorts.

The blinds had been closed and the cabin lights turned off on the flight to allow the sensible passengers to sleep. Richard had slid into the middle seat, ostensibly so they could continue chatting without disturbing the passengers around them.

Four hours into the flight they were kissing, her tongue snaking in and out of his mouth. She was hungry.

Five hours down and she was sucking her belly in so he could unbutton her jeans and unzip her. 'It's been months,' she breathed into his ear. She slid down the seat and he parted her with his fingers.

He moved the thin blanket over them as he found her clitoris, circled it, then moved his finger up and down, pushing against her. Her short, sharp nods encouraged him, and she reached for him under the blanket as her breathing quickened. She squeezed him and whispered, 'I want to ride you, Richard.'

She unzipped his cargo pants and freed him, her hand

encircling him as she massaged his natural lubricant into him. They paused, breathless, when Katrina saw the flight attendant coming down the aisle. The woman glanced at them, and Katrina pulled the blanket over her head and started giggling.

'Shush,' he said, and would have laughed himself if she hadn't lowered her mouth to him. Richard had done a mental inventory of his daypack and could have kicked himself.

Katrina emerged from under the blanket and placed her lips against his ear as her hand replaced her mouth. 'Let's go. To the loos.'

'Oh, bollocks.'

'What?'

'I didn't pack any condoms.'

She groaned again, but not in a good way. He went back to kissing her and touching her, and she orgasmed, grinding into his hand, then fell asleep. He was frustrated, and passed the time with another in-flight movie, drinking alcohol served by a flight attendant who winked at him. He was angry at himself for forgetting the protection, and for letting himself fall for her. He knew he had a problem with women and casual sex, and he knew he'd be shot of Katrina within twenty-four hours.

When she'd woken, smiling sheepishly, they'd kissed again, tenderly this time, and the passion had been reignited, despite their fatigue, when they'd shared a cab to her hotel in Sydney.

Katrina pulled up the covers and shaded her eyes with her forearm. 'What are you doing?'

'I'm going out for a run,' Richard said. 'I need to clear my head.'

'I'll be here when you get back, as long as you're not running a marathon.'

'Thanks.'

He took his mobile phone, left the darkened room and shut the door behind him, then took the lift down to the ground floor.

Richard nodded good morning to the concierge and doorman and went outside into the cool dregs of the night. Most of the traffic on George Street was taxis whose tyres hummed and hissed on the wet road. But the rain had stopped, replaced with fog. A young Asian man on the footpath turned his face from the stiff breeze coming off the harbour.

Richard didn't really know Sydney, but figured if he stuck to the water's edge he'd be fine. It was a big harbour. He ran along Circular Quay, which had been crowded with tourists and commuters and buskers when their cab had pulled up to the hotel last night, but was now quiet and barely lit. His running shoes slapped on the pavement as he passed the giant white sails of the Opera House. Headlights buzzed along the Harbour Bridge, up to his left, but Richard turned his back on the distinctive structure and carried along on the water's edge, down the eastern side of the Opera House and along the waterfront edge of the Botanic Gardens.

He was alone, for the first time in what seemed like years. He'd run away, more than once, but always ended up in the arms of a new woman, and in the throes of another difficult situation. When he thought about it, everything that had gone wrong in his life, and the one thing that had been good, could be traced back to Rwanda. Liesl had called him a coward at the airport in Johannesburg and she was right. He ran and he ran and he ran. But he knew it would have to end one day. What Richard wanted to make sure of was that when his final reckoning came it was more or less on his terms.

He passed only two other runners, hardy souls or fellow insomniacs, as he rounded a point. On the far side he saw three Australian naval ships at anchor, and remembered the Garden Island base. He'd been to the base for a tour and cocktails there when he'd first arrived in Australia, before he'd been sent to Rwanda. It had been meant as a sunshine posting – six months on the beach in Queensland – and he'd put his hand up for a raft of pointless courses around the country so he could get in some paid sightseeing. He'd gone to Sydney for a course in marine medicine. Along the way, he'd met Carmel Shang, fallen for her, and been sent to Rwanda. And then his life had been put into a form of cryogenic suspension.

He thought about her as he ran. He had pursued her and won her love. Sure, later he'd worried about settling down too soon, but he knew now that what he'd had with Carmel had been, Juliet notwithstanding, the real deal and not just a passing infatuation. Most of his memories of Carmel were of her wearing a spotted camouflage uniform; he found it hard to imagine her as a civilian prosecutor in corporate armour. He remembered her in Rwanda, so torn over the powerlessness of her official role, so stung by the callous remarks of the soldier who couldn't understand the nightmare of being a lawyer in a country with no law. His beautiful, fragile Carmel. Of all the bad things he'd done in his life, and there had been plenty since then – the drugs, the affairs – there was nothing he felt more guilt over than cheating on Carmel.

'Fuck.' He'd lost her. He'd told himself at the time that he would end it with Juliet and be good and true to Carmel. And then he'd slept with Liesl.

He increased his pace, punishing his exhausted, booze-soaked body. He was breathing hard as he followed a pathway inland, past an art gallery and then through the lawns of a park. Eventually he made his way back into the central business district and found George Street, which he knew would take him back to the hotel. A knot of clubbers emerging from an all-nighter cheered him, but he ignored them and focused on the footpath. A street-sweeping machine rumbled past him and a garbage truck clanked along, keeping pace with him for a while.

By the time he made it back to the hotel it was after five-thirty and the sun was just rising. He took the lift up to the room, the ammonia-like stench of perspired alcohol filling the small space. He heard the shower running. The bathroom door was ajar, steam leaking out. Richard was in a quandary. He wanted a quick, clean exit, but he needed to wash his stinking body. The smart thing to do would be to slip out and hit the hotel pool for a swim. It'd be cold, but it would do him and his libido good.

'Richard, is that you?' she called.

He pulled off his soaked T-shirt and slid out of his running shorts and opened the bathroom door. Fuck it, he thought. Katrina slid open the curtain and grinned at him. 'Come on in, the water's fine.'

'I'm not staying, Katrina, and I probably won't see you again after today.'

She reached for the soap as he joined her, and started lathering his chest, running her fingers through the curls. 'I don't care,' she said.

19

Collette Clemenger had grown into a tall, beautiful twenty-nine-year-old woman. Her surname was from her adoptive naturalised Australian parents, but her skin was the colour of polished ebony. She rose from her seat in the cafe in Surry Hills to meet him and Richard took her hand and kissed her cheek.

'Hello, Doctor Dunlop, how are you?' she said.

'I'm fine,' he said, smiling. 'Please, call me Richard.'

A waitress came over and relieved the awkwardness as they took their seats. Richard ordered a short black, and Collette a second latte. He checked his watch. 'I'm sorry I'm late. I thought a taxi would be quickest.'

'Not in Sydney peak-hour traffic. You're staying near Circular Quay?'

He nodded.

'A train to Central would have been best, it's only a two-minute walk from here.'

He looked into her eyes. 'I hardly recognise you from the skinny little girl you were.'

She gestured around the cafe. 'Well you couldn't have mistaken me for anyone else. No other black women here.'

He smiled. 'I don't suppose there are many Rwandans here in Australia?'

'No. I think at last count there were thirty in New South Wales. I don't socialise with them, though.'

'No.' It was a good idea, he thought.

'So, Jason and Denise tell me you're a lawyer.'

The waitress brought over their coffees. 'Yes. Tax law by day, and I do some pro-bono work as a refugee advocate.'

'I'm sorry, Collette, I lost track of your life over the years. I wanted to stay in touch, but . . . I feel like I turned my back on you.'

She shook her head and reached across the table, putting a hand on his. 'No, you mustn't say that. Jason and Denise took care of me and provided a life for me that I could never have dreamed of in Rwanda, especially after the genocide.'

'I see. Thanks.' She was giving him an easy out.

She withdrew her hand. 'You saved my life. I didn't need anything more than that.'

He swallowed, then took a sip of the rich, strong coffee. It helped steady him a little. He found it hard to look at her, though he could feel her eyes searching him for more, for a reason for this meeting.

'I haven't seen Jason or Denise. Are they well?'

Jason Clemenger had served with the Australian Army during the time Richard had been on exchange in Australia. Jason had been a radiographer, but had long since left the army. He'd been based in Townsville and Richard had known that he and his wife, Denise, had been talking about adopting a child. They'd had no luck conceiving by natural means and IVF had failed them. Jason had joked, when Richard had been deployed, that perhaps he could send them a baby back from Rwanda.

But it had been no joke. It had happened. Richard had smuggled Collette out of Kibeho by placing her on the floor of an Australian Army ambulance and covering her with blankets. It was just as well he'd hidden her, as the vehicle had been stopped by an RPA checkpoint. The soldiers had grudgingly let the vehicle through, filled as it was with seriously injured Hutus, but if they'd found the uninjured little girl it could have caused a serious incident. It was ridiculous, Richard thought, that the UN mission could be compromised because he'd chosen to rescue a child, but such were the rules under which they had operated. Richard had handed Collette on to a refugee agency that arranged for her to be taken out of Rwanda to an orphanage in Nairobi, and he'd followed her progress even after he'd returned to the UK. He'd put Jason and Denise in touch with the orphanage and they'd flown to Kenya and begun the process of adopting her. They'd wanted a baby or a small child, but when Richard had explained how he'd seen Collette's father die, they'd decided to try to adopt her. Richard had planned on telling Carmel about Collette, the night after he returned from Kibeho, but their break-up had put paid to that. He'd glossed over mentioning Collette to the prosecutor, Ioannou, not wanting the man to find her and dredge up painful memories from her childhood.

'Yes, my parents are fine,' Collette said. 'Richard, I don't wish to seem rude, but why are you here, after all this time?'

He saw her discreetly checking her watch. He had done a good thing for her, all those years ago, but she must be asking herself why this bedraggled man had walked back into her life. Now it was time for him to do what he'd prevented Ioannou from doing.

Richard took another sip of coffee. 'I need to talk to you

about the camp at Kibeho, Collette, about the day we rescued you, about the day . . .'

She closed her eyes and lowered her head. 'About the day my father died.'

'I'm sorry.'

'I knew it would come back, that I would be forced to remember.' She opened her eyes and stared at him. 'But of course, I've never forgotten. I can't forget.'

'I know how you feel.'

She sat back in her chair and tilted her head, regarding him in a different light; perhaps as one adult to another for the first time. 'Yes, I suspect you do. I don't imagine it was easy for you peacekeepers, you soldiers, but I lost everything. My entire natural family was murdered.'

'Yes.'

'And you know the worst thing about it, Richard? You know what tears me up inside every time I think about those days, every time an Australian teacher or a family friend or another schoolkid asked me about them as I was growing up?'

'No. Tell me.'

'They all think, all these good people here who wanted to care for the poor little refugee girl from tragic Rwanda, that I was an orphan of the genocide, that I was a Tutsi whose family was killed by evil Hutus. They want to think of me as the innocent victim, just as you and the other soldiers who saved me wanted to think of me like that.'

Richard knew this wasn't going to be easy, but he hadn't given too much thought for the trauma Collette would have carried all these years and, yes, perhaps the guilt. It made sense that Collette had wanted to hide her Hutu background; after all, despite the mass killings at Kibeho, the world's perception after the 1994 genocide was that the Hutus were the perpetrators of evil. Many people didn't want to acknowledge the bloodshed that the Tutsis had been responsible for with revenge killings once they'd taken back control. 'So, you're Hutu?' he confirmed.

She looked away for a second and drew a breath before she could face him again. 'You didn't know? What do you think my father was doing hiding in that squalid camp in Kibeho, living among all that filth?'

Richard shrugged. 'There were many Hutus in those camps who were there simply because they feared the wrath of the RPA when they swept through the country. It was on the local radio station, we'd been told. Radio-Television Libres Milles was telling all the Hutus that they'd be killed for being complicit in the genocide.'

'If my father had been innocent – truly innocent – he would have voluntarily resettled us rather than staying in the camp months after the genocide was over. I've read a lot about those times, Richard. I know that what the RPA did that day, shooting and mortaring us, rounding us up like cattle, was wrong, but I also know there were many bad people hiding in the camp.'

Richard could feel himself losing control of the situation, and the last thing he wanted was for Collette to storm out on him. He reached into the inside pocket of the rumpled blue blazer he'd put on over his T-shirt and jeans for the meeting – to look somehow more respectable, more doctorly for her – and took out the copy of Liesl's photograph of the picture Collette's father had been holding. 'Please, Collette, it doesn't matter about your father, who he was or what he did, but I need you to look at this.'

She took the picture from him. He could see her eyes were rimmed red and her face set in a scowl as though she was angry at him for forcing her to dredge up these barely suppressed memories and emotions. 'These are my father's fingers, holding this, aren't they?'

He nodded. She caressed the edges of the print, placing her fingers on her dead father's, the tops of which showed at the edge of the shot where he was holding up the creased photo to the camera.

'Do you know who any of the men are in this picture?'

She pursed her lips. 'Well, there is my father.'

Richard thought she had misunderstood. 'Well, yes, his fingers. But I meant the men in the picture he's holding.'

She looked at him over the rim of the photograph and shook her head. 'My father is one of the men in the picture.'

'He is?' That was news to him.

'He's the one with his back to the camera. You wouldn't recognise him as you can't see his face, and the beret is hiding his greying hair. But even all these years after his death, without having seen him, I know his bulk, his stance. There is no doubt that this is him.'

Richard nodded. His recollection was of a patient dying despite his best efforts, and of the man's pleading words and the agony in his face as he fought to pass on what he thought was important information. 'He's in a camouflage uniform.'

Collette stared at the picture. 'Yes. He was a colonel in the FAR – the Rwandan national army.'

'What was his job in the army? Do you know?'

'Military intelligence.'

That figured, Richard thought. 'Do you know who the white man is in the picture?'

Collette chewed on her lower lip as she stared intently at the picture.

'Or the other man?' Richard prompted.

'I was only twelve years old when my father died.'

Richard slumped in his seat and sipped his cooling coffee. 'I know. I wouldn't have come all this way if it wasn't important, Collette.'

She set the picture down on the table. 'I didn't think you'd come just to see me.'

Richard closed his eyes and realised what an arse he'd made of himself. 'Collette, I'm so . . .'

'Forget it. I'm just being selfish. You gave me my life, Richard. You and your colleagues risked a great deal to get me out of Kibeho alive – I know that. And I am so very grateful to you for that, and for getting my parents to adopt me from the orphanage in Kenya. I'm being silly. It's just that . . .'

He reached across the table and it was his turn to lay his hand on hers. 'You are scared?'

She blinked. Once, twice, then used the back of her other hand to wipe her eyes. 'All the time,' she said in a small voice. 'For years I was afraid they would come for me. I knew they wanted to kill me.'

He squeezed her hand. 'But you are safe here in Australia. And in Kenya I had people I knew keeping watch on you, sending me messages.'

She nodded, but looked down at the table. 'I know all that, but you don't know what they are like, these people.'

Richard wondered if she was talking about the genocide and the revenge killings that followed it, or if she meant a particular group of people. 'Were you worried about the men in the picture coming to get you?'

She stared at it again, then put it down and slid it back across the table to him. Collette looked up at him, straight in the eye this time. 'No. I have no idea who the other men in this picture are.'

There was something about the way she said the words and her blank gaze. She was trying to meet his eyes, but actually looking through him. She was being evasive. He thought he understood why.

'I should have visited you before this.'

'I'm not your responsibility, Richard. For sure, there were times when I was growing up when I thought of you, often. I saw you coming to get me, to take me away from Jason and Denise – particularly when we were fighting, during my teenage years. But I love them very much, even though sometimes I wanted the man who rescued me to come save me again.'

It was Richard's turn to stare at the table. He felt as though he had wasted the trip to Australia and once again disappointed someone who had cared for him. He slid the picture back around so he could look at it, for the hundredth time. 'There's nothing more you can tell me?'

'Richard, I have an appointment, a client.' She checked her watch for emphasis. 'I'm sorry.'

'No, Collette. I'm sorry. Truly sorry.' He stood for her, took her hand and kissed her cheek. 'Goodbye.'

He watched her walk out of the coffee shop and out of his life again. He picked up the photograph and paid the bill and wondered what on earth he should do.

'Do we follow the man or the woman?' Nguyen asked his cousin, Tran. They were seated in a low-slung Subaru WR-X.

'Buggered if I know.' Tran scratched his scalp in between

his heavily gelled spikes of hair. 'All I know is Uncle Minh told us to stick with this guy after he got off the flight from Africa and report what he does and who he sees.'

The men were of Vietnamese origin but both spoke English with the nasal twang of southwestern Sydney. Nguyen said, 'I vote we stay with the black chick. She's hot. I'd like to give her one.'

'This guy gets around, man. He was supposed to be single and then he ends up in a cab with a white woman, and now this one. He's the target,' Tran said. Tran van Duong was Nguyen van Lo's elder by four years. At the age of twenty-two he had already done six months in Long Bay Jail for assault occasioning grievous bodily harm after he'd beaten the shit out of a senior member of a rival Vietnamese gang. Tran considered himself lucky, as the police didn't know that it was him who had killed the Lebanese boy in the drive-by in Lakemba a year earlier.

His boss, Nguyen's father Minh, knew Tran was lucky too. Uncle Minh had given him this important job – it was a favour to a supplier from Africa – and he had entrusted Nguyen into his care. Tran was worried about fucking up. Nguyen was a hothead with a big mouth. Tran had seen the inside of prison and while it had made him stronger, he didn't want to go back. Tran took out his iPhone and scrolled to Uncle Minh's number and called him on Viber, so there would be no record of the call on his bill.

'Yes?' his uncle said.

'Hurry, he's leaving now,' Nguyen whispered.

Tran held up a hand to silence his cousin. 'He met a black woman. They talked for half an hour, then she left. She's on foot. He was in a taxi.'

'I will report back to our supplier,' his uncle said. 'What do you think you should do?'

Tran thought about it. His uncle was putting him on the spot. He knew that with his form he was being considered for higher things in the organisation. He had proven his strength, by delivering punishment to his rival, and his will, by killing the Leb, but his uncle wanted to know if he had brains as well. 'The man has no luggage with him, so he will have to return to his hotel sometime soon. The room is in the name of the woman he met on the plane, and she has only booked for one night. Assuming check-out from the hotel is ten or eleven, then he will be heading back there pretty much straightaway.'

'Good, so you know where he is going.'

'And our instructions were to see who he met.'

'And who did he meet?'

'A black – Ah, I see. Yes, Uncle. We need to know who she is.'

'Precisely,' Minh said.

'I will send Nguyen to the hotel, to wait and watch the man, and I will follow the woman and find out who she is.'

'Very good. I'll text you when I have further instructions and you will call me then.'

'Yes, Uncle.' Tran ended the call.

'I could hear,' Nguyen said. He frowned. 'How come I get the dude and you get the hot chick?'

'Rank has its privileges, Cuz.'

It was after midnight in Kigali and the Indian restaurant was empty but for Liesl, Henri, a waiter, and a tired-looking manager.

Liesl was shattered, but buzzing from the alcohol. She'd

felt like this many times before – overtired but cruising on her reserve tanks. It was sometimes the most fun, just before a crash. She was trying to figure out the Frenchman. She lit another cigarette. She was nearing the end of the packet, partly thanks to Henri who had bummed three since Miss Prissy had left to go to bed.

'So, you're here to bring back a chimp?'

'Yes, as I said before. I think. That was two bottles ago.'

She laughed. 'I think there's more to you, *Monsieur* Bousson.'

He shrugged. 'Perhaps this is it. What you see. What do you hope to find here?'

Their talk had been of travels in Africa, of their respective jobs, of their upbringings. Both were children of Africa, restless, kindred, and they had seen their share of sorrow. Henri had asked her about Afghanistan, and she'd told him, candidly, about her breakdown.

'You know how it is – people are always bemoaning the state of Africa, but tribalism, civil war, corruption, senseless killing aren't the sole preserve of Africa.' He'd nodded and she'd wondered what demons he had lurking in his head. They'd been dancing around the real reasons for their being in Rwanda, but the alcohol was loosening Liesl's tongue and she hoped it would have the same effect on him.

'So you are not just here to take pictures of the mountain gorillas?'

She smiled. 'I'd be lying if I said I was. The truth is, I don't know where to start looking, but there's a story in all of this. If there is someone, or some group of people who are prepared to carry out multiple assassinations in three countries to stop people finding out what the significance of my photograph is, then it has to be because of something pretty big and something pretty secret.'

'Such as?'

'You've seen the picture. You've been around. The men in that photo are posing with a Russian-made surface-to-air missile launcher – the kind of weapon that was used to shoot down the plane carrying the presidents of Rwanda and Burundi back in 1994. There's been a lot of conjecture as to which side – the Hutus or the Tutsis – fired that missile. And there's a white man in the picture, which makes me think there's some credence to rumours that there was a western country involved in the killing.'

Henri scoffed. 'You media people are always good at finding conspiracy theories, yes?'

'Well you only have to google this one to find plenty of them. There's the most popular theory that even though President Juvenal Habyarimana was a Hutu, and several of his senior Hutu military staff were on board the aircraft, it was other Hutus that shot down his plane.'

'Yes,' Henri agreed, waving a hand in the air as though he'd heard it all before. 'There is strong evidence that the more radical Hutus, the ones behind Hutu Power and the Interahamwe militia, were concerned that Habyarimana was about to agree to the Arusha Peace Accords which would pave the way for all the Tutsis who'd been living outside the country to move back. That was at odds with Hutu Power's stated aim of wiping out all the Tutsis in Rwanda.'

'Yes, and then there's the theory that it was actually Habyarimana's wife who was behind the killing. She was apparently the grande dame of an ultra-extremist faction of Hutu Power called the Akazu. Some people say that she had given up on her husband, considering him a moderate and a sell-out.' Liesl had learned about the Akazu, which meant 'little house', when she was in Rwanda. This close-knit band of relatives and supporters of the late president had been unable to countenance a deal with Paul Kagame and the Tutsis under any circumstances. She wondered at the callousness – or was it conviction – of a woman who could have her husband murdered in the name of racial politics.

'Of course,' Henri continued, 'there is also the possibility that Kagame, or some element in his Tutsi RPA, shot down the president's aircraft. After all, the RPA had been at war with Rwanda's army for years. Perhaps General Paul Kagame or his subordinates were secretly as worried about the prospect of peace as Habyarimana's extremist supporters.'

Liesl shrugged and drained the last of her red wine from her glass. 'Possible. Kagame was winning the war and the RPA actually had forces billeted in Kigali in the lead-up to the signing of the peace accords. They were a whisker away from military victory. Habyarimana's death was the spark that reignited the war – a war that Kagame and the RPA eventually won.'

Henri looked dubious. 'Yes, but what a price to pay. Shooting down that aircraft was the spark that ignited the genocide and led to the deaths of nearly a million people.'

Liesl was happy to continue as the devil's advocate. 'Yes, but perhaps Kagame didn't expect the Interahamwe and the FAR to go as far as they did . . . perhaps a few pogroms, some isolated killings . . .'

'This is too deep a discussion to be having after too much red wine,' Henri said. 'A nightcap at the hotel, perhaps?'

'I think the hotel bar is probably closed, and I didn't buy

any duty-free booze – more's the pity given the price of wine in this country.'

Henri called for the bill and insisted on paying for all of it.

'What about the lawyer? She should be putting it on expenses,' Liesl said as Henri counted out a stack of Rwandan francs.

'A gentleman always pays.'

'*Ja*, well you've just seen how much I drink, so I hope you've got plenty more where those francs came from. But seriously, it's on me next time. So, you and Carmel, what's going on there? You two an item?'

'A gentleman never tells.'

Liesl laughed out loud. She felt even more inebriated when she stood up and they began walking towards the gate, no doubt to the relief of the waiting staff.

'But actually,' he added quickly, 'we are just friends.'

Interesting, Liesl thought.

Carmel was mad at Henri. It was silly, she knew, for her to allow the South African woman to get to her after all these years, but Carmel had bridled when Liesl had breezed in unannounced and forced Henri to buy another bottle of wine. He would have been fine with just one, she was sure.

I could use a drink right now, Carmel thought. In fact, she was craving it. The smell, above the food, of the red sloshing in their glasses; their carefree easy manner with each other; the red glow in Liesl's cheeks as the alcohol quickly freed her. Carmel felt imprisoned by her sobriety right now, not uplifted by it. She felt miserable and denied rather than righteous and healthy, as she knew she should. She licked her lips.

Carmel went to the fridge and grabbed one of the three

cans of Coke Light she'd ordered from room service – she hadn't wanted the waiter coming backwards and forwards all evening. She had a fridge in her room but, thankfully, it wasn't stocked. Sometimes, when travelling on business, she was fine to stay in a room for a night, or even a couple of nights, in the company of a full minibar, but at other times, like now, she would have to call housekeeping and have them remove all the alcohol. She didn't want to fall off the wagon – not after so many years.

But she envied them. She envied the way the drug could allow two strangers to end up conversing as though they'd known each other for years. She envied Liesl, the bitch, her ability to flirt and distract Henri's attention from Carmel, and the seriousness of the situation at hand.

And what, Carmel wondered, was she to do with Liesl now that she had stormed into Rwanda like a typical nosey journalist? It was not only inappropriate and irresponsible, it was downright dangerous.

Carmel leaned back in the chair, stretched, yawned and checked her watch. It was after two in the morning. She knew she should get some sleep as she would need her wits about her tomorrow morning. Although her laptop was open and her iPhone had a note-taking app, she'd always been a list maker. Writing out what she needed to do, on paper, was the best way to focus her thoughts, and she always gained a small frisson of pleasure from striking through a task once it was completed.

1. *Meet Jean Paul at prosecutor's office, Avenue de l'Armée, 10.00 am*

2 *Kigali Central Prison*

3. *Gorilla permits*
4. *Genocide Memorial – time permitting*

Carmel tapped the pen against her teeth while she thought of what else she needed to do or, more importantly, what she could do in Kigali. She sighed. She really had no idea where this investigation was going. If the people who were trying to kill her, Liesl and Richard – presumably the same people who had killed Mike Ioannou – were Hutus, they may not even be in Rwanda at all. They could be in exile across the border in the Democratic Republic of Congo. If they were Tutsis – say, some extremist faction of the government – then her enquiries at the prosecutor's office and central prison would soon filter back to them. Alternatively, it could all have been one long string of unrelated coincidences.

But she could feel it in her insides. It was what was keeping her up, functioning on adrenaline; it was what was jangling her nerves and tingling her fingertips. She was on the trail of something big here. It was bigger than her and bigger than the ICTR. She was the first to admit she was going outside the accepted channels and that she needed help and top cover, which made it even more frustrating that her superiors were not responding to her messages. She would call Arusha in the morning.

Carmel heard voices in the corridor outside her room. The door of the room next door to her, Henri's, opened and closed. She checked her watch again and silently tut-tutted his late return. She needed to go to the toilet anyway so she stood and stretched. There was laughter from the hallway; a mix of deep bass and a high-pitched girlish giggle, almost a shriek. Then the man spoke and Carmel moved to the peephole in the door.

As she looked out she saw Henri, his bulk magnified by the distortion of the peephole glass. He was lingering in the hallway, and not in his room as she'd thought. Perhaps he had stopped in there for something. His back was to her, but his left arm was bent across his body as though he was holding something she couldn't see. Across the corridor a door was open. The light inside the opposite room came on and Liesl was standing there.

Liesl smiled, and Carmel swore it looked like she was coming on to him. She crooked her finger and although her voice was muffled through the door Carmel could read her lips. 'Come in,' Liesl said.

Henri entered Liesl's room and the door closed behind him.

Carmel thumped the bathroom door and it swung back on its hinges hard enough to slam against the tiles.

20

Collette walked quickly up Elizabeth Street through Surry Hills, striding back to the sanctuary of her work and the life she had made for herself. The demons of her past were following her, just behind, reaching out their cold, dead hands.

She was scared.

Richard had asked her if she wanted him to send her a copy of the photograph so she could have a second look at it, but she didn't need to. She knew all three people, at least by sight if not by name. Even before the genocide, their evil had touched her. The men had come to several meetings in her father's country house at Gisokoro, in southwestern Rwanda, not far from the shores of Lake Kivu and the border with Zaire, which was now called the Democratic Republic of Congo.

They'd thought her just a silly girl, but she was smart – the cleverest in her class – and she was curious. She'd lingered in the garden, by the open window under the bougainvillea, when the men drank their beer and smoked their cigarettes and talked in hushed tones, even that far from the capital.

She'd been there the day the photograph had been taken, in the forest near their home, where her father and his brothers and their friends sometimes hunted for bushmeat and live animals to trade with the white man.

A taxi driver stabbed his horn. Collette stopped short and took a step backwards onto the pavement again. She'd almost been run down crossing Devonshire Street. The shopping housewives and office workers spinning out their coffee and cigarette breaks milled around her, but Collette was in another world and another time. She wanted to escape it, but it was engulfing her.

She remembered the day in early 1994 – it must have been March sometime, just before the madness began; the camera's flash going off, illuminating the gloom under the jungle canopy. It had been hot and wet in there on the edge of Nyungwe National Park, as oppressive as always. She feared the hills and the jungle and the animals that lived there – elephants, buffalo, and the wily chimpanzees that raided the banana crops and were hunted and killed for their meat and their body parts. Sometimes they were captured, especially the babies, and sold to the white man who came often to Collette's father's house.

The trade in wildlife had slowed as the talk of a Tutsi invasion and the litany of publicly broadcasted hate increased. Everyone spoke of the imminent invasion by General Kagame and his Tutsi army, the RPA. The radio broadcast a continuous cacophony of hatred and this filtered into people's day-to-day conversations and attitudes. Collette had never needed to think much about Hutus and Tutsis. Her mother was a Tutsi, but Collette was classified as a Hutu like her father, and this made her happy – especially at school when the other children began picking on the few remaining Tutsis from the village, calling them cockroaches and snakes. When she'd told her mother what had happened at school her mother had told her not to be a part of such terrible behaviour. That, Collette thought, was easy for her mother to say. Better to be part of the majority than suffer the insults and beatings the Tutsi girls endured. It was hard enough being the brightest girl in school: Collette didn't want to stand out from the crowd any more by sticking up for a few stems of 'long grass'.

Collette screwed her eyes shut, to try to close out the terrible images from that time. The rapid pinging of the 'walk' signal brought her temporarily back to the here and now of Sydney. She had ten minutes to get to her meeting; plenty of time.

She remembered seeing the anti-aircraft missile launcher. She was smart enough as a child to know it was different to the weapons her father's soldiers carried on the streets and around the barracks. But it wasn't until the president's aircraft had been downed, and she'd overheard her mother and father arguing, that Collette had put together the pieces of what she had seen.

So much time had passed since then, and she'd tried hard to put all those memories and the nightmare that followed out of her head. Now was not the time, she chided herself as she checked her watch. She always made sure she was five minutes early for a client meeting. A woman was walking towards her leading a little girl by the hand. Collette thought the child was not much younger than she had been when she had lost her mother. This girl, maybe ten, clearly didn't want her mother to be dragging her. She wriggled in her parent's grasp, a look of stubborn annoyance on her little face. If only the girl knew, Collette thought, how fragile such bonds were.

They had been in Kigali when Habyarimana's Dassault

Falcon executive jet had been downed. Collette remembered, vaguely – for there was so much in the days after to cloud such a seemingly small recollection – a noise like a clap of thunder, and looking outside to see fire lighting the night sky.

'It has happened,' her mother said, looking accusingly at her father.

He studied the carpet. 'It has.'

'How?'

'It was always going to happen,' her father said. He was dressed in his uniform, his pistol in the canvas holster at his side. 'We need to leave.'

'My sister . . . her children,' Collette's mother said.

Collette thought of her Aunt Cecile and her cousins, Jean Paul, Gregoire and little Angelique, and was worried. The baby was like a little doll, and Collette loved playing with her. Uncle Alphonse was Tutsi, as was Aunt Cecile, and he had been killed a year earlier, just before Angelique was born, in one of the regular outbreaks of anti-Tutsi violence.

'No, Yvonne,' her father said to her mother. 'We leave tomorrow. I will be back in the morning. Do not leave the house, whatever you do.'

Collette's father left their home and got into his army Land Rover. The shooting started not long after, along with the sound of shouted male voices and women screaming. The killing began, and ever since Collette had wondered what part her father had played in it.

Her mother tried calling Aunt Cecile, but the telephone was not working. 'Mama, what's happening? Are the Tutsis invading?' Collette asked.

'No!' Her mother ran a hand through her bouffant hairdo

and then dabbed her eyes with her handkerchief. 'I'm sorry, *chérie*. No, not yet. I think this is worse than civil war or an invasion. I think this is very bad, what is happening. *Chérie*, Mama has to go out for a little while, but I want you to stay here and wait for Papa. *D'accord?*'

'No, Mama, I don't want to be left alone.'

'Shush, shush, *chérie*,' her mother said as she fetched her coat and belted it on. 'I have to go to Aunt Cecile's place. I'm going to get her and the kids. I won't be more than an hour.' Her mother took Collette's face in her hands and kissed her. 'I love you, *chérie*.'

'I love you too, Mama, but please—'

'Be brave, my good girl. I will be back soon, I promise.'

That was the last she had seen of her mother, and she never again saw her aunt and cousins alive. All were butchered.

Collette cursed herself and blinked away the tears. She had a meeting to get to. She took out a tissue and blew her nose. She switched her iPhone to silent so it wouldn't bother her during her discussions with her client.

'Are you serious, Uncle?' Tran said into his phone as he walked along Elizabeth Street, keeping the woman in sight.

'I'm not the joking kind,' Minh said tersely.

'Yeah, but all the same – in broad daylight, in the middle of downtown Sydney?'

'The man said soon as possible. Tran, listen to me, boy. There is more money on offer for this deal than we can make in six months.'

Tran thought about it. As much as he wanted to protest the insanity of kidnapping a woman off the street in the busiest city in Australia, he was also excited by the prospect. He'd snapped a picture of the woman with his phone and sent it as an SMS to his uncle and had expected to be told to keep an eye on her for the rest of the day; to find out where she worked and where she lived and so forth. But then he'd got lucky. He'd got close to her and been within eavesdropping distance when she'd received a call and answered it.

'Hello, this is Collette,' she'd said into the phone. Tran had quickly followed the picture message with a text to his uncle which said, *First name Collette.*

Within fifteen minutes the word had come back, from wherever his uncle's client was, that they had been offered a contract to kidnap the woman. 'OK, Uncle. Your son is with the Anglo man. I'll need him to do the job – he's got my car.'

'Just do it. The man said as soon as possible, Tran. These are not people we fuck with, OK?'

'OK, Uncle. What's my cut?'

His uncle's laugh was like glass being ground underfoot. 'We'll talk about that later on, boy. For now, you do job and don't fuck up.'

Tran turned instinctively when he heard the hoot of a car behind him. It was Nguyen in the WR-X. Nguyen pulled into the bus lane and Tran jumped in. 'Why are you so stupid, man?'

'What do you mean? I came as soon as I got your text. What's up, Cuz?'

'I'm following the bitch and you go honking your horn. You're lucky she didn't make us.'

'*Make* us, Cuz? You been watching too much *Hawaii 5-0.*'

'Whatever. Your dad wants us to grab her.'

'All *right!*' Nguyen thumped the steering wheel.

'Settle, dude. She's up ahead. Lucky the traffic's slow, so just stay with it.'

'OK, but how we gonna do this? We can't just pull over and grab her, Cuz. There's like a million fucking witnesses and probably security cameras everywhere.'

Tran had already thought about all that. His cousin was right. It was all very well for Uncle Minh to dangle the prospect of promotion and money, but he and Nguyen were the foot soldiers who were expected to risk their own arses putting the general's crazy plan into action. Tran reached across, under his cousin's legs.

'You trying to blow me, Cuz?'

'Just keep driving, smart mouth.' Tran felt for the angular weight of the pistol and pulled it out.

'Awesome. I didn't know you had that under there. Cool.'

Tran held the pistol low and pulled back the slide and let it go, chambering a round.

'Look, she's turning down that alley, man,' Nguyen said, pointing at the woman. 'Perfect.'

Tran slipped the 9mm pistol into the waistband of his jeans in the small of his back and pulled his T-shirt down over it. 'Follow her in. It looks quiet.'

Nguyen checked his rear-view mirror and indicated to the left. The laneway veered off so that a second after they'd made the turn the woman went around to the right, past a rubbish skip, and they lost sight of her. That was good, he thought, as they wouldn't be seen from the main road. 'Stop just around the corner.'

The woman had increased her stride and checked her watch, as though she was late for an appointment or something. Tran noted from the clock on the dashboard that it was 10.54 am. If she had an eleven o'clock then she was close to her destination. He could follow her to wherever she was going, but if she'd taken the laneway as a short cut she might be less inclined to use it after her meeting. No, it was time to act now. Tran's black bomber jacket was on the back seat of the car; he reached behind and grabbed it. Nguyen stopped the car and Tran got out. He closed the door softly so as not to alert the target.

He scanned the doorways and windows above him as he moved. He could see no cameras and there were no other people about. There was a broken beer bottle on the ground and a patch of dried vomit. Further along he smelled piss. This was where people came in the city when they needed to disappear for a while. Perfect. Tran quickened his pace and closed the gap between him and the woman. His basketball hi-tops were silent on the pavement.

As he walked Tran did up the zip of his jacket, without putting it on. He came up behind the woman, lifted his arms, and slipped the zipped jacket down over her head. She screamed and flailed as her face was covered, but Tran was ready for this. He wrapped his left arm around her neck from behind and pushed his knee in behind hers, causing her to buckle. As she fell he reached around and slid the pistol from his jeans. The woman reached back and before Tran could get the barrel of the weapon into her temple her thumb was in his eye. He screamed.

From behind them came the noise of an engine revving and the squeal of slick tyres. Tran saw stars, but managed to swipe across at the woman's covered head with the butt of the pistol and smashed it into her. She was writhing in his weakened grip, though, and clawing at the jacket. The car door slammed and Nguyen leapt out. He kicked her hard and fast in the ribs and she sagged in Tran's grasp.

'I've got a gun, you fucking bitch,' Tran hissed in her ear. 'Keep still or I'll kill you now.'

'Let's get her in the car,' Nguyen said. He kicked her again for good measure then grabbed the sleeves of the jacket and wrapped them around her face and neck and tied them in a knot. The two men dragged the woman, still kicking and trying to cry out through her makeshift gag, into the back of the car and forced her down on the floor.

Richard retrieved his backpack from the left luggage room in the hotel and thought about what he should do next. He knew Katrina would have checked out and left for the airport to catch her flight to Brisbane. He'd timed his meeting with Collette so he wouldn't see the South African woman again. Richard couldn't afford to stay in this hotel so he would have to find a backpackers' or a hostel until he worked out his next step.

He'd been foolish to think Collette would have all the answers. She'd been a scared little girl when her father had died. There was no reason to think she would have been privy to any special knowledge her old man had. It was interesting, though, that the man with his back to the camera was her father, the same man who had died in Richard's arms.

Richard left the hotel and decided to walk for a bit. He yawned. The jet lag had really screwed his system. He turned left and started walking towards Circular Quay.

As he started down the street, he replayed the meeting with Collette in his mind. She was holding something back. He stopped at a park bench, shrugged off his pack and took out his phone and the business card Collette had given him.

He dialled the mobile number listed on the card but it rang

out before going to voicemail. He left a message, asking her to call him back. Collette would more than likely have known who was calling, from the South African number that would have appeared on her phone screen. She'd left the meeting rattled and he wondered if she was deliberately avoiding his call. He dialled her law office's landline.

'Livingstone, Ward and Company solicitors, may I help you?' the receptionist said on the other end.

'Hi, I'd like to speak to Collette Clemenger, please,' Richard said.

'Sorry, Ms Clemenger isn't available at the moment. Can I ask what it's regarding and take a message, please?'

'It's quite urgent. I'm a client of hers and I was hoping to speak with her now; can you interrupt her please?'

'I'm sorry, sir,' the receptionist said. 'Can I get your name, please?'

Richard decided to keep bluffing it out. 'Look, I had a meeting with Collette this morning, and—'

'Oh, I'm sorry, sir,' the receptionist said. 'You're involved in the Lloyd matter? I've just had a call from one of the other parties and they're also looking for Ms Clemenger. I've tried her phone four times and can't get through. I can't imagine what's keeping her.'

Richard took a breath. A chill rippled through him. The jet lag had fogged his brain and he now remembered her saying she had a meeting to get to. Had she missed it? 'She's not at the meeting . . .'

'Yes, sir. Sorry. As I've said, I've been trying to call her,' the receptionist said.

'She was walking to the meeting,' Richard said, stating a fact.

'Umm,' Richard could hear the receptionist turning pages. 'Yes, sir, that would make sense. I'm just checking her diary now. She had a ten o'clock in Surry Hills and, as your offices are close by, I'm sure she would have walked. Unless she got held up at her ten o'clock . . .'

'Does she make a habit of forgetting meetings?'

'No, sir,' the receptionist said, sounding defensive. 'Never. Perhaps you can give me your number and I'll call you and Mr and Mrs Lloyd as soon as I hear from Collette. I'm terribly sorry for the inconvenience, and—'

Richard ended the call. He grabbed his backpack, got up, looked around and ran across the road. He hailed the cab and read from her business card. 'Mount Street, North Sydney. Quick as you can, driver.'

The driver looked young and was Middle Eastern, with his head shaved on the sides leaving an oval of gelled bristles on the top. 'Settle, man, you're not on TV. I'll go as quick as the speed limit allows.'

'For Christ's sake, a woman's life is at stake here. Get a move on!'

'Serious?'

Richard reached over and grabbed the man's shirt front. 'Do I look serious?'

'OK, OK.' The driver brushed Richard's hand away and stamped on the accelerator.

Richard tried ringing Collette again. There could have been any number of reasons why Collette had missed her meeting. She could have been run over by a car, or tripped over, or had a seizure, or stopped to help someone in trouble. Normally any such matter would have been bad enough, but given what had happened to anyone else with a connection to that bloody picture, Richard could only assume it was worse than all those calamities put together. He swore. It was as if that bloody picture had been cursed.

It seemed to take ages to turn into Bridge Street, but after missing two green lights the cab driver was able to accelerate again as he entered the approaches to the Sydney Harbour Bridge. Richard paid no interest to the iconic structure, or the surrounding harbour. The North Sydney exit was just over the other side of the harbour. The driver turned left and then took a right up Walker Street. 'What number?'

Richard checked the card. 'Ninety.'

'Mount Street's a mall and ninety will be up there,' he said, pointing to the left as he pulled over.

Richard gave the driver a twenty-dollar note and when the man began counting out change, he said: 'Can you wait for me?'

'For how long?'

'I don't know.'

The driver looked at him. 'There's really some chick's life at risk?'

'Yes.'

'OK, mate, I'll wait around the back, in the laneway.'

Richard got out and slammed the door shut, leaving his pack in the backseat as a deterrent to the driver getting bored and leaving without him. He ran up the pedestrian mall, dodging office workers out for an early lunch. He took a flight of steps to the building where Collette worked and found a name plate with *Livingstone, Ward & Company* on it. Richard got into a lift and pressed the button for the sixth floor.

'Good morning,' said the receptionist when he stepped into the foyer.

'I called before. I'm looking for Collette Clemenger.'

'Oh, I assumed you'd be at the meeting, Mr . . .?'

'My name's Dunlop, Doctor Richard Dunlop. I'm worried something very serious has happened to Collette.'

'Well, Doctor Dunlop, I'm afraid I can't help you. As I said on the phone, we've been unable to reach Collette. It's quite a mystery. After you got off the phone Collette's PA, Isabelle, came back from a break and she has no idea what might have happened to her either. We're just hoping that if she's had a little mishap or something on the way to the meeting that it's nothing too serious. I've left a message there for her to call us once she gets there.'

'She's not going to *get* to the meeting!'

'How do you know?' asked the receptionist.

A young woman with blonde curly hair walked into the foyer and addressed the receptionist. 'Emily, did I hear you asking about Collette?'

'Yes, it's very urgent,' Richard interrupted. He could see by their body language that these two women were about to close ranks on him. 'I'm a doctor. I was seeing Collette at ten o'clock. It wasn't a social meeting, it was an appointment.'

'Really? I'm Isabelle Robertson, Collette's PA. Forgive me for saying, but I haven't seen too many doctors who wear Clash T-shirts and jeans when they treat their patients.'

'Shit,' Richard said, running a hand through his greasy hair. He reached into his pocket and took out Collette's business card and threw it on the reception desk. He took out his phone, called his message bank, put the phone on speaker and dialled. There was only one message and it was from Collette. *'Hi Richard, I can meet you at ten am at a coffee shop in*

Surry Hills.' She gave the name and address of the place and directions to nearby Central Railway Station.

Isabelle put her hands on her hips. 'You had an appointment in a coffee shop?'

'I'm a friend of the family. Look, listen to me. I'm very worried that something very bad may have happened to Collette in between when she left me and when her meeting was supposed to start.'

'What time did she leave your meeting?' Isabelle asked.

Richard thought about it, and remembered her checking her watch. 'Ten-fifty.'

Isabelle nodded. 'Plenty of time to walk to the Lloyd conference.'

'Call the police,' Richard said.

'Really?' asked the receptionist.

'Yes, really,' Richard said. 'Is there any other way we can contact her? Like, I don't know, do people still use pagers? Can you email her?'

Emily, the receptionist, called 000 and asked to be put through to the police. 'Umm . . . twenty-five minutes,' she said into the phone. 'Yes, but her doctor's here and he says something serious might have happened to her.'

Richard could tell the police thought Emily was crazy for reporting someone missing because they'd failed to show up for a work appointment and were only twenty-five minutes late.

'Lost phone!' Isabelle said.

The receptionist put a hand over her ear to drown out the other conversation while she persisted with the police.

'What do you mean?' Richard asked Isabelle.

'Collette's super-organised, but she does have a problem

with phones. She's lost two – one in a cab and one in a restaurant – so I downloaded this app to her iPhone that allows us to find her phone, wherever it is.'

'What if it's switched off?' Richard asked.

'It still works, we've tried it.'

The receptionist got off the phone. 'The police say it's too soon to report someone missing. They suggest we call the nearest hospitals to see if she's been admitted.'

'Move over, Emily.' Isabelle sat in a vacant office chair and rolled in front of Emily's computer monitor as the receptionist took another call using her wireless headset. 'All I have to do is log into Collette's Apple account – I know the password for emergencies like this – and log into Find My iPhone.'

Richard watched, slightly amazed, as Isabelle's ruby nails fluttered over the keyboard. 'Searching now,' she said, then turned the flat screen monitor side-on so that by looking over the reception desk counter he could see it. 'There it is.'

Richard looked at the streets on the map on the screen. As Isabelle magnified the image street names appeared. He grabbed a pen off the desk and scrawled them down. 'Cadogan Street, just off Sydenham Road, Marrickville.'

'That's miles away from where her meeting was supposed to be. And I don't know if there's a hospital in that part of Sydney. What on earth would she be doing there?' Isabelle said.

'What sort of place is it?' Richard asked.

'Marrickville?' Isabelle shrugged. 'Used to be a working-class suburb, now getting trendier. There were a lot of Greeks there, but the Vietnamese have taken the place over in the last few years. Good restaurants.' She opened another window and called up a satellite view of the same street on

Google. 'This looks like the industrial area – old factories, warehouses, that sort of stuff.'

Richard suddenly remembered the young Asian man with the spiky hair standing on the wet, near-deserted street corner early that morning, smoking a cigarette, when he'd gone for his run. 'Thanks, Isabelle. I can't tell you how important this is. Here's my number.' Richard wrote it down and passed it to her. 'Can you keep an eye on this thing and call me if Collette starts to move again, or if she calls.'

'I'm worried,' she said.

Richard thought she had good reason to be, but he didn't say so. He left before she could ask him any more questions.

21

Collette saw the devil when the pullover was lifted from her head. It took a moment for her eyes to adjust to the minimal light around her, but the red devil's face loomed in front of her, causing her to recoil. It was a mask. The men had been speaking in an Asian language as they'd dragged her from the car, the gun pressed painfully into her back. Her first thought had been that they were going to rape her, but they'd placed her on a hard wooden chair and taped her hands to the frame. She'd smelled spices and now that her face was uncovered the odour was stronger. All around her were pallets piled high with cardboard boxes with Asian writing on them. She could hear a faint buzz of traffic beyond the walls of the warehouse they'd brought her to.

'What's your name?' the man in the devil mask asked.

'What do you want with me?'

The hand of the man snaked out and slapped her face, hard enough to make her rock on the chair.

'Answer him!' Behind her, another man, with an Asian accent like the first man's, slapped the back of her head, knocking her forward.

'You've got my handbag. You must have looked in there.'

The man in the mask chuckled. 'Clemenger. Don't sound black. What's your real name, bitch?' Another slap followed before she even had a chance to answer.

'That is my real name.' She tasted blood in her mouth. God, now she was really worried. Why was this creep asking about her real name on the same day Richard had come back into her life and started asking questions about her childhood? What hadn't Richard told her?

'Bullshit!' Devil-man placed both of his hands on the collar of her blouse and ripped outwards, exposing her bra. The buttons popped easily and she felt even more afraid. 'Hey! Shit! Look what the bitch is hiding in her tits.'

Collette cringed as the man groped in her bra and pulled out her phone. He slid his finger across the screen to activate it and scrolled down the list of numbers. 'Lot of same incoming missed calls,' devil-man said to his accomplice, still out of sight. 'All in the last half-hour. Somebody's missing her already.'

'Better be quick,' said the man behind her.

Devil-man's hands were empty – she presumed the man behind her was covering her with the gun. The masked man reached into the back pocket of his jeans and moved his hand to her face. The blade of the flick knife sprang open, the point arriving just millimetres from her left eye.

'No!' She'd seen what blades could do to human flesh. 'Please.'

The devil laughed again. Collette winced and tried to slide the chair back as he moved the point between her eyes.

'Stay still,' the man behind her said, and checked her movement with the hard point of the gun at the back of her neck.

Devil-man touched the point of the blade to her face, between her eyes at the bridge of her nose. He slowly traced it down, his soft words following its path. 'Shame to mess up such a pretty face.' Collette shivered in her seat as the blade scratched down her nose, between her nostrils and paused on her top lip. She squeezed her eyes shut, but the tears forced their way out.

'Please. I told you my name. It's Collette Clemenger. I was adopted, as a baby. I don't know my real name.'

The devil moved close enough for her to smell the stale cigarette smoke on his clothes. The knife moved over her quivering lips. He took a handful of her hair and whispered into her right ear: 'Liar.' He pushed the tip of the blade up into the soft skin under her chin.

Collette screamed as the blood spurted down over her bared chest.

'Faster,' Richard said, checking their progress on the screen of his phone and on the cab driver's GPS.

'I'm going as fast as I can, all right,' said the driver, who had told him his name was Bilal, and that he was Lebanese–Australian. He indicated to pass a truck as they drove down King Street through Newtown, avoiding a car in front that had suddenly stopped to turn right.

'Hey, is this some kind of dangerous shit you're getting into?' Bilal asked as he planted the accelerator again.

'Yes, and when we get to where we're going I want you to drop me about a block away and then drive off.'

Bilal glanced at him, then back at the road as a bus loomed in the windscreen. Bilal accelerated and darted around it. 'No way. I mean, if something's going down you're going to need a getaway, right?'

Richard hadn't had time to think through his plan. He didn't want to involve any more innocents, but maybe Bilal was right. 'How easy will it be for me to get another cab?'

'In that part of Marrickville? Take you hours, mate. Better if I wait.'

'OK,' Richard said.

'Someone's in trouble, right? I heard you talking on the phone. You call the cops?'

'Someone else did.' Isabelle had phoned to tell him she'd called the police and reported a suspected abduction. She'd given the police dispatcher the address and the police had agreed to send a car to check it out, but not before speculating that perhaps Collette simply had an appointment she didn't want her workmates to know about – the inference being she was cheating on a boyfriend or involved in something criminal. 'And, yes, a friend of mine is in big trouble.'

'GPS says we'll be there in three minutes. If we had more time I could have got you a gun, mate.' Bilal turned down a street that took them into what looked like a light industrial area. They passed a self-storage place, a mechanic's garage and a couple of warehouses. 'Should be just up in the next block,' Richard said, checking Bilal's GPS. 'Drop me off here.'

'OK. I'll wait for you.' Bilal pulled over and Richard opened the door to get out. 'Hang on, mate. I got something for you.'

Richard stuck his torso back inside the cab as Bilal leaned forward and reached under his seat. He pulled out a wide-bladed hunting knife in a sheath and held it out. 'Thanks,' Richard said. As he walked he slid the knife into the back of his jeans and pulled his T-shirt down to conceal it.

Richard walked down Cadogan Street, which was empty of people at this time of day, between morning tea and lunchtime. Nearby he heard traffic from busy Sydenham Road and the high-pitched squeal of an angle grinder from the mechanic's shop. He moved quickly, trying to relate the pinpoint on the online map to the real thing. The older buildings were red brick and he came to one with a saw-toothed roof that looked like it might have been a factory or machine shop back when it was built, in the forties or fifties. What had looked like a solid city block on the online map was in reality divided by a narrow lane. Richard slowed as he neared the laneway and peeked his head around the corner. Parked halfway down was a boy-racer sports car that looked very similar to the one he'd seen parked near the hotel this morning. According to the online map, Collette – or her phone, at least – was somewhere in this building. He reached behind him, undid the press-stud fastening on the leather loop around the knife's handle and slid it from the scabbard.

Sticking close to the wall, Richard moved towards a metal roller door set into the brickwork. The car was parked close by. Richard dropped to his knee and stabbed the front right-hand tyre. As the air whooshed out he moved to the rear and punctured another. There was a Judas gate in the roller door, but it was closed and Richard figured there was no way he could open it quietly. He carried on past the car until he came to a garbage skip. He re-sheathed the knife and climbed up onto the skip. From there he could reach up to a window ledge. He saw the window was cracked and it appeared from scuff marks in the grime that someone had climbed in this way not long ago. The window was hinged down one side. When Richard slipped his fingers between the glass and the frame and pulled, it squeaked loudly. He froze. He was worried someone might have heard him, but his thoughts were drowned out by a piercing scream.

'It's Ingabire. My real name is Collette Ingabire.' She wept as she felt the wetness drip down from under her left ear. The devil bastard was serious – he was going to cut it off. 'Are you happy now?'

The man behind her eased off the pressure of the pistol, which he'd dug into her spine while the devil-man set to work on her again. Her chest was covered in blood from the wound to her chin and she could feel the hot blood sliding down her neck. Collette's tears mixed with the blood. For the first time she realised the chair was actually sitting in the middle of a heavy-duty nylon tarpaulin that had been spread across the floor. There were soft beeps behind her and the other man then started talking in the Asian language again. The devil stood there, his eyes bright through the mask, as if he was smiling in anticipation as his accomplice spoke on the phone.

Collette could only understand one word of what the man behind her said. Her surname. Her captor waited for the person on the other end of the line and when he spoke again his voice was lower. He asked the devil something in their language. The devil cocked his masked face to one side, and then back to the other, as if he was weighing up how to comply with the order he'd just received.

'My friend wants to know what you told the Englishman you met with this morning,' the devil said in his mask-muffled voice. He held the knife loose in his right hand.

Collette thought about the question. This was, as she suspected, to do with Richard's visit. He had shattered the safe world she'd created in Australia. There had been so many years of fear and guilt at first, but as she had become accepted in school on her merits and excelled at university, she had come to believe that she really had put Rwanda behind her. Despite the nightmares that still came, she had convinced herself she would be all right. But Richard had destroyed that.

'What did you tell him?' The devil hooked the blade of his knife under one of her bra straps and pulled it towards him. The strap snapped, exposing her breast. The devil placed the point of the knife on the skin of her breast and traced a line down towards her nipple. Collette whimpered.

She closed her eyes. If she was in danger, then Richard was in danger too. These men could not have known about her until he arrived in Australia. They must have been following him. She wondered if he was still alive. Her mind flashed back to Kibeho, to that terrible place where her father had been taken from her. She heard the screams of the other refugees, heard the explosions of the mortar bombs and the crack and thump of the machine-gun bullets. She saw the bloodshed and the bloated Tutsi corpses in the river and the streets in the months leading up to that fateful day. Amid all that sorrow, all those tears that had shaped her childhood in Rwanda, the only moment of hope was when Richard had picked her up and carried her to the army ambulance.

When the light had passed from her father's eyes she had fallen beside him, distraught and wailing the last tears left in her slight body. He had come for her and her mother, and he had been angry when Collette had told him that her mother had gone in search of Aunt Cecile and her children. They were all that was left of the family and her mother's line. And then it was just her. She was sure, at that moment in 1995 at

Kibeho, that someone would finish her off. She was a smart girl and she had seen how the Australian and Zambian peacekeepers had fended off the refugees. They were not there to take care of able-bodied Hutus. If she had been shot, or struck with a machete, they might have taken her into their care, but she knew they would pass her back over the razor wire to meet her fate at the hands of the RPA or the other men in the camp who had also tried to kill her father. What she hadn't told Richard was that her father had been shot not by an RPA man, but by a member of the Interahamwe militia who had been sheltering in the refugee camp along with many of his comrades and co-conspirators in the genocide. They had seen her father running towards the UN compound and a man had raised his hidden revolver and shot him. She should have told Richard that.

Collette looked at the mask and sought out the eyes peering through it. She felt the blade under her nipple and the point pressing into her flesh. She knew the plastic sheet on the ground was there for a reason. Death had robbed her of her childhood, and she had often felt, in the dark recesses of her consciousness, that it would find her in the same bloody manner to which it had taken her whole family. They had died for nothing. She, however, had a chance to protect the one person who had given her the many years of peace and happiness she had known with her adoptive parents in a new country.

'Go to hell,' she said to the devil, and forced a smile at her joke.

Collette could no longer feel the other captor's gun in her back, so as the devil pressed home the knife Collette threw herself backwards. As she fell she kicked out as hard as she could, catching the masked man in the crotch. He doubled over and yelped as Collette crashed onto the plastic sheet and the unyielding concrete beneath it. She felt the wind knocked from her lungs and a stabbing pain in her back as the wooden chair cracked and a splinter of wood dug into her flesh. She looked up, expecting to see the other man pointing a gun at her head. She was well aware that many Rwandans killed in the genocide would have thanked God for the mercy of a bullet.

She kicked with her feet and one of her high-heeled shoes fell off. Scrambling for purchase on the slippery sheet she barely made it a metre from the devil, who was still on his knees, his head down as he fought for breath. There were footsteps behind her.

'Stupid girl.'

Collette craned her head back and saw a young Asian man standing over her, his arm outstretched and a pistol pointing at her face. He had no mask, this one, and she realised that seeing his face had signed her death warrant, whatever she said.

'Last chance. What did you tell the Englishman?'

'Nothing.'

'OK, fine. If that is your answer then my orders are to kill you.'

'We fuck her first!' the devil gasped through his pain.

Collette was glad she'd hurt him. She closed her eyes and prayed to God that Richard had escaped and that a bullet would end it for her, rather than the knife.

Richard weaved his way through the maze of stacked pallets as quickly and as quietly as he could. He heard a crash and a desperate scream of pain. As he poked his head around a pile of cardboard boxes, he saw Collette sprawled on the ground, one man on his knees and doubled over in front of her, and a man standing behind her pointing a gun at her. He heard what the men said to her.

Richard ran from cover, his arm extended, and came up behind the gunman just as the shooter turned his head, searching for the source of the noise behind him. Richard, who was left-handed, drove the blade into the man's back, up and under the rib cage and into his heart, just as he'd heard an instructor describe it to a disinterested class of officers half a lifetime ago. He knew the Latin names for the organs he was destroying; he could visualise the path the knife was following. He knew exactly what he was doing and how he should do it.

The man stared, his eyes wide, as his blood gushed down over Richard's hand. Richard felt a primal hatred for him and twisted the knife, pushing it deeper still. The pistol clattered from the man's hand.

'Cuz!' The man in the devil mask jolted up straight and sprang to his feet, lunging towards Richard and the dying body he was clutching in an obscene dance. Richard tried to pull the knife free, but it was stuck, held in place by the suction of the man's innards. He pushed the dying man away from him, towards his attacker, and at the same time Collette kicked out and tangled the devil-faced man's legs, sending him sprawling. Richard saw that Collette's fall had cracked the frame of the chair she was bound to, and as she rolled away from the fallen Vietnamese she shrugged at her bonds. Richard wanted to help her, but the man in the mask was still a threat. He saw his chance and kicked the fallen man in the face as he started to get up. He looked around for the discarded pistol but couldn't see it.

The mask slipped down, revealing the young, spiky-haired man Richard had seen on his run. Richard put his foot on the back of the dead man, grasped the handle of Bilal's knife and heaved it out.

The other man recovered from the kick and sprang to his feet, spreading his arms in the stance of an experienced knife-fighter. Richard moved so he was between Collette, still struggling on the ground, and the armed man.

'First I'm going to kill you, then I'm going to gut that bitch. Slowly,' the man taunted. He lunged at Richard, who jumped back, out of reach. The man laughed.

Richard glanced at Collette. She was struggling frantically with her tape bindings and the wreckage of the chair. Richard didn't know how long he could hold off the younger man, let alone if he could defeat him in a fight. The man feinted to the left and Richard darted to the right, but before he could move out of range the Vietnamese had followed him. His right hand shot out and across and Richard felt the burning sting of a line drawn across his chest before he could move out of range and slash with his own blade.

Richard touched the fingers of his right hand to his T-shirt and saw the blood well into the weave of the fabric. He was sure it wasn't a deep cut, but the man had got under his guard before Richard had realised his mistake. The man grinned at him. 'You got any last words, now's the time to say them.'

'Your cousin's the second man I've killed this week. I think I'll try for a hat-trick.'

The man danced to the left on the toes of his black canvas

slip-on shoes and delivered a short, sharp kick to Collette's side. She yelled and curled in pain. 'Stop moving, bitch.'

Richard charged at the man, enraged at the sight of him tormenting Collette. The man nimbly twisted to avoid Richard's lunge, then shot his foot out again. Richard's shin connected with the man's leg, and Richard lost his balance and fell into a stacked pile of boxes. Cartons dislodged from the top of the pallet tumbled down around him and probably saved him from immediate execution. His attacker stayed just out of range as Richard fended off two more falling boxes of Asian noodles. The man laughed with glee.

Richard kicked up with his right leg as the man moved towards him. The gangster sidestepped then slashed Richard's outstretched leg and jumped back out of range again.

Richard struggled to his feet, his leg nearly buckling as the pain of the last slash registered with his brain.

'I'm sick of this game. Time to finish you off.' The man spun and kicked and Richard felt his forearm and knife hand go numb as the man's foot sent the blade spinning from his hand. Richard dropped back down and tried to roll, but the man's second kick caught him in the chest and drove the air from his lungs. Before Richard could move, the younger man was on top of him, knees astride his torso and the point of the knife at his throat as he struggled to drag a breath into his pain-racked body. 'Time to die, hero. This is for my cousin.'

Richard could sense movement on the other side of the man but did not want to alert him. Instead, he closed his eyes as he felt the pressure of the knife increase against the skin of his neck. 'Do—' He coughed. 'Do it!'

The gunshot exploded in the confines of the warehouse and Richard felt wet matter spatter his face. He opened his eyes and pushed away the falling gangster. Collette was standing, the pistol extended in her hands. Her mouth was open wide and her eyes were wild. Richard rolled the man off him and got to his feet. The single shot had left a small entry hole in the back of the man's skull and blown away a good chunk of his face. He'd died before he hit the ground. Richard winced as he put his weight on his lacerated leg and saw the blood oozing down over his soaked sock and shoe and onto the floor. Collette let the gun fall to the ground and Richard hobbled to her and took her in his arms. She started to sob.

'It's OK. You saved my life.'

She looked up at him. 'And you, mine. But what now? This is Australia, not Africa, Richard. What have we done?'

Blood oozed from under the body, spreading across the concrete floor. Richard wiped the blade of the knife on the shot gangster's jeans and then picked the pistol up from the floor. He realised he was shaking. Collette looked as stunned as he felt as she pulled her ripped blouse together and knotted it at the front. Both he and Collette turned when they heard a metallic clanking. He saw the handle on the steel door at the end of the warehouse start to jiggle. It sounded like someone was working a key in a stubborn lock. Richard sheathed the blade, tucked it into the back of his jeans and grabbed Collette's wrist. 'Come on, let's go.'

He limped to the Judas gate and unlocked it. In the distance he could hear a police siren. There was a squeal of tyres and Richard looked up the laneway to see Bilal's taxi whizzing towards them. The vehicle pulled up with a skid. 'Get in!'

Richard put his arm around Collette and bundled her into

the back of the cab, then jumped in the front passenger seat and slammed the door. 'Go!'

Bilal checked his rear-view mirror as he planted his foot on the accelerator. The car fishtailed until its rear tyres found purchase. The cab bounced over a speed bump, jolting them all in their seats, and Bilal swung left onto the main road. 'Get down!'

Richard and Collette lowered their heads as a police car sped past them. Bilal turned right onto Sydenham Road and slid into the parade of traffic. Richard and Collette sat up.

'Shit, man, I heard a gunshot. You got blood all over your face. What happened?'

Richard looked at him. 'Do you really want to know?' He folded down the sun visor and checked his face in the mirror. It wasn't just blood; there was also brain and some small bone fragments.

'No way. To tell you the truth, I'm on parole.' He looked back over his shoulder. 'You the one who got kidnapped?'

Collette blinked away her tears. 'Yes. Richard did nothing wrong.'

Bilal held up a hand. 'That's OK. It's all good. You got my knife?'

Richard pulled the knife and sheath from his jeans and held it up. Bilal looked at it, saw the blood that stained it and Richard's right hand. He noticed the gun in Richard's other hand. 'Shit, man.'

'Indeed.'

'So where do you want to go?'

Richard looked into the backseat. Collette wiped her eyes and shrugged. 'They know I'm here, Richard. I can't hide anywhere now. They'll find me, wherever I go. What am I going to do? My parents . . .'

Richard closed his eyes and laid his head against the head-rest of the car seat. He wanted to run, but Collette was right. They'd killed two men, and there was the man who had tried to kill him in South Africa, and the other assailant who'd tried to murder Carmel. The bodies were piling up all around the world. Whoever was behind this had money, reach, connections and intelligence. He and Collette would never get ahead of the game this way.

They could turn themselves in to the local police, but that was risky. With his record of drug abuse he could see the police thinking this was some gangland deal gone wrong, and if he and Collette stayed put, how long would it be before there was another attempt on their lives? He needed to get out of this country, now.

'I'm coming with you, wherever you go, Richard,' Collette said from behind him, breaking into his thoughts.

He reached down and felt his leg. The blood was still flowing. 'We need a pharmacist.'

Bilal nodded, his eyes alternating from the traffic ahead to his mirror.

Richard turned around in his seat again. 'All right, Collette. You can come with me if you want, but when we get to the airport you tell me everything. And I mean everything. Got it?'

She nodded. Then she started to cry again.

He needed her to hold it together a little longer. 'You'll need your passport.'

She sniffed back her tears. 'I live on the other side of the harbour, but it's no problem as my passport's at my parents' house with all my other important documentation. They live at Bexley, it's close to the airport.'

'OK.'

'Flights? It's short notice.' He was feeling a little light-headed. It was shock and blood loss.

'I can use my phone – book online.'

He pulled his wallet from his pants and passed her a credit card. 'Good. We can change my return flight; travel tonight, via Perth, get you on the same one with a bit of luck. You book us two tickets to Kigali – the South African home affairs people won't let you into the country on a one-way ticket unless you've got an onward flight.'

Bilal drove them to a park on the edge of a narrow water-way. A sign said it was Cooks River. They got out and Bilal looked around to make sure no one was nearby. 'Dump the knife and the gun in the river.'

'OK.' Richard limped close to the water's edge and threw both weapons out into the middle of the murky-looking stream. When he was done they got back in the cab and Bilal took them to a pharmacy.

'I'll go in,' Bilal said. 'You two got too much blood on you. People will remember you.'

'Get me some steristrips, Betadine, gauze, pressure bandages . . .'

Bilal held up a hand. 'I done this before, OK, mate?'

Richard nodded.

When he came back, Bilal drove around until he came to a deserted alley, where he pulled up. He got out and from the boot of his car pulled a plastic five-litre water container. 'I keep this for the radiator.' He helped Richard out of his jeans and washed down his leg. While Richard bandaged himself, Bilal helped Collette wash the blood from the cut under her chin. Richard cleaned his hands and his face. When she saw what he was doing, washing the gore from his face, Collette threw up beside the car. Richard found a clean T-shirt for Collette in his pack, and a change of clothes for himself. Bilal turned away modestly while Collette changed out of her blood-soaked blouse into the baggy shirt. When they were done, Bilal balled their soiled clothes and tossed them into a rubbish skip.

He drove them to Bexley and Richard waited in the cab, eyes closed and head back. She returned with her passport and a hiking pack. 'I had some old clothes I left with them. I wanted to leave a note, but then I thought better of it.'

When they arrived at the passenger drop-off zone outside the Qantas domestic terminal at Sydney Airport, Richard checked his watch and saw it was less than an hour since they had killed the two kidnappers. He got out and Bilal retrieved his bag from the boot of the cab. 'Thank you.'

Bilal shrugged. 'Broke the monotony, mate.'

'If the police find you . . .'

'Mate,' Bilal said to him, his mouth curling in a smile, 'I'll sing like a canary – tell them everything I know about you.'

'I'd expect nothing less. Thank you.'

'As long as the lady's OK.'

Collette moved to him and kissed him on the cheek. He blushed and got back into his car. 'Good luck.'

Richard had a feeling they'd need it.

22

Liesl stepped out of the lift and saw Carmel, who was sitting down to breakfast at a table in the Hôtel des Mille Collines' restaurant on the sixth floor. She walked over to her. If Carmel had seen her she gave no indication.

'Mind if I join you?'

Carmel raised her eyes from the iPhone beside her plate, then looked around. Liesl sat opposite her anyway.

'Coffee, please,' Liesl said to a passing waitress.

She looked out at the city. Kigali tumbled down the hill into the valley below and struggled up the hills on the other side, before the city petered out into the endless green hills that stretched into the morning mist. A squadron of yellow-billed kites dived and wheeled above the construction site across the road.

'My coffee?' Liesl asked the same waitress. The woman nodded, turned and walked away. 'Sleep well?' she said to Carmel.

Carmel looked up again from the phone screen. 'I'm not much of a morning person.'

Liesl slumped back in her chair. This was always going to be trying. 'Sorry you had to leave early last night. Were you not feeling well?'

Carmel sighed. 'I don't drink alcohol. I wasn't in any mood to sit around and watch you and Henri get hammered. It was a long day. All right?'

'All right.'

Defeated, Liesl got up and went to the egg station where she ordered an omelette with cheese and chopped chilli from the African cook. It was one of her staple hangover cures. That and vodka. Reluctantly, she made her way back to Carmel's table via the fruits and yoghurt. She heaped melon and pineapple into her bowl.

'Any sign of Henri yet?' Liesl asked as she sat down again.

Carmel chewed her food and looked out over the city. When she was finished she took a sip of orange juice. 'I would have thought you'd have a better idea of his movements this morning.'

'What?'

Carmel stared at her from across the table, as if daring her to break eye contact. 'You know what I mean.'

Liesl clenched her jaw. She held Carmel's gaze. 'No, I don't.'

But she did. Shit, she thought to herself. She'd invited Henri into her hotel room after they'd returned, drunk, from dinner. He'd wanted to borrow what appeared to be the hotel's only multi-plug power board. She'd finished charging her phone and laptop and topping up her camera batteries and she could have just passed the power board to him through the door. Instead, she'd faffed about unplugging stuff and told him to come in and get it. Once inside, he'd leaned against the wall and looked at her.

'What?' she'd asked him, smiling.

'Nothing. I'm just looking at all the stuff you have to charge. You're like a one-woman electrical store.'

She'd laughed. 'I'd offer you a drink if I had one.'

Henri had moved his hand from behind his back and held up a bottle of cognac.

'Bad man,' she'd chided, wagging a finger at him.

He'd shrugged. 'Sometimes.'

She'd seen the look in his eye. Maybe it was just the drink, but she was sure he would have stayed in her room for the night, given half the chance. He'd been probing her all night, asking questions about her life, her work, her plans for her trip in Rwanda. He'd offered to help her with contacts in the country and had suggested she stay close to him and Carmel, for safety's sake, while she investigated who was behind the apparent plot to harm them.

Henri was handsome, and he liked to party, and as far as she knew he was single. Ordinarily there would have been nothing stopping her having a nightcap with him, and perhaps more. But she'd thought of Carmel, and the business with Richard all those years ago. 'I think I should get to bed,' she'd said to Henri.

'But of course,' he'd smiled. He'd even bowed a little as he'd taken the power board and wished her goodnight.

Carmel's dark eyes felt like lasers, boring into her conscience. She had nothing to hide and, now that she thought about it, no reason to feel bad. 'Tell me something, then, since you don't believe me – are you and Henri an item? Or were you?'

Carmel flinched. 'Your omelette's here.'

Liesl turned to see the waiter hovering behind her. 'Thank you,' she said. She was trapped now. She couldn't very well get up and take her food to another table.

Carmel leaned forward on her elbows and lowered her

voice. 'You've got a thing for men I'm involved with, don't you? Or perhaps any man is fair game to you, Liesl.'

Liesl leaned back, away from the attack, and folded her arms. The woman was a professional victim. As far as Liesl was concerned, Richard could have called a halt at any time. It wasn't up to her to monitor his relationship status. Besides, he'd been two-timing Carmel, so what did it hurt if she'd had sex with him as well? That day, after the things she'd seen, she just wanted to feel another human next to her.

'It was easy for you,' Carmel continued. 'He was just another lover for you. But I'd planned my life around Richard. I had to come to terms with the fact that he'd lied to me twice over and that he'd never had any intention of coming back to Australia with me. I was a fool and you just made it that little bit worse for me.'

There was more Liesl could have told Carmel. She wanted to, but she knew it wouldn't help. She'd felt no sense of victory, sleeping with Richard. It hadn't been about taking him from someone else. It had been all about her – the need to fill the emotional gulf that day at Kibeho had ripped from her soul. Carmel was taking it personally, which was understandable, but she could never know just how much Liesl regretted her liaison with Richard.

The hell with it, and the hell with her, Liesl thought. She pushed her plate away and got up. As she turned and started walking out of the restaurant she saw Henri emerging from the lift. He smiled his crooked smile at her and raised a hand to his brow as though his head was aching.

'Morning,' he said.

Liesl strode past him and into the lift. In her room she made a cup of instant coffee while she waited for her laptop to boot up. As she sipped the bitter brew she opened her emails and had her first good news of the day.

It was a message from Pierre Rwema, a Rwandan Tutsi who'd worked as a driver and fixer for herself and a number of other freelance journalists and photographers in the aftermath of the genocide. Pierre said he was happy to hear from Liesl and looked forward to meeting her again. Liesl was pleased, although she also felt a little guilty. The reason she had Pierre's email was that he had contacted her – and presumably many of the other whites he'd helped back in the old days – about six years ago, asking for money. Liesl recalled a story about wanting to put his children through school. She'd ignored it.

Liesl used her mobile phone to call the number Pierre had emailed. He answered after only two rings. She went through the ritual of asking him how he was, and he her.

'Pierre, I need some help. I'm looking for some people here in Rwanda and I also need to get to Ruhengeri to see the mountain gorillas, and Nyungwe to see the chimps.'

'I can help, for certain. By the way, I emailed you some time ago. Did you not get my message?'

Liesl had been expecting this. 'I was overseas at the time, covering the war in Afghanistan, Pierre. I couldn't call you from there and I had no money, but I can pay you for your help now.'

'It will be fine. We can discuss that later. You are staying at the Mille Collines, yes?'

'Yes.'

'When would you like me to come around? I can be there in half an hour if you wish.'

'That would be perfect. Thanks so much, Pierre.'

She hung up and got her camera bag ready. She was on

assignment in Rwanda, as well as trying to work out who was trying to kill her, so she checked her cameras and her batteries, and her digital voice recorder. It took her back to the days when she'd been preparing to go out and document another day's worth of atrocities. While she waited, she thought about the confrontation with Carmel.

The Australian woman didn't know anything about her. They'd all been confused back then. Half the press corps was sleeping with each other, and the hotel staff were prostitutes for the UN workers and cameramen. It was as if the horror provoked some primal need to procreate. She guessed it was a similar phenomenon to the baby boom after the Second World War.

She'd been crazy not to use a condom with Richard. Even back in 1995 everyone was aware of the scourge of AIDS. It was as if she'd suffered a bout of temporary insanity. Liesl screwed her eyes shut and placed balled fists to her lids to try to force away the images.

The sex.

Carmel bursting in.

Richard leaving.

The clinic.

The tears squeezed out, finding their way to the surface despite her best efforts. She got up and went to her backpack and found the bottle of vodka buried in her clothes. She unscrewed the cap and took a decent slug. The spirit warmed and soothed her. She'd lied to Henri last night because she didn't want him to polish off her emergency stash of liquor.

She'd been too embarrassed and guilt-ridden to find Richard and tell him about the pregnancy that had resulted from their afternoon together. She had thought she was doing the right thing for her career, getting an abortion at a private clinic in Nairobi, but she'd carried deep feelings of guilt and loss ever since.

The confrontation just now with Carmel had shaken her. That bitch. What did she know about anything? Carmel didn't want her in Rwanda, which was fine with Liesl. As a photojournalist she was used to doing her own digging, and she was no stranger to danger. It was time, she thought, to forget about the others – Richard, Carmel and the handsome Henri – and take matters into her own hands.

Liesl dried her eyes on the back of the sleeve of her bush shirt, hefted her heavy camera bag and walked out of the room.

'You're quiet this morning,' Henri said to Carmel.

'Am I?'

'Yes. You've hardly said three words – and they were "pass the sugar".'

She didn't smile. She was so angry at Liesl, and him, right now, that her breakfast had given her heartburn. Carmel was confused, too. She didn't know whether to confront Henri about what had happened last night, or not. If she did, it might seem as though she had thought there was more to their relationship than there actually was. If she said nothing, then there was no way she and Henri could ever be more than acquaintances. The thought of making a fool of herself over a man again was tearing her up inside. Despite all of the work she had done to put her life back together and to become someone who was functional and in control of her demons, she was obviously utterly hopeless when it came to men. *Jesus,* she thought, *what's wrong with me?*

'Do you need a power adaptor, for your laptop or camera or whatever?' Henri asked, then sipped his coffee.

The streets below were alive with the rising hum of traffic and the ever-present blare of moto horns.

Carmel figured it was a safe enough question to answer. 'I brought a multi-adaptor with me. It works for all countries, so I'm fine thank you.'

'Very organised. Just as well, as Liesl had the only one in the hotel, apparently. I borrowed it from her last night, after we got back from dinner. We were both pretty drunk, so I hope we didn't disturb you when we came back to the hotel.'

'No, not at all,' Carmel lied. 'So did the party carry on when you got back?'

Henri raised his eyebrows, then leaned back in his chair as he regarded her. 'Ah, so you think there was some of the hanky-panky last night? Between me and Liesl?'

She folded her arms. 'None of my business.'

Henri smiled. 'I went to her room to get the adaptor board and I offered her a cognac, but sensibly she refused and sent me on my way. That's probably the only reason I am awake at all this morning.'

'Really?'

'Carmel, did you really think I had feelings for Liesl after just meeting her?'

'No, I . . .'

He leaned forward, resting his elbows on the table, and put his palms face down on the starched white tablecloth. 'Carmel, I like to think that we are friends, yes?'

'Yes, of course.'

'Even though we have only just met in person, I like you, Carmel. Very much. You are strong and brave, and you care for wildlife, as I do. I do not presuppose anything, but I would like to continue to be your friend and perhaps, well, perhaps when we sort this business out, then maybe you and I might spend a little time alone, getting to know each other better?'

'I . . .' Carmel felt the burn in her chest again and found the words wouldn't come.

'It is all right. Perhaps I have been too forward.'

'Not at all,' she said.

Carmel had interviewed enough criminals and witnesses in her time to come to the conclusion that she was about ninety-five per cent sure Henri was telling the truth – that nothing had happened between him and Liesl. She hoped he was telling the truth. He smiled at her, perhaps reading her thoughts, and she could feel her cheeks cool a little. She didn't particularly care that Liesl had left in a huff because Carmel had never forgiven her for the way she had broken up her relationship with Richard. Also, while she was concerned for Liesl's safety, it was actually a hell of a lot simpler if she didn't tag along with them to this morning's meeting with the Rwandan chief prosecutor. Carmel knew the power of the media, and had discreetly briefed journalists on occasion when she thought it would serve her interests or those of her clients, but she failed to see how having a South African photojournalist in tow could make it any easier for her to enlist the help of the prosecutor.

'You're planning on seeing the chief prosecutor today?' Henri asked as he pulled apart a croissant and spread butter on it.

'Yes,' Carmel said.

'I've seen the concierge already and ordered us a car and a driver. I would like to come with you, but I understand that it will not help having a stranger along, so I will wait outside while you have your meeting, and then perhaps I can assist you around Kigali, depending on what happens with the prosecutor. I still know my way around and, although it's a little rusty, my Kinyarwanda is passable.'

Carmel nodded. 'That sounds perfect, Henri, thank you.' She was wondering what she was going to do with him and how she would explain his presence and role to the prosecutor. In fact, Henri didn't have a role in any of this except that he genuinely wanted to help her. She was impressed by his tact and his concern for her.

She looked at her watch. 'My meeting with the chief prosecutor is in twenty-five minutes. We should get moving.'

'Of course,' Henri said. He stood and nipped around to her side of the table to pull her chair out for her.

'Thank you,' Carmel said.

'My pleasure.'

'Liesl, it makes my heart so happy to see you.' Pierre Rwema shook her hand and then clasped both of his over his chest. 'I have my car outside, but I thought perhaps you would first like to hear what I have found out.'

'Of course, we can sit over there.' She ushered Pierre towards a lounge suite near reception. Liesl noticed he was walking with a pronounced limp. 'What happened to your leg, Pierre?'

He shrugged. 'I was shot.'

'Really? When? What happened?'

'The trouble in Rwanda did not end with the return of the RPA and change in government,' he said as they took their seats. 'Hutus who fled to the DRC still cross the border occasionally and mount revenge raids against Tutsis. I was in one of the western border towns reporting on a flooded river when some rebels crossed and attacked the village I was in. They opened fire indiscriminately and four people were killed. Myself and seven other people were wounded. It was terrifying.'

'Hell,' Liesl said. 'Most people think Rwanda is at peace these days.'

Pierre shrugged again. She remembered, now, his Gallic indifference. 'It is, by and large, but the Hutu extremists still dream of returning and wiping out us Tutsis. There is a new generation of hate and it's hard to imagine that the old enmities will ever truly die out.'

He had aged well, Liesl thought, although middle age had brought with it quite a bit of bulk beneath the cracked black leather jacket he wore. The broad smile was still the same as it had been back in 1994 and 1995 – something that amazed her considering the horror they'd both witnessed – and his moustache was in better shape than the wispy growth he'd sported as a twenty-year-old university student. Pierre was tall and broad-shouldered, a handsome guy. He was now a subeditor on Rwanda's daily English-language newspaper the *New Times*, and Liesl hoped his contacts and street smarts would help her out.

'I'm sorry, Pierre, for not getting back to you when you emailed me,' she said.

'Forget it,' he said. 'I didn't have a job at the time – the newspaper I'd started on had closed down and I was pretty desperate, but it was embarrassing having to ask my old friends for help. It is me who should be apologising.'

'Not at all. So, did you recognise anyone in the picture I emailed you last night?'

'I showed it to a colleague who has also reported on the prosecution of *génocidaires* – I hope you don't mind.'

'No,' Liesl said, though she now wished she'd told him to keep the picture private. People who had seen it were becoming targets. She felt guilty, too, about not telling Pierre her fears, but she desperately needed his help. Besides, she thought, he was a survivor who knew how to take care of himself.

'My friend confirmed what I initially thought, that one of the men was a Colonel Jean-Baptiste Menahe who served in the FAR, the old Rwandan army that was dominated by Hutus. He was captured by Kagame's RPA in 1994 and accused of multiple counts of genocide.'

Liesl felt her hopes sink. She knew that the death penalty had been imposed on those senior figures in Hutu Power, the FAR and the Interahamwe militia who had been arrested. 'Is he still alive?'

'Remarkably, yes. He was convicted of organising genocide, but he appealed and a stay of execution was granted, much to the government's annoyance. His surname means "young warrior", and while he's not so young any more, he's still reportedly in good health and running a large part of Kigali Central Prison. Menahe has maintained all along that he didn't personally kill any Tutsis and that his activities were confined to fighting the RPA. He says that as an officer in the FAR, the national army at the time, he was simply doing his duty by engaging in lawful battle with the RPA, which was technically an invading force.'

'What do you think?'

Pierre shrugged. 'The prosecution's evidence was sketchy, but it's hard to imagine a senior FAR officer *not* taking an active role in the genocide. Menahe is a Hutu, but if I played devil's advocate I'd be asking why he didn't flee to Zaire with the other senior *génocidaires*. The fact that he stayed and fought the RPA and was captured on the field of battle at least shows he was taking his duties as an officer seriously. Do you know what the weapon is in the picture, the one the white man is holding?'

Liesl nodded. 'A surface-to-air missile.'

'You believe this has something to do with the assassination of the president?'

'Honestly, Pierre, I don't know. We can't think of anything else that people would go to such lengths to cover up.'

Pierre glanced across at her. 'Who is *we*?'

Liesl knew there was no way she could keep the truth from Pierre. He had put his life on the line to help her several times in the past, negotiating a path for her and the other reporters through checkpoints manned by angry, vengeful RPA soldiers and shepherding them away from firefights. 'Pierre, I should have told you earlier, but myself and a doctor and the lawyer currently investigating the significance of this photo have all recently been the target of murder attempts. It's like there's some giant conspiracy going on here. We don't know if it's just coincidence or if there is someone, or some group, who wants to kill anyone who's seen this picture. I'm sorry for not telling you.'

He shook his head. 'Don't worry, Liesl. I am a journalist. I would have wanted to investigate this with you anyway. Now you have me even more interested, although I should warn you that discussing theories about who shot down the president's aircraft in 1994 is a taboo subject in Rwanda.'

'Really?'

'Yes. The current president is, I believe, by and large a good man. He wants to put the past behind us, but that sometimes means burying some things. As journalists we like to dig, and that upsets the authorities.'

Liesl sighed. 'We don't even know if the missile launcher in the picture was the one used to shoot down the president's jet, or if the men in the picture were involved. So, you said your car is outside. Where are we going now?'

'To Kigali Central Prison, to see Colonel Menahe.'

When the lid on his wooden prison was prised open, with a squeak of bending nails, Vite was too dehydrated and exhausted to cry out. A pale face haloed by bright lights peered down at him and Vite blinked at the glare.

The man spat angry words at someone out of sight and Vite slumped in the white hands that lifted him out of the crate.

23

Collette helped Richard wash the last of the dried blood from his leg as they both stood in the shower room of the Qantas Club lounge at Sydney Airport's international departures terminal. Richard had his pants off and as he patted the wound dry with paper towel Collette took out the new pair of jeans she'd bought for him in one of the duty-free shops downstairs.

Richard inspected the fresh steristrips he had applied and squirted Betadine over the wound before applying a fresh bandage. He rested his hand on Collette's shoulder as she helped him slide his wounded leg into his pants. He winced in pain.

'Are you going to be all right?' she asked him.

'I might still need a couple of stitches when we get to South Africa, but I'll be OK for the flight.' Collette had been able to change Richard's ticket online to an evening service from Sydney via Perth, at a price, and she had been lucky enough to get last-minute but expensive flights for herself to Johannesburg and both of them on to Rwanda.

'Oh, Richard.' Collette's lower lip started to tremble. 'What have I done?'

He squeezed her shoulder. 'You've done nothing wrong,

Collette. It's not too late, you know – you can stay here in Australia if you want.'

She shook her head. 'No, I want to come with you, back to
Africa. I cannot have whoever is after us targeting my parents. I want to meet Carmel and tell her everything I know
about the men in the picture. These people need to be pros-
ecuted and put behind bars.'

He admired her bravery. Richard zipped up his new trousers and buckled his belt and they went back out into the
lounge. He scanned the room, fearing he might see some
more Vietnamese gangsters or, almost as frightening, some
uniformed New South Wales police or detectives in suits
come to arrest him and Collette. He thought of the blood
rushing down over his hand when he'd killed the first man,
and when he inspected his fingernails he could see traces of
the dark stain. He felt light-headed and steered Collette to
the first available lounge chairs.

'Can I get you a drink? Some juice?' Collette asked him.

'Tomato juice, please. With vodka, Tabasco and Worcester
sauce.'

'Is that good for you?'

'I'm the bloody doctor.'

Collette walked off and returned soon with the bloody
mary and a glass of water for herself. 'You didn't tell me
everything you knew about the picture, did you?' he asked.

She looked away from him. 'No.'

'Why not, Collette? It could have been important.'

She looked down at the carpet. 'I know, but seeing the
faces of those men brought it all back to me. I wanted the
memories to go away, but now I know the fear is real again
and that I must face it.'

'Who are they? You have to help me understand what's at play here.'

She sagged back into her chair and cast her eyes upwards, as though the memories were playing on some invisible plasma screen mounted on the far wall. 'I do remember that day, as I told you. My father found me, after his meeting with the men in the jungle, and scolded me for sneaking around. He told me I was to say nothing of what I'd seen and, in particular, he told me to forget I had seen the white man with the blond hair. White men, foreigners, came to see him on several occasions. But the one I remember most is the one in the picture, with the white, white hair. He had such blue eyes. He was almost like an albino, though not quite.'

'Where was he from, the man with the missile launcher?'

'I'm not exactly sure. I remember once he spoke to us – my brother and I – and that made my father angry, too. The blond man seemed particularly interested in my little brother, asking him what he studied at school, what sports he liked playing, that sort of thing. I knew the man wasn't Belgian or French, because of his accent, and I thought he might have been South African. There was a lot in the news at the time about Mandela's release from prison and the first multiracial elections. I asked him if he was from there, and he said something like, "Not from there, but near there." He said his family were German.'

'South-West Africa? The former Namibia maybe?'

Collette nodded. 'Yes, that's what I think now.'

'What was his name, Collette?'

She looked at Richard again. 'I *wish* I could remember. I've been trying since you showed me the picture. It's on the tip of my tongue; you know the feeling where something's just out of reach, hovering close by but you can't quite grab it?'

He nodded. 'Try, Collette. It's very important.'

'I *know*, Richard. I am trying.'

'Why was your father so angry that you and your brother had spoken to the blond-haired man?'

'He didn't say – he just told us never to speak to him again, and to go to our rooms next time he came to visit. The next time was when the picture was taken, and I disobeyed my father by sneaking into the bush and watching them with the missile launcher. It was as if the blond man was giving them all a lesson on how it worked. I remember him putting it up on his shoulder and aiming it at the sky, through the trees. What I do remember about him, and it came back to me when I saw the picture, was how much he scared me.'

'Why? Did he do something to you, or your brother?'

Collette reached into the pocket of her suit jacket and pulled out a crumpled tissue. She dabbed the corner of her eyes. 'No, he didn't. But you know what, I am sure he would have if he'd had half a chance. I can see him now, touching my brother's hair. It scares me even now, Richard. It's all coming back to me. I went to the bush to watch him because I wanted to keep tabs on him to make sure he didn't hurt my brother.'

Richard thought about the new information. 'Namibia had been independent for a few years before the genocide occurred. I wonder what this man was doing in Rwanda. Maybe he was an arms dealer?'

'I honestly don't know,' Collette said.

'And what about the other man in the photo? The Rwandan man? Do you know him, too?'

'I have no idea who he is. A colleague of my father's, I imagine.'

'I wonder if the white man is the key to what's been happening to us – the assassination attempts and your kidnapping.'

Collette checked her watch. 'We're boarding soon. I want to get away from here, but I don't know where we can be safe, Richard.'

'Neither do I.' And that was the problem. Whoever was after them had a worldwide network of contacts that could be paid to kill people. To draw on those sorts of resources you needed to be working for one of two organisations: a global crime syndicate, or a government.

Pierre parked his Nissan on the grassy verge of the street, two hundred metres past the entrance gate to Kigali Central Prison. 'Ready?' he asked Liesl.

'Not really, but let's go,' she said. She'd read about Rwanda's chronically overcrowded prisons in the years following the genocide. 'Do we have official permission to meet this guy?'

'Ah, no,' Pierre said. He smiled. 'But this is Rwanda. I have a cousin who is a senior warder here. We're going to meet him. All we're doing is visiting a prisoner at 1930, right? There is no law against that.'

'Whatever you say,' Liesl said. She remembered now that 1930 was the common local name for the city's prison.

As they approached the entrance gate, Liesl swung her camera bag around from her shoulder and started to unzip it. Pierre laid a gentle hand on her arm. 'No,' he said quietly. 'No pictures here please, Liesl. The guards are jumpy.'

She nodded. 'Understood.'

The prison gates, flanked by brick towers that reminded Liesl of a medieval castle, were on the crest of a ridge line overlooking the prison, a collection of red-brick buildings set down the hill in front of them, with the city of Kigali as a backdrop. Pierre and Liesl walked past a queue of prisoners' wives and children that stretched from the gates to the road. The women, many of them carrying baskets of food on their heads and paper shopping bags, were waiting patiently to be checked by a guard with an AK-47. Pierre spoke in French to a warder in a blue uniform with a green woollen jumper. The man carried a swagger stick under one arm, which Liesl guessed denoted some seniority. The warder eyed Liesl coldly, but eventually gave a curt nod and Pierre motioned for Liesl to follow him to the gate office.

In the office they signed their names on a register in front of a bored-looking female guard, and a younger prison officer was summoned to take them inside.

'This prison was built for two thousand inmates, but at its peak, after the genocide, there were eleven thousand men and women in here,' Pierre explained as they followed the guard.

Liesl couldn't help but feel unnerved by the stares of the men, young and old, who milled about in a muddy open area they passed through. Those whose relatives had arrived already sat at long wooden tables in the open, their spouses and children on the other side. Scores of eyes tracked her progress. Incongruously, Liesl thought, given their crimes, the prisoners' uniform was pink shorts and short-sleeve shirts.

'Pink?' she whispered.

Pierre nodded. 'Yes. The inmates are given cloth and needles and thread and told to make their own clothes.'

'*Inyenzi*,' a skinny prisoner whispered as they walked by. The comment earned the man a short, sharp stream of what sounded like abuse from the young warder.

'What was that about?' Liesl asked Pierre.

'He called me a cockroach. It was one of the names the Hutus had for us Tutsis at the time of the genocide. Some things never change.'

They moved deeper into the ramshackle maze of buildings and there seemed to be inmates everywhere. 'Even now there are still about six thousand men and women here. Obviously, we are in the men's section. That open area, over by the left there, is for the dysentery patients.'

Liesl saw a dozen or so men sitting or lying on the bare red dirt, resting. They looked even more gaunt than the rest of the prison population. An open drain passed through the courtyard, and she guessed this was why those with the debilitating diarrhoea were there. The stench of faeces wafted over, further sullying the omnipresent odours of wood smoke and sweat.

'You can go this way,' the warder said to her in English, pointing ahead. He turned and started walking back towards the gate.

'Where's he going?' Liesl asked, unable to mask her alarm at their armed escort's departure.

'We're entering another country, Liesl,' Pierre said. 'Follow me.'

'Another country? What do you mean?'

'The main part of the prison is ruled by the old regime – by the strong men of Hutu Power; at least those of them who are still alive because they have not been sentenced to death or because they are still awaiting trial. The warders are too scared to venture further into the prison. Also, the prisoners run their own affairs in a fairly orderly manner. There are systems of government in here. You have to remember that people from all walks of life were involved in the genocide.'

As they walked people continued to stare at them, but Liesl felt the absence of the warden had lessened the tension as they made their way down a slippery lane between the red-brick buildings. 'Is it violent in here?' Her knowledge of prisons was mostly based on what she'd read or heard about places such as Polsmoor, in Cape Town, where murder, rape and drug abuse were everyday occurrences.

'Sometimes, of course,' Pierre said. 'It is a community so there is crime and violence, but the *génocidaires* also police themselves and look after themselves. There are teachers who give lessons, ex-police and ex-soldiers who enforce the rules, doctors to treat the ill with rudimentary care, lawyers to represent the accused, and every other profession you can imagine.'

'Amazing.'

Now that she had overcome her initial fear and shock, Liesl took time to surreptitiously inspect the inmates she passed. She noticed that the uniform of pink shorts and shirt was actually not as uniform as it had first appeared. Some of the men's outfits were frayed at the hems, with gaping seams where their hand-sewing was coming undone. Others, however, had neatly pressed outfits with perfect stitching and, in some cases, embroidered with decorative designs. Clearly the prison society was stratified into haves and have-nots, rulers and serfs. She was fascinated, and wished she could follow her instincts and start shooting some pictures to record her experience, but she'd been made to leave her camera bag at the office after signing in.

Pierre stopped a couple of times to ask directions and was met with a jab of a thumb and a toss of the head. The men he asked also took their time to look Liesl over. Inwardly she shivered under their stares, but she forced herself to stand up straight and look them in the eye.

'We are close. It is this next building.'

Pierre led her into a building and the smell inside almost overpowered her. Urine and faeces competed with body odour, smoke and dank mould to see which could make her gag first. They passed men leaning against walls or standing and sitting in communal cells. As they climbed a flight of stairs, the smell lessened a bit, and weak sunlight filtered through the narrow slit windows.

'Colonel Menahe?' Pierre asked a slight, effeminate-looking youth who emerged from a doorway and walked quickly down the corridor towards them, head down. The boy looked over his shoulder and pointed to a door, outside which stood two smirking, hulking inmates. '*Il est là.*'

'*Merci.*'

Pierre approached the men, who appeared to be guarding the room, and spoke to them rapidly in French. They replied with a few words and one of them went into the room. Liesl suffered more ogling in silence as they waited for the guard to return. He spoke to Pierre, who then translated. 'He says we can go in. The colonel will see us.'

'That's very good of him.'

Pierre didn't comment on her sarcasm. She saw him draw a breath as he followed one of the bodyguards inside. The cell was the same as the others they'd seen, except that instead of being crammed with bunks for thirty it had two double bunks on opposing walls and a large office desk in the centre. A well-fed man in neatly stitched pink stood from behind the desk and extended a hand. Pierre shook it while Liesl cast a glance at one of the lower bunks with its rumpled blanket and sheets. The three other beds were neatly made.

'I am Colonel Jean-Baptiste Menahe. Pierre asks that I speak English, how do you do?' the man said to Liesl. She shook his moist hand.

'Fine, thank you. Has he told you what this visit is about?'

'I received a message earlier today from Pierre, telling me you are a journalist from South Africa who is doing an article about human rights abuses in Rwandan prisons. You have come to the right place and the right man.' He smiled across the desk at her and motioned for them to take a seat.

'Thank you for agreeing to meet with us, Colonel,' Liesl said. Pierre had filled her in on the cover story he had invented for her.

'My pleasure. There are so few distractions in prison. Pierre has been a fair and independent reporter on the justice system, or what passes for a justice system here in Rwanda. His articles locally and his commentary to foreign media have shown the world that many people incarcerated here in Rwanda – myself included – are innocent.'

Liesl nodded. She'd often heard it said by crime reporters that there was no such thing as a guilty inmate in a prison – they all maintained they were innocent.

'What is happening with your appeal, Colonel?'

'My lawyer says I have an excellent chance of acquittal, but then they always say that. But I am quietly confident I will be released soon. You see,' he said, directing his attention back to Liesl, 'I played no part in the genocide. Indeed, on several

occasions I stopped the troops under my command from join-
ing in with the Interahamwe militia. I was brought here on
trumped-up charges simply because the new regime believed
all in the national army were war criminals. I was a soldier who
defended the legitimate government of the day, nothing more.'

Liesl reached into the pocket of the fleece jacket she wore
and took out the print of the picture the dying man had given
Richard. She placed it on the desk and slid it across the table
towards the colonel.

The smile fell from his face. He lowered his head to better study the picture, but kept his hands under the table, as
though he was too scared to touch it. After a few seconds he
looked up, his eyes drilling into Liesl. She shivered. 'Where
did you get this?'

Liesl took a breath. People had been trying to kill her over
this picture, so it was pointless hiding the truth. 'I took it. At
the Kibeho refugee camp in 1995. The man holding the picture – you can see his fingertips at the edge – died that day.'

'As well he should have,' the colonel said.

Lisa felt her courage weakening under his malevolent
gaze. 'That's you in the picture, on the far left, talking to the
white man.'

Menahe's mouth widened into a grin but his eyes remained
steely cold. 'This picture was taken seventeen years ago. This
may or may not be me.'

'You've been identified, Colonel.'

The ex-officer turned his eyes on Pierre, who shifted in
his chair. Liesl glanced behind her and saw the bulky bodyguards filling the doorway. Whether or not they understood
the conversation, they had sensed the change in mood and
were watching the conversation with interest.

'If this is me, what of it? It is a group of men in the bush, nothing more.'

'A group of men with a surface-to-air missile,' Liesl said, waiting for his reaction.

Menahe pushed the picture across the desk to her, then leaned back on his chair, causing the legs to creak. He kept his hands out of sight. 'So what? We used surface-to-air missiles in the army. There is nothing unusual about this.'

'Then why would someone want to kill me and everyone else who has seen that picture? And who is the white man in the picture, Colonel?'

'I don't have to answer your questions.' The colonel's tongue darted out and moistened his lips. He looked over their heads towards the bodyguards. 'I think it is time for you to leave now.'

'Colonel,' Pierre said, 'we are not looking to cause trouble. But what Miss Nel says is true – there are people whose lives are in danger because of this picture. We merely wish to find out why.'

'My advice to you both,' Menahe said, leaning forward again, 'is to burn this picture and forget you ever saw it.'

'That's not possible, and besides, it's the subject of an investigation by the ICTR. You're probably going to get a visit from one of their investigators and the national prosecutor today,' Liesl said, playing her trump card. He could dismiss her and Pierre, but not the law, and she wanted to see his reaction.

'You shouldn't have said that,' the colonel said.

'Why not?' Liesl glared back at him defiantly.

'Because now I am probably going to have to kill you.'

24

Carmel got out of the car and closed the door. A light drizzle was falling and she zipped up the waterproof spray jacket she'd brought with her. She knew how changeable the weather could be in the hills of Rwanda. The meeting with the prosecutor had gone well. He had immediately identified Colonel Jean-Baptist Menahe in the picture and told Carmel she could find him at Kigali Central Prison.

Henri opened the back door of the small sedan and pulled his cigarettes from his shirt pocket. He lit one. 'Are you sure you're going to be OK by yourself?'

'I've been here, and other prisons, plenty of times. I know what I'm doing.' She had been into the prison in the company of an interpreter on many occasions, without the need for armed guards so she was probably safe enough, though in the light of recent events she did feel more nervous than if she were going to interview an accused any other time. All the same, as much as she liked Henri she was not convinced it was appropriate for him to sit in on this interview.

Henri shrugged as he lit and inhaled. He exhaled a long stream of smoke, adding to the fog of wood fires and exhaust fumes that were settling over Kigali under the low cloud. 'I don't doubt that, but given what has happened lately . . .'

'Given what has happened lately, inside the four walls of a prison is probably the safest place for me.'

Henri nodded. 'What makes you think this colonel will be willing to talk to you?'

'The chief prosecutor thinks he's hiding something. The colonel's probably going to win his appeal and his freedom soon, but the government investigators have always thought he was holding back.'

Henri waved his cigarette in a circle in front of him. 'That is my point. Why would he talk to you and not them?'

'I can offer him something the Rwandan government can't – his life. If we can find out what's behind all this and it implicates the colonel further, the Rwandans will keep him in prison and, if he's found guilty of a capital crime, they'll quash his appeal and hang him. If I can cut a deal with him, for information, I can probably pull some strings with the prosecutor to get his appeal decision expedited and when he's out of prison I'll get him out of the country. If he cooperates I might be able to get him into witness protection, and if he's guilty of something heinous then at least he'll be banged up in The Hague in a cell that would be five-star compared to this place, and certainly better than being hanged.'

Henri leaned back against the car and looked at her, his head slightly cocked.

'What?' she asked.

'You are a tough woman, Carmel Shang. And devious. I would not want you as an enemy.'

She nodded. 'Just as well we're friends then.' She checked her watch. 'If I'm not out in an hour, send in the SAS, OK?'

'Consider it done. But I'll bring some legionnaires, though, as I think it should be Frenchmen who save the day.'

'Very funny. I'll be back soon.'

Carmel walked across the road to the prison and joined the throng of men, women and children queuing to visit those inside. A warder in a green jumper, carrying a swagger stick under his arm, walked up to her, a guard armed with an AK-47 in tow. It had been a couple of years since she'd visited the prison, but he looked familiar. 'Can I help you?' he asked.

'I'm here to see one of your prisoners. Colonel Jean-Baptiste Menahe.'

'He is a popular man today. I have seen you before, yes?'

Carmel nodded. 'My name is Carmel Shang. I am a prosecutor for the ICTR. What do you mean, he's *popular today*?'

'Two other people are visiting him right now.'

'A white woman?'

The warder nodded. 'This is very irregular. You must wait here while I call my superiors.'

Carmel looked skyward and held out her hands, palms up. 'It is raining. Are you going to make me stand out here and get soaked while you ask your superiors for permission to do your job?'

The man looked over his shoulder at his office, and Carmel caught the faint smirk of the guard with the AK-47. She'd successfully managed to shame him in front of his subordinate. 'You can go inside,' he said with an imperious nod. 'And sit with the prisoners' relatives while I clear this with the chief warder.'

'Thank you,' Carmel said, and walked to the gate where she signed in, ahead of the waiting families. The women in the queue, in particular, had watched the exchange and followed her every move as she strode through the gates into the busy courtyard.

Once inside she noted two other warders who were watching over the men receiving visitors. Carmel walked up to one of the guards, who had a pistol in a holster on his belt. 'I've come to see Colonel Jean-Baptiste Menahe. I'm with the other white woman who is with him, but I was running late. Do you understand what I'm saying?'

The man nodded. 'I speak English, yes. I saw them go in about twenty minutes ago.'

'I need to get to them.'

The warder looked at his colleague, who just shrugged. 'I am not supposed to leave my post.'

Carmel maintained her bluff. 'That's fine. I will go in myself. Which block is the colonel in?'

The man looked past her, as if hoping to spot a more senior officer. 'You should not go in there alone.'

'So, show me the way. How long will it take? My friend had a man with her, yes?'

'Yes, madam, she did.'

'Then take me to them. He can escort me out.'

The man said a few words in French to his counterpart who, again, just shrugged. 'Come with me,' he said. 'Quickly.'

Carmel followed the guard through a maze of ambling male prisoners in matching pink outfits. Her nose rankled at the stenches that came from the prison and she looked straight ahead, ignoring the stares of the inmates. The prison was just as depressing as it had been last time. She'd outgrown her initial fear of the place, but all the same it was still overcrowded and borderline medieval. The soldier in her thought these men were lucky not to have been killed for their crimes, but the lawyer in her recoiled at the abuses of basic human rights, no matter what crimes the inmates had committed.

The sound of a melodious choir wafted from a brick building with a rusted tin roof. Carmel marvelled at the beauty of the massed voices in such a setting, and shivered at the contrast of this beauty with the crimes the singers may have committed. Her escort pushed his way through a throng of men and Carmel quickened her step to keep up with him. Ahead, past the guard, she saw half-a-dozen men running towards them. One of the men had his hand behind his back and started to bring it into sight.

'Look out,' Carmel cried, 'he's got a weapon!'

The warder turned to look back at her, perhaps not having heard her properly, but in the time it took to do so, the clutch of men was on them. The man Carmel had spied raised his hand and lashed out with a homemade club fashioned from a broken wooden chair leg reinforced with strips of iron. As the warder fumbled for the clip of his holster the club caught him on the side of the head and he fell. Carmel caught the guard just before he hit the ground.

Again, the prisoner with the chair leg struck down at the warder as two other men reached down for him. Carmel found herself pinned under the guard, and as she tried to slither away from the rain of blows and the hands that groped for her, she felt the angular butt of the warder's pistol dig into her belly. She reached out and grabbed the gun as she felt another hand reaching for the weapon. Carmel had the grip first and, hoping the warder had the pistol loaded and cocked, she swivelled it, still in its holster and slid her finger into the trigger. The prisoner trying to get the gun punched her in the face and Carmel needed no further justification. She pulled the trigger.

The gunshot echoed off the cell block walls and the bullet exited the base of the canvas holster and blew her assailant backwards, off her and the fallen warder. The man with the chair leg straightened and backed off a step as Carmel slid the gun fully from the holster and scrambled to her feet. She raised the pistol, wrapped her left hand around her right and adjusted her stance to distribute her weight over both feet. It was the first time she'd held a firearm since she'd left the army. The man who had punched her was clutching his stomach and screaming.

'Get back!' she shouted.

The other prisoners regrouped, a few paces from her, as Carmel swung the barrel of the pistol left and right, keeping them at bay. She slowly lowered herself to one knee and checked for a pulse in the neck of the fallen prison warder. She found it, though it was weak. The wounded man writhed on his back, but she could do nothing for him.

Carmel started edging backwards, but when she risked a glance over her shoulder she saw a phalanx of men in pink blocking the laneway between the cell buildings. She heard shouting and the slap of sandals on mud and looked to her front again to see a new crowd moving towards her.

At the head of the mob were three boys who barely looked eighteen. They ran straight at Carmel. 'Stop!'

The first boy slowed, nearly tripping as he saw the gun. 'Don't shoot!'

'What's happening?'

'One of the *chefs*, the chiefs, he has a hostage,' the second boy said.

God, Carmel thought. 'A white woman?'

'*Oui,* madam.'

A siren started to wail. Carmel looked behind her, back up the alley towards the visitors' compound and the entrance to the prison, and saw the gates starting to swing shut.

Liesl had seen the anger building in the colonel, but she had been totally unprepared for the speed and violence of his attack.

In one fluid move he had drawn a homemade knife, fashioned and sharpened from an offcut of metal, from under the desk, which he'd flipped up and wielded in Pierre's face, knocking Pierre back off his chair. Colonel Menahe was on top of Liesl with the point of the knife pressing into the soft skin of her neck before she could let loose a scream. The bodyguards moved in on some silent signal and began pummelling Pierre with their fists.

The colonel drew her to her feet, his arm around her neck constricting her flow of oxygen, and walked her out into the corridor and down the stairs of the crowded cell block. Men gathered in his wake and started chattering. Some laughed and others cheered.

'What are you doing?' Liesl asked, struggling for breath.

'You have caused this to happen.'

Liesl stumbled, half deliberately, in a bid to slow the colonel. He let her fall and she slid painfully down three stairs. He kicked her in the ribs and she screamed. He bent and picked her up again, returning her to his iron embrace. 'Try and delay me again and I will kill you slowly, after I have given you to my men. If you do as I say, I will release you when we are free.'

'You're trying to break out?' Liesl gasped.

'If I stay in prison now I will be killed.'

It hurt to breathe. Liesl's mind was racing. She was terrified of what would happen to her, but at the same time she was desperately trying to piece together this new information. 'But why? It looks like you run this prison.'

'Because of you. Because of that stupid photograph. It should never have been taken.'

'Let me help you, I can—'

Menahe increased the hold on her throat and Liesl started seeing pinpricks of light in her peripheral vision as he dragged her out into the muddy laneway between the cell blocks. More men joined the procession, but others, perhaps not wanting to suffer the consequences if the colonel's bid for freedom failed, sprinted ahead of the mob.

Liesl realised the colonel was going to use her as a hostage. She twisted in his embrace, to lessen the pressure on her neck and to look for Pierre. She saw him, blood streaming from his nose and from a cut on his forehead, being carried barely conscious between two other inmates, also armed with shivs, homemade prison knives.

'Who would kill you?' she asked the colonel again, coughing as the words caught in her bruised neck.

'If you don't know then I am not going to tell you. Perhaps I'll take you to him when I get out, in exchange for my life. Who else knows about the photograph?'

'Go to hell,' Liesl said. The colonel squeezed tighter and Liesl felt the point of the knife dig into her skin.

'Colonel!' yelled one of the men in the vanguard of the surging mob.

'What is it?'

'Another woman!'

Liesl looked past the scouts and saw Carmel Shang striding, alone, towards them. She held her hands up high.

'Liesl!'

'Carmel!'

Liesl's call was silenced by yet more pressure and she felt herself start to grow dizzy in Menahe's arms. She blinked and saw Carmel had started to run towards them.

'Release her!' Carmel shouted.

The colonel stopped and his entourage followed suit, a few at the rear bumping into those in front who were blocking their view ahead. 'Colonel Jean-Baptiste Menahe,' Carmel yelled, 'my name is Carmel Shang. I am a prosecutor with the International Criminal Tribunal for Rwanda. If you let that woman go I will see you are not mistreated.'

'Pah! Your United Nations tribunal is a sham. I have committed no crime of genocide and have nothing to answer for. Get out of my way or I will take you with me as well.'

'You're committing the crime of kidnapping now. You will stay in prison whatever the result of your appeal.'

Liesl felt Menahe's grip loosen a little. 'Get out of my way,' he said.

'I need to talk to you, Colonel. I need to know who the white man in the photograph is.'

The colonel started to walk forward again and his men, impatient for their freedom, started moving with him. 'I will tell you who he is. He is the devil. Grab her!'

Four of Menahe's men broke from their ranks and moved to grab Carmel. She reached behind her and pulled out the guard's pistol from the waistband of her jeans. She brought it up in front of her in a two-handed grip. The inmates sent to grab her stopped and backed away, but the colonel kept walking, dragging a pale-faced Liesl with him.

'Hah! You dare to pull a gun on me, woman.'

'Stop right there and let her go,' Carmel said.

Menahe laughed as he kept walking, slowly closing the gap between them as he talked. 'You are a woman, and a lawyer. Even the court you serve is too soft to impose the death penalty. You people know nothing of my country, of my people, of my Africa. You are soft. You will not shoot me.'

Carmel tightened her grip on the pistol to still her shaking hands. She had shot one man today already, possibly killing him. The army had taught her to shoot, and to aim for the centre mass of a target around the stomach and chest to ensure the best chance of a hit. Shooting guns out of people's hands or wounding them in the leg was the stuff of action movies.

'Stop!' she shouted once more.

He shook his head. 'No. You will give me the gun and you will become my second hostage. I will walk out of here with both of you and give you to the devil as a peace offering.'

'Stop or I'll shoot.' The siren continued its mournful wail from the gatehouse.

He mocked her again with his laugh, then stopped, ten metres from her. 'I've changed my mind. I'm not going to take you hostage, woman, I'm going to gut you. You put down your pistol and kick it to me or I'm going to kill this one now, in front of you.'

Carmel sneered back at him. 'Do what you want to her. It's you I want now.'

Menahe chuckled. 'One of you has to die now. Take her!' He let go of Liesl and pushed her into the arms of another prisoner armed with a shiv before she had a chance to run. The colonel advanced on Carmel, his knife up and ready to strike.

'Stop, Colonel. For God's sake, don't make me kill you.'

'I have been responsible for more deaths than you can possibly imagine. And I have killed with my bare hands. You will not shoot me.'

He ran at her and Carmel squeezed the trigger twice, in the double tap she'd practised at the firing range. The bullets knocked the colonel backwards. Carmel swung and aimed at the head of the man who held Liesl. He let go of her and turned and ran, as did the now fragmented crowd that had been following the colonel. From the gate they heard more gunshots and the *pop* of exploding tear-gas canisters.

Carmel ignored Liesl, who fell to her knees and started dry-heaving as the shock of her ordeal began to sink in. Carmel knelt beside the wounded colonel. Blood frothed and gurgled from a hole in his chest. The other bullet looked like it had grazed his rib cage. 'Talk to me,' she said.

He wheezed as he tried to speak. 'No . . . you must kill me now. Quickly.'

'Why should I give you an easy way out? Did you kill President Habyarimana with the missile launcher in the picture? Were you part of Hutu Power, or the Akazu elite?'

'It . . . it was him . . . he is the devil . . .'

'Who, the white man? What is his name?'

'Devil.'

'Who did he work for? The president's wife and her supporters in the Akazu?'

'He . . .'

'Kagame? Did the Tutsis do it?'

'Kill . . . me . . .'

'No, damn you. I'll get you witness protection. I'll save you.'

'You cannot save me. I am damned. All of us . . .'

'For God's sake!'

'Yes. Maybe . . . maybe neither.'

Colonel Menahe raised his right hand and Carmel dodged quickly out of the way, thinking he was trying to slash her with his knife. Instead, the colonel raised his torso a little, wincing with pain, and stabbed the shiv into his own throat and drew it across his jugular vein.

'No!' The spray of blood hit Carmel in the face and she wrestled with him as he used his ebbing strength to fend her off. Carmel reached for the gory wound and tried to get her fingers onto his artery as he grabbed her wrist to prevent her. 'Help me!'

Liesl kneeled by her side and started coughing as the tear gas made its way up the alleyway. Carmel, too, started coughing as the blinding chemicals stung her nose and eyes. The colonel's strength ebbed away, and Carmel knew she was too late. The flow of blood was reducing with each final beat of his heart.

Liesl felt rough hands grabbing her and looked up through her streaming tears to see two warders in gasmasks, armed with shotguns. More uniformed men fanned out past them, firing shots into the air and tossing tear-gas grenades ahead of them.

'Leave this man,' she heard a warder say to Carmel, his voice muffled by the rubber mask.

'No. You have to get an ambulance. We must revive him.'

Liesl looked down at Menahe's body and remembered the point of the knife and his choking grip. She glared at Carmel. 'You would have let him kill me.'

Carmel got up and they both started walking back towards the gate, under the escort of the warders. Two other prison officers had retrieved a groggy Pierre and were helping him walk. 'No,' Carmel said.

'I don't believe you,' Liesl said, wiping her eyes.

Carmel shrugged. 'Well, maybe.'

Liesl reluctantly smiled, and so did Carmel.

Other prisoners, who had not taken part in the mini riot, cowered down muddy laneways and back into their cell blocks to escape the noxious gas, and the very real possibility of guilt by association. Teams of riot-squad guards were darting into the crowds that had gathered and dispersing it with shouts and by thrashing batons if they detected the merest hint of resistance.

Liesl and Carmel let the phalanx of armed officers escort them back to the gate, coughing and dry-retching from the after-effects of the gas. Liesl felt groggy and light-headed, as though recovering from an anaesthetic or just waking from a confusing dream. She needed a cigarette and a brandy and Coke as soon as was humanly possible. She looked at Carmel, her stride long, head up, dark eyes darting from side to side. She seemed unfazed by the ordeal they'd just been through, and by the act of killing a man. No matter what their differences were, Liesl had to admit she was gutsy.

When they reached the gates they were opened for them, just wide enough to let them out, and Liesl saw a line of armed police and soldiers waiting outside in case any rioters suddenly poured out. Liesl saw the Frenchman, Henri Bousson, dart through the traffic that had slowed to ogle the smoke above the prison, despite the barked orders of police to move on. Henri came to them.

'Carmel . . .'

Liesl saw Carmel's resolve start to crumble as soon as she spotted him, and felt a sudden pang of jealousy. He spread his arms and she moved to him. Liesl stopped as Henri enfolded Carmel in an embrace. They didn't kiss, but she buried her face in his neck.

'My God,' he said, 'I just heard. The guards told me.' He held Carmel back out at arm's length. 'Are you all right?'

'I'm fine,' she said, but Liesl saw her lip start to tremble. Henri wrapped her in a bear hug again, and Liesl felt lonelier than she had in a very long time.

'I wouldn't have forgiven myself if anything had happened to you,' Henri said to her. 'The man you were seeking is dead?'

'Yes,' Carmel said. 'And he told us nothing.'

25

'What do you think the colonel meant by *maybe neither* the Hutus nor the Tutsis killed the Rwandan president?' Liesl asked. She took a big gulp of her wine. They sat around a table by the pool at the Hôtel des Mille Collines.

Carmel stirred her Coke with her straw, trying to make it last. The way she felt after the business at the prison, she could have killed for the numbing buzz of a double gin and tonic or two. 'A third force, a foreign power, perhaps?'

'The stuff of conspiracy theories,' Henri ventured. Carmel noticed he was sticking with sparkling water tonight. She doubted he was doing it out of politeness to her, but she was pleased he was staying sober while they tried to work this thing out.

'I'm not so sure,' Carmel said. 'There were several international powers with an interest in the outcome of the Arusha Peace Accords in Rwanda.'

'Like who?' Liesl asked.

'Belgium, as the former colonial power in Rwanda, had always had an influence in who was in power. The Belgians still have a strong business presence here. They supported the Tutsis initially, then switched that support to the Hutus after the country gained its independence, in a ham-fisted attempt to atone for some colonial guilt. That resulted in the rise of Hutu Power. Then there's the French, of course.'

'Who like to assert their power just because they can, I suppose you're going to say?' Henri said, tossing his nose in the air.

'Don't take it personally, Henri,' Liesl said.

'I don't.'

'But the French did supply the Rwandan government with arms before the genocide, and their Operation Turquoise, in the immediate aftermath of the genocide, did proclaim safe zones that allowed hundreds of thousands of Hutus, including many *génocidaires*, to escape to Zaire and avoid prosecution,' Carmel said.

Henri waved a hand as though swatting an imaginary fly. 'To say the French government would protect mass murderers is insulting.'

'Well, they did,' Carmel pointed out, 'even if it was unintentional.'

'And what good would it do France to foment genocide by shooting down President Habyarimana's aircraft? Carmel, that jet was a Dassault Falcon 50, French-made and a gift to the Rwandan government from President Jacques Chirac.'

'Yes,' Carmel continued, playing devil's advocate, 'but Habyarimana had agreed to implement the Arusha Accords, which would have allowed Paul Kagame and the RPA back into Rwanda, along with the return of a million English-speaking Tutsis. Rwanda would be at risk of becoming an Anglophile country instead of a Francophile one, and the return of the Tutsis would have paved the way for more American involvement in Rwanda.'

'America?' Liesl said. 'Why would America have been interested in a little country like Rwanda back in 1994?' Liesl beckoned the waiter over and ordered another glass of wine.

'It mightn't have seemed likely at the time, but the history of the region since the genocide has given some weight to this theory.'

Henri shook his head. 'I'm not convinced.'

'Let her talk, Henri,' Liesl said. 'I'm interested in this.'

Carmel continued: 'Paul Kagame, who went on to become president, received his military training in the Ugandan Army. He was studying as an exchange officer at the US Army's Command and General Staff College at Fort Leavenworth, in Kansas, in 1990 when the RPA first invaded Rwanda. When the invasion began, Kagame returned home immediately, resigned his commission and went to fight with the RPA. He had close links with the Americans, and after the RPA took over Rwanda and Kagame became president and head of the Rwandan Patriotic Front, the American presence in Rwanda increased.'

'Why?' Liesl asked.

'As it turned out, after stabilising his own country, Kagame turned his eyes on Zaire, where ethnic Tutsis were being persecuted by the Zairean military and by Hutus who'd escaped from Rwanda. The Americans had previously supported the Zairean president, Mobutu Sese Seko, but he'd become a madman by this stage, and an embarrassment to the Americans. There were vast mineral resources there that America and the west was worried about losing. Mobutu had outlived his usefulness and the Rwandans were arming and supporting a viable opposition army led by Laurent Kabila. The Americans decided to help Kabila through Kagame. I was back here in Rwanda in 1996 when the civil war in Zaire was hotting up. The American Club – the Indian restaurant where we ate the other night – was full of CIA people and US special forces soldiers who were using Rwanda as a jumping-off point for Zaire. In the end, Kabila's forces were victorious over Mobutu and the country became the Democratic Republic of Congo, largely thanks to Rwanda's help.'

'So,' Liesl said, nodding, 'it's possible the Americans were secretly backing Kagame so that he could eventually help bring about a regime change in Zaire.'

'Yes.'

Liesl frowned. 'But killing Habyarimana sparked the genocide. Do you think the Americans would have been cynical or foolish enough to back an assassination if they thought that might happen?'

Carmel just looked at her.

Aston sat at the bar of the Hôtel des Mille Collines nursing a dewy half-litre glass of Primus beer. He looked at the knot of white people, the man and the two women, sitting at a circular table on the far side. The other patrons, high-heeled prostitutes fluttering about Belgian and French businessmen, were drinking and laughing, but the trio sat away from the Thursday-night happy-hour merriment.

Aston took another sip of beer, got off his seat and walked around. 'Aha, we meet again,' he said to Liesl Nel.

'Oh, howzit,' she said after a short pause.

That was good, Aston thought, that she had not automatically recognised him. He had been tailing them at a distance, but it had been made impossible when the two women had gone their separate ways. He had stayed with the Nel woman and waited outside the prison to see what happened. He hadn't been surprised to see Carmel Shang and the French-man arrive a short time later.

It had been logical that they would find their way to the colonel. He'd heard the prison siren and seen the commotion among the warders as they turned away the queue of inmates' relatives and shut the gates. He'd seen the riot-squad officers arrive and toss their smoke grenades, and heard the crackle of muted gunfire from deep inside the prison, and he'd dared to hope that this muddled situation had sorted itself out within the prison walls.

'I am fine, and you?'

Liesl shrugged.

'Hello, my name is Henri Bousson,' the white man said, sliding off his bar stool and offering a hand.

'Aston Mutale.'

'Can I help you with something? The ladies have had rather a trying day, I'm afraid.'

'No, nothing in particular. I met Liesl at the airport in Johannesburg. I am a fan of her photographic work.'

'I see,' Bousson said, staring at him. Clearly Bousson did not want him hanging around. Aston knew that to push further to join them in their drinks might arouse suspicion. Aston had heard on the local radio that Colonel Jean Baptiste Menahe had been shot during an escape attempt from Kigali Central Prison. What Aston didn't know, but needed to know, was if the colonel had provided the women with any salient information before he died. Somehow, Aston doubted it. 'Well, nice to see you again, and enjoy your drinks.'

'Wait a minute,' Liesl said as he turned to leave. 'You said you had a wide network of business contacts in Rwanda in the import-export business.'

'I did, and I do,' Aston said.

'Does that extend to arms deals?' Shang interrupted.

Aston pursed his lips. 'I can assure you, madam, that I am involved in nothing illegal. I deal in legitimate business only.'

'I didn't mean to offend you,' Carmel said.

'No offence taken. However, while I operate above the law, my visits to Rwanda have, occasionally – how shall I put this – brought me into contact with certain people who are not so scrupulous. Why, if I may ask, are you interested in illegal arms deals?'

'No reason,' Liesl said. She looked at the other two, asking some unspoken question.

'I don't know if it is a good idea to involve more people in this business, given how much trouble the photograph has caused,' Bousson said.

'We're getting desperate,' the lawyer said to Bousson and Liesl. 'No one need know his name and I'm running out of leads.'

Aston knew exactly what they were discussing. The woman was tough, and he reluctantly admired the way she was potentially endangering an 'innocent' bystander in her quest.

'Would you take a look at this picture for us, please?' the Australian asked Aston.

Liesl slid the picture across the table and Aston picked it up and pretended to study it.

'What is it?' Liesl asked. 'Do you recognise any of those men?'

Aston rubbed his chin. 'When was this taken?'

'Sometime around 1994, we think,' Carmel said.

'A terrible time. I know; I was here not long after the genocide.'

'You were?' asked Carmel. 'You're not Rwandan, are you?'

'No, Zambian. I served here with the Zambian infantry peacekeeping battalion. I was a corporal at the time. I have never seen such horror before or since.'

'UNAMIR II?' Carmel asked.

'Yes. You know of it?'

'Amazing.' Carmel reached across the table, offering her hand. 'I'm Carmel Shang. I was here with the Australian contingent. I was the legal officer to AUSMED and, as it happened, to all the other UN contingents as none of them brought their own legal officer. I handled a couple of investigations you guys did.'

'This is all fascinating,' Liesl interjected, 'but we can save the army buddies' reunion for later. What do you see in this picture, hey?'

Aston pushed his glasses up the bridge of his nose and made a show of studying the photograph again. 'This white man, he looks familiar to me. I'm trying to imagine what he looks like now. You say he is an arms trader?'

'To be honest,' Carmel said, 'we don't know. It's all just an assumption at this stage. The two other men in the picture are dead.'

'What makes you think this man still lives in Rwanda?' Aston asked.

Liesl shrugged. 'We had to start looking for him somewhere, and as a result of what happened to us today, we think the white man is close.'

'What happened today?' Aston asked.

'We'd rather not say, if that's OK. It's the subject of a police investigation. Who is this man?'

Aston rubbed his chin again. 'I have met him, though his name escapes me.'

'Really?' Liesl asked.

'Yes. I've seen him somewhere, maybe here, maybe elsewhere in the country. I think he owns a lodge or a safari business. I'm not aware of him being involved in anything illegal, though, if that was what you were inferring before.'

'That's incredible! We don't know if he's involved in wrongdoing now or in the past,' Carmel said. 'But we'd like to talk to him.'

'Maybe we should just hand this over to the Rwandan police,' Liesl suggested.

'And tell them what?' Henri interjected. 'That we're looking for a man who we think was in a photograph taken seventeen years ago and may have been behind at least one murder and several attempted murders?'

'It is a bit flimsy,' Carmel said.

'But this *oke* tried to *kill* us,' Liesl said.

Carmel nodded. 'We can't be a hundred per cent sure, Liesl. Also I'm worried that if it turns out that it was the RPA that shot down President Habyarimana's jet, and that the current ruling party was involved, then this will all just be covered up anyway.'

'Hang on,' Liesl said. 'You think the Rwandan government might be behind all this, trying to keep us quiet?'

'I just don't know, I don't think we can rule it out.'

'There is nothing to stop you making some discreet enquiries and perhaps then going to the police if you know for sure that this man has done something wrong, although I must confess I am concerned by all of this talk of murder and attempted murder. Perhaps I should just leave you in peace now and get back to my business here.' Aston picked up his beer and made to leave. 'Ladies, I am glad if I have been of assistance, but—'

'No, wait,' Liesl said.

'Yes, please. Stay and have a drink with us,' Carmel said.

Aston noticed that Bousson had retreated into silence again and was sitting with his arms folded and his lips pursed. He was clearly not happy that Aston had insinuated himself into their conversation. Aston didn't care. He would deal with the Frenchman as and when necessary. If he wanted to act as these women's bodyguard, he would find himself with a bullet in the back of his head. 'Very well,' he said, dragging over a chair from a neighbouring table. 'But please allow me to get the next round of drinks.'

Over the next hour Carmel Shang explained that she was an investigator with the ICTR, which Aston already knew, and that she had investigative powers under the tribunal's auspices and that she agreed it would be better to conduct a low-key investigation at first. Aston was pleased she had played so easily into his hands. He knew well of the animosity between the Rwandan government and the ICTR. Carmel was on the trail of a major scalp and she would not want the man she was looking for to end up in a Rwandan prison.

'Are you sure you can't remember this guy's name?' Liesl said.

Aston looked at the picture again, squinting at it. 'I hope it will come to me. It was as if it was on the tip of my tongue. Most of the white people I meet seem to have some connection to tourism or aid. I travel to Ruhengeri often, so I am thinking that could be where I met him. He does not look like the NGO type, though I suppose people do change their colours.'

'I've got to go to Ruhengeri and the Volcanoes National Park anyway,' Liesl said. 'We've got a cover for being in the area – we can say we're all going to see the mountain gorillas.'

'Good,' Aston nodded. 'There are always many western tourists in Ruhengeri, so you won't stick out. I just wish I could remember this man's name.'

'Please try, Aston. It's very important.'

'I understand, particularly if, as you say, this man was responsible for supplying the weapon that sparked the Rwandan genocide. I will do my best to find him for you.'

'Thank you,' Carmel said.

He called the waitress over. 'My pleasure.' In fact, it would, he knew, be a pleasure for the man they were seeking, when Aston delivered them to him. He almost pitied them; instead of taking an assassin's quick, clean bullet, their ends would be slow and painful, and Aston would reap a bountiful harvest of organs and parts from their bodies.

Rain pattered on Jan Venter's green poncho. His fatigues were soaked and he wiped the condensation from the eyepieces of the binoculars and refocused on the Nel family farmhouse below. Another man might have complained, but Venter still considered himself a soldier.

It had been the wettest summer since 2000, and while the floodwaters had not been as high as they were then, they had caused disruptions. The helicopter they had planned to use for their criminal purposes had been called up to rescue people stranded around Hoedspruit by a flash flood, and then the aircraft had been grounded by an electrical storm.

Ironically, the crooked vet who was supposed to have been here by now to dart the wild dogs was busy saving stranded wildlife on game farms around the Lowveld, according to the rushed call Jan had received from the man. Their plan had been pushed back by at least a day, maybe more.

But delays in military operations were like the rain, inevitable and unavoidable. Venter would wait as long as he had to. The money was worth it.

Richard finished securing the fresh bandage on his wounded leg in the toilet of the Qantas 747 as the captain announced that the aircraft was beginning its descent. As he walked down the aisle he saw Collette jump up, a broad smile on her face.

'What is it?' he asked.

'I remembered.'

He was tired. They were into the eighth hour of the flight and he'd been too wired and in too much pain to sleep. He'd taken some paracetamol to take the edge off, but he had no intention of arriving back in South Africa too drugged out to deal with any potential threat. 'Remembered what?'

'That man's name.' Collette stayed standing and Richard paused in the aisle. The other passengers around them were snoozing or engrossed in in-flight movies. 'I was just watching a documentary about the Second World War. They showed some footage of Hitler and it triggered something in my memory.'

'How so?'

'I was studying the war, in history, at the private school I went to in Rwanda around the time that the men started coming to my parents' place for meetings – the ones in the pictures. And I remembered reading something about one of Hitler's deputies, and his name was the same as one of the men my father had been talking about to my mother – without me knowing – and when I saw that man, the one who had such an interest in my brother, I asked my father if he was German, because he had the same name as a famous Nazi.'

'What was his name?' Richard asked.

'Hess, as in Rudolf.'

'What was his first name?'

'Karl.'

Carmel, Henri, Liesl and Aston ended up eating at the hotel bar. Carmel toyed with the fish on her plate. Her stomach was turning and she had little appetite.

It was, she imagined, mostly due to the trauma of her day that she found it so hard to relax. She'd replayed the day's events over and over in her mind, and if she put herself in the position of an investigator or lawyer cross-examining her testimony, then she found it hard to find any fault in her actions. It was, she realised, not only the fallout of killing the colonel, and possibly the other man that had her on edge, it was also the very close presence of Henri.

He sat next to her, close enough for her to feel the heat of his body through his jeans and her cargo pants. His leg, she reckoned, was no more than a few millimetres from hers. When he'd reached across the table to get to the salt, her leg had actually touched his and she'd felt a frisson of excitement jolt up her body. He was telling a story now, of his childhood in Rwanda, and in doing so he was leaning close to her and putting his hand lightly on her arm, as if to empha-sise a point to her.

Carmel sucked in a deep breath. She could smell the raw, slightly acrid odour of his long day, but it aroused as much as offended her. He had been there for her when she had emerged from the horror of the prison siege and she knew enough about psychology to understand that the attraction she was feeling for him now was probably the same kind of base animal lust that had caused Richard to sleep with Liesl back when they'd all been in Rwanda the first time. 'Survivor sex' it was called – a primal need to fornicate and procreate after exposure to danger. When she'd first read about this phenomenon she'd wondered if that was what had gone on between Richard and Liesl, after they'd both been through the horrors of the Kibeho massacre. But Carmel, too, had seen horrors in Rwanda, and hadn't felt compelled to fuck the first man she'd seen. Perhaps that was indeed what she was feeling now, but if she was honest with herself, she had to admit that her attraction to Henri had been growing steadily since she'd first met him.

She looked at Liesl, to see if she was taking an unusual interest in Henri. Liesl smiled back at her, as if somehow reading her mind.

Liesl raised a hand to her mouth, tilted back her head and yawned. 'I'm tired, and we've got to get up early tomorrow to get our gorilla permits and get on the road.'

'Yes,' Henri agreed. He had called for the bill earlier and now started counting out Rwandan francs.

'Let me,' Carmel tried.

He looked at her, and as Liesl gathered her daypack and jacket, Henri said quietly, 'You can get breakfast.'

Carmel felt heat rush through her body to her extremities as she looked into his eyes and saw what she hadn't seen for a very long time.

'Well, if you will excuse me, I'm going to bed,' Liesl said.

They both wished her goodnight and Aston, too, announced

that it was time for him to turn in. Then they were alone. 'I would offer you one more drink . . .' Henri said.

'But I don't drink alcohol and if I have another Coke I'll be up all night,' she said.

'You say that like it's a bad thing,' he said.

She kept her smile in check. He was definitely flirting with her now and she had to evaluate how she felt about that. On the plus side, he was tall and handsome and she had felt marvellously warm and safe in his arms when she'd emerged from the frightening chaos of Kigali Central Prison. He was passionate about wildlife conservation, as was she, and she had the skills and, yes, even the money, to help him continue to realise his dream of rehabilitating wild animals into the wild. He was, in short, almost the perfect match for her, except that he lived in Zambia and she lived in Australia, and there was no time for romance in her life while there was someone still out there trying to kill her.

'Shall we go?' he asked.

They left the poolside restaurant and walked up the stairs to the lobby. Carmel felt a warm flush spreading up through her body, to her chest, neck and face as they waited for the lift to descend. Henri was behind her, close enough for her to hear his breathing. The chime pinged and the door opened.

It was a small lift and when Carmel walked in and turned around, she saw that he was looking down at her. She swallowed. She saw the small smile on his lips. He reached out with his hand and gently laid the back of his fingers on her cheek. It felt as though he'd scorched her.

'I was worried about you today.'

'I'm fine,' she said.

'I know. You are strong. But all the same, maybe you'd like me to come in and sit with you for a while.'

She knew what he meant, but he'd couched it as though she needed babysitting, like a helpless little girl. She didn't want his faux concern. Carmel stood on her toes and placed a hand behind his neck and kissed him. Henri dropped his daypack, which fell with a heavy clank on the floor of the elevator, and kissed her back, passionately. She felt his tongue in her mouth and she drew it in. God, she wanted this. He put his hand under her arse and backed her against the wall. She could feel his erection, hard through his jeans, and she lowered a hand between them to caress it.

The door pinged open again.

Henri took a breath and stepped out into the hallway. Mercifully, there were no other guests standing there waiting for the lift. 'My room or yours?' he asked.

'Fuck it,' she said. 'Who cares?'

Henri's was closer. He quickly inserted the key card and they were embracing again before he'd even kicked the door closed. He began unbuttoning her shirt and Carmel undid his belt and the top button of his jeans. She reached a hand inside and gloried at the weight and feel of him.

'Let's go to bed,' she whispered into his ear.

26

Dust hung in the thin, weak beams of light that penetrated the cracks between the timbers of the crate. Vite had been taken from the foul-smelling shack where he had been held captive with other animals, but now a new range of horrors was confronting him as his wooden prison rocked from side to side.

Vite's ears were assaulted by the bleating of the goats tethered around him in the back of a truck. One was perched just above him, its hooves clattering as it scrambled for purchase.

The vehicle they were travelling in juddered in and out of ruts and potholes. His family and the warm breast of the woman who had rescued him, then abandoned him, were just confused memories. He had yelled until he could yell no more, his cries masked by the goats, who seemed to make even more noise when he tried to outdo them. How would his family hear him now?

Further and further from his home he travelled, until at last the machine stopped. A man climbed into the back of the truck, weaving his way between the goats. He rapped on the wood of the crate, but there were many other human voices.

Vite cried and the goats made their *beeehing* noise, and no one rescued him.

He didn't know it, but he'd just crossed into Rwanda.

It was overcast and misty when they met in the hotel car park the next morning. Carmel had returned to her room before dawn, to shower and pack her bag for the trip to Ruhengeri. She'd felt deliciously achy as she let the hot spray pummel her body.

For the first time in years she felt alive. Her existence had for so long been based around her work. It was how she defined herself. Her life was the prosecution of the people who had caused the genocide and she questioned, now, if that was enough. If she could somehow close this chapter in her life and the troubled history of Rwanda, by finding the men in the picture and possibly discovering for certain who was responsible for the act that sparked the mass killings, then she could allow herself a fresh start in life. Perhaps with Henri. She pressed the replay button of her mind and smiled to herself.

Henri had laid her on the bed and got down on his knees on the floor. He'd dragged her bum to the edge and opened her, and kissed her until she'd come, again and again. They'd cuddled and kissed and later in the evening they'd made love on the bed, slowly and gently. Before she'd left this morning she'd climbed on top of him, and afterwards had snoozed for an hour in his arms. She was exhausted and wanted to sleep all day in his arms, but they had to leave this morning.

She'd dried herself, dressed and grabbed a quick continental breakfast, then taken her bag down to the car, which was waiting for them. A local tour operator, organised by Henri, had arrived with a Toyota RAV4 that looked like it had seen better days. A quick walk-around revealed a low-hanging exhaust pipe, bald tyres, and several dents.

'Where's the paperwork?' she asked the slightly built African man as he lifted a big old-fashioned stereo speaker from the boot of the four-wheel drive. He untwisted the wires linking it to the car's sound system. A scratched CD dangled from the rear-view mirror.

'There is nothing to sign, it is all fine,' the rental man said.

'Really?' Carmel, the lawyer, would have been appalled. This morning, however, she didn't care. It was kind of liberating, she thought, to know they could get in this car and drive to Cairo if the mood took them, with no paper trail to track them down. Of course, it was highly unlikely the vehicle would make it that far.

'Now that the formalities are over, shall we go?' Henri asked.

Liesl put her backpack in the boot, where the speaker had been, and Henri loaded his and Carmel's bags. Liesl had said little this morning, Carmel noted. She felt her cheeks colour a little. 'Do you want to sit in the front?' she asked the South African.

'Ag, no, it's fine. I'll sit in the back. I'm tired, so I might snooze. Wake me if you want me to do some driving.'

Liesl hefted her camera bag into the backseat and climbed in beside it. Carmel got in the front next to Henri, who took the driver's seat. She tried to look straight ahead, but she was acutely aware of his body. She'd seen all of it. Memories of its feel and tastes filled her head. She tried to force them away by studying the map of Kigali and Rwanda.

'I remember the way,' Henri said to her, smiling.

'Oh, OK.' She felt like a teenager, lost for words.

'It will be fine.'

She nodded.

They waved goodbye to the rental man and set off out of the hotel gates. As quietly joyous as Carmel was over her night of passion, the reality of the mission ahead sobered her. They turned right and then left, heading down the hill into the maelstrom of Kigali's morning traffic.

Motos beeped on either side of them, and Carmel felt again the slight disorientation of driving on the opposite side of the road. It seemed every oncoming vehicle was about to plough into them, and when Henri took a right onto a roundabout, it felt downright wrong. He weaved his way across several lanes and then exited right, towards the valley below. Carmel snuck a peak in the back and saw Liesl had already drifted off to sleep. Her head was lolled back and her mouth half open as she quietly snored. Just then a white Coaster bus with *Omega* painted on its side came close to sideswiping them and Henri was forced to use his horn to warn a pedestrian in a suit to hurry out of his way.

Despite her lack of sleep, Carmel was alert and aware of her surroundings – and of the man next to her. She focused on the passing traffic and scenery to stop from staring at Henri. Elections were coming around again in Rwanda and she spotted soldiers, in pairs, dressed in camouflage jump-suits and carrying AK-47s, standing on street corners. As they descended into the valley she saw a full section of ten men in uniform patrolling the street. There had been criticisms of Paul Kagame, as president, for being too heavy-handed in dealing with political opposition, but Kagame had seen his country – his people – almost wiped out. Carmel wondered what repercussions there might be for the RPF at the polls if it was revealed that their leader, and not some radical Hutu, had shot down the former president's aircraft, thus sparking the murder of nearly a million Tutsis and moderate Hutus.

Henri's mobile phone rang and he answered it while he drove. 'Hello? Yes, we'll see you there.' He ended the call. 'That was Aston,' he said to Carmel. 'He will meet us at the turn-off to Ruhengeri. He's been out doing some business this morning.'

'Okay,' Carmel said. She wasn't sure how far they could trust the rotund, rather affable Zambian, but she stood by what she had told him – that she'd been impressed with the Zambian soldiers and officers she'd met. It was an amazing coincidence that he claimed to recognise the white man in the picture, perhaps too amazing. She wondered if he might be a con man who would ask them for money before revealing what he supposedly knew, then give them the slip, but she was prepared to take that risk.

Liesl stirred, but the phone call and their talking hadn't fully woken her. Carmel was glad.

They reached the turn-off a short while later and Carmel could see Aston sitting on the bonnet of a silver Corolla. Henri pulled over and both he and Carmel got out.

'You are ready?' Aston asked. As he stood, the car rose a little as his weight was lifted from its front suspension.

'As ready as we ever will be,' Carmel said. 'Who's this?' She pointed through the windscreen of the Corolla to another man.

'He is my driver, Alphonse. I use him every time I come here on business. He knows the way.'

'OK,' Carmel said. 'Let's get this show on the road.'

Kigali was not a big city by African standards and they were soon following Aston's Corolla out into the rural landscape. Carmel noted, as she had before, that there seemed to be not a single native tree left on Rwanda's rolling hills. The hills themselves were mostly terraced, and what vegetation there was tended to be straggly banana plantations or stands of Australian gum trees. Ironic, Carmel thought, that this little piece of Australia was all that was keeping the soil of many of these hills from tumbling down into the creeks and rivers that wound through the rumpled landscape.

As they passed a roadside brick-making operation Carmel saw a toothless woman carrying a stack of eight house bricks on her head. The raw product was laid out in row after row on the ground, wet bricks drying in the sun before being finished off in a roadside kiln. The clay used to make them was blood red, and stained the hands and forearms of the boys who slopped mud into wooden moulds and then tipped them out. It was a timeless operation, she thought.

The villages clustered along the main road consisted of houses made, presumably, of the same mudbricks she'd seen the woman carrying, but the walls were rendered smooth and painted a pale khaki. The roofs were terracotta half-moon tiles, echoing the country's European colonial history. It could have been, Carmel thought, a village in medieval Belgium, complete with architecture that was inspired by some faint memory of Roman invaders. Long-horned cattle roamed the roadside here and there, and dogs darted out of the way of the vehicles. The road was good for the most part, but the steepness of the hills prevented the traffic from reaching dangerous speeds, and the downhills, more often than not, led to the next village where blue uniformed police with AKs kept watch for speedsters.

Carmel saw a billboard promoting the Rwandan national cycling team and privately marvelled at how hard their calves must be, training in this rollercoaster topography. She imagined the strength and stamina of the farmers who climbed and descended their terraces every day and wondered, not for the first time, how such smiling, industrious people could have been whipped into such a frenzy of hate and killing. As long as she lived she knew she would never truly understand it.

These streams had been choked with bodies, the roadway drenched with blood at the checkpoints where the Interahamwe had carried out the ceaseless, tiring work of hacking apart their neighbours. The green fields in the valleys probably still held mass graves whose bones would appear during the seasonal rains, then be deluged in new flows of red topsoil. Remnants of the killing would be coming and going for years.

Liesl yawned loudly from the back seat. 'What do we do when we find this guy?' she asked, as she lifted one of her cameras and clicked off a rapid burst of frames as they passed a trio of smiling, waving children.

'Firstly we identify him and learn as much as we can about him,' Carmel said. 'And then I'll try and question him.'

'You? Alone?' Henri asked.

'You don't have any authority to question a potential witness or suspect in an ICTR investigation, Henri,' Carmel said.

'No, but this man, if he is the one who ordered the assassinations . . .'

'If he is the man who was behind the attempts on our lives, then I'll exercise every caution around him,' she said.

'I'm not sure, Carmel,' Henri said.

She looked over her shoulder and saw Liesl had lost interest in the conversation and had put the white buds of an iPhone in her ears so she could listen to music. She showed no sign of being able to hear them. 'Henri. I can't let what happened interfere with my work,' Carmel said softly.

'I don't want to see you hurt.'

'And neither do I, but we've come so far. This man, he's like a ghost. We haven't been able to find him, yet he's been haunting us all along. This lead from Aston is the only concrete lead we've had since the colonel's death to find out who is behind this thing. It's my duty to find this man and to question him and, if needs be, to bring him to justice.'

Henri risked looking away from the winding road that climbed through the gum-covered hills to stare at her for a couple of seconds. 'You don't have an army or a police force on your side, Carmel. Is there any way you can forget this – drop this investigation and go back to practising law in Australia, or maybe somewhere else?'

'Somewhere else?'

He shrugged and looked back out the windscreen. 'Maybe Zambia.'

Carmel was taken aback. 'What are you saying?'

'Carmel,' he said as quietly as the vehicle's small whining engine would allow, 'how would you like to come and stay with me?'

'For how long?'

He shrugged. 'Indefinitely. I could protect you. I know people in Zambia. There would be work for you – I could arrange it. I am sure if we leave this man, if we leave this country now, you would be safe.'

It was a tempting fantasy. 'What makes you think that whoever's tried to kill us all would stop now?'

'You don't *know* who's been trying to kill you, or why. It could all be one grand coincidence, Carmel. Come with me. I'll take care of you. Leave this place of death now.'

She looked at him staring fixedly out at the road, his hands tight on the steering wheel. She remembered the feel of those hands on her body, strong when they'd needed to be and soft as a woman's when their loving had called for it. 'I don't need protecting, Henri.' She risked laying a hand on his arm for a moment. 'But thank you. Perhaps when this is all over . . .'

'That's precisely what I'm worried about,' he said, his voice cracking as he indicated to pass a slow-moving petrol tanker, 'that it will soon be *all over* – for all of us.'

Liesl glanced up from the screen of her iPhone just long enough to see Carmel withdrawing her hand from Henri's arm. Liesl felt Carmel's eyes on her from the rear-vision mirror. She knew guilt when she saw it. Liesl was sure the pair had slept together last night.

Liesl wasn't jealous – well, not overly. Henri was a good-looking guy and Liesl had noticed Carmel smiling to herself over breakfast, and then forcing a straight face when she'd seen Henri emerge from the elevator. It all made sense.

Instead of selecting music, Liesl had been SMSing Pierre, who was using his cellphone from a bed in Kigali Central Hospital. The colonel's thugs had roughed up Pierre big-time, and he'd been battered and bruised and pissing blood when the police took him to hospital. He was in for another day at least, pending some tests. Liesl had stopped by to see him and told the attending physician she and *Escape!* magazine would be paying all of Pierre's medical costs.

Liesl typed a message to Pierre as Carmel and Henri resumed their conversation. *Any luck finding out who the white man is in the pic?*

Her phone was on silent, so as not to attract Carmel's attention. Liesl felt the ordeal in the prison had broken down part of the barrier between her and the frosty lawyer, but she also knew Carmel was not the type to share information. Carmel had taken her aside the previous evening and read her the riot act about passing on anything she learned that related to their investigation. 'You should have told me you were going to the prison with Pierre,' Carmel had said.

'I never received a call or SMS from you telling me you were going to the prison either,' Liesl had retaliated.

The phone vibrated and Liesl opened a new message from Pierre. *Have emailed pic to a friend in Ruhengeri. If the man is a tour operator or lodge owner, my contact will know of him.*

Liesl had messaged Pierre in hospital that morning and passed on the information they'd gleaned from Aston, that the white man was somehow connected with the tourist industry in the region around the Volcanoes National Park. The inference was that he would be involved in one of the lodges or tour groups that made their money organising trips into the park to track the mountain gorillas. She'd warned her journalist colleague to be careful who he sent the picture to, but Pierre seemed to have ignored that. Liesl felt bad enough that Pierre had been beaten, and she didn't want to be responsible for more injuries or deaths, but she also thought Carmel's by-the-book approach was doomed to fail. The man they were hunting did not play by the rules, and neither would Liesl.

She looked at her hand after she had sent the text and noticed the tremor. She checked her watch. It was ten in the morning. A little early, but by no means her earliest. She unzipped her daypack and found the half-jack of vodka she'd bought duty free at OR Tambo Airport. She unscrewed the cap. A glass would have been good. She raised the neck of the bottle to her lips and saw Carmel's eyes in the rear-view mirror. Liesl licked her lips as the fiery liquid radiated through her body. 'Want some?'

'No, thank you. Do you think that's wise, given where we're going?'

Liesl shrugged and removed the buds from her ears. 'I thought I wasn't invited to this party. As far as I'm concerned, we've got to sort out our accommodation today and I'm going on a gorilla trek tomorrow morning. This is pretty much a free day for me since you've no intention of letting me interview the man who's trying to kill us.'

'Don't be smart, Liesl,' Carmel said.

'I can't help it.'

Henri gave a small laugh and Carmel looked at him admonishingly. 'What?' his return glance seemed to ask her.

Liesl rolled her eyes. 'This is bizarre. I don't know what I'm doing tagging along with you guys. I should just head off somewhere safe, like Afghanistan.'

But she did know why she was here. Above and beyond the need to find out who was trying to kill them, Liesl sensed she was on to the biggest story about Rwanda since the genocide. She needed to be there, and she needed to get the story first, even before Carmel and the ICTR, or the

Rwandan police. It would be dangerous, but she didn't care. She took another slug of vodka then replaced the cap. That would have to do for now, she thought, though it was like saying goodbye to an old and trusted friend when she slid the bottle into her bag. When she checked into her room at the guesthouse she would make a show of needing to sleep. Carmel wouldn't miss her for the rest of the day, which would give Liesl the opportunity she needed to quietly slip out and find their man – assuming Pierre came through with a name.

Liesl's phone vibrated and she opened the new SMS. It was from Richard. Liesl hadn't told Carmel they'd been in touch again, but was beginning to think she should come clean. He'd messaged her from Australia, apologising for his sudden departure. He'd assured her he was following up a lead over there, but could tell her no more. She'd wondered, briefly, if he was delusional as well as being a coward and a cad.

Just landed in Joburg. Have a name for our man. Karl Hess, the message read.

Liesl looked at the back of Carmel's head. She would tell her the news, in good time. This Aston was supposedly taking them to the man. The more she thought about the Zambian's timely arrival, with his offer to take them to find Hess – or whatever his name was – the more she thought it was too coincidental. She reached into the pocket of her jeans and found the crumpled card Aston had given her last night. Aston Mutale listed his occupation as Traditional Healer and Chief Executive Officer, Best Imports, Private Limited. The address listed was in Roodepoort, Johannesburg. Liesl SMSed Aston's name, occupations and details to Richard, with the addendum, *Check this oke out.*

Will do. Be careful, Richard messaged.
You too.

As soon as they cleared customs and immigration, Richard found a seat in the arrivals area and sat down, grateful for the chance to take the weight off his wounded leg. There was a stain on his jeans where a little blood had seeped through and he knew he would have to change the bandage again.

'I need to go to the bathroom, and I'll get us some coffee as well,' Collette said.

Richard nodded as he scrolled through the contacts on his cellphone. 'There's a Mugg and Bean upstairs. Make mine a double shot.'

Collette left and Richard dialled Sannie van Rensburg. Sannie was a former detective inspector who lived on a banana farm at Hazyview, near the Kruger National Park. Richard had delivered her third child, an emergency breech birth, when she had gone into labour during a game drive in the Kruger National Park. The last time he'd seen Sannie she'd told him she'd gone back into the police, as a reservist, having heeded a nationwide call for experienced officers to return to the ranks. Many whites had taken early retirement or been made redundant in the push to Africanise the police force, but the authorities had recently realised they were suffering from losing so many experienced officers.

'Sannie, hello?' she said.

'Hi, it's Doctor Richard Dunlop.'

'Richard! Good to hear from you. Are you all right? I heard about the problem at your house, hey.'

'Yes, I'm fine thanks. And you, and your son?'

'*Ja, lekker* thanks, and little Tommy's doing fine thanks. He turns two next week.'

'That's great. Sannie, are you working today?'

'*Ja,* I'm doing a shift in Nelspruit, covering for a guy whose wife is having a baby.'

'I know this is unusual, but I need some help. I need you to check out a couple of names for me – a criminal record check.'

There was a pause on the other end of the line. 'Richard, it's not like the movies, hey. We're not allowed to give out information on people's records to just anyone.'

'This is really important. It's related to the shooting – the guy who tried to kill me at my home.'

'OK, Richard, but you must talk to the detectives handling that case. That is the correct protocol. Maybe you should come into the office and see them.'

Richard sighed. 'I'm in Johannesburg. I can't come to Nelspruit and I don't have time to explain what this is about to the detectives. Sannie, please, you have to help me.'

'No, Richard, I don't.'

He gritted his teeth. His leg throbbed. 'When you called 1011 they wanted your husband to drive you to the Mediclinic in Nelspruit to have the baby, didn't they?' Again, there was a pause. Richard hated resorting to this.

'Richard, this is not about my son . . .'

'They didn't understand what was happening. If I hadn't been driving past and seen Tom standing there, frantic, yelling into the phone, little Tommy would have died.'

'Richard, this isn't fair. You did your job and we thank you, with all our hearts for it, but . . .'

'Have you never broken the rules, Sannie? I heard you had

a reputation for following your instincts. I don't want to sound dramatic, but there are people right now who may be heading into grave danger, and all I'm asking you is if these two men whose names I have share a common connection or have any criminal connections.'

She swore, under her breath. 'Give me the names.'

'Karl Hess, probably Namibian-born, aged about mid-fifties now, I would guess, and an Aston Mutale, a Zambian living in Johannesburg.' Richard read Aston's address and heard Sannie's fingers tapping on a keyboard.

'*Jislaaik*, Richard. A Namibian and a Zambian? What do you think our central criminal records are going to have on these guys?'

'I don't know.'

'Give me a couple of minutes. The computer system here is not so *lekker*.'

Collette came back with two takeaway cups of coffee. Richard nodded his thanks to her and sipped the strong, slightly bitter brew. He knew the fatigue would kick in soon, but he couldn't afford to rest.

'OK, Richard? Are you still there?'

'Yes?' He had nowhere else to go.

'This is interesting, hey,' Sannie said.

'What is?'

'This Mutale has one conviction, for smuggling wildlife. Four years ago. He was fined ten thousand rand for trying to send an African rock python out of South Africa to Germany via a courier. The investigating officer was a Captain Fanie Theron. I know him – worked with him not long ago on a case of someone stealing plants from the Kruger Park. He's head of the Endangered Species Unit.'

'Smuggling wildlife?' Richard was vaguely aware that the trade in wildlife was big business, but he wondered if it was something worth killing over. He couldn't understand what connection Aston Mutale could have to someone who wanted to kill everyone who'd laid eyes on Liesl's photograph. 'What about the other guy, Hess?'

'Dead.'

'Serious?'

'Yes, but here's the interesting thing. Hess was wanted for the murder of a woman and a park ranger in Mozambique, and for the poaching of an elephant and theft of ivory. The investigator was the same Captain Theron, but a note on the record said Hess was believed killed in Zambia in 2004.'

Richard thought about possible connections. If there was a link between Mutale and Hess, then it seemed to be the trade in wildlife or wildlife products. Was it possible that Hess was smuggling wild animals out of Rwanda at the time of the genocide, and importing weapons, such as the surface-to-air missile in the photograph, to some splinter military or political faction? And how did the Zambian come into it? In any case, it seemed he'd hit a dead end as Hess, if he was the man in the photograph, was apparently dead.

'You say you know this Captain Theron. Can you give me his number?'

'Richard, I don't know . . .'

'Sannie, please. Like I said, this is important. I need to talk to Theron. I know Mutale, the Zambian, is in Rwanda right now and I've got a suspicion he's up to something illegal there – something dangerous. Also, some people I know are right this minute also in Rwanda looking for this man Hess.'

'But he's dead, Richard. I just told you.'

'*Believed* killed, you said. He could still be alive.'

'All right, I'll give you Theron's number, but don't tell him where you got it, hey?'

'Thanks, and believe me, I won't tell him it was you.' If Hess was alive, he seemed hellbent on killing anyone who got close to him, so Richard had no intention of involving Sannie any further. As soon as he'd taken down Theron's number he ended the call.

He called Captain Theron on the cellphone number Sannie had given him. Collette took a seat next to him, on the bench. People passed by them, pushing trolleys laden with baggage, hugging and kissing friends and relatives, or walking briskly to flights. Richard wished he could be one of them – coming home or running off to somewhere exotic.

'Theron, hello.'

'Captain, you don't know me, but I understand you were involved in the investigation of a man named Karl Hess, for murder and wildlife-related crimes several years back.'

There was a pause. 'Who is this? What do you know about Karl Hess?'

Richard heard the excitement in the pitch of the officer's voice. He guessed it wasn't every day a policeman who investigated smuggled reptiles and plants got involved in a double murder. 'Captain, what would you say if I told you I had information that Karl Hess was alive and living in Rwanda?'

There was an intake of breath. 'I would say, where are you? I'd need to see you right away.'

'First I want to make sure we're not wasting each other's time. Can you give me an email address?' Theron gave him his police email. 'I'm sending you a photo, now.' Richard paused to scroll through to the copy of Liesl's photo he had on his iPhone and then sent the image to Theron.

When Richard got back onto the phone the detective asked him again for his name and his whereabouts, and demanded he explain further what information he had about Hess. 'Just check the picture, Captain.'

'*Ja*, OK. It's through now. I'm looking.'

Richard waited, and looked at Collette. She had been eavesdropping.

'It's an old picture, but it's him,' the captain said. 'I'd recognise him anywhere. Where was this taken? Zaire?'

'Close. Rwanda. I think about 1994.'

'Makes sense,' Theron said. 'But this man was killed in 2004.'

Richard played a hunch. 'But let me guess, you never found a body?'

Again, Theron paused. 'Listen, whoever you are, tell me where you are. I need to speak with you.'

'OK, my name is Doctor Richard Dunlop. I'm at the arrivals hall at OR Tambo International Airport. Some friends of mine are on their way to possibly meet with the man in that picture, in Rwanda. He's been spotted there, alive, recently. This might sound crazy, Captain, but do you think it's possible that this Hess, if it is him and he's still alive, would have the ability to order hits on people on three continents?'

'Doctor Dunlop . . .'

'Yes, Captain?'

'This man is the devil incarnate.'

27

White man's name is Jurgen Pens. Owns a half-share in Mist Tours gorilla trekking lodge. Based in South Africa, visits Rwanda occasionally, said the message from Pierre that buzzed onto Liesl's phone screen.

Liesl took a *Lonely Planet* guidebook from her daypack and found the chapter on gorilla trekking in Rwanda. The names of several lodges clustered around the entrance to the Volcanoes National Park were listed on a map. She found the Mist Tours lodge. Judging by the scale it looked no more than two or three kilometres from the guesthouse where Henri said they would be staying.

She SMSed the updated information about the white man's identity to Richard, who responded back less than a minute later:

Must be an alias. I have positively identified him as Karl Hess. Namibian mercenary and big-game hunter, wanted for murder and poaching crimes. Be very careful, Liesl. SA Cops say this man is extremely dangerous. Aston Mutale has criminal record for wildlife smuggling. Suggest you all pull back to Kigali and await South African extradition of Hess. We've got him now.

Liesl slumped back in the car seat and looked out the window. They'd slowed as Henri navigated his way through a substantial town. 'Is this Ruhengeri?' she asked.

'Yes,' Henri said. 'We're nearly there. Have you been sleeping?'

'No.'

Liesl thought about how things would unfold if the South African Police became involved. There would be local cops and prosecutors brought in, and if Hess was wanted for murder there would be publicity. She would lose her scoop and Carmel would lose the high-profile scalp the ICTR needed to show it was doing its job. Liesl wondered if the fact that she was considering endangering herself and her travelling companions by going ahead with a meeting with a killer in order to get a story was, ironically, a sign that she was getting some of her old passion back.

She'd been coasting at *Escape!*, taking mediocre pictures and filing bland stories about luxury game lodges to repay junkets she'd been given as free holidays. She'd lost her journalistic integrity and her edge. She wanted to investigate and uncover, and to make a difference again. But was it worth risking the lives of the other two people in the car?

Liesl had hurt Carmel badly back in 1995, but that would be nothing compared to what might be waiting in store for them if they bumped into this Pens, or Hess, or whoever he was. The Zambian, Aston, was also a criminal and she was sure he must be connected to the white man somehow. Liesl knew she had to speak up, even though it might cost her the story of her lifetime.

'Carmel, I've just had a message from Richard.'

Carmel turned to look at her, the anger immediate and barely concealed in her eyes. 'What about?'

'He's in South Africa. He's been following a separate lead about the man in the picture. He says his name is Karl Hess. I've also heard from my contact in Rwanda, Pierre. He says the blond man's name is Jurgen Pens, but Richard thinks that's an alias.'

Carmel looked stunned. 'How long has this been going on for – this *lead* that Richard has been following?'

'Umm, I'm not sure. He's only just got to SA from Oz, and I still don't know exactly what he got up to in Australia.'

Carmel sighed. 'Why didn't you tell me this before, Liesl? We have to communicate.'

Liesl bit back her reply. Carmel was not in the business of sharing. She should have been grateful. 'There's more. I got Richard to check out that guy Aston with the police in South Africa. Turns out that he has a record in wildlife smuggling, and Hess was also wanted for murder.'

'Was wanted?'

'He was reported missing presumed dead in 2004 the last time the police tried to get him. That was in Zambia. Prior to that Hess was an arms smuggler and a mercenary. I was too hasty inviting Aston to talk to us in the bar. I think now that he was following us, Carmel. If he's been keeping tabs on us all along then maybe now he's leading us into a trap.'

Carmel closed her eyes while she digested the information. 'It could just be another coincidence. If Aston's been involved with wildlife smuggling, that might be how he knows Hess, but if he knows about past murders, and if they were both working together and planned the attacks on you, me and Richard, then why would he have made contact with us so overtly? It's almost like he's asking to be caught.'

'Look around,' Liesl said, and gestured out at the streetscape. 'We're in the middle of nowhere. If he's Hess's decoy and his job is to draw us into a trap, there's hardly a more remote place to spring it. Maybe Aston and Hess want to find out just how much we know, and if it turns out we know too much, then they might just finish us off up here.'

Carmel was suspicious as well, but she wanted to see this thing through to the end. If Aston was crooked they would just have to find a way to play him and wrap him up when they found Hess.

'Carmel,' Henri interrupted, 'listen to Liesl. Is there any way you can drop this now – close off your investigation and forget about the photograph? If we stop the car and tell Aston we don't need to find this Hess or Pens or whoever he is, and that we're all going home, perhaps that will be the end of it. If Aston is working for the white man, then he can get a message to him without us having to confront him face to face.'

'A colleague of mine was murdered, Henri,' Carmel said calmly. 'You don't have to be involved here if you don't want to be.'

That settled it, Liesl thought. There was no going back. Ahead of them a towering dormant volcano rose violently from the otherwise gently undulating landscape. On its slopes, and on the similar neighbouring peaks, lived the last of the endangered mountain gorillas. When Liesl had been in Rwanda back in the nineties she'd thought these gentle primates the only thing good about this screwed-up, torn-up country. Rwanda was at what passed for peace now, and the gorillas' numbers were, by all accounts, increasing. She'd hungered for action and adventure when she was younger and here she was again being drawn into danger. Part of her wished she could be happy just photographing Africa's majestic wildlife, but the other side of her was riding high on risk.

Liesl unzipped her bag and wrapped her fingers around the cool glass of the vodka bottle. She started to take it out, but then relaxed her grip. She wanted to do this without the numbing fuzz of alcohol. Her hands started to shake and she looked down at her trembling fingers, hidden by the fabric of her bag. It was just like the old days. She was as excited as she was terrified.

Henri pulled into the driveway of the guesthouse and crunched down the gravel to where a woman stood waiting to greet them. A porter was already taking Aston's bag to his room, which was set in a circular building with a red terracotta-tiled roof. The grounds of the small lodge were carpeted with lush green grass and flowering bushes.

Carmel got out of the RAV4 and went to the back to start unloading. Henri popped the boot door release button and Carmel raised the hatch. Deliberately, she went for Henri's daypack first. She'd remembered the unfamiliar weight of it, and the way something had clanked on the hotel reception floor when he'd set it down. It was possible he had a bottle of booze in there, but she didn't think so. She ran her hand over the nylon exterior until she felt the hard, angular shape. It was a pistol. *I knew it*, she thought. He no doubt had connections, still, here in Rwanda – people he hadn't mentioned to her. They were lovers but they hardly knew each other. She didn't want to go into a meeting with Karl Hess armed, but it was comforting to know there would be back-up close by. Hess, too, would have connections if he had managed to carve out a life here after the genocide, perhaps with the local police. She knew the textbook thing to do would have been to contact the police or hand the case over to the Rwandan prosecutors, but she had no proof of any wrongdoing by Hess, and she could only imagine how long it would take to explain the situation to the local authorities and convince them to come along on a raid. In any case, she wanted Hess's scalp for the ICTR. Carmel licked her lips. As foolhardy as this mission was she was looking forward to this, she realised.

Henri came to the back of the vehicle and she passed him his bags and unloaded Liesl's and her own. 'Thanks,' Liesl said.

'No problem. What's your plan?'

Liesl shrugged. 'I'm going to take a walk up to the national park gate, where the gorilla treks will leave from tomorrow; do a bit of a recce. Also, from what I remember, there's a village up the road. I might wander up there and take some pics for the magazine. Good local colour.'

Carmel nodded. 'All right, but don't go too far.'

'Yes, *Mom*.'

Carmel put her hands on her hips and stared at Liesl. She let the comment ride. It was hard for the photojournalist, she knew. She wanted in on the investigation, but knew that Carmel couldn't allow that. Carmel, for her part, was pleased that Liesl had volunteered the new information about the man they sought, but she also suspected Liesl hadn't told her everything. 'I'll come up to the gate with you once we've checked in. I could use a leg stretch after the drive.'

'Then it's one for all and all for one,' Henri chimed in. 'Let's all meet back here in ten minutes, yes, after we drop off our luggage?'

The room was tired-looking, Carmel thought. It had a double bed that was saggy and lumpy, and a bathroom with a leaky cistern. The floors were bare concrete and the place smelled damp. It was the sort of place tourists on a budget spent one night before blowing five hundred dollars on a permit to spend an hour with the mountain gorillas the next morning. Carmel went to the toilet, washed her face and hands, and headed back out.

She, Henri and Liesl, who was festooned with two Nikons and carried her camera bag on her back, walked up the road to the entrance gate, which was about three hundred metres from their guesthouse.

'Hello?' called a voice behind them. Carmel turned and saw Aston waving and waddling up the street towards them. 'Where are you going?'

'None of your business,' Henri said under his breath.

'Just to the park gate,' Carmel called back.

'I will come too.' Aston was panting by the time he caught up with them.

When they'd arrived the sky had been relatively clear, littered with a few skerricks of white cottonwool that hung around the tops of the volcanoes; but now the clouds had coalesced into towering grey thunderheads that blotted out the afternoon sun and brought a chill to the air.

The four of them crossed the deep stormwater drain and walked to the national parks office. A man in civilian clothes greeted them warmly and asked if they were coming to see the mountain gorillas the next day.

'Yes, we are,' Carmel said.

'You are most welcome.' The man explained to them that

they should assemble back at the entrance at seven the next morning, and cautioned them not to be late. He ran through a well-rehearsed checklist of what to wear – long trousers and sleeves, and gloves if they had them to ward off stinging nettles, and a hat to keep off the sun.

'Do you know a Mr Pens?' Carmel asked the ranger.

'But of course. He owns Mist Tours. Are you part of his group for tomorrow?'

'I'm not sure exactly who we've booked with,' Henri said.

'All I know,' Liesl added, 'was that one of the local tour operators offered permits for me and my friends here as a favour to *Escape!* magazine. I didn't even look at the name of the operator.'

Henri pulled from his pocket the gorilla permits he'd collected from the Rwanda Development Board office. 'I didn't check either.' He looked at the top one, then turned to Carmel. '*Merde.*' He handed her the slip of paper.

'*Mist Tours,*' she read.

'Let me see that.' Liesl snatched the permit from Carmel. 'Oh my God. He's been behind this all along. He knew we were coming.'

The fear gripped Carmel's insides and chilled her. She looked at Aston, who simply shrugged. 'You know the name of the man you seek now?'

'Yes,' Carmel said, deliberately not revealing her source.

'Then perhaps you don't need my services any more. I don't recognise the name Pens, though.'

Carmel regarded him. If he was in on this, with Hess, aka Pens, then Aston would have wanted to stay with them, to make sure they didn't run or try to contact the local police. Perhaps it was just a coincidence that both Aston and Hess were guilty of wildlife smuggling. 'How about the name Hess?' she said to Aston.

The Zambian tapped his chins with a podgy index finger, then shrugged. 'No, I am afraid I don't recognise that name either. What do you know of this man?'

'Virtually nothing.'

'Well, if I am not needed, I think I might see if my driver can get me back to Kigali this evening.'

'I'm sorry if we've inconvenienced you,' Carmel said.

Richard and Collette had jumped in a taxi and checked into the Metcourt Hotel at the Emperor's Palace casino complex, a couple of kilometres from the airport. The Metcourt was the cheapest of the three hotels at Emperor's.

Richard stepped from the shower and wrapped a towel around his waist. The room was small but functional and the shower door swung around to enclose the toilet. There was a knock on the door.

'It's me,' Collette said.

Richard undid the security latch and opened the door to let her in.

'Oh, I can come back when you're ready,' she said.

He waved a hand. 'No, it's fine. Make yourself comfortable.' Richard went back into the bathroom, shut the door and applied a fresh dressing to his leg wound and checked the scratch on his chest wasn't bleeding. He changed into the cleanish clothes he'd salvaged from his bag. He walked back into the room barefoot, and buttoned his shirt.

'So what do we do now?' Collette was sitting on the bed. She crossed her legs.

It occurred to Richard, now that they were alone, that

she'd matured into a beautiful woman. It was a measure, he thought, either of the gravity of the situation or his own maturity that it had taken him this long to appreciate her. Her hair was damp and she'd changed into jeans and a T-shirt she'd bought along with the new clothes for Richard before leaving Australia. 'I don't know,' he said.

He'd tried Kenya Airlines and Rwandair when they'd arrived, but neither airline had seats available that night for a flight to Kenya or Rwanda. Instinctively, he thought he should be with Liesl and Carmel, on their quest to track down the man in the picture, but logically he knew that he and Collette would not be able to catch up to the others before they found Hess.

'I'm pleased we couldn't get a flight to Rwanda,' Collette said.

'I understand why you don't want to go back.'

Collette shook her head. 'I don't understand any of this. I don't know why I agreed to come this far with you. I should have stayed in Australia and explained to the police what happened. What if there's an investigation and they won't let me back in the country, Richard?'

He felt helpless and ashamed that he, too, felt the same as Collette about going back to Rwanda. He wondered if he should have stayed with Liesl. But she was like a hyena tearing at a carcass – relentless and fearless. He thought about Carmel, and the memory of what they'd had, prior to his cheating, was like pulling a sticky plaster off a partly healed wound. He'd been an idiot all his life, and the one woman who might have healed him was heading into danger while he languished in an airport hotel. He had to do something. His phone beeped from the bedside table. He picked it up and read the SMS.

'Who is it?' Collette asked, as impatient as he.

'It's Theron, the endangered-species cop. He's just pulled into the car park.'

They left the hotel and walked through the convention centre, across the road and into the covered mall where the complex's shops and restaurants lined a faux-Italian piazza under a roof painted to look like a blue sky dotted with clouds. A replica of Michelangelo's David stood in the centre, wearing a hard hat and a tool belt. Richard and Collette walked past some tourists who were snapping David, and into the Tribes steakhouse. A white man wearing jeans and a golf shirt stood up from his table as they entered.

'Doctor Dunlop?'

'Captain Theron?'

'Yes. Howzit.' He clasped Richard's hand in a grip that might have cost him his living if he was a surgeon. Richard introduced Collette and Theron nodded to her. 'Take a seat.'

Richard noticed the policeman was drinking Coke, so he ordered a sparkling water from the waiter and Collette asked for a Sprite.

'Tell me what you know about Karl Hess,' Theron said without preamble.

Richard spread his hands. 'Not a lot. Collette recognised him from the photo I sent you. She remembered his name.'

'My father was an officer in the Rwandan Army,' she explained. 'This man Hess visited us a few times. I was scared of him.'

'You were right to fear him,' Theron said, 'but please continue.'

Collette looked at Richard, who took up the story and explained about the attempt on his life, Collette's kidnapping and the failed hits on Carmel and Liesl.

'If Hess was behind all this, you've been incredibly lucky,' Theron said. 'He was a ruthless killer.'

'Was?' Richard asked.

'I was chasing Hess, when he worked as a professional hunter back in 2004, along with a Russian client of his named Orlov. I suspected them of being involved in the killing of a big bull elephant from the Kruger Park and later they tried to kill a protected black rhino in a national park in Zimbabwe. I was part of an undercover operation that tracked them into Zambia. Orlov was arrested and charged with poaching and the murder of a ranger in Mozambique. Hess left a string of bodies as he tried to cover his tracks – a woman he shot in cold blood in Mozambique, a man he stabbed to death in Zimbabwe and a South African pilot who had helped him. He's ex-military, special forces, and he kills with ruthless efficiency. I almost had him, but he fell out of a helicopter during a struggle to apprehend him. I was on the helicopter – flying it – but I had wounded on board and couldn't land. I went back the next day with the Zambian police to the spot where Hess had fallen out, but we never found his body. There were lion and hyena tracks in the area – it was in the Game Management Area on the border of the South Luangwa National Park – and the locals speculated that Hess's body had been cleaned up by animals. I wasn't convinced.'

'Well, it seems he's alive and well and living in Rwanda,' Richard said.

'And you have friends up there looking for him?'

'Yes,' Richard said to the policeman. 'They've found someone who recognised him from the picture and says Hess – who goes by the name of Pens – owns a trekking lodge near the Volcanoes National Park.'

Theron nodded. 'That's a plausible place for him to end up. I did a good deal of research into Hess's background when I was investigating him. I spoke to ex-military people who served with him in the Rhodesian SAS and later in the elite *Koevoet* police unit during the war in the old South-West Africa. After South-West became Namibia, Hess left the country – the new government would have arrested him for war crimes in any case, and he ended up in Rwanda and Zaire. There were rumours that he'd been dealing in arms, and your photo of him with the surface-to-air missile seems to indicate that he was. I know, too, that it was around that time, when his work as a soldier started to dry up, that he also began focusing on making a reputation for himself as a professional hunter who would go to any lengths to get his clients the trophies they wanted.'

'Who was he working for in Rwanda and Zaire?'

Theron shrugged. 'We don't know. Himself, mostly, making money by dealing in weapons, but there were rumours mentioned by people who knew him that he was also an asset for a foreign intelligence agency. Some said the Americans, others the French. If he was working for the Americans he could have been assisting Kagame and the Tutsis behind the scenes, but there's always been talk about the French propping up the Hutus. Who knows? Perhaps he was working for more than one political paymaster. He eventually moved to South Africa where he bought a hunting farm up in the Limpopo Province – a big place with a fancy lodge. Whatever he was doing in central Africa, he must have made some serious bucks. If he did survive his fall from the helicopter in 2004, then Rwanda would be as remote a place as any for him to set himself up with a fake identity. If your friends can positively identify him, I can get a warrant to extradite him back to South Africa. It could take a couple of days.'

'We don't have a couple of days,' Richard said, draining his water. The waiter, who had been hovering nearby, refilled his glass. What he really wanted was a beer, but there was work to be done. 'What about this man Mutale?'

Theron smoothed his moustache with his fingers. '*Ja*, this one is closer to home. I have his address in Joburg. But apart from his earlier conviction for smuggling wildlife, I've got nothing on him.'

'He's connected, I'm sure of it,' Richard said. 'It's too coincidental, him making contact with Liesl Nel – the photojournalist I told you about – and him knowing where to find this Pens. I'm worried that my friends are walking into a trap. Can you search his home or his office?'

'Not without probable cause,' Theron said. 'I have no evidence he's committed a crime.'

'You could check his phone records – see if he's made calls to Rwanda recently.'

'What would that prove? We know he's in Rwanda for business. It could be legitimate,' Theron countered.

Richard thumped his hand down on the table, making Collette start. 'Sorry,' he said. 'I've got his address.'

Theron leaned back in his seat and regarded Richard through narrowed eyes. 'What are you planning?'

'Do you really want to know?' Richard asked back.

'We have to do something,' Collette said as the two men eyed each other.

'Do you have a car?' Theron asked.

'I could rent one.'

'Do you know how to break into a building?' Theron said.

Richard shrugged. 'How hard can it be?'

The policeman's mouth turned in a hint of a smile. 'Maybe I can give you a lift.'

Liesl opened the door of her room at the guesthouse and looked out. There was no sign of Carmel or Henri, so she slipped out, shouldering her camera bag. She walked briskly up the driveway and turned left, retracing their earlier walk.

She passed the park entrance and carried on until the tarred road became a potholed dirt track as it entered a village. She presumed this was where most of the park rangers and trackers lived. Barefoot boys and girls in school uniforms waved to her, and a woman with a plastic jerry can of water balanced on her head gave a shy smile in reply to Liesl's, 'Good evening.'

A late-afternoon downpour had left the road muddy and the fields on either side of her soaked. A few shafts of golden sunlight struggled through the thinning clouds and the mist that was skirting the nearest volcano. Liesl was wearing her waterproof jacket, in case of more rain, and it warded off the growing chill of the evening.

'Mist Lodge?' she asked a woman with a baby tied to her back with a brightly printed *kikoi*. The woman nodded and pointed over her shoulder, in the direction Liesl was headed. 'Thank you.'

Men sat outside a whitewashed shebeen, drinking beer from half-litre Primus bottles, and Liesl ignored their leers as she strode through the village. The houses gave way to a straggly plantation of gum trees that blocked the light completely and shrouded her in a spooky darkness. She shivered.

According to the rough map in her guidebook, Mist Lodge should be about two kilometres further on.

'Pencil pen, pencil pen,' two small boys called to her, their hands outstretched as they jogged past her. She smiled and shook her head. A sign told her the entry to Mist Lodge was just five hundred metres ahead. She trudged on through the gloom. When she emerged from the gum forest she saw the clouds had cleared a little more, giving her the benefit of more light.

Liesl weighed up whether to go off the road and circle around the lodge through the fields of beans and maize, or to just walk in through the front gate. As the lodge entrance came into sight she saw two women in brightly coloured rain jackets standing by the entrance, taking pictures of the sun setting behind the mountains. Liesl paused and unslung her pack and took out one of her two camera bodies. She put her pack back on and slung the camera around her neck. Security around the lodge looked minimal, just a low fence augmented with a trimmed hedge. What looked like the main building was a stone structure with a thatch roof turned green with moss which had flourished in the cool, wet climate. Smoke curled from a chimney.

'Glorious view, isn't it?' she said to the women.

'Oh, yes. It's simply gorgeous,' a woman with short grey hair replied.

'Getting cold, though,' Liesl said. 'Can't wait to get in and sit by that fire!'

'Y'all got that right,' the woman drawled in a southern United States accent.

Liesl raised her camera and shot a few frames to keep up appearances. When the women turned to re-enter the lodge

Liesl tagged along behind them. There was a security guard who eyed her curiously for a few moments, but when Liesl said good afternoon to him and smiled, he returned the gesture and greeting.

She had bluffed her way past the security guard, but Liesl doubted her ability to fool any reception staff inside the lodge. She walked up to the building but when the grey-haired tourist walked in and held the door open for her, Liesl reached into her jacket and drew out her cigarettes. 'Thanks, but I'm going to have one of these before I come in to that fire.'

'OK,' the woman said, and closed the door behind her.

Liesl looked back up towards the gate and saw the guard had retreated into the small wooden gatehouse, which was illuminated by the weak light of a paraffin lantern from inside. She ducked into the shadow cast by the lodge in the dying rays, and carried on, past a row of five accommodation units. A man and a woman emerged from one and said good evening to her. Liesl nodded and carried on. Beyond the huts she could see a gate in the fence and hedge, and another large stone and thatched house beyond. A sign above the gate said, *Private Residence, Staff Only. No Entry.*

Liesl checked over her shoulder again and pushed open the gate, which was unlocked. Her heart started pounding when she saw the silver Toyota Corolla that Aston had been driven in from Kigali parked at the end of a driveway leading to another gate. Aston's driver was sitting on the bonnet smoking a cigarette. He turned his head at the sound of the squeaky gate. Liesl ducked back behind the hedge and ran, as the gate, which was hooked to a spring, slammed shut.

She darted along the hedge line looking for another way in; when she came to the corner of the yard she found a stretch where the wire mesh of the fence between the lodge and the private residence had been peeled off the pole and bent over. She guessed this was a short cut created by staff wanting to pass from the lodge to the residence and then out the residence gate, which was just on the other side. Liesl squeezed through and stayed in the shadows, catching her breath. She could see the glow of Aston's driver's cigarette. The man didn't seem to have been alarmed by the closing gate. Liesl bent double as she moved down another decorative hedgerow that flanked a path leading to the house. A light shone through a crack in the curtains of the nearest window and, like the main lodge, the smell of wood smoke told her there was someone inside by a fire. A new Land Rover Discovery 4 was parked outside the house. Liesl went to the window and dropped to one knee.

Inside, the Zambian, Aston, was standing in front of a roaring fire, his nose in a brandy balloon. Opposite him, gesticulating and stabbing a finger at him, was a man with short-cut white hair. The right side of the man's face was creased by a puckered scar that ran from his hairline all the way down through the empty socket of his eye and down to his chin.

Despite the frightful disfigurement, and the addition of about eighteen years to his age, there was no doubt this was the man in the photograph – Karl Hess, aka Jurgen Pens. Liesl raised the camera and set the ISO to 6400 to increase the light sensitivity and avoid the need for a flash. She fired off eight rapid frames, focusing on Hess's battered face.

'Got you,' she mouthed. Liesl had the photographic evidence that Aston was in cahoots with Hess, but she needed to know more now, like what they were talking about. She moved along the outside of the lodge and smelled cooking food. She came to a door in the back with a lit glass pane. She heard women chatting in Kinyarwanda and the clang of metal pans. This must be the kitchen. Looking out into the gloom, she saw the fence at the rear of the property was much higher than the perimeter barrier. This one stood about three metres and was topped with razor wire. Beyond it, in a separate compound, was a long, low building made of stone with a corrugated-iron roof.

Liesl carried on around the outside of the lodge until she came to a pair of shuttered French doors. She tried the door handle and it was unlocked. She slung her camera over her shoulder and eased the door open. Inside this room she saw a double bed, side tables, and an open door leading to a darkened corridor beyond. From the lack of clothes or clutter in the room she supposed this was a guest bedroom – a lucky find. She crept into the hallway, moving silently on a thick Persian runner. She could hear the crackle of the fireplace and feel the warmth radiating through the wall beside her. She guessed the lounge area where she'd seen Hess and Aston was just on the other side. The long corridor led to another entrance and around the corner to the right would be the kitchen she'd passed earlier. Dark wooden Congolese masks adorned with strands of hair stared down at her. She heard the men's voices and moved closer towards the sound, until she stopped by a doorway.

'They are not going anywhere. They are in the guesthouse and waiting to go on a gorilla trek tomorrow,' Liesl heard Aston say.

'We'll get them tomorrow morning. You know this will signal the end of my operation up here, once they go missing,'

Hess said in reply. 'Your mistakes have cost me dearly, Aston. I'm not happy about this.'

'The errors were not of my making.'

'No,' Hess persisted, 'but you chose the men who failed. You are lucky I don't dispose of you.'

'You need me,' Aston said. 'What will you do about the Frenchman?'

'We have to take him, along with the others tomorrow. He has to disappear as well. We can't have him being interviewed by the press. There cannot be any witnesses left, Aston.'

'I understand. But there will be much media coverage anyway. The lawyer is Australian, and even the South Africans will want to know what happened to their famous photographer. That will draw attention to you, surely?'

Liesl's eyes widened. They were talking about killing all of them – her, Carmel and Henri.

'I've thought about that,' Hess said. 'You should know by now that *I* leave nothing to chance. I'm going on the trek as well. I've already told all the staff here that I'm going to see the gorillas tomorrow and that they should take the day off. My Rwandan business manager back in Kigali will have to deal with the fallout of my "disappearance", and that of his clients.'

'What about me?' Aston asked.

'There will be no one left alive to link you to the missing westerners. You can take your harvest with you back to South Africa and oversee the shipment of the dogs. I hope I can trust you not to fail at that mission, as you have failed at everything else. You're late, already, with the dogs.'

'An unavoidable delay. You must have seen the media coverage of the floods in South Africa. But it is arranged, and, no, I will not fail,' Aston said, bridling. 'I have my man on the scene and he has been monitoring the farm. The veterinarian should be on his way to him by now. The wild dogs are still in their enclosure in Letsitele and they will be in the air within twenty-four hours, on their way to Dubai.'

'Good,' Hess said. 'And the same thing goes there, on the farm – no witnesses left alive.'

Liesl put a hand against the wall to steady herself. She felt as though she was about to faint. She and Richard had known there was someone watching them at her parents' farm at Letsitele, but what she hadn't realised was that her parents, and by the sound of it the painted dogs they were caring for on behalf of the state, were also a target. It all made sense. Hess and Aston were still involved in wildlife smuggling, as well as whatever else they were mixed up in previously. If the dogs were to be shipped to Dubai there would be a huge amount of money involved. She'd seen stories in the newspapers about the illegal trade in live wildlife, and remembered that private zoos and collectors in the Middle East and Asia paid serious money for African wildlife. She took out her cellphone and started tapping out a message. She heard the scratch of claws slipping on polished stone floors and looked up to see a black Doberman running towards her. The dog growled, low and menacing, and then ran at her. She tried to escape, but screamed as she felt its massive jaw close around her leg.

28

Richard felt the phone buzz in his pocket. He took it out and the screen illuminated his face in the darkened hallway of the former residential house in Roodepoort where Aston Mutale operated his traditional healing 'surgery'.

'Turn that off,' Theron hissed.

Richard shook his head. The only person he'd been sending and receiving messages from in the last few days was Liesl, and this one was from her. He held up a hand to Theron, who was beckoning him down the hallway, and quickly read the message: *Hess and Mutale working together. Plan to kidnap us and raid my parents farm and kill them and steal do . . .* He read it again. 'Shit,' he whispered.

'What?' the detective asked. Richard handed the phone to Theron so he could read it for himself. 'What's *do*?'

'I don't know, but we have to get to Letsitele now. That's where Liesl Nel's parents live.'

Theron nodded. '*Ja*. I know of the Nels. Everyone in the wildlife conservation world does.'

'We have to leave now.'

They'd broken into Aston's office, Theron using a lock pick to open the door. Richard had asked him first if he was worried about an alarm, but the detective had assured him that no thief would break into the residence or surgery of a traditional healer, for fear of the evil that would befall them. Theron had posted Collette at the door as a lookout and, despite her years of western education, she'd been happy to wait by the door. 'No way I'm going inside that place.'

'We've come this far, let's have a look,' Theron said. 'We don't know when they plan to kill the Nels, or what for. Something here might tell us.'

Richard took a deep breath and exhaled. 'All right. But I want to call them to warn them. Can you get police to their farm?'

Theron shrugged. 'Maybe. They don't call Letsitele the "slow veld" for nothing, and resources are short everywhere. I need firm evidence a crime is about to be committed.'

'All right then, what are we waiting for?' Richard said.

They moved through a waiting area, furnished with cheap wooden lounge chairs with foam cushions. A coffee table carried the last few days' tabloids and some old copies of *Drum* magazine. The air smelled of stale cigarette smoke. The lock of the first door yielded almost instantly to Theron's pick. 'Looks like the reception area. Have a look in here,' he said to Richard, 'but leave everything as you find it.'

Richard nodded. He was wearing thin latex surgical gloves that Theron had pulled from a bag in the boot of his Mercedes. They'd driven through the night streets of Johannesburg to get to Roodepoort, which was in the western part of the city. Richard had never grown used to the big city and had a healthy respect for its reputation as a crime capital. Far off he heard the wail of an ambulance or police siren. The house itself was in a quiet street where most of the residents had been forced out – perhaps because of crime or falling property values, or both – and businesses had moved in. A dog barked in a neighbouring house.

'I'm going to check Mutale's office and the rest of the house.'

'OK.' Richard rolled back the office chair pulled up to a timber veneer desk. He smelled perfume in the air. On the desk, next to the screen of a desktop computer, was a studio picture of three small children. The woman's desk was clean, but for a desk calendar blotter and black and red pens, and a small bottle of Gilbey's gin with three wilted flowers in it. Richard slid open the large filing drawer on the right. Inside were two trays – Aston's inbox and outbox.

He lifted the trays and slid out the contents, keeping them in piles. In the outbox were three sealed envelopes – one addressed to Eskom, the electricity authority, and two to men with African names. All needed stamps, so Richard assumed this was the next day's post. He shuffled through the inbox and found junk mail, bills for the renewal of a car licence and water rates, and an invoice from the cargo division of a Middle Eastern airline.

'Hello,' Richard whispered. The invoice was for the shipment of twelve dogs from Maputo, Mozambique, to Dubai. The breed of the animals was listed as 'German Shepherd'. The cost was staggering, but Richard had never heard of someone transporting so many pets at one time. He thought of the *do* at the end of Liesl's unfinished SMS message. He got up and moved as quickly and as quietly down the hallway as he could.

Collette looked back at him and he nodded to her, then went in search of Theron. What was clearly Aston's office was empty, so Richard headed to the back of the dwelling. The kitchen of the house was as it must have been originally, but Richard was assailed by a strong smell of meat almost at its use-by date as he entered. Theron was standing over a large deep freeze, the lid raised.

'I've found it,' Richard whispered to the detective's back. 'I know what they're after.'

Theron turned and looked at him, and blinked. 'What is it?'

Richard handed Theron the bill of lading for the dogs. 'Liesl's parents have twelve African wild dogs on their farm that they're looking after until they can be released back into the wild. Judging by Liesl's SMS, they're going to steal the dogs and kill her parents. That makes sense, as her mum and dad have also seen the picture of Hess in Rwanda. The shipment date for those dogs is tomorrow afternoon. I think they're going to hit the farm tonight, if they haven't already.'

'*Eish*,' Theron said. 'And have a look in here. We're messing with a bad *oke*, all right.'

Richard peered around the bulk of the detective, who shone a Maglite torch with a red filter into the freezer. Inside was a human arm, severed at the elbow, with the hand and just three fingers left on it. Next to it was a plastic bag with what looked very much to Richard like someone's heart and lungs. '*Muti*.'

'*Ja*. God knows what else we'll find in here.'

'Liesl said Aston's planning on kidnapping her and the others. What do you think he's going to do to them, Captain?'

Theron closed the lid of the freezer. 'I don't want to imagine. But at least she's on to them, so hopefully they can turn around and get away from Hess and leave him to us.'

'I'm worried about the way the message cut out,' Richard said.

'Send her one back, man.'

Richard nodded. He tapped out, *Are you all right?*

Theron opened the freezer again and rummaged inside it. He found the head of a baboon, which he lifted out to show Richard. 'These guys are definitely still into wildlife, as well as people.'

Richard's phone beeped. *All fine here. Sorry re last message. Have SMSed my folks. They are fine. Not at farm – staying at friends' place. Poppa released dogs into wild yesterday. Emergency averted, but can you go there and wait for me to return tomorrow?*

'What does she say?' Theron asked, closing the freezer again.

'She says everything's all right and that her parents are now fine.'

'What do you think?' Theron looked at him.

Richard tapped another message and pressed send.

Aston stuffed a handkerchief in Liesl's mouth and tied it tight with a length of cord he took from a curtain in Hess's lounge room. It was worrying that the woman had been eavesdropping on them, but he was pleased that they would soon be rid of her and the other witnesses.

Hess told his dog to sit, patted its head for the good job it had done savaging Liesl's leg and arm, and then went to the kitchen and dismissed the staff, telling them that nothing was wrong; he had caught an intruder but would deal with it. The cooks wiped their hands, turned off the food, took their coats and hurried off to the staff compound.

As Hess came back into the room where Liesl lay, face

down and bound, he held up the reporter's phone. 'I've just been exchanging messages on this young lady's behalf with Doctor Richard Dunlop in South Africa,' he said to Aston. 'I've sent him an SMS telling him to go to the Nel farm. I'm sure he'll comply.'

'My man will stay behind and take care of him when he arrives,' Aston said.

Liesl's phone beeped and Hess checked the screen. 'Hmmm.' Hess squatted and grabbed Liesl by the hair, turning her head so she was facing him. 'He says he will go to the farm, and that he loves you, Liesl. Isn't that sweet?'

The woman glared up at Hess, and Aston saw the mix of hatred, fear and impotent rage. Hess thumbed the phone's keypad and spoke slowly as he typed. *And I love you too, Richard, with all of my heart. X, O, X.* How's that?' Hess allowed himself a chuckle.

Aston took out his phone and SMSed Jan his new orders. His phone beeped in reply a minute later. 'He says affirmative. He's about to go in now and get the dogs – and the old couple.'

Liesl writhed and screamed into the gag. She replayed Hess's words . . . *He loves you, Liesl.* Richard didn't love her, nor she him. Clever Richard, she thought. If he'd messaged her telling her he loved her, she would have replied, *Get over yourself*, or something similar. He was suspicious, and now he would know it wasn't her on the other end of the phone.

Hess looked down at her, hands on his hips. He lashed out with the toe of his boot and Liesl winced and tried to curl into the foetal position as he connected with her ribs. 'You want her alive, I presume, to do your business?'

Aston nodded. 'Yes. I can't tell you how valuable she is. I'm thinking I might video her as well.'

Hess rocked his head from side to side, weighing up the comment. 'Cover her face with a hood then. You don't want a videotape identifying her doing the rounds of the internet or porn websites.'

'Yes, of course. I'm not an idiot,' Aston said.

'I just hope your superstitions don't bring you undone.'

'Where can I do it?' Aston asked.

'Outside, in the storage building with the rest of the stock.' Hess dropped to his knees beside her and touched her cheek with the back of his hand. 'Just another animal to be traded. Shame. That's what you get for sticking your pretty nose where it shouldn't be. I'm afraid you're going to wish you'd been killed by the man who carjacked you in Jozi.'

Liesl kicked and writhed as the two men grabbed her, taking an elbow each, and lifted her painfully to her feet. Her hands and ankles had been bound with electricity extension cords. To move her, they dragged her along on her toes. Her arms felt like they were being torn out of their sockets. As they went outside she caught a glimpse of the lodge behind her, full of well-heeled tourists who had come to see the endangered mountain gorillas. Hess and Mutale took her the other way. Aston steadied her while Hess unlocked the gate in the high razor wire-topped fence that led to the low stone building in the next yard. As they dragged her through the gate Liesl tried to throw herself to the ground, hoping she might somehow loosen her gag or bindings by rolling in the wet grass. Hess caught her, stopping her from falling, and rewarded her effort with a slap to her face that left her ears ringing.

'We should drug the bitch,' Hess said. 'I'll give her some Ketamine.'

Aston shook his head. 'No. I want her conscious. It's better for the *muti* that way. Her fear and pain are the power source. She needs to be aware of what's happening when I operate.'

'Very well,' said Hess. 'I'll indulge you on this because I want to see it myself, but make sure she's well gagged. I don't want the staff barging in.'

'Of course.'

Hess opened the door to the stone building and Liesl heard the screech and chatter of birds and animals inside, and smelled their mess. It was almost overpowering. They dragged her in and Hess flicked on a fluorescent light. There were rows of cages and the light and the movement set the reptilian, avian and mammalian captives into a renewed frenzy of squawking, hissing and chattering. Liesl saw a rare golden monkey; a black and white colobus; a python as thick as her leg, raising its big head to check out the commotion; and a dozen different types of birds. Leathery black fingers poked through the chicken wire of a wooden cage and shook the door. As she focused on the creature, Liesl saw it was a young mountain gorilla. The fuzzy infant was probably no more than a year old. Hess had collected a goldmine of endangered fauna.

Beyond the animal cages was a wall that looked like it was made of steel, or aluminium, and set into it was a heavy door. Both the door and the frame were cushioned by thick rubber seals. Through the door Liesl could see a stainless-steel operating table, and a trolley next to it that was glittering with a terrifying array of surgical instruments, syringes and medicines. Nearby was a large deep freeze.

Hess and Mutale dragged her into the next section, where

the floor was slippery and off-white, instead of the compressed earth of the animal-holding area. 'For your information,' Hess said, 'this is a completely soundproof refrigerated shipping container once I close the door, so no one is going to hear your cries for help.'

Mutale had mentioned the word *muti*. Traditional medicine. From her time working on South African newspapers Liesl knew that human body parts regularly went missing from morgues and hospitals across the country, and graves were robbed so bodies could be dismembered. *Muti* could be made from plants and animals and birds, but the most powerful medicine came from human beings. She knew that even more powerful than organs and limbs and eyes that had been harvested from the dead were those that had been cut from a living, screaming person, just before their tortured death.

'Let's get her on the table.'

Liesl kicked out at Hess and yelled into the rag in her mouth. But as fit as she was, she was no match for the two men, who hefted her onto the veterinary operating table and secured her ankles to rails on the side with thick leather straps. Hess grabbed a handful of her hair in one hand and, holding the tip of a scalpel against her jugular, forced her to sit up. 'I'll happily kill you now, but there's a chance you can walk out of here if you tell us what we want.'

Liesl didn't believe him, but she did know she needed to stay alive as long as possible if she was going to have any chance of escaping. She decided she would die trying to get out of this hellhole. Mutale told Hess to ease her down as he used leather straps with buckles to secure first her left and then her right wrists to the security bars. Liesl quietly tested the bonds.

Hess closed the heavy door to the container then turned on an overhead light, forcing Liesl to blink. 'I used to be a professional hunter. Taxidermy was my hobby.' He set the scalpel down on the side trolley and pulled a pair of rubber gloves from a packet. He snapped them on, then took up the surgical blade again. He moved to her face and Liesl turned away. 'Hold her, Aston, please.'

Aston grabbed her hair and rotated her head so she was looking up into Hess's cold blue eyes. The light haloed him like an angel of death. Hess sliced through the cord that held her gag in place, and then removed the saliva-soaked handkerchief and tossed it on the floor. She coughed. He laid the flat of the scalpel blade on her forehead, stilling her.

'Please . . .' she croaked.

'Shush. There will be time for begging later. First, let me tell you what's going to happen to you.' Hess turned the blade so that the blunt rear edge rested between her eyes. 'You're going to tell me who knows of my identity, and what you know of my time here in Rwanda.'

'*Fokoff.*'

'Ah, it's been too long since I heard Afrikaans. I think I need to go back down south.' Hess dragged the point of the scalpel on to Liesl's lips and let it rest there. 'But quiet for now. As I said, you're going to tell me what I want to know, and then I'm going to hurt you, a little, just to make sure you're not lying. If I believe you, I'm going to let you go, as long as you promise not to report me to the police, OK?'

He lifted the scalpel. Liesl licked her lips. 'I . . . I don't believe you. You're not going to let me go.'

He smiled down at her. 'Smart girl. No, I'm not going to let you go. You're going to die here, Liesl. But I am going to give you a choice in how that happens. My Zambian friend here is a traditional healer, of the very bad kind; a man who believes his human *muti* needs to be harvested from a living, screaming victim. I'm curious to see how that might happen, but I'm not a monster. If you tell me what I want to know, then I'm prepared to deny Aston his pleasure by killing you quickly. The choice is yours.'

Liesl screwed her eyes shut. She felt the point of the scalpel trailing down over her chin and along her neck. She felt the metal lifted from her sternum, between her breasts, as he began slicing open her T-shirt. A tear squeezed from her eyes.

'I'll tell you everything,' she said in a whisper.

'I always knew you would.'

29

Theron was talking on his car's hands-free phone, trying to organise a police team to meet them at Letsitele, when Richard got through to Lourens van der Merwe at the Kruger National Park. It seemed like months rather than days since he'd been shot at in his home, fearing it was Lourens, the jealous husband, come to get him.

'Doc, howzit?' Lourens said, as though he didn't really care for the answer.

Rapidly, and hopefully coherently, Richard explained that armed poachers were about to break into a farm at Letsitele, near Phalaborwa, kill the inhabitants and capture twelve wild dogs. 'Lourens, are you there?' Richard asked, hearing no reply from the man.

'I'm thinking. This farm is out of our jurisdiction, technically, but those dogs probably came from the Kruger Park originally, yes?'

Richard had no idea where the dogs were from. 'Undoubtedly. Can you help us, Lourens? I'm with a Captain Fanie Theron of the endangered-species unit. He's trying to get the local cops to respond but I'm worried they won't make it, and they'll be outgunned.'

'Outgunned, you say? You expecting a big fight?'

'Lourens, I'm not exaggerating when I say the guys we're dealing with are killers.' Richard wondered whether he'd just talked Lourens out of risking the lives of himself and his men.

'In that case, we're in. Are you driving now? Where are you?'

'Just passing Benoni, heading east.'

'Benoni? Why are you heading east? You'd be quicker taking the N1 north and turning off at Polokwane.'

'I know,' Richard said, 'but there's been a major accident between a taxi and a truck on the N1 northbound and it's closed.'

'Shit, man. You'll be over five hours to Letsitele if you take the N4. I'll meet you at the Alzu Services – halfway to Kruger. Shouldn't take you more than two hours. You know the place?'

'Yes. See you there.' Richard had stopped off at the motorway service station a few times and knew where it was. Richard told Theron the new plan, and the fact that the policeman didn't object told him he'd had little luck marshalling the local police.

'There was a double murder in a shebeen on the outskirts of Phalaborwa. Somebody opened up with a nine mil and three people were wounded as well. Half the local police service is there and the other half is out. They're going to send a car to check on the farm when they can.'

Richard nodded. It felt good to be doing something. To a large extent, Liesl, Carmel and her French friend were on their own, and they'd made their choice to go after Hess. Liesl's parents, however, were bystanders in all of this, and their lives were threatened by association with the rest of them. 'Do you have a spare gun?'

Theron glanced at him. 'Do you think you're going to go in all guns blazing? You're a doctor, man. You're probably better off staying with the girl. Pardon me, miss,' he said, looking back at Collette. She waved away his concern.

'I was an officer in the parachute regiment for five years. I know how to handle firearms.'

Theron shook his head. '*Eish*. Check the glove compartment.'

Richard opened the glove box and under the vehicle's papers he found a snub-nosed .38 revolver. It was under-powered by South African standards, but it was better than nothing. He checked the cylinder and saw six rounds were loaded.

'There's a speed loader in there as well, with another six shots. You'd better take it.'

Richard felt as though he was going to war, which was ironic as the other conflicts he'd gone into, in Rwanda and later Kosovo, had been pretty much over by the time he'd arrived. He'd been in the business of cleaning up the bloody pieces of other people's battles, always arriving too late. If they were lucky, they might just get to Letsitele before the killing began, for a change.

Traffic mostly yielded to Theron's high-speed run, but when he came up behind a dozy driver who hadn't noticed his flashing light he had to sound his horn. Richard braced himself for impact with a futile hand on the dashboard, then breathed a sigh of relief as the startled driver pulled over to the left into the yellow lane.

The phone rang and the captain answered it on speaker phone. 'Captain Theron.'

'*Ja*, Captain, howzit,' said a slow-talking African voice.

'Fine. What have you got for me, hey?'

'Captain, it's Warrant Officer Manzini here from Phalaborwa. We managed to get to the Nels' place earlier than expected. I'm at their farmhouse now, and they seem fine. Can we go back to the station or must we wait here for you, sir?'

Theron looked at Richard, who shook his head. 'Shit. Liesl's SMS said her folks were staying with friends. If they're at home, then that means Liesl definitely didn't send that message at all. It was worrying enough with her saying how much she loved me – she wouldn't have even joked about that. This confirms what we feared. The Nels are at home and they don't know what's about to hit them.' Liesl's phone was obviously in someone else's hands and he feared for her safety. He had tried calling Carmel, but his call could not be connected. Hopefully they could save Liesl's parents, but what of her?

'They have to leave the farm,' Theron said.

Richard knew that was the sensible thing, but he shook his head. 'Old man Nel's a stubborn guy. He won't leave his staff in danger, and he won't want whoever's after them to know that their plan's been compromised. I think he wants a showdown, even if it places his life and his wife's life in jeopardy.'

'Afrikaners,' Theron sighed. 'Manzini?'

'Here, sir.'

'Stay there with the Nels, in the house with them. Make sure the old man's armed and call for back-up as well. You're going to get hit with a farm invasion just now.'

'Serious?'

'*Ja*, my friend. Very serious.'

*

Jan Venter guided the helicopter in by radio, reeling off land-marks for the pilot to spot in the dark. When he heard the chopper approaching the big kopje he switched on his high-powered torch and started flashing it.

'*Ja*, OK, I see your light, over,' the pilot said.

'There's a clearing in front of me. You're safe to put down, over,' Jan replied.

The helicopter loomed out of the darkness, blotting out the stars. The only illumination on the aircraft was the wink-ing red light above the engine housing. Jan played his beam on the ground to assist the pilot. As soon as the skids touched the ground the veterinarian jumped out, a backpack over his shoulder and a dart gun in his right hand. Immediately, the pilot took off again, powering up into the night.

'Why the rush?' the vet asked when the whine of the engine had receded.

'Shit's happening somewhere else. And you're late. I'll be glad when it's done, so I can get off this hill.'

The vet wrinkled his nose. '*Ja* man, you're *foofy*. You've been up here too long without a bath.'

'Keep the noise down,' Jan said. He led off, holding his R5 assault rifle at the ready. He'd fitted an Mkonto silencer to the end of the barrel, in preparation for the assault that was to take place on the farm, once they had bagged the wild dogs.

'Don't move!'

Jan froze and closed one eye as the beam of a powerful torch picked out the vet, who immediately dropped his dart gun and raised his hands. Jan raised the R5 to his shoulder, took aim at the light and fired. The silencer reduced the noise of the round to a dull bang. The light fell to the ground.

Jan ran forward at a crouch, his weapon still up in the

ready position. A white man in a khaki uniform coughed and writhed in the dirt. 'Sorry, China,' Jan said. He pointed the barrel of the R5 between the man's eyes and fired again.

'Jesus Christ, you killed him!'

Jan turned to see the vet standing over him, empty-handed. 'Go get your *fokken* weapon. What did you think we'd be doing here?'

'Darting some painted dogs and putting them on the helicopter. Bloody hell. Aston never said anything about cold-blooded murder. I'm out of here.'

Jan turned and pointed his rifle at the man. 'I've got orders to leave no witnesses tonight. If you want to go, then technically you're no longer one of us. You're a witness.'

The vet looked down at the dead ranger. He coughed, and then started to retch. He vomited in the dirt beside the body.

Jan walked off and retrieved the Dan Inject dart gun. When he returned the vet was wiping drool from his mouth. He held out the gun. 'Here, take it.' The vet just stared at him.

'*My fok*, man. Take the bloody gun before I kill you.' The vet slowly reached for it.

'Come on, let's go.' He grabbed the vet by the arm and dragged him. 'We need to get to the enclosure. This *oke* probably wasn't alone, and if he heard the helo then others would have as well.'

They moved at a jog through the mopane forest that blanketed this part of the farm, soft butterfly-shaped leaves brushing their faces. Jan had reconnoitred the area and knew his way cross-country to the pen where the dogs were kept. They passed Tokkie Nel's sable antelope breeding enclosure on the left, and Jan knew there were white rhino about five hundred metres off to the right. The rhino on this part of the farm were watched over twenty-four hours a day, but from what Jan had seen there were no permanent guards on the dogs. Why would there be? Unlike the rhinos, the dogs' value was their rarity, not their price as a commodity. Technically, the Nels didn't even own them. If it all went well this evening, and the killing was done quickly and cleanly, Jan thought he might see if he could convince the vet and the helicopter pilot to wait while he shot a couple of rhino – and their guards if need be. It would give them all a healthy bonus.

'Up ahead,' he said to the vet. He heard high-pitched yapping as the dogs, sensing their approach, started calling.

They reached the gate and the alpha male, who wore a reflective orange collar, climbed onto a low termite mound to get a look at them. Jan thought it ironic that the orange collar with the silver reflective strips was so visible. Out in the wider world it was meant to allow the dog to be seen by motorists from a long way off, but in here it provided them with a perfect aiming mark. Jan felt for the dogs a little. He loved his country's wildlife and was more troubled at the prospect of killing a rhino, later in the night, than he had been killing the ranger. But this was business, and it was just a shame that animals sometimes had to die. He consoled himself with the knowledge that these dogs would be far better protected and cared for in some rich sheik's private zoo in Dubai than they would be if they were let loose to run through the surrounding farmlands.

The vet was silent, but he was on his knees preparing the tranquillising darts. He laid out a towel and on it was a fishing tackle box with his needles, syringes and drugs, and strips of cloth he'd cut to use as blindfolds for the tranquillised animals. Jan kept watch for other rangers or security guards and periodically checked his watch. 'You finished yet, man?'

The vet looked up at him and nodded. Jan hoped the man didn't go to water. Sure as nuts he'd put a bullet in the vet if it even looked like he wanted to make a run for it, or if he slowed him down in any way. 'OK, get on with it.'

The vet stood and slid the first of the darts into the stock of the dart rifle, then closed the cap on it. He checked the pressure gauge, raised the rifle, took aim and fired at the alpha male. It was an easy shot as the curious animal was standing in plain view. When the dart hit the dog he yelped and jumped, then ran in circles. He reached back with his teeth, trying to rip the dart from his rump. Jan heard the shrieks and yaps of the rest of the pack as they trotted up in response to the male's calls.

'Open the gate,' the vet said.

'Aren't you going to dart them all first?' The other dogs were clustering around their fallen leader.

'Don't tell me you're scared? There's never been a recorded incident of a wild dog attacking a human.'

Jan licked his lips, wondering if the vet was telling the truth, or perhaps setting him up to be mauled, so he could make his escape.

'Do you want to take the risk of me hitting them all from here? They'll lose interest in the male soon, once he doesn't wake.'

Jan brought the rifle back to his shoulder, aimed at the padlock on the chain securing the gate and fired. The silencer muffled the noise of the shot to that of a loud clap. The dogs started at the noise, but were soon back to sniffing and scratching around the male. The vet had already reloaded and he walked in until he was no more than ten metres from the downed dog, and shot the alpha female, the true leader of the pack, who was also collared. The pups and older dogs scattered, but within seconds were back, prancing and sniffing in confusion. The vet unrolled the towel, into which he'd bundled the remaining darts, and methodically tranquillised each of the dogs. Such was their devotion to their fallen pack members that right to the last dog they held their ground.

'All right, call in the helicopter. Let's get out of here,' said the vet.

'Not yet. You stay with the dogs. I have some other business to attend to. I'll be back in fifteen or twenty minutes.'

'But what if someone comes?' the vet protested.

Jan shrugged. 'Tell them you're clipping their nails. But if you run, know that we'll find you and kill you.'

Theron pulled into the Alzu service station and pointed through the windscreen to the open grazing land behind the restaurant complex. 'There's your helicopter.'

Richard got out of the car and saw Lourens van der Merwe and the national parks helicopter pilot, Andre, standing beside the aircraft, smoking cigarettes. Richard waved and Lourens lifted a hand and nodded, then continued smoking.

'He doesn't exactly seem overjoyed to see you,' Theron said.

'We have some history.'

Theron raised an eyebrow.

'Let's go,' Richard said to Collette.

They made their way down to an electrified fence where a man in a two-tone farmer's shirt introduced himself as the resident gamekeeper.

'Game?' Collette asked.

'Yes,' Richard said. 'They've got rhino and buffalo here, and some ostriches and antelope. Tourists stopping here to refuel can look out the windows of the service station area and see their first rhino, even before they get to the park.'

'They're over there,' said the man, pointing for Collette's benefit.

'Crazy country,' she said.

Andre had climbed into the cockpit and now had the engine whining and the rotors starting to turn. Richard, Theron and Collette made their way quickly to the helicopter. After hasty introductions, Lourens took a seat next to the pilot, and Theron, Collette and Richard got in the back. An African field ranger was snoozing in the rear compartment, an FN rifle laid across his knees. He opened his eyes as they climbed in. 'Ah, Doc. Good to see you again.'

Richard shook hands with the ranger, whose name was Musa, and introduced him to Theron and Collette.

'The doctor, he saved my friend. He is very brave under fire,' Musa yelled to Collette over the escalating noise of the helicopter's engine. Soon they were airborne, the headlights of the N4 disappearing as they cut across darkened farmland and headed northeast towards Phalaborwa and Letsitele.

Lourens indicated that they don headphones. 'What's the latest?' he asked via the intercom.

'I've got two police officers at the farmhouse,' Theron said. 'We're expecting a raid on the farm tonight, with the intention of darting and taking the pack of wild dogs. As Richard predicted, the Nels have refused to leave their house while they still have staff out on the ranch. I've told our officers to stay with them, and the Nels are trying to contact all their rangers and other staff and tell them to move to secure areas. It'll be another hour or two before I can get back-up from Phalaborwa.'

'OK,' Lourens said. 'I think we should fly over the dog enclosure and check it out from the air, then put down at the farmhouse and check on the Nels. Richard, do you know the layout of the farm?'

'I've been to the enclosure. It's not far from the road. I can show you.'

They settled into silence as they crossed the Blyde River Canyon. 'How do you like the Squirrel?' Theron asked the pilot, using the common name for the Eurocopter helicopter.

'*Ja*, she's a *lekker* machine, hey. Do you fly?'

'When I can. I flew Alouettes in South-West, back before I joined the police,' Theron said.

'Cool, man,' Andre said.

'Not at the time, but looking back on it, I had my share of adventures.'

'I'll bet. You'll have to tell me over a beer once tonight's over.'

Richard clasped his hands together to stop the shaking. He felt for the pistol stuffed in his belt and prayed that he wouldn't have to use it. He remembered the shudders of the Vietnamese gangster dying on his hand as he drove the knife into him. It seemed like a long time ago, but what was it? Hours? Days? It suddenly all seemed hopeless. They'd been on the back foot from the start, ever since the prosecutor Mike Ioannou had tied them all to Liesl's photo. Rwanda would claim them just as it had claimed a million other souls. It was like a vortex of death, sucking them all in.

'Richard?'

He opened his eyes and saw Collette staring at him. She had her hand on his arm and he hadn't even noticed her touch. 'Richard, are you all right? You're shaking, and your face looks pale.'

Theron looked at them, able to hear her words. Richard nodded to him. 'I'm fine,' he said to Collette. It was a lie. If they weren't here he'd be on the floor of the helicopter, in the foetal position. The noise of the engine and the mixed smells of sweat, oil and old vomit reminded him of other helicopters he'd been in, in other third-world countries. He gagged on the tears that threatened to rise up and gush from deep inside him.

She touched him again, taking his arm in her hands, holding it tightly, and looked into his eyes. She held him like that for a few moments, steadying him, then moved one of her hands in order to remove her headset. Collette pointed at his headphones and he took them off. She leaned close to him and yelled into his ear: 'I remember the last time you and I were together, before you came to Australia.'

He stared back at her.

'You saved my life, Richard. Really. I wouldn't have had all that I have now without you. I was crying and shaking, but you picked me up and you were strong for me, Richard. I'll never forget that.'

He smiled at Collette and patted her hands, still clasping his arm. He was just pleased she had survived Rwanda and had studied hard and made a good life for herself. It seemed like saving her was the only good thing he'd done in his life. She leaned over and kissed him on the cheek. He separated himself from her then donned his headset.

'Five minutes,' said the pilot over the intercom.

Musa grasped the cocking handle on his FN and yanked it back. Theron took his Glock from the pancake holster threaded on his leather belt, slid back the slide and checked there was a round in the breech. Richard knew his six-shooter was loaded, but all the same he checked it. They were going to war.

'They have the dogs. Jan's just going to finish the job now,' Liesl heard Aston say.

Hess leaned over the veterinary examination table and slapped Liesl's cheeks. 'Liesl? Liesl, did you hear that?'

She kept her eyes closed and willed her body to be still, as though she was unconscious. The pain was like a blanket now. It rolled over her body, sheathing her, and was no longer confined to any one part of her. The burn and the jolt of the electric shocks, the lines of fire carved by blades and the seemingly endless slaps all blurred into one now.

Hess drew the tip of the scalpel along the sole of her foot and she couldn't stop the reflex reaction. 'Ah, I thought you were still conscious.' He stooped, picked up the bucket and tipped the water over her face. Liesl coughed and spluttered, almost choking as some of the water slid back down her throat. 'Did you hear what Aston said? We have your father's wild dogs. We're going for your parents next. We're going to kill them.'

'No!'

Hess laughed. 'Now you're awake. You can save your mother and your father, Liesl, if you tell me everything.'

'Have . . .' she coughed. 'I told you everything.' The tears came again. He'd been coming and going for hours. The waiting in between the sessions was almost as bad as the torture itself. Her mind reeled with thoughts of what he would do to her next. When she strained her head against the leather restraint tied around her forehead, she could see blood on her bared body, where he'd sliced away her clothes and tormented her skin, though she couldn't tell just how badly she'd been mutilated.

'What's happened to the Englishman – the doctor – and the Rwandan girl, Liesl? You keep saying you don't know, but I know you're lying.'

'I . . . told . . . you. He went to Australia. He left me.' She cried. She really did still hate Richard for leaving her at Johannesburg. She'd thought he was going to stay by her side. She wondered if she would have got herself into this situation if he *had* stayed with her. Carmel had shut her out, and Richard had left her. She'd been foolish to go off by herself and now she was paying the price for her stupidity. Her tears were real. So why, she asked herself, was she protecting him?

Hess lowered his face to hers and whispered into her ear. 'Liesl, I'll make you a deal. I'm going to have to kill you, but I can save your parents. No, shush . . . don't say anything yet. I want you to believe me. Aston has a man at your parents' farm. He and his accomplices have drugged the wild dogs and they're about to be taken away. Aston has told his man to go to the farmhouse and kill your parents, but I can rescind that order, if you let me.'

'What? How?' Her brain was fuzzy with the pain. She was beyond fantasising that she might be saved, but what if Hess was telling the truth? What if she could save her mother and father?

'Liesl,' Hess whispered. 'I know Dunlop went to Australia and I know he met a Rwandan woman there. I want them both – the doctor and the woman. I am prepared to give your parents their lives in return for these two. The doctor and his friend have disappeared from Australia, leaving a couple of bodies in their wake.'

Liesl wanted to smile, for Richard. He'd told her that some guys had tried to kill him in Australia but he'd dealt with them. Richard had said nothing to her about a Rwandan woman, though. They'd all been compartmentalising information – Richard, Carmel and herself – hiding things from each other. Liesl knew Richard was in South Africa and, hopefully, he was on his way with the police to Letsitele to save her parents.

'Is he in South Africa, Liesl? Is he on his way here?'

Liesl blinked through her tears. She tilted her head as much as the restraint would allow her. She saw Hess's scarred, twisted face, just a few centimetres from her own. He smiled a crooked smile. Her parents had seen the photo. There was no way he would let them live. She hawked in the back of her throat and spat at him.

He wiped his face and then the pain came to her again, much worse than before. Liesl screamed.

'Keep an eye on her,' Hess said at last to Mutale. 'I have to go. Make sure she doesn't die before I get back.'

30

'Captain, I'm in contact with your officers on the ground now, I'm going to put them through on the intercom,' Andre said.

'All right.'

'*Ja*, Captain, are you there? It's Warrant Officer Manzini, over.'

'Go ahead Manzini, I read you, over,' Theron said.

'The Nels just tried to contact their head of security. No answer, hey. Last we heard from him he told them on the radio he was going to investigate the sound of a helicopter coming close to the property. You're not close yet, are you?'

'No,' Theron said. 'We're still a few minutes out. It wouldn't have been us that he heard. I'm worried, man.'

Richard, who was listening in, ran his fingers across his neck. 'Get them out,' he mouthed to Theron, who nodded. 'OK, Manzini, listen to me. Get them out. Take them in your car or *bakkie* or whatever and get to Letsitele police station. Put the cuffs on them if you have to. We'll do a low pass over the farm and see if we can see any intruders, then we'll come to the station. Understood?'

'*Ja*, affirmative, Captain. We're leaving now.'

'Roger. Take care, Manzini.'

*

Jan looked left and right down the main road that divided the game farm from the Nels's citrus farm. There was no traffic. He sprinted across the tarmac and took cover under the first of the decorative palm trees that lined the long driveway up to the grand farmhouse.

When he was sure there were no security guards patrolling the gate or fence line, he moved forward, darting in bounds from tree to tree. He paused when he heard a car engine. Jan brought his rifle up into a firing position as he saw headlights flickering through the trees ahead of them. He closed one eye and took aim. As the vehicle rounded a bend, he saw the lights on the top of the double-cab *bakkie*. It was a police car. Shit, he thought. The cops must have arrived after he'd left his surveillance position and gone to meet the veterinarian. This wasn't good. The vehicle was accelerating.

As the vehicle came closer he could see two black faces in front. Perhaps the two officers were making a check on the Nels. There had been extra patrols earlier, so this might be routine. He was about to lower his weapon and move back into the shadows of the palm's trunk when he saw the white face appear between the two policeman. It was old man Nel, leaning forward to say something. The driver slowed a fraction and glanced back to answer the farmer's question. Jan knew that he would have one chance, and it had just been presented to him.

He stepped into the open to ensure a clear shot, curled his finger through the trigger guard and thumbed the selector switch to automatic. Jan steadied his aim and pulled the trigger, loosing off a four-round burst.

The first two shots slammed into the radiator, bringing forth an immediate geyser of steam. The *bakkie* slewed as the driver returned his attention to the front, swerved and then overcorrected. At least one of Jan's bullets starred the windscreen. The *bakkie* looked as though it might slide off the raised embankment on the side of the driveway, but the driver regained control and floored the accelerator. Jan fired at the tyres and first one and then the other blew out as the vehicle passed him. The officer in the passenger side had his pistol out and was firing blindly out of the window. The driver lost control and weaved, overcorrected again, and then slammed into a tree. The horn started blaring.

Jan ran up to the vehicle and fired more shots into it from behind. The policeman in the passenger seat opened his door and dived out. As he rolled he raised his gun arm and started firing. A bullet plucked at Jan's sleeve, forcing him to dart behind another tree.

The police officer who had escaped the vehicle popped up out of the grass searching for a target. Jan fired and hit him. The man dropped to the ground. Jan ran towards the truck again, moving to the next tree. He saw the officer wriggling on the ground, wounded but not dead. The horn was still sounding its screeching single note, and Jan hoped that meant the driver was lying dead on the steering wheel. He was almost there.

Jan shifted his aim to the wounded officer and was about to deliver the coup de grâce, an easy shot from just twenty metres away, when a bullet slammed into the tree beside him. Four more shots bracketed him, driving him to take cover behind the tree. He peeked around the trunk and saw old man Nel fire off a shot at him from behind the *bakkie*.

Nel was a bushman of note, Jan knew, and had been an accomplished professional hunter before dedicating his life to conservation. Jan fired two quick shots in return and dropped to the ground. He started leopard-crawling to the next tree, his R5 in the crook of his arms. He used the long grass at the edge of the road as partial cover. As he crawled he heard the clatter and whine of a helicopter. He looked up and saw the beam of a landing light snaking up the road towards the farm. What was the fool of a pilot playing at? He should have still been orbiting out of range until the veterinarian called for a pick-up.

Jan reached the base of the next tree and peered around it. He had a better view of the crippled *bakkie* now. It was empty, but he saw Nel's head poke up from the other side. Jan fired a snap shot, but missed. The wounded policeman was crying in pain, not far from him.

The helicopter was heading straight towards him. Bloody vet must have panicked and called in the chopper too early. The pilot was coming in to land, flaring the nose up as he approached the stricken truck and sending a hail of sand and grass and twigs into Jan's face. 'Idiot!'

Jan blinked away the grit and saw old man Nel get up and grab his wife by the hand and stumble towards the helicopter – the Nel woman must have been ducking down in the back during the firefight. *Fools*, Jan said to himself. They thought the chopper was their salvation. He stood and ran to the police *bakkie*, leaning across the bonnet to steady his aim. He put the red dot of the sight on top of his R5 in the centre of Nel's back.

Bullets ricocheted off the metalwork of the vehicle and Jan's first shot went wide. He ducked as he saw a beefy man with a grey moustache leaning out of the helicopter's rear cabin, pointing a police-issue Z88 pistol at him. It wasn't the vet or anyone Jan knew. As he blinked again he saw the helicopter was painted in the orange and green of the South African National Parks. Jan raised his rifle and fired a burst at the helicopter, but a second man was now firing at him and bullets pinged off the *bakkie* dangerously close to him.

Jan knew he had no choice but to retreat; he was surrounded and outnumbered. His face was blackened and he hadn't been close enough to the Nels for them to identify him. The veterinarian would lie low, if he was smart, or try to escape on foot, which was what Jan now planned on doing. He could survive for days in the bush. His only fear now was of failing their overlord, Karl Hess. Hess and Mutale had been counting on him to steal the dogs and eliminate the witnesses. The presence of the national parks helicopter told him the smuggling part of the operation had probably been compromised. It was time for him to disappear, perhaps across the border into Mozambique, and hopefully start a new life as far away from Karl Hess as possible.

Jan turned to run at a crouch, remembering as he did that he had to at least finish off the wounded police officer. The black warrant officer had raised himself, painfully, into a seated position. He raised his arm and the last thing Jan Venter saw in his life was the flash from the muzzle of Manzini's Z88.

Richard leapt to the ground just as the skids touched. He sprinted to the police *bakkie*, Theron's .38 in one hand and the helicopter's medical kit in the other.

Tokkie Nel had his arm around his wife's shoulder. 'Liesl? Is she all right?' Tokkie yelled over the noise of the helicopter's engines.

'I hope so,' he called back, but he couldn't stop to talk

now. They had seen the gunman fall and Richard prayed there wasn't a second lurking somewhere. He put his fingers to the neck of the officer slumped over the blaring horn and ascertained he was past help.

Richard ignored the man in the camouflage fatigues who'd been shooting at them moments earlier – he had a bullet hole between his eyes and the shocked look of a man killed because he had underestimated his foe. He ran to the African policeman who had slumped onto his back. The man's eyes were closed. The name tag on his shirt said Manzini. This was the warrant officer Theron had been speaking to.

'Please,' Richard said to no one in particular. He'd brought this on these brave men. Richard checked for a pulse and found one, though it was weak and erratic. The man was bleeding out from the hole in his stomach.

Richard ripped open Manzini's shirt and the first-aid kit. He tore open a dressing with his teeth and placed the bulky pad on Manzini's injury. He rolled him over to tie the bandage ends of the dressing and searched for an exit wound at the same time. There was none. This was bad.

Theron, Lourens and Musa had quickly swept around the farmhouse and were now standing over Richard. The Nels joined them. 'OK, let's get him on the chopper, quickly,' he said. 'We'd better take him to Phalaborwa – that's the nearest hospital. We can radio them when we're in the air. What about the other officer?'

'Dead,' Lourens said.

'We will pray for both of them,' Elize Nel said.

'Ambulance, coroner and more local police are on their way, finally,' Theron said. 'They're close.'

By the time the four men had carried Manzini to the

waiting helicopter, sirens were heralding the belated arrival of the local authorities.

'We're staying,' Tokkie Nel said.

'We need to talk to you,' Theron said.

'Then you can come back here and talk to me and my wife later. This is our home. Thank you for arriving when you did – you saved our lives, but I'm not going to be scared away from my farm. I have staff here I need to take care of, and my game-farm manager is still missing.'

Theron cautioned Nel not to go anywhere without a police escort, and briefed the two cars of detectives and uniformed officers that had just arrived. 'Let's go,' Richard said.

'*Ja*,' said Theron. They laid Manzini on the floor of the helicopter and Richard hooked the IV drip onto the bulkhead. 'We'll take him to hospital, then I want to come back and find out what's happened to the dogs.'

Tokkie Nel grabbed the sleeve of Richard's shirt. 'What has happened to my daughter? Where is she?'

'Rwanda. She tipped us off about the plan to raid you and kill you and Elize and steal your wild dogs.'

'She did? How . . . Is she safe?'

'I don't know, Mr Nel. I hope so,' he said. The truth was that Liesl had sent the SMS messages to him under duress, or someone else had her phone. All that stuff about them loving each other and sending hugs and kisses had tipped him off that all was not right on the farm. 'I'm sorry, we have to go. The policeman needs surgery.'

'You'll tell me, as soon as you hear from my daughter?'

'Yes.' Richard climbed into the helicopter.

'Go, go, go!' he said to the pilot as the sun came up over Africa.

31

Carmel woke before dawn, showered and dressed in long pants, boots and a long-sleeved shirt for the gorilla trek. She'd seen the gorillas before and wasn't convinced it was necessary to go through the whole rigmarole again for the sake of maintaining their cover as tourists. She was itching to find Hess and question him.

They'd been told to be at breakfast at six, but Carmel arrived early. The African chef on duty took her order for a fried egg – all that he was offering – presumably so he could get ahead of the rush. She helped herself to strong coffee out of an urn. It was clear outside, but chilly. Henri walked in, rubbing his hands together.

'Morning,' he said.

'Have you seen Liesl?' Carmel asked.

'No.'

'I knocked on her door as I came past – several times. I called for her but there was no noise from her room.'

'Good morning, madam,' said the Rwandan woman who had checked them in the day before. She carried a folded piece of paper, which she held out to Carmel. 'Miss Shang, I have a letter here, from your friend, Miss Liesl Nel.'

'Really?' Carmel unfolded the note and read it. Henri cocked an eyebrow. 'Bizarre. She says she's gone back to Kigali with Aston and his driver, and she's going to fly back to South Africa. She says she's sorry she got cold feet and that she hopes we stay safe.' Carmel passed the letter to Henri, who read it for himself.

'It's odd, I must admit. We've come so far . . . but you've said yourself she was more of a hindrance than a help. Take that business at the prison, for example, where she got herself kidnapped.'

Carmel nodded. 'Hmm. Still, it's strange that she would go from being so keen to find Hess to turning her back and running home.'

'She did suffer a breakdown of sorts after being wounded in Afghanistan.'

'Did she?' Carmel said. 'I didn't know that.'

Henri nodded. 'She told me over drinks that first night in Kigali. She was wounded when the vehicle she was travelling in was hit by an IED. She famously kept taking pictures, even as they were pulling her out of the burning wreck, but afterwards she fell apart. Perhaps this brought back too many memories – of being under pressure to deliver the picture and story, but knowing that you're facing death in the process.'

Carmel shrugged. 'I guess so.' The waiter appeared with her egg on toast and she sat down to eat it.

After breakfast they went back to their rooms. Henri waited in the doorway of his room as Carmel came out of hers and closed the door. 'Come here,' he said, nodding to the interior.

'*Henri*, we don't have time for this.'

'We do.' He took her hand and led her into the gloomy

interior. He pulled her into his arms and kissed her, hard. When he broke from the kiss he brushed a strand of hair from her face. 'I don't want to see you hurt, Carmel.'

'I'm going to be fine. *We're* going to be fine.'

Carmel's phone beeped. She eased herself out of Henri's embrace. She took it out of her pocket and saw it was a new email.

'Ignore it.'

'I can't,' she said, opening the message and reading it. She sat down on Henri's bed. 'It's from the head of the ICTR in Arusha. I can't believe it; they're ordering me to drop the investigation. I emailed them the day before yesterday asking for guidance and back-up from our local investigators. They've been slow to give me any information on this case all along. It was almost like they were stalling or blocking me, and now she says that I am to come back to Arusha and that any investigation into the shooting down of the president of Rwanda's aircraft is out of our remit. I'm supposed to close Mike Ioannou's file for good.'

Henri placed a hand on her shoulder. 'It's probably for the best, Carmel.'

'Maybe you're right. We're in over our heads. The ICTR could just be following the letter of the law, but perhaps there's more to this.'

'Like what?' Henri asked.

'I really don't know. Perhaps the ICTR is worried about upsetting the current government, or perhaps some other UN member country is bringing pressure to bear. It could be the French, or the Americans, or the Belgians. I just don't know.' Her shoulders sagged under the weight of confusion. She wished she was back in Australia.

She sat her phone down on the bed and it rang. Carmel answered it, wondering who would call at this time. She didn't recognise the number on the screen, but from the prefix it was not from Arusha, Tanzania. 'Hello.'

'Carmel, it's Richard. I'm in a hospital in South Africa . . . I've been trying to get through to you for ages.'

'Are you OK?'

'I'm fine, but listen, Liesl is in trouble. Have you seen her?' Richard asked.

'No. We got a note from her telling us she was going back to Kigali. And I've just been ordered off the case by the ICTR.'

'Carmel, that note's a fake. I got some weird text messages from Liesl that convinced me she was under duress or someone had her phone. There's been a shootout at her family farm. More people are dying, Carmel. You've got to try and find Liesl.'

'Hess?' she said.

'It's all pointing to him.'

'It is. It turns out we're booked on a gorilla trekking trip with the company he owns, under an alias. I was just about to pack up and go back to Kigali.'

'Carmel, I don't want anything to happen to you. Can you call in the local cops? Tell them Liesl's been abducted or something like that?'

'There might not be time. She could have been gone from yesterday evening. What if they have her, Richard? We can't just turn around and leave her. I have to go through with this now.'

'Carmel . . .'

'Yes?'

'Carmel, I . . . just be careful, OK?'

'OK.'

She ended the call and told Henri what Richard had said. Henri took his daypack from the bed and unzipped it. 'I have this.' He reached in and pulled out a Russian Makarov semi-automatic pistol.

'Where did you get that, and when?'

'I went shopping when I was in Kigali. I still have some contacts there. Do you know how to use it?'

She took the gun from him and turned it over in her hands. 'I was in the army for eight years. I know how to shoot.'

'We know this man Hess is dangerous and he has tried to have us all killed. I can't imagine he is going to come quietly,' he said.

'If you want out, Henri . . .'

'No. I want to be with you, to see if I can help, or at least protect you.'

She laid a hand on his forearm. 'I'm going to find Hess and try and get Liesl. If I judge it too risky, I'll pull out and call the state prosecutor in Kigali and get him to involve the Rwandan police and let them take it from here.' She looked up into his eyes, marvelling at his handsome face, as he reached for her and stroked the hair at the back of her head. She did feel safe with him. 'There was a time in my life when I thought I would have been better off dead, Henri. I felt empty for so many years, and I was in pain. I tried drowning myself in alcohol and after that I tried burying myself in work. I want more than that now. I want to live for a change. And Liesl . . . I don't like her, but if she's in trouble we have to help her. I have to go.'

'Me too.' He bent his head and kissed her again, more tenderly this time. 'Come, the gorillas and Hess await.'

He led her out of his room and into the sunshine and they walked up the road the short distance to the national park entry gate.

A man with white hair – neither the grey of age nor the fake white of peroxide, more a strange cross between albino and platinum – strode across the grass from the car park at the gorilla trekking base camp. He waved.

'Hello,' the man called. 'I'm Jurgen Pens. You must be Liesl Nel?'

Carmel shook her head. 'No, I'm Carmel Shang, but I know Liesl. Can I have a word with you, Mr Pens?' Her heart was pounding. She was face to face with Karl Hess.

'It looks like we are about to leave, yes?' The man was smiling, and he rubbed his hands with anticipation. Carmel tried not to stare at the disfiguring scar on his face. 'I have seen the mountain gorillas many times, but I never tire of it. We must go now.'

'About Liesl . . .' Carmel began.

'Yes, where is she? I've organised this trip for you and your friend, on the basis that Liesl will be doing a story on my lodge for *Escape!* magazine. Do you know where she is? The guides, the gorillas, they won't wait for her.'

'I was just about to ask you the same question. Liesl left a message with the receptionist at our guesthouse last night saying she'd gone back to Kigali.'

Hess frowned. He was playing the part of the safari company owner very well. 'I'm sorry, I have no idea where she is. These permits are worth five hundred dollars each. I was counting on Liesl's story in her magazine.'

'We don't need to see the gorillas,' Carmel replied.

Hess waved a hand in dismissal. 'No, it's fine. They're

non-refundable and I never miss a chance to see the gorillas. Even though I live here I don't often get the chance. Come, you'll be my guest and we'll go back to my lodge for brunch afterwards.'

'That's very kind, and I need to talk to you anyway.'

Hess raised his snow-white eyebrows. 'I can't imagine what about, but we can talk on the walk. I'm in a separate vehicle to you. Once your national parks guide has given you a briefing you'll travel with him to the jumping-off point, where our walk will begin.'

Carmel wanted to stop him now and quiz him, but he turned and strode back to the black Land Cruiser he'd arrived in. 'Bizarre,' she said.

'Quite,' Henri said.

'He's as cool as. He's either a consummate chameleon or he's innocent.'

Henri shrugged. 'It's your investigation, Carmel.'

Carmel stopped to consider her options. She knew their current course of action was risky, but she hadn't come this far to turn back now that they'd found Hess. Even with the grotesque scar that crossed one side of his face, there was no doubt in her mind that he was the man in the photograph. But what did that mean? Perhaps Hess was an arms dealer, but did that mean he had supplied the weapon that sparked the genocide, and was responsible for the attempts on their lives to cover his tracks? Perhaps this was a dead end and there was someone else out there still after them. If Hess was out to get them, why hadn't he killed them in their sleep in the guesthouse? Why had he made no attempt to hide from them? It was as though he was taunting her.

A national parks guide came up to them and introduced

himself as Aubert. He was young and looked supremely fit, which was no wonder as his job entailed climbing up and down rainforest-covered volcanic mountains every day. Aubert wore a pressed green uniform and black gumboots. He carried a handheld radio and a folder. He explained they would be tracking the seventeen-strong Amohoro troop of mountain gorillas.

Carmel was too busy mulling over thoughts about how she would interrogate Hess to pay too much attention, but she did pick up that this troop of gorillas had recently crossed from the Democratic Republic of Congo side of the Virungas into Rwanda. Aubert explained that they should not get closer than seven metres from a gorilla, but added that sometimes the mighty apes came closer than that to their human visitors.

When the briefing was done, Carmel and Henri got into their RAV4 with Aubert and drove out of the national parks compound and turned right. Hess's driver waited until they had passed him, then pulled out and followed them. The tar road ended within a few hundred metres and deteriorated progressively from graded dirt, through the village near the national parks camp, to a rutted, eroded track that looked like a solidified lava flow. Aubert told Henri to turn right and they started climbing the slopes of a mountain. Here the surface of the road was littered with volcanic rocks worn smooth by years of bouncing tyres. Several times the little four-by-four, with its low clearance, bottomed out and there was the tortured sound of its underparts dragging over rocks. Carmel looked over her shoulder and saw the menacing shape of Hess's bigger vehicle, its windows tinted black, never far behind them. She consoled herself with the thought that even if Hess was their man, there was no way he would try to harm them in front of a national parks guide and the team of three trackers that Aubert told them would be with the gorillas. Besides which, she didn't plan on outing herself to Hess straight off the bat; as far as he knew, they were just a couple of tourists blagging a free mountain-gorilla trek from their journalist friend.

'Are the trackers armed, Aubert?' she asked, to reassure herself.

'Yes. They have AK-47s. They spend all day with the gorillas and leave in the evening, once the troop has made its night nests in the trees. The females, babies and young males sleep in the trees, and the silverbacks, who are too big for the branches to support, sleep on the ground in order to defend the family. The trackers return each morning, around dawn, to the same spot and are there when the gorillas awake. This way we always know where the gorillas will be.'

'That's good,' Carmel said. Surely not even Hess would try something around three men armed with automatic weapons.

They bounced along until they came to a small village set midway up the cultivated slope leading to the rainforest. The road petered out completely and Aubert told Henri to pull off to the left, into a muddy plain that functioned as a car park. Hess pulled in behind them. When they got out Aubert pointed to a young boy who was carrying a sheaf of wooden sticks. 'Take a walking stick, please, and tuck your trousers into your socks because of stinging nettles and leeches,' he said.

Carmel noticed that Hess, when he got out of his vehicle, was wearing waterproof gaiters that came down over his socks, and chamois leather rigger's gloves to protect his hands from the nettles. A couple of villagers greeted him and he replied in Kinyarwanda. It was clear he was well known and apparently well liked by the locals. Carmel wondered again if she was heading for a dead end in her investigation. Hess seemed afraid of nothing and no one.

'Let us go,' said Aubert, leading the way up a pathway that passed between fields of beans and flowers. Laid out on the ground, blocking their way, was a plastic tarpaulin strewn with the heads of white flowers.

'Daisies?' Carmel asked. She hadn't remembered seeing flowers here on her last visit.

'These are pyrethrum daises,' said Aubert. 'They are dried and then the chemical extracted from them is used in insect repellents.'

They walked around the drying flowers and up the steepening trail until they reached a waist-height dry-stone wall. 'This is the border of the national park,' Aubert said.

It was no barrier to a mountain gorilla, or a poacher, Carmel thought. The intensely cultivated and terraced fields ended at the wall, and a thick forest of bamboo and tall trees began on the other side. Aubert told them to form single file behind him, and to stay as quiet as possible. They climbed over the wall and the ascent immediately became steeper, tougher and more slippery. Carmel realised that the main reason the jungle, the national park and its attendant wildlife still existed here was because the land was simply too steep to build on or farm.

Carmel found she was using her walking stick with every step, pushing it into the muddy path and using it like an anchor to drag herself up. A couple of times Henri, who was in front of her, lost his footing and almost slid down the slope into her. She managed a laugh, despite the tension she felt in her chest. Hess had placed himself in front of Henri in the queue, as if he was deliberately avoiding her.

Aubert stopped and Carmel, although she prided herself on her fitness, was grateful for the chance to catch her breath. 'Buffalo,' he said, pointing to a pat of dung on the ground.

'I am surprised there are any left,' Henri said, puffing a little.

'Yes,' Aubert agreed. 'The poachers come into the foothills and the bamboo at night-time and set snares. Our patrols pick up thousands of snares each year, but some small buck and buffalo are still caught. Also, the snares are a danger to the gorillas when they come down to the bamboo zone to feed on the new shoots.'

'That's terrible,' Carmel said. She'd dealt for many years with the evil that men inflicted on each other, but the thought of an innocent animal such as a gorilla being injured or killed by a snare upset her deeply. It was why she devoted much of her spare time and cash to wildlife conservation charities, and now, she reflected, this interest had led her to Henri.

She watched his broad, sweat-dampened back as Aubert led them back up the hill. She remembered the touch and the smell of him as they'd made love. She wanted more of him, and to get to know him better. Perhaps once this was done, if such a goal were achievable, she would take him up on his offer of an extended stay at his riverside mansion in Zambia.

But first, there was Karl Hess to deal with.

Liesl came to and the pain washed over her again, making

her nauseous. She blinked and turned her head as far as she could. Aston was sitting in a corner of the shipping-container surgery, his legs crossed. He was reading a copy of *Escape!*.

'Ah, my patient is awake. Good. You know, as well as taking exceptional photographs, you also write very well.'

She blinked again. 'Water . . .'

He frowned. 'Well, I suppose that's possible. We shouldn't have too long to wait.'

Aston went to the stainless-steel side counter and poured a glass of water from a plastic bottle.

'I'm afraid it's not cold.' He tipped the glass to her lips, but the restraint tied around her head prevented her from sitting up enough. She coughed and spluttered out what little liquid Aston had managed to tip in. 'Here, let me loosen that for you.'

He undid the buckle on the restraint strap and Liesl was able to lift her head enough to be able to drink from the glass. She was parched, but she was also able to get a view of the cuts on her body. She laid her head back down again as another wave of nausea passed over her. 'Why . . . why don't you just kill me now?'

Aston smiled at her. 'If it were up to me, I would. You and your friends have evaded death too many times. However, I understand Hess's strategy. He's going to show you to your friends, when they get here, to scare them, and he's going to threaten to kill you if they don't reveal where the Englishman and the Rwandan girl are.'

'You want me . . . my body, don't you?'

He looked down at her and brushed a sweat-dampened lock of hair from her forehead. Liesl cringed. 'Yes, but not in a sexual way. I want your spirit. Your body will heal a great many people. Think of yourself as one big organ donor.'

'I've got money,' she said. 'Back in Cape Town.'

'So have I, Miss Nel. I daresay I have a great deal more than you. In the new South Africa there are people who will pay almost any price for the right kind of *muti*. I'm going to make more from your body than you could afford to pay me as a bribe to let you go.'

'How can you be so . . . evil?'

He shrugged. 'You were here, in Rwanda, after the genocide, as was I. You can't lecture me about evil. I have my beliefs, in the power of the *muti* I harvest. Yet what was done here was for no reason, other than jealousy and hatred, and the instinctive evil that lives in all men. I simply worked out a way to profit from it, as did you.'

'I did not.'

Aston laughed. 'Of course you did. You media people, you feed like vultures and hyenas on Africa's death and sorrow, and then you regurgitate it to feed the squealing masses who consume your filth.'

'I . . .'

Aston put his hands on his hips and looked at her. Liesl began shaking in her restraints and her convulsions increased until the whole operating table was shaking. Her head, now all but free of the restraints, thrashed from side to side.

'Stop!'

Liesl's body continued to writhe and jerk. The bed began moving on its wheels, juddering and shaking from the force of her fitting.

'Don't die!' Aston commanded again.

Liesl's body sagged. Her head flopped to one side and she was still.

'No!' He placed two fingers on her neck, feeling for her carotid artery. 'A pulse. Are you conscious?' He slapped her face, but she gave no response. He hit her harder.

Liesl parted her eyelids a little, then fluttered them. Her lips moved.

'What? What are you saying, woman?'

'F—'

'What?'

'F—'

'I can't hear you. Were you having a fit? Is that what you were saying. Are you epileptic?'

'F—'

He lowered his head and turned it so that his ear was close to her lips. Liesl opened her eyes and said, 'Fuck you!' Her head shot up to meet his and she grabbed his ear between her teeth and bit down as hard as she could.

Aston screamed like a dying animal. He lashed out at her, but Liesl held on to him with her teeth like a hyena ripping into its prey. She tasted the tang of blood in her mouth, but still she bit and shook. Aston tried to get away from her, which was what she had hoped he would do. The gurney was old and the leather strap restraining her left hand was looped around a purpose-made sliding steel pole set into a tube on the side of the table. It was locked, to stop it sliding, but Liesl had been quietly jiggling the pole since Hess had left, while Aston had been engrossed in the magazine. Liesl thought that the locking mechanism might be worn as the pole felt loose in its socket. She'd staged the fit to pull at the anchor point even more. It was nearly free.

Aston flailed at her, but Liesl had endured so much pain in the last few hours that the fat witchdoctor's blows felt girlish and ineffective. Aston fell into the side table, sending a metal tray of surgical instruments crashing to the floor, then slipped over. In doing so his foot connected with one wheel of the operating table. Liesl felt the gurney start to tip, which was what she hoped for. Blood ran down her face and for a second she had the terrible thought that Aston's ear might come off in her mouth before the table fell. Aston, however, kicked out with his foot, which just helped put the trolley further off balance and it, and Liesl, toppled over onto him.

Liesl wrenched furiously at the pole on the left side as Aston screamed underneath her. The table must have buckled a little in the fall because suddenly the pole slid loose and Liesl's left hand was free. She let go of his ear, but swiped down straight away on the big man with her free hand and drove two fingers straight into his eyes. Aston squealed at the new pain and started lashing out at her. Liesl pushed harder and tried to scoop his eyes from his head.

Aston finally recovered from the shock of nearly losing his ear and then having the trolley and the girl fall on him. He was overweight and slow, but he was also strong; he reached under Liesl and heaved her off him. She'd put all her effort into hurting him and still only had one limb free. Aston put a hand to his blurry eyes and kicked at her as he tried to get away.

Liesl was on her side and the air was forced from her lungs as Aston's shoe connected with her chest. She knew Hess had given him a pistol and she'd seen Aston put it down on the side bench. He was on his knees, hauling his heavy body up. She groped on the floor around her and her fingers closed around a bloody scalpel Hess had used on her. She grabbed it and reached up and plunged it into Aston's back, around where she thought his kidneys would be.

Aston bellowed and fell backwards on top of her. Liesl pulled the scalpel out just before he crushed her, and got her free hand out of the way. Aston writhed on top of her, but before he could hit her or push himself free of her, Liesl plunged the scalpel into his neck and dragged it crossways.

Blood and air gushed from the wound, but Liesl continued to saw the blade through his skin and windpipe.

As the strength rushed from him, Liesl rolled the dying man off her and started to undo her restraints. Her pain subsided as adrenaline recharged her tortured body. She'd kill that bastard Hess, too, when he got back.

32

Aubert put a finger up to his lips. 'We are very close to the gorillas. Listen. Hear the branches snapping? They are feeding.'

Despite the stress of the situation, Carmel couldn't help feeling a twinge of excitement. Henri turned to look at her, took her hand and gave it a squeeze. God, Carmel thought, I hope I can have a normal life once this is all over. She let him help her up a slippery stretch of the pathway that had been hacked through the rainforest vines and stinging nettles by the trackers. Henri grinned and pointed.

Carmel saw the young gorilla lying on a tangle of tree branches. It was light enough not to fall through. It lay on its back with its head lolling down, looking at her through upside-down eyes. It blinked twice. She felt her heart move. There was beauty here, in the dark heart of Africa, despite all the killing and chaos that had gone on. In this moment, Carmel knew there was and always would be hope for the future.

'It is a young female,' Aubert whispered. He arranged them so they could take pictures, but none of them was minded to. Hess and his chauffeur appeared to be more interested in looking for other gorillas. Carmel saw the blond man's head bobbing as though he was doing a count of the troop. The African man with him leaned on his walking stick and looked bored. Henri seemed mesmerised, first by the young gorilla and then by its mother, who climbed out on a limb and offered her baby her hand. The young one went to her mother and followed her down the trunk of the tree. The pair passed between Carmel and Henri, barely a metre from their legs as they knuckle-walked down the path.

'Come, we will follow them.'

The order of march was now reversed as they retraced their tracks a little way down the path. Carmel was the first of the tourists, just behind Aubert, followed by Henri, Hess's man, and then Hess himself, who now brought up the rear. The two trackers, who had found the gorillas early that morning, slung their packs and AK-47s and fell in behind Hess.

'This troop of gorillas recently crossed from the Democratic Republic of Congo,' Aubert said quietly to Carmel as he moved briskly after the gorillas. 'They lost a baby and its mother over the border to poachers not long ago. We believe the troop was too frightened to stay on the Congo side.'

Carmel nodded. She wondered how much thought went into the gorillas' movements, which she imagined were more seasonal and to do with vegetation than with fear or an understanding of danger. Still, perhaps she was wrong. Maybe the gorillas really did think it was safer on this side of an imaginary line drawn through the Virunga Mountains.

Aubert turned to the left and began hacking through vines and bushes. He was soon joined by one of the trackers, who had overtaken them. Aubert held up his hand and Carmel paused. He pointed up with his machete. A juvenile male gorilla had climbed a tree trunk and was looking down at

Carmel. As her eyes became accustomed to the gloom in this darkened part of the forest, which lay under a thick canopy of vegetation, she eventually made out the black forms of the rest of the troop as they munched on leaves and here and there paired off to groom each other.

'The silverback,' Aubert said. 'His name is Kajoliti.'

Carmel nodded. 'He only has one hand?'

'Yes, he is the one who lost a hand in a poacher's snare. He is no less able as a result, and he is very strong and very protective of his family. The trackers have reported that he is very temperamental, quite aggressive, since the loss of the baby.'

As if on cue, Kajoliti stood and took three paces towards them, beating his leathery chest with his good hand as he advanced. Carmel flinched and bumped into Henri behind her as she instinctively stepped backwards.

'Still,' Henri whispered to her. 'You must not run.'

He folded his arms around her, from behind, and she felt safe and comfortable in his embrace. Gradually her heart rate slowed to normal again. It had been a short, sharp shock to see how fast the big silverback could move. From her reading and previous visit she knew the gorillas were basically gentle creatures, but the one-handed Kajoliti had just reminded her he was more than capable of killing if he had a good reason.

'I can't believe people are still killing gorillas and taking their babies,' she murmured to Henri.

'It is money,' Henri said.

'It is evil.'

'Yes, you're right,' he whispered to her. He hugged her and kissed the side of her face. Carmel reached up and put her hand around his.

Behind her, Carmel heard a noise like two paper bags being burst. She pulled away from Henri, turned towards the sound and saw Karl Hess striding along the trail with a pistol in his hand. On the end of the weapon was a long silencer. He raised it, looked past her and Henri and fired two shots. Aubert's head snapped back and he fell in the mud.

The noise was nowhere near as loud as a normal gunshot, but the suppressed bang was still enough to frighten off the gorillas. Several of the females screamed and babies ran to them and jumped into their arms and onto their backs. Kajoliti turned to face the humans and grunted and beat his chest again as the family began scampering away. He stayed until all had disappeared into the thick undergrowth, then turned and ran after them, all the while glancing back over his shoulder to make sure the humans weren't following.

'Down,' Hess barked at Carmel and Henri. 'On your knees. Hands on your heads. Do it!'

Hess's accomplice was right behind him. He carried the AK-47 that Carmel knew must have belonged to the other tracker. She realised the man was dead. Carmel wanted to scream in frustration. She had known the risks inherent in confronting Hess, but had decided to go after him anyway. Everything she had done had been against her nature, but she had followed her heart, not her head, to try to find Liesl, the woman who had ruined her life.

'Do as he says,' Henri whispered, dropping slowly to his knees.

'Shut up.' Hess struck out and pistol-whipped Henri across the face, drawing blood from his cheek with the butt of the weapon.

'Hello?' the first tracker called out as he retraced his steps back to the group. He began frantically unslinging his AK-47 from his back as soon as he saw Aubert's body. Hess raised his pistol again and shot the tracker. The man was screaming as he fell. Hess stepped over Aubert's body and fired two more silenced shots into the tracker's head.

'Tie them,' Hess said to his man.

From his daypack the driver produced a roll of duct tape, which he used to bind Carmel's and Henri's hands behind their backs. He tore off two strips of tape and used these to gag them. When he was done he dragged them to their feet and gave Carmel a shove in the small of her back.

Hess caught her, by the hair, before she fell. 'I'm more than happy to kill you here, on the mountain,' he hissed into her ear. 'But I want to talk with you first and find out what you know. If you cooperate there's a chance I'll let you live, in return for my freedom. Understood?'

Carmel nodded. They headed off down the mountain, and she imagined how the scene would be reported. The fact that Hess and his henchman had done nothing to hide the bodies of Aubert and the trackers gave her a preview of the story that would play out in the media. Two foreign tourists and Hess, or Pens as he was locally known, the wealthy lodge owner, would be reported as missing, presumed kidnapped by armed bandits or rebels. There would be a search – something like this could not be covered up – but by the time the police got organised Hess would be long gone, probably in another country, and she and Henri would be dead and buried, literally.

Carmel looked back over her shoulder and was rewarded with a slap in the face from Hess's man. 'Eyes front.' She hadn't been able to see Henri, which meant Hess was keeping them separated. She wondered what had happened to Liesl – if she had really left them and gone to Kigali. Carmel prayed she had, because if she'd been kidnapped by Hess then she was probably dead already.

There was nothing more Richard could do for Warrant Officer Manzini after the surgeon and nurses at Phalaborwa Hospital had loaded him onto a gurney and taken him into the operating theatre. The sun was up, but the sky was grey with low cloud as Richard, Theron and Collette stood outside the building. He could only hope Carmel had found Liesl in Rwanda.

'We're going back to see if those wild dogs are still there,' Theron said to Richard. 'Are you coming with us?'

Richard nodded, and looked to Collette. She nodded. 'I want to come too.'

'After this, we'll go back to Kruger with the helicopter. I still have a house there and I'm sick of running.'

'That sounds good to me,' Collette said. 'I need a bath, and I need to sleep.'

'Come, let's get this done,' Theron said.

It was a short ride back in the helicopter to Letsitele and as they approached the Nels's farm Andre spoke into the intercom so they could all hear. 'Funny, there's another helicopter overhead, hovering over the farm. He's low. I don't have visual, but I can see him on my radar. He's in the mist and low cloud.'

'Get there, fast,' Theron said. He slid his Glock out of its holster and ejected the magazine. He counted his remaining bullets and decided to replace the magazine with a fresh one.

'Poachers?' Richard asked.

'In a helicopter?' Collette said, sounding surprised.

'*Ja*. It certainly wouldn't be the first time around here. We've suspected a couple of local pilots have been working with poachers. There's even evidence a vet has been involved in the poaching of rhinos inside the Kruger Park and in the private reserves bordering it.'

'It should be over here,' Andre said, pointing out the right side of the helicopter. 'But I can't see any navigation lights.'

'Come right a bit more,' Richard said. 'We're almost over the enclosure where I saw the dogs.'

Andre flicked on his landing spotlight, to make himself more visible as he approached the mystery aircraft through the cloud. 'Holy fuck!'

The helicopter rocked to the left as the pilot threw the machine over. A darkened bulk and spinning rotors passed by them, momentarily blotting out their view of the ground.

'Crazy bastard!'

'That's them!' Theron said.

Richard had time to glimpse a white face in the rear of the other helicopter as it flitted past them. His heart was pounding. If Andre hadn't switched on his landing light at that moment they would have probably collided with the other machine, which had been in the process of taking off, but showing no lights.

'After them!' Theron said.

Andre brought the helicopter around in a sweeping turn, increased the throttle and headed after the rogue aircraft.

'Bring us alongside,' Theron said into the microphone. His door was open and wind rushed into the rear cabin. Richard drew his .38 as well, and turned his torso to further shield Collette from the passenger or passengers of the other helicopter.

Lourens couldn't bring his gun to bear, as he was sitting in the co-pilot's seat, on the opposite side of the pilot to the other chopper, and Musa, the armed ranger in the back, was sandwiched between Theron and Richard on a bench seat along the rear bulkhead.

'The man in the back's got a gun!' Richard said. 'He's aiming.'

Theron fired twice. He had a clear shot from his side of the helicopter, but both machines were bucking in turbulence as they crossed a range of hills. His bullets flew wide.

'Aaagh!'

The national parks helicopter started to lose speed and altitude.

'What is it?' Theron asked Andre. 'Are you hit?'

'*Fok!*' Lourens swore. 'There's a bloody dart in his arm!'

'Get him out of the pilot's seat,' Richard said. 'If it's a dart intended for the dogs, then it could be M99, which will kill him in minutes.'

'Lourens, help me get him out of the pilot's seat. I'll fly,' Theron said.

It was an awkward shuffle. Lourens scrambled out of the co-pilot's seat and Theron climbed over the back and into it. Andre was losing consciousness and he slumped forward.

'Get him off the stick!' Theron wrenched on the control column, trying to fight the near dead weight of the pilot as Richard and Lourens each grabbed one of the pilot's shoulders and heaved. The helicopter's nose dropped and the machine slid towards the ground. 'Hurry. Get him off!'

Richard and Lourens heaved back, fighting against the g-forces as the helicopter plummeted. Collette leaned over to help as well and the three of them were finally able to drag the pilot out of his seat. Theron levelled the helicopter as the skids brushed the tops of a stand of gum trees on a farm plantation. 'Too close,' he said. 'Back to the hospital?'

Richard checked the pilot. He had stopped breathing. 'No, Fanie. We don't have time. It must have been an M99 dart, from how fast he has lost consciousness. He'll be dead before we get there. The only thing that'll save him is Naltrexone, to reverse the M99. If there's a vet on board that helicopter he'll have some. You've got to get them to land.'

'*Ja*. All right.'

Richard launched into CPR, breathing hard into the pilot's mouth. Collette got down on the floor of the cabin. 'I studied first aid in Australia. Let me do the compressions.'

'OK,' Richard said in between compressions.

Theron lowered the helicopter's nose and increased speed. He tried calling the pilot of the other aircraft on the radio, but there was no response. 'I've got him on radar. He's heading east.'

'Mozambique?' Lourens said.

Theron shrugged. 'Maybe. If they've got the dogs on board it would be easier for them to get them past customs from Maputo than out of South Africa. Also they'll be in international airspace soon and technically we won't be able to follow them.'

'That's one of my men, a national parks officer, on the floor,' Lourens said.

'I said *technically*. I'm not letting that bastard get away.'

Richard and Collette kept up the CPR. It was exhausting work, but it was the only thing keeping him alive.

'I see him,' Theron said. 'He's flying much slower than us, thankfully. He might have a heavy fuel load.'

Theron drew up close to the helicopter, until he was just aft and to the left of the other aircraft. 'Unidentified helicopter,

I say again, this is Captain Fanie Theron of the South African Police. I order you to land immediately. Give yourselves up.'

The pilot of the Bell 412 turned to the right sharply and dived for the ground. This told Theron he could hear him and was deliberately trying to avoid him. Theron followed him. Collette yelped in the back as the manoeuvre knocked her off her knees onto her side.

'Keep up compressions!' Richard said.

'All right, all right,' she said. Collette righted herself and placed the heel of her hand on the pilot's sternum once more and began pushing down.

Theron stuck to the other aircraft and narrowed the distance between them. 'Lourens, Musa, ready?'

'*Ja*,' each said in return. Lourens and Musa had positioned themselves on the right side of the aircraft.

'OK. When I come up beside him, let this *poes* have it. Blow him out of the *fokken* sky.'

As Theron eased himself alongside the other helicopter the white man in the back slid open the door and started firing at them. This time, he was armed with a pistol rather than a dart gun. A bullet pinged off the skin of the chopper, forcing Theron to jink.

Musa was aiming at the engine. He fired round after round from his rifle, and after six shots, smoke started to stream from the Bell's jet exhaust. The man in the other heli kept firing back and Lourens cried out, 'Shit. I'm hit.'

The Bell was losing height and Theron broke off the attack and circled the stricken helicopter. 'Are you all right, Lourens?' called Musa.

'Got me in the arm. Not serious. Through-and-through wound.'

Musa pulled a field dressing from the helicopter's diminished first-aid kit and wrapped it around Lourens's arm.

'I'm going down,' Theron said. 'He's auto-rotating by the look of it, putting down in that clearing. We're somewhere in the Kruger Park, between Orpen and Satara, I think.'

Richard looked at Musa. 'Do you know CPR?'

'*Yebo.* We learn it as part of our training, but I've never done it.'

'Collette will show you, but keep it up. Don't stop.'

'Let me . . . let me come with you, Doc,' Lourens said.

The anti-poaching ranger had probably taken a bigger knock than he thought. His face was white and beaded with sweat. Richard shifted to let the other man take over the CPR. He lifted Lourens's arm and took a quick look at the wound. There was blood on both sides of the dressing, tied just above his right elbow, confirming the bullet had passed through the muscle. Lourens couldn't hold a weapon and might fall over if he got out of the helicopter.

'Take this, Doc,' Lourens said, passing him his Z88. 'More stopping power than that peashooter you've got.'

Richard nodded and braced himself in the door of the helicopter. Looking out he saw the Bell land heavily and tilt to one side as its right skid collapsed under the impact of the powerless touchdown. The rotor blades slammed into the ground and sheared off.

Theron touched down a couple of seconds later and Richard jumped out and ran towards the other craft. The pilot's door opened and Richard raised Lourens's pistol. 'Don't shoot, don't shoot!' the pilot said as he stepped out. He dropped his weapon on the ground and raised his arms.

Richard lowered his handgun a little, but then the man who

had been shooting at them staggered out of the rear of the crashed helicopter. There was blood on his face. He raised his pistol and Richard fired twice. But Richard was still a good fifty metres away and the man ducked, so both shots went wide. The man pointed his pistol at Richard again, but was unsteady on his feet. Richard kept his own pistol trained on him, waiting for the man to stop lurching so he could take a clean aim.

The man let off two shots, both of which skewed way off to the right. He adjusted his aim and went to let off another shot in Richard's direction, but nothing happened. He was out of ammo.

'No!' the man screamed, realising he was done for, and threw his pistol towards Richard. 'Please don't kill me.'

Richard felt the blood lust rise up inside him, as it had when he'd killed the gangster in Sydney. He wanted to kill this man, but first he needed to save Andre. 'I need Naltrexone, now, to counteract that dart you put in our pilot.'

'Yes, yes, of course. I'm a vet. I have it in my bag.'

'Then bloody well get it, man. Now! And if you try anything I'll shoot you in the fucking back.'

The man limped back into the cabin of the Bell. He dragged out a plastic fishing tackle box, opened it, and rummaged inside.

Looking over his shoulder Richard could see the still forms of a dozen African painted dogs, lying heaped on the floor of the crashed helicopter. Richard thought the veterinarian, driven by greed, must have decided to push on with the plan to steal the dogs even though he surely knew from the gunfire and police cars at the Nel farm that his partner in crime was dead. Richard would get to the dogs in time and force the vet to revive them, but his most pressing concern right now was the pilot.

'Hurry!'

'Here.' The vet held out a syringe and Richard grabbed it from him. Richard turned and ran back towards the other helicopter, where Theron was climbing down from the pilot's seat.

'Richard! Look out. Behind you!'

Richard looked over his shoulder. In his haste to get back to revive Andre he'd forgotten the discarded pistol. The veterinarian had run to it and picked it up.

'Don't be an idiot!' the pilot yelled to the veterinarian.

'Here's the Naltrexone!' Richard waved it and kept running. He had to get the syringe to the dying man. He braced himself for the impact of a bullet in the back.

The shot exploded in the damp morning air, which was quiet now that the helicopters' engines had shut down.

Richard kept running. The bullet had missed. He made it to the helicopter, anticipating another shot hitting him at any moment. He pushed up Andre's sleeve, took the cap off the Naltrexone, shot a little into the air to clear any bubbles, and then plunged the needle into the man's skin. There was no time for finesse. Almost immediately, Andre coughed and tried to sit up.

'Thank God. Lie still,' Richard said, putting a gentle hand on the groggy pilot. Only then did he turn around. Fanie Theron was standing over the vet, who was lying in the grass with a hole in the side of his head, blood soaking the ground beside him, the pistol still in his hand.

'Richard,' Collette exclaimed. 'You saved him!'

Richard stood by the chopper. He felt so exhausted he thought he might collapse. Collette climbed down out of the cabin and wrapped her arms around him.

33

Liesl had blocked out many of the things Hess had done to her while he was torturing her, but she could see the blood on her skin and she knew she was going into shock.

She leaned against the cages and had to reach out twice to find the latch of this cage. It was hard to open and the bolt swam in her vision as she tried to slide it across. She'd already freed birds and lizards and a pair of golden monkeys, and before she'd felt too weak she'd been able to drag out the cage with the fat python in it and set it free. It had slithered, almost reluctantly, into the long grass behind Hess's private zoo. She finally managed to open the door to this cage and a colobus monkey sprang out, nearly knocking her over.

All that was left now was the baby gorilla. She'd wondered if she should let it go. It would need special care if it was to survive. She had Aston's gun tucked into her pants, which she'd pulled back on, along with a lab coat. She really needed to lie down. She wasn't thinking straight.

She'd first staggered, bloodied and battered, to the lodge and walked in on Hess's high-paying guests having breakfast. A couple had shrieked when they'd seen the gun in her hand.

'Call the police,' she'd demanded of a waiter. When the

man had hesitated Liesl had fired a shot into the floor in front of him. He had run off, presumably to the nearest phone. The guests had stampeded. Dazed and sapped from her fight with Aston, she had then returned to the stone building in the rear compound and Hess's container of evil to see if there was anything else held captive there. She'd set about releasing the animals and birds he'd been planning on selling. She hoped the police arrived soon, but part of her also hoped Hess would get back first. She wanted to kill him. She heard a shriek from a cage at the end of the room.

The door swung open.

A man stepped inside and Liesl clutched at the side cabinet. The man had an AK-47 in his hand and a green uniform. She wondered if he was a government soldier or policeman.

'Get her! Tie her up now,' came a voice from beyond.

Hess. Liesl raised her pistol, which she'd been holding behind her back, and shot the black man in the chest. He pitched backwards.

'Liesl!' Carmel cried into her gag. Liesl sank to her knees, unable to stand any longer.

Liesl's hand swayed as she fired another round, but Hess had the instincts of a leopard and the speed of a striking snake. His pistol was already up and he fired twice. Both bullets hit Liesl in the chest and she fell backwards.

Hess pushed Carmel and Henri to the floor, so they were kneeling. Carmel stared into Liesl's lifeless eyes. She turned to Hess.

He leered down at her and tugged the gag from her mouth. Looking down at Liesl, she retched.

'I wanted to know just how much you knew about me,' he snarled.

'You bastard. You're going to hang for this,' she said.

Hess laughed. 'Your ICTR doesn't condone the death penalty.'

'No, but Rwanda does.'

Another African man ran into the shed and through the connecting door into the container. He surveyed the blood and death, but didn't comment on it. 'Boss, some of the guests have called the police. That woman,' he pointed at Liesl on the floor, 'told me to, but I didn't.'

Hess nodded. 'OK, Claude. Thank you.' He raised his pistol and shot the waiter between the eyes.

There was one thing Carmel didn't know about Hess. 'You supplied the surface-to-air missile that shot down Juvenal Habyarimana's presidential jet.'

Hess shrugged. 'So the photograph you found would seem to indicate. What of it?'

'Who was behind the assassination? Who bankrolled it, who planned it? Who started the Rwandan genocide?'

Hess laughed. 'It doesn't matter. The genocide started long before you or me or President Habyarimana himself was born. It was born of us all, of mankind, of greed and hatred. It doesn't matter who pulled the trigger or why.'

'Tell me.'

He shook his head. 'Sadly, Miss Shang, this isn't a James Bond movie.' He chuckled again at his own joke. 'I don't reveal my secrets, and you don't save the world. Not even this little corner of it. And now, I have to go.' He raised his silenced pistol yet again and pointed it between Carmel's eyes.

'All this killing . . .'

Hess shrugged. 'There will be more.' His finger curled around the trigger and began to tighten.

A door slammed and Hess looked over his shoulder. 'My God—'

Hess fired but the blur of black hair and muscle and yellowed teeth and screaming was too much to be stopped by the single shot he was able to get off. The room filled with more shrieking and beating and the slap of huge feet on the linoleum floor. Carmel and Henri curled themselves into a ball and rolled away from the terrifying onslaught. There was the smell of animal everywhere and the crash of surgical instruments falling. The fallen operating table was picked up and then brought crashing down. Hess yelped and there was the sound of breaking bones. He screamed again as a huge hand swiped down on his head.

From the last occupied cage the baby gorilla shrieked and poked its stubby black fingers through the wire mesh of the door so it could shake it. Kajoliti, the one-armed silverback they'd seen on the mountain just a couple of hours earlier, took another swipe at Hess and then ambled to the cage, grabbed the mesh and ripped the door from its hinges. He scooped the squealing baby into his arms and glared at the frozen forms lying curled on the floor before trampling over Hess's body and ushering the rest of his troop from the confines of the room.

The invasion was over almost as fast as it had begun.

Henri rolled over and Carmel saw he'd been able to pick up a fallen, bloodied scalpel and had been using it to slice through the tape around his wrists. He wrenched his arms apart and stood. He looked down at Carmel.

'Watch out for him. He's not dead,' Carmel said. Hess groaned.

Henri rubbed his wrists and scanned the wreckage of the

container until he saw Hess's silenced pistol. He picked it up and looked down at the man. Hess coughed blood and stared up into Henri's eyes.

'OK, free me, but keep him covered,' Carmel said, her head still reeling from the commando-like raid the mountain gorilla had carried out. She'd once heard of lowland gorillas coming into a village in Congo to take back a stolen baby, but never had she heard of a mountain gorilla conducting such a rescue.

Henri ignored her and continued to stand over Hess. She looked up at him. 'Henri . . .' she began. She wanted to repeat her order, and to tell him to tie Hess up so he could be arrested and tried. She did not operate under the law of the jungle; she was a lawyer, dedicated to the execution of legal justice. Then she looked at poor Liesl's ravaged body. Liesl, who had clearly suffered so much, had presumably stuck around to release the animals that Hess must have had captive here. 'Henri . . .'

'He has caused too much suffering, Carmel. He does not deserve to live.'

Hess looked up at him. 'You won't do it,' he said.

Henri aimed the pistol at Hess's head and killed him with a single shot.

He undid Carmel's bound hands and she threw her arms around his neck and sobbed into his chest.

'It's over,' he said. 'It is over.'

EPILOGUE

Franschhoek, South Africa, two weeks later

Richard and Collette sat in the downstairs lounge of the Plumwood Inn guesthouse in Cabriere Street, where they were staying. Richard had helped himself to a sparkling water and poured Collette a glass of Graham Beck shiraz.

'I don't know about you, but I need this,' Collette said.

'I need a clear head.'

'I'm scared, Richard.'

He reached over and put his hand on hers. 'You'll be fine.'

Richard sat back and checked his watch. 'We need to go in about fifteen minutes.'

Collette nodded.

Carmel and Henri had been unable to make it back to South Africa in time for Liesl's funeral, but Richard and Collette had gone, along with Captain Fanie Theron. Liesl's parents had, understandably, been distraught. The knowledge that Liesl was facing death just as Richard and the South African Police were saving them made their loss even harder to bear. They took some consolation from the fact that her last act had been to release a menagerie of endangered animals.

The police in Rwanda and the team of ICTR investigators who flew to Kigali from Arusha, belatedly, had prevented Henri and Carmel from leaving until their statements had been taken, several times over. Carmel had begged the investigating officers to be allowed to fly to South Africa for the funeral, but she had been stonewalled.

Henri, it turned out, had a wine farm just outside Franschhoek, in the Western Cape, about forty minutes' drive from Cape Town. He and Carmel had eventually been allowed to leave and had flown there from Kigali, via Nairobi and Johannesburg. This would be the first chance Richard would have to see his former lover in seventeen years. He downed his water and wiped his hands on his trousers. 'Let's get this over with.'

Collette set down her glass, which she'd barely touched. 'My stomach is churning. You're right, let's finish this.'

Richard nodded. They walked outside and got into the hire car they'd picked up yesterday. Franschhoek, he was learning, was the sort of place that could experience four seasons in a day, even in summer. The low misty cloud they'd encountered when they arrived had cleared to reveal a clear view of the craggy grey faces of the mountains that flanked the Franschhoek Valley. They headed to the end of Cabriere Street, where Richard turned left and then right into Huguenotweg, the little town's main street. The police station was on the corner. He looked at Collette and she said nothing. Richard gripped the wheel tighter. He could feel his heart racing.

He turned right at the memorial to the town's founders, French Huguenot refugees, glancing at the statue of a young woman on a pedestal and the semicircular parade of arches behind her. Franschhoek had been a refuge for the people who came here and the woman held a broken chain and a Bible in her hands, signifying religious freedom and the breaking of bonds. His heart ached when he thought of Liesl, and how she had died. She had stayed on in Hess's macabre torture chamber, trying to save the animals imprisoned there, and God alone knew what she had been through before her death. Her life had been troubled, but she had been courageous to the end and while he wished he had been with her, he now knew that Collette had needed him, too.

The vineyards began as soon as he cleared the town. Richard checked his rear-view mirror and saw two Mercedes sedans. The road began to climb into the foothills of the mountains. It was spectacular countryside and Richard wondered how much a wine farm here was worth. More than he could ever afford, that was for sure.

Four kilometres further on he took a turn-off to the right, through a gate and along a red dirt road. Rows of grapes flanked the driveway, which led up a slope towards a grand Cape Dutch farmhouse. Richard stopped about two hundred metres from the building, turned off the engine and got out. He started walking the rest of the way towards the house.

A dark-haired woman walked out of the house and raised her hand to shield her eyes. Richard recognised her immediately. His pace faltered. She put her hands on her hips and he saw her face. She was as beautiful as he'd thought her the day he'd met her, at an army base in the tropical north of Australia. She stood there, looking at him.

He couldn't turn back. There was too much at stake. Richard resumed his stride and as he came closer Carmel took a couple of tentative steps down the wide stone staircase that led down from the stoop. Henri Bousson walked out, shrugging off a white cook's apron. He wiped his hands on it and followed Carmel down the steps.

'Hello, Richard,' she said, and stopped out of his reach.

'Carmel, hi. I—'

'Save it.'

'Yes. All right.'

'Hello. You must be Richard?' Henri moved past her and extended a hand. He squeezed Richard's hard. It was the grip of a woman's new lover meeting her former partner, a test of strength. Richard looked him in the eye.

'It is good to meet you,' Henri said. 'I heard what you did here in South Africa, for Liesl's parents. She died a brave woman.'

'Yes, she did.'

'Where is your car, Richard? You should have driven all the way up.'

'The road's steep, and wet from this morning's rain. I wasn't sure if it would make it all the way up here. It's parked down in the vineyards.'

Henri waved a hand. 'Ah, no need to be so timid. The road here is fine. We can get it later, but for now I have made coq au vin for lunch, so you must come in and eat.'

'Yes.' Richard stood there, looking at him.

'A shame I couldn't meet your travelling companion – the Rwandan girl. What was her name?'

'Collette. Collette Ingabire.'

Henri didn't blink and Richard held his stare.

'She has gone back to Australia, yes?' Henri said.

'Yes.'

'I am sure she will be safe there.'

Richard wondered how the man could be so calm. 'Why shouldn't she be now Hess is dead?'

Henri shrugged. 'I don't know. It is a safe country, from what I know, yes?'

'Unless you hire some local muscle to kidnap someone, torture them, then try to kill them.'

Henri looked over his shoulder towards his grand home. 'I don't know what you are talking about, but I need to go check on my chicken.'

When Henri turned back around Collette was walking up the road towards the farmhouse. He looked at Carmel, back at the house, and then at the woman walking towards him. Finally, Richard saw Henri's resolve flicker. He blinked.

'Is this him?' Richard shouted, not daring to take his eyes off the Frenchman.

Collette came up behind him. 'Yes, it is him.'

'I don't know this woman,' Henri said. 'Is this your Rwandan?'

'Don't speak of her like she's an object, Bousson, or whatever your real name is. She's a person. A human being, just like the million people who were killed by the people you and Karl Hess were working for.'

'Preposterous. I know nothing of what you say. I am going inside. You should leave.'

'Stay where you are.' There was the warning blip of a siren and two BMW M3 sedans roared up the driveway. The doors opened and a mix of uniformed and plainclothes police, headed by Captain Fanie Theron, bundled out and surged forward.

Bousson looked from Richard to Carmel. His body sagged a little. 'How did you know?'

'It took a while,' Carmel said.

Richard couldn't read her expression, but he thought she looked sad and weary.

'I thought you were genuine, the real thing, Henri. But you made some mistakes, and so did your business partner, Karl Hess. When Hess kidnapped us the sensible thing for him to do would have been to kill you. You had nothing to do with the investigation and the photograph. He had no reason to keep you alive, but you were accomplices. I've also been doing some checking of your wildlife "orphanage". I had an investigator talk to some of your past volunteers. There were several stories of people turning up to work to find that perfectly healthy animals had died in the night and had been removed under cover of darkness. Captain Theron also found your phone number, and one that was subsequently linked to a phone found in Hess's house, in Aston Mutale's mobile phone records. I took a picture of you on my phone, when we were still in Rwanda after Liesl died, and emailed it to Richard, who showed it to Collette. I stayed with you long enough to make sure you didn't disappear.'

Bousson snorted. 'This would have all been around the time you stopped letting me fuck you.'

Richard's fist shot out and took Bousson square in the middle of his face. Blood spurted from his nose as he staggered back.

The police advanced, guns drawn, before the fight could escalate. 'Henri Bousson, you are under arrest for contravention of the endangered species trafficking act, and you are also wanted for questioning over the shooting of a Robert Banda in Livingstone, Zambia.' Theron read Bousson his rights as two policemen moved to him and took an arm each.

Bousson stared at Collette. 'You recognised me.'

'Yes,' she said. 'You were the other white man who used to come to our house. You were the friend of that man Hess. You were the one who took the picture.'

'Yes, OK, I was there, but I played no part in downing the Rwandan president's aircraft. I don't know who Hess was working for, or who the men he met with were working for. I was Hess's guide in the mountains and I dealt with him in smuggling out wildlife before the genocide . . . that's all.'

'That's all?' Richard shook his head.

Bousson wiped blood from his nose and turned beseeching eyes to Carmel. 'You saw me, I killed Hess. He was a madman.'

'Yes,' Carmel said. 'That was what made me think you weren't who you pretended to be – the way you killed Hess. He was an animal, but I don't believe in summary justice and I couldn't love a man who does. Several of his bones were broken by the gorillas and he wasn't going anywhere, but you shot him in the head, for no reason other than to protect your identity. And then, after the police investigation, you said the chimp you'd gone to Rwanda to rescue had died in captivity and you didn't need to see the people who'd been caring for it. You were going to get the baby gorilla, weren't you?'

Bousson simply stared at her.

'You also killed the man who came to your lodge in Zambia – a man you set up or Mutale set up on your behalf – just to make me trust you. Plus, you and your business partners killed Mike Ioannou, and set up the raid on Liesl's parents' farm. Hess's man tried to kill the Nels and you *knew* Hess was going to kidnap and torture Liesl to find out what we knew about him. You thought you'd covered your tracks, Henri, that I'd be fooled by your lies.'

Richard admired her steel, as she stared Bousson down and the man turned his face away from her. She had stayed with him to ensure his arrest, placing herself at greater risk in order to do her job. She had honoured Liesl's sacrifice and her courage made him reflect on his past weakness.

Theron cuffed Bousson and he and the other officers led him to the waiting cars. When they were almost at the car Bousson said something to Theron. The policeman nodded and Bousson stopped and turned. 'Collette?'

She looked at him.

'For the record, a week after the meeting when I took the picture, I overheard Hess and Colonel Menahe discussing your father. Your father was there as a military intelligence and weapons expert and they thought they could trust him. But he was opposed to the plot to shoot down the president's jet. He fled his post and went into hiding, but I heard he was eventually tracked down and killed at Kibeho. He played no part in fomenting the genocide or carrying it out, as far as I know.'

Collette nodded, and Theron led Henri by the arm to the waiting police car.

Carmel and Collette formally introduced each other and shook hands. 'I feel like I know you,' Collette said, sniffing and wiping her eyes.

'How so?'

'Richard has talked of little else these past few days.'

Carmel looked at him. 'Really?'

Richard extended his hand to Carmel and after a moment's hesitation she took it. Collette stepped back from them and looked out at the mountains that surrounded them, tilting her face to the afternoon sunshine. She wiped a tear from her cheek.

Richard didn't let go of Carmel's hand. 'Yes, really. I was a fool to cheat on you, Carmel. I didn't love Liesl, I loved you.'

'Yes, well, that's all ancient history, isn't it?' she said.

'It is. I'm sick of going over the past – all the terrible things that happened and all the stupid things I've done in my life. Collette's flying back to Johannesburg and then on to Sydney this afternoon. I was wondering if you'd like to have dinner with me.'

She held on to his hand and looked into his eyes. 'Maybe.'

ACKNOWLEDGEMENTS

This is a work of fiction based on some tragic real-life events and a mystery. I do not know who shot down President Juvenal Habyarimana's aircraft in 1994 and even as late as 2011, when I was researching this book, another enquiry was re-examining circumstances of this event, which is widely regarded as the spark that ignited the Rwandan Genocide.

Likewise, the UN International Criminal Tribunal for Rwanda (ICTR) was still recording prosecutions of high-profile *génocidaires* while I was writing this book, some seventeen years after the massacres took place in 1994.

I visited Rwanda in 2011 while researching *Dark Heart* and found it to be a pleasant, orderly, safe, clean (plastic bags really are banned in Rwanda, and it shows) and well-run country. My wife, Nicola, and I had a wonderful experience tracking mountain gorillas in the Volcanoes National Park and at the time of writing I would recommend a visit to this beautiful country in a heartbeat.

In the capital, Kigali, we visited the genocide memorial and museum. While this excellent facility gives some historical context to the genocide I think that we, like most visitors to peaceful Rwanda, were still left confounded as to how such horror could have transpired there.

In the course of my research I read several books about the genocide and spoke with Rwandan survivors of the genocide; men and women who had served with the United Nations Assistance Mission, Rwanda (UNAMIR); and civilian and military photographers who documented the terrible events of 1994 and 1995. Some of these people wish not to be named, and I thank them and respect their desire for privacy.

I would like to particularly thank the following: Craig McConaghy QC, who served with the Australian Army as the legal officer for UNAMIR II and later as a prosecutor with the ICTR; Kevin O'Halloran, who witnessed the Kibeho massacre as a platoon sergeant with the 2nd/4th Battalion of the Royal Australian Regiment and later documented that event and others through the eyes of Australian veterans of the UN mission in an excellent book, *Pure Massacre*; and photographers Steven Siewert and Robyn Bird.

Doctors Neil Bonginkosi, Lawrence Taverner and Gary Peiser read and corrected the passages concerning medical procedures and the life of a doctor in the Kruger National Park (and some of my Afrikaans). As with the other areas where I have sought research assistance any mistakes are mine not theirs.

John Lemmon of the Australian-based wildlife NGO Painted Dog Conservation Inc and Emma Loewenson provided information about the illegal trade in endangered wildlife. I drew on various media reports for information about the trade in animal and human body parts for use in traditional African medicine. While such reports are an almost daily occurrence in parts of Africa, I should point out here that at no time in my research did I ever uncover any suggestion of illegal or improper conduct by members of the Zambian Battalion (ZAMBATT) deployed to Rwanda as part of the UN peace keeping mission; indeed, the opposite is true.

Keili Jefferies and Di McGill filled in the gaps in my memories of Townsville, Chris Lloyd suggested the location of the gangsters' lair in Marrickville, and Amanda and Edward Vorster kindly allowed me to draw on descriptions of their wonderful home and lands at Letsitele in my description of the Nel family's fictional property. Rupert and Barbara Jeffries' lovely home bears a striking resemblance to Henri Bousson's pad on the Zambezi.

As in my previous books a number of good people paid money at charity auctions to have their names used as fictional characters. I would like to thank the following and the organisations that they supported: Richard Dunlop and Carmel Robertson née Shang (courtesy of her daughters Isabelle and Emily), Painted Dog Conservation Inc; Rick Green and Katrina Driver, The Grey Man; Michael Ioannou, ZANE (Zimbabwe, a National Emergency); Collette Clemenger (courtesy of Jason and Denise Manning), St Michaels Catholic School, Hertfordshire, UK, which supports a school in Rwanda.

As usual my heartfelt thanks go to my unpaid unofficial editors, Nicola Park, Sheila Hawkins and Kathy Dowling, who read the book and made many valuable suggestions. Thanks, too, to Annelien Oberholzer and another wonderful person (who wishes to remain anonymous) who read the entire manuscript and corrected my cultural and linguistic errors.

At my publishers, Pan Macmillan, I would like to thank my friends, publishing director Cate Paterson, managing editor Emma Rafferty and freelance copy editor Julia Stiles.

Writing is, as they say, a lonely business so it is nice to be able to socialise and kick ideas around with some great Aussie authors, especially Peter Watt, Di Blacklock and David Rollins. If you like my books, buy theirs.

And thank you. You're the one who counts the most.